BONDS OF BLOOD

D1521054

J.N. CHANEY
TERRY MIXON

VARIANT
PUBLICATIONS

LAS VEGAS, NV

CONNECT WITH J.N. CHANEY

Don't miss out on these exclusive perks:

- Instant access to free short stories from series like *Backyard Starship*, *Sentenced to War*, and more.
- Receive email updates for new releases and other news.
- Get notified when we run special deals on books and audiobooks.

So, what are you waiting for? Enter your email address at the link below to stay in the loop.

https://www.jnchaney.com/last-hunter-subscribe

CONNECT WITH TERRY MIXON

Check out his website
https://terrymixon.com

Connect on Facebook
https://www.facebook.com/TerryLMixon

Follow him on Amazon
https://www.amazon.com/Terry-Mixon/e/B00J15TJFM/

JOIN THE CONVERSATION

Join the conversation and get updates on new and upcoming releases in the awesomely active **Facebook group**, "JN Chaney's Renegade Readers."

This is a hotspot where readers come together and share their lives and interests, discuss the series, and speak directly to J.N. Chaney and his co-authors.

facebook.com/groups/jnchaneyreaders

CONTENTS

1

Commodore Jack Romanoff stood in the gargantuan engineering compartment aboard the Confederation Navy battleship *Delta Orionis*—which they called *Hunter*—and watched as his makeshift engineering crew worked on the two failed fusion plants.

They'd managed to restore a third to operation, but it was only generating partial power because they didn't fully trust it just yet. It was enough to keep the lights on, the gravity working, and even power the defensive lasers they'd gotten back into service, but nothing more.

There was a lot of work ahead of them if they were going to get out of this unnamed system before the Locusts caught up with them, and he had no doubt the robotic motherships would eventually come. They'd be easy pickings if Hunter didn't get enough power back online to use her independent quantum drive.

Another problem—albeit a very serious one—to add to his ever-growing list.

His chief engineer, Lieutenant Kelly Danek, walked over from the operational fusion plant. Her face looked even paler than usual under the dark smudges she'd picked up while inside the machine.

"Give me some good news," Jack said. "I could use some about now."

The thin officer shrugged and brushed her somewhat out of regulation length brown hair behind her ear. She'd changed out of the standard duty uniform—standard for *Hunter*, anyway—and into a set of blue work coveralls.

"I have *some* good news, sir, but I'm afraid it's not good enough. I think we'll be able to get this fusion plant back up to full power, but I want to baby it. The damned thing is hundreds of years old, and you never know when some part is going to break unexpectedly."

She sighed and moved her shoulders in what looked like an unconscious attempt to stretch her back. "That'll be more than enough for us to run everything aboard *Hunter*, except for the quantum drive. We need the full output of two fusion plants to make a jump, and we're not going to get that.

"One of the plants we had operating at partial power is scrap now. That leaves us two down. The third can probably be brought back to partial functionality. Added to this one, it's not going to be enough."

Jack looked around the massive compartment and easily

picked out the four fusion plants as they were arrayed across the exterior of the cylindrical chamber. With artificial gravity, it was easy enough to make the center of the cylinder feel like up and the curved walls feel like down.

That gave the designers a lot of space to pack in the machinery required to move a nickel-iron asteroid more than a kilometer long and jump between stellar systems using their independent quantum drive.

A month ago, *Hunter* had been a decaying museum. The Confederation Council had paid good money every year to ensure it was kept in mothballed condition, ready to be restored to active service in an emergency, but Vice Admiral Suzanne LaChasse and an unknown number of others had been siphoning that money off for a very long time.

Honestly, his best guess was that someone had started the scheme about a hundred and fifty years ago, so *Hunter* was in terrible condition. That wouldn't have been such a problem if the Locusts hadn't chosen this moment to invade again.

Jack's father, a former Grand Admiral of the Confederation Navy, had pulled strings and done shady deals to get his son assigned to command the battleship division when LaChasse had tried to force him out of the service.

That made it his job to do the impossible and get this ship back into fighting trim. A job he just hadn't had enough time to execute. If the engineering crews aboard *Hunter* hadn't been maintaining the engines since the beginning, *Hunter* would still be stuck in orbit around Faust.

As it was, he'd managed to pull together a makeshift crew and get the ship to the Perseus Cluster just in time to see the Locusts completely overwhelm it.

They'd managed to pull two hundred and six civilian vessels and one wrecked Navy cruiser—his ship until a month ago—out of the trap the robotic invaders had sprung on the Confederation Navy, but expanding the quantum bubble to take those extra ships with them had crippled *Hunter*.

Jack used his functional hand to rub his face. His other arm was still in a sling from where an assassin had tried to kill him. Well, technically, Lieutenant Selter had wanted to kill Commodore Sara Nastasi from the Judge Advocate General's office, but Jack had jumped the man first.

"So, the bottom line is that we only have three quarters of the power we need to jump," Jack said to be sure he had it straight. "Is there any way we can scavenge a fusion plant from the civilian ships to bridge the gap?"

Kelly pulled a rag out of her pocket and wiped her face. If she'd intended to clean off the smudges, her efforts only made things worse. She didn't seem to notice or care.

"Maybe, but I wouldn't hold my breath. While we might be able to jury-rig something, it wouldn't have the redundancies we'd need to make sure it kept functioning under unusual strain or even shut down properly if something went catastrophically wrong.

"The three operational power plants we had went offline when we overstressed them during the jump, but they failed in a manner that didn't destroy the ship. I'm not sure I'd trust a civilian fusion plant to do the same."

That was about what Jack had expected to hear, but it was still disappointing. He had another option, but it wouldn't be an easy one to arrange.

They'd brought the cruiser *Hawkwing* along for the ride after the drones had shot her up. She still had power, so it was conceivable they might be able to salvage her fusion plant. It wasn't as big as *Hunter*'s units, but it might be enough to make this work.

Unfortunately, Captain Ronnie Magri—his replacement—hated his guts and was determined to assume command of *Hunter* for himself. He didn't believe Jack had really been promoted to commodore and had tried to have him arrested when he'd made the trip to offer *Hunter*'s resources to help with damage control.

Honestly, Jack couldn't blame the man for being suspicious. The last Magri had seen of Jack, he'd had his discharge papers in hand. The man hadn't been at headquarters for any of the chaos that followed Jack finding out about his secret orders, so he was probably right to be skeptical.

Still, he hadn't needed to be an ass about it.

In the end, whether the man believed him or not, he'd eventually have to accept this was the way things were. *Hawkwing* was disabled and undoubtedly had some seriously injured people aboard. Magri would be a fool not to take advantage of the medical facilities aboard the battleship.

And even if the man was a fool, *Hawkwing*'s executive officer —Commander India MacKinnon—was *nobody's* fool. She'd browbeat her captain into accepting help before very long.

"Well, do the best you can," Jack finally said. "The soonest the Locusts could get here is about four months from now at the speed we've estimated their hyperdrive works. If we're going to be conservative, maybe we should halve that. If we get *Hunter* operational enough to get out of here within a month, we can be long gone by the time they arrive."

"If we don't have things fixed in a month, we won't ever have them fixed," Kelly declared.

Jack didn't disagree with her gloomy assessment, but he'd do everything in his power to see them beat the odds. "If anything changes, call me no matter the hour."

She snorted. "I think I'd be better off calling David Chen and letting him decide whether it's worth waking you up. You look like hell."

That would've been out of line on a regular Navy ship, but Jack wasn't concerned with shipboard courtesy right now. Kelly had her own unique and prickly way of dealing with people, but as long as she made the magic happen, he'd tolerate just about anything.

Chen was the civilian steward his father had hired to get Jack's new life organized. Thankfully, he was a lot more than just that. He was also a retired analyst with the Office of Naval Intelligence and had the brains to know when something was important enough to wake him.

"Fine," he said with a sigh as he started toward the lift. "Tag him if the situation changes and make sure whoever has the bridge watch gets notified as well."

"Done and done, Commodore," Kelly said, promptly turning

back toward the damaged fusion plant, having already dismissed Jack from her mind.

He got into the lift, pressed the button to take him to the appropriate deck, and leaned against the wall. He was exhausted and emotionally drained. He'd seen a dozen Navy cruisers destroyed in the fighting and couldn't begin to imagine how many friends and colleagues he'd lost today.

The defeat was a terrible blow to the Confederation as a whole and the Perseus Cluster in particular. The annihilation of those ships meant *Hunter* was all that stood between the alien invaders and far too many innocent people.

When the lift opened, he found Christine Hooghuis waiting for him. The muscular young woman was dressed in her usual civilian clothes and wearing her special belt with its numerous pouches. He even spotted one of her ever-present drones hanging behind her shoulder and recording them.

"Are you stalking me?" he asked with a slight smile as he stepped into the corridor.

She shrugged. "Is it *really* stalking when I'm your official videographer?"

"Technically, the Sons and Daughters of the Locust War hired you as the *ship's* videographer. Shouldn't you be bothering one of the other five thousand people aboard right now? I'm a little busy."

He didn't feel nearly as grumpy as he made it sound, but he had far too many things that needed his immediate attention to be distracted right now. He made that clear by marching past her and heading toward the bridge, forcing her to keep up.

"I could, but everybody else is busy, so figured I might as well bother you," she said with a smile as she matched his stride. "Besides, your mother asked me to tell you she wants to check your wound later today and make sure you've been using the sling like she ordered."

His mother—Jesse Romanoff—had basically forced her way on board with a number of retired medical professionals she'd scrounged up at the last minute to help man *Hunter*'s almost nonexistent medical department.

Jack had been *very* tempted to send her home, but he'd decided her skills outweighed the worry of having her aboard. Besides, both her husband and son were going to war. She wasn't going to stay behind no matter what he said.

And truthfully, she was far better at nagging him into doing things than any of the other doctors would've been, which was probably the only reason he was still wearing the damned sling. His shoulder was fine.

Well, as fine as any shoulder that had been shot three days ago could be.

Not that he suspected he'd be wearing it shortly. He couldn't afford to show weakness when he confronted Magri. If the man scented blood in the water, it would make Jack's task much harder.

As he walked, Jack glanced over at Christine. She had dark circles under her eyes even though he could see where she'd used makeup to help cover the effect. She wasn't getting much sleep either, and he suspected he knew why.

"How's the professor doing?" he asked.

He wasn't sure whether he expected her to deny she'd been spending time at Professor Alan Prescott's bedside or not. She'd been in the aid station every time he'd stopped in to check on the man, and it seemed his suspicions that she was romantically interested in the older man were accurate. Still, would she deny it?

"They cut him loose about an hour ago," she said. "If this is your idea of subtly asking exactly what our relationship is, I've moved him to my quarters so I can keep an eye on him. That's how the situation is."

"Well, I suppose that puts me in my place," Jack said with a chuckle. "I wasn't trying to pry, but I could see you were interested. I just wasn't sure whether he reciprocated the feelings or even noticed the attention. He's a scientist and can be a bit dense when it comes to social niceties."

She laughed. "Isn't that the truth? I just about had to beat him over the head to clue him in that I'd like to spend a little more time together. That spooked him for a bit, but he seems game. I wouldn't say we're a couple just yet, but we're certainly headed in that direction."

Jack nodded and slowed his pace to pay more attention to this conversation because it was important. "It's none of my business, and feel free to tell me that, but this is kind of quick, isn't it?"

She nodded, not seeming the least bit embarrassed. "It is. Under normal circumstances, I'd probably get to know him better before I made my feelings known, but these aren't normal times, are they? If you leave something unsaid now, it might never be heard."

"Well, I wish you both success in your relationship. Everyone deserves all the happiness they can get. There's a lot of misery, suffering, and death going on in the Perseus Cluster right now, and our situation isn't exactly the most stable."

"Things must be worse in engineering than I thought," she said after a moment. "I don't want to know the details because you don't have time to tell me, but is there a solution?"

"Yes, but it won't be an easy one. I have a plan to get us out of this system before the Locusts catch up with us, but it requires me to make nice with the man who replaced me in command of *Hawkwing*.

"He's a jackass, and I don't imagine trying to convince him to give up his fusion plant will go over very well. Nevertheless, if we want to get out of the system before we asphyxiate or the Locusts come to kill us, that's what we need."

Christine raised an eyebrow. "You're the senior naval officer in the cluster, aren't you? Can't you just order him to do what you want?"

"If only things were that easy. I command the battleship division, not the fleet they set up to fight the Locusts. He's got a completely separate chain of command.

"That doesn't mean I can't put some pressure on him or come up with some other maneuver to get what we need. It's not as if *Hawkwing* will ever move under her own power again. I haven't checked the regulations to see what happens to a ship that's been damaged so badly that it has to be abandoned during wartime, but that's an option."

"Then I think you've found your answer," she said. "You should discuss the potential ramifications of this with

Commodore Nastasi. While she's not necessarily going to be able to beat someone into submission with regulations, she should be able to verify your new rank.

"And if this guy doesn't want to cooperate, she might be able to come up with a means of compelling him."

"That's a good idea," he agreed. "Now, if you'll excuse me, I need to get moving."

"Don't forget to eat something," she advised. "Catch you later."

He smiled and shook his head as he turned back toward the bridge. He'd only taken a few steps when his communicator chimed, so he pulled it off his belt and answered.

"Romanoff."

"This is Midshipman Calvo on the bridge, sir. The Marine recruits at one of the forward airlocks have an away party from *Hawkwing* requesting to see you."

Well, at least they hadn't made him wait until the middle of the night before they'd showed up. "Escort them to my office and slow walk them, Derek. I need time to get things set up the way I want."

"Will do, sir."

Jack ended the conversation and immediately called Sara. Once she answered, he laid the situation out for her.

"It looks like we've got visitors from *Hawkwing*, and I'd like you to join me in my office to meet with them. This won't be a fun conversation, and I think having a neutral third party with some authority present would help calm the waters."

"I'll need a guide," she said. "I still can't find anything aboard this ship."

"I'll send Tina Chen to go get you. Having her listen in will also prove useful."

"Works for me. See you shortly."

He called David Chen next. "I'm meeting with a delegation from *Hawkwing* in my office. It would be helpful if you could provide refreshments and have your wife bring Commodore Nastasi there. I suspect I'll need all of you to get this situation settled."

"Of course," his steward said. "I'll make the arrangements, and we'll be there shortly. I suggest you have whoever's bringing them take their time."

"Already done. Thanks for the support."

"No need to thank me. It's my job. See you in a few minutes."

Jack changed course for his office. He needed to get things set up just right. Magri already hated his guts, and he didn't want to give the man even more of an opportunity to lash out. This was too important.

He'd get the fusion plant he needed one way or another because the future of the cluster depended on it, but he'd rather not have to violate every regulation in the Navy or use force to do so. For once, he had the upper hand.

That said, he had to be careful how he worked this, or he'd screw things up in a way that would be disastrous for both his crew and the people of the Perseus Cluster. No matter the cost, he had to keep his temper under control and be as reasonable as possible under the circumstances.

As impossible as that sounded when thinking about Magri.

Well, miracles did occasionally happen. Still, it might be best to have Mac Turner and his retired force recon Marines on standby. Hell, having the man in the room might keep things from spinning out of control. He'd make that happen, too.

It was time to get the Magri situation settled once and for all.

2

MIDSHIPMAN DEREK CALVO hurried toward the front of the ship but slowed when he got closer to the airlock where the visitors were waiting. The commodore had been very clear that he wanted time to get ready for this meeting, so he needed to stall.

Until recently, Derek's only experience with the military had been at the Naval Academy. Dawdling there was a punishable offense, so people hurried to wherever they were going. Breaking that habit was a bit nerve-racking.

He used up some of the time by going over his uniform. This meeting was going to be important, and he wanted to be sure he looked his best. With the old-style uniforms, he was already bound to get some strange looks, but he had to admit the old Navy had certainly made uniforms with panache.

Derek felt like a kid playing at being a naval officer in a video game. And since his skills at Locust War Online had gotten him where he was, that wasn't an unreasonable comparison.

Even so, it was very different from the standard Navy duty uniform, and he felt confident the officers from *Hawkwing* would have something to say about that.

Derek waited ten minutes to be sure he'd delayed long enough and then turned toward the airlock. The visitors wouldn't be happy at cooling their heels, but he didn't work for them.

When he made the final twists and turns to arrive at the airlock, he found six people waiting for him. Two of them were Marine recruits pulling guard duty at the airlock. He recognized them by their old-style Navy work coveralls with the red piping down the arms.

The other four had stripped off their vacuum suits and were dressed in standard Confederation Navy uniforms. Two of them were enlisted Marines, and the other two were officers.

The more interesting of the latter was a tall, dark-haired woman wearing commander's tabs. The other was a thin man whose dark hair was slicked back with some type of product. It made him look like a used vehicle salesman.

Derek quickly put that comparison out of his mind because that wasn't how a midshipman needed to be thinking about a Navy captain, no matter how accurate the description seemed. That was a quick way to find himself busted down to enlisted rank and tossed off *Hunter*'s bridge.

The man was the first to speak, his eyes wide with disbelief. "What the hell are you wearing?"

Derek stopped and came to attention. He didn't salute the man, which was something of a slight, but the Navy had some relatively lax rules about when saluting was required. Being respectful should be enough, even if only barely.

"Welcome aboard *Delta Orionis*, sir, ma'am. I'm Midshipman Derek Calvo. Commodore Romanoff sent me to escort you to his office. I apologize for the delay, but it was a rather long trip from the bridge."

That only made the man blink. "That raises so many questions, Midshipman, that I'm not sure where to start. Now, what the hell are you wearing? Did someone interrupt you playing dress-up?"

Derek felt his eyes narrowing and stopped himself before it became worse than it already was. The man's insulting tone made him want to snap back, but that wasn't his place. It was astonishing how different the commodore and this man were.

"It's the standard duty uniform aboard *Hunter*, sir. What other questions can I answer for you before I take you to meet with the commodore?"

The man said nothing, only walking slowly around Derek and eyeing his uniform from every angle. "That has to be the most ridiculous thing I've ever seen. I can't imagine how anyone would want to humiliate themselves by wearing something that made them look like a dictator from some small fringe planetary government. Aren't you ashamed, Midshipman?"

"Sir, I'm not sure we have time for this," the woman said. "It's not exactly Mister Calvo's decision to wear this uniform, so does asking questions about it really serve a purpose? Shouldn't we be moving a bit more expeditiously?"

The man gave her a look that was both withering and dismissive. "I'll decide what's important. Answer the question, Midshipman."

"I don't feel the least bit ashamed wearing the Confederation Navy uniform that was in use the last time we beat the Locusts, sir. It lends a sort of history to what we're doing now."

The man grunted. "And why were you coming from the bridge, Midshipman? Were you bringing someone coffee?"

"No, sir. I was sitting bridge watch. If I might be so bold, we do need to get moving. We wouldn't want to keep the commodore waiting."

He heard a sound behind him before the officer could respond and partially turned to see one of the men acting as Commodore Romanoff's guards arrive. He wasn't alone, having two of the few fully trained Marines at his heels.

All three wore the Marine version of the old-style uniform, with the scarlet stripe down the outside of the legs twice as wide as the stripes on his own uniform pants. The ends of their tunic sleeves were also twice as wide, though that wasn't apparent with their greatcoats on. Also, their hats were scarlet rather than white. The tabs on the officer's greatcoat indicated he was a major, and his nametag said Turner.

He took their arrival as a cue to continue. "Major Turner, this is… I'm sorry, sir and ma'am. I don't know your names."

"I'm Captain Ronnie Magri of the Confederation Navy

cruiser *Hawkwing*," the man said, looking as if he'd rather not answer. "This is my first officer, Commander India MacKinnon."

"Captain Magri, Commander MacKinnon," Turner said. "Welcome aboard *Hunter*. You're welcome to keep your Marine guards with you, but I have to ask for their sidearms. Security is at an elevated state, so I'm afraid that's nondiscretionary."

"That's outrageous! As the commanding officer of an *actual* Navy warship, I'm not going to be dictated to by some dressed-up actor. Not only is your supposed commodore not a serving Navy officer, but this is also not a Navy vessel. Is that clear, Major? If, of course, that is your actual rank."

"I have more time in service than you do, Captain, so I'd suggest you keep a civil tone," Turner growled. "If you're not willing to surrender your Marines' sidearms, then I'll have to insist that you return to your vessel."

The Marines behind the major stepped to the sides and put their hands on their sidearms. Based on their expressions, they weren't going to take no for an answer.

Derek cleared his throat. "Perhaps it isn't my place to say so, but our sensor readings indicate that your vessel was badly damaged, Captain Magri. If part of your trip here is to secure the use of our medical facilities, cooperation might be in order. You're in no danger here."

Magri poked a finger into Derek's chest. "I will not be lectured by someone that isn't old enough to shave. Get out of my way right now, boy."

As much as Derek wanted to let Turner take the heat, he was

the Navy officer on the scene. It was *his* duty to carry out the commodore's orders, not the retired Marine officer's.

It took all his willpower, but Derek stepped forward, crowding the captain's personal space and forcing him back a step. "My apologies, Captain Magri. Major Turner has made Commodore Romanoff's orders quite clear. If you're unwilling to abide by the conditions necessary to be aboard this vessel, I'll have to insist that you leave.

"Should you resist, I shall instruct my Marines to dress you in your vacuum suits and put you out of our vessel. I would regret taking those steps, but make no mistake, I *will* do so if required."

Based on the color of his face, Captain Magri was in danger of suffering a stroke. He couldn't seem to form words even though his mouth was moving. It was kind of entertaining, in a truly terrifying way.

"You will regret your insolence, boy," Magri said in what might have been a sinister tone if it had been pitched a little lower. As it was, it sounded kind of... whiny.

"Be that as it may, sir, if you will instruct your Marines to surrender their sidearms to my Marines, they will be returned when you depart. If not, then I must insist you leave."

Magri spat out orders to his Marines to give up their pistols, and they did so, looking a bit relieved at not having to be the point of contention any longer.

Once that was done, Derek turned on his heel and marched back the way he'd come, trying not to stagger with relief or move too quickly. It felt like Magri's eyes were burning a hole in his spine.

When they reached the main corridor, he gestured for the senior officers to go toward the ship's center and walked alongside them. They were bracketed by their Marines, who were in turn bracketed by *Hunter*'s Marines. Major Turner brought up the rear.

When they arrived at the commodore's hatch, he was relieved to see another set of Marines standing guard outside, fully armed. They were part of Turner's retired Marine force recon personnel. If there was any trouble, they'd be more than capable of dealing with it.

He pressed the admittance chime and stepped inside as soon as the hatch opened. The commodore was seated behind his desk —minus his hat and greatcoat—and David Chen stood off to the right-hand side. Commodore Nastasi—dressed in civilian clothes —sat in a chair off to the left.

"Sir," Derek said, coming to attention. "Captain Magri of *Hawkwing* and his executive officer Commander MacKinnon."

Before anyone could say anything, Magri stalked into the office, glaring at everyone. "It's time to put an end to this charade, Romanoff. You're no commodore, and as the senior naval officer in the Perseus Cluster, I'm assuming command of this museum right now."

It surprised Derek that there was only a tiny twitch of the commodore's eye in response to that provocation before he gestured toward the hatch. "You can return to your station, Mister Calvo."

Derek didn't hesitate to walk out of that meeting. Under other circumstances, he might have wanted to be a fly on the wall, but this wasn't the sort of thing a young officer wanted to be present for. Things were going to be said that couldn't be unheard.

He honestly hoped the old man ripped the bastard's head off.

3

JACK LET Magri's words hang in the air before he steepled his fingers on his desk and responded. "It's good to see you again as well, Captain Magri. I expect this to be a spirited meeting, so please don't hold back on my account."

That caused the man to sputter, but Jack could see the beginnings of a smile on India's face. Apparently, his former executive officer didn't mind seeing her new commanding officer put in his place.

"I won't have you making light of this, Romanoff!" Magri snarled. "I saw you being discharged, so this is all a lie. No matter how you try to play this situation, you're a washed-up naval officer, not a commodore, and this is a museum. Nothing more!"

Jack crossed his arms and leaned back in his chair. "I'd be happy to share a copy of my orders so you can verify them for yourself. Being as we're trapped inside the Perseus Cluster, I'm afraid you're not going to be able to access any of the more recent updates to the Navy databases, but we have them in our computers.

"In any case, your system should be able to validate the orders as at least being authentic. Also, I happen to have someone from the Judge Advocate General's office here to clear up any potential misunderstandings. Seated off to my right is Commodore Sara Nastasi, the head of JAG at Faust."

"You'll forgive me if I don't rise, but I was shot in the leg just a little bit ago, and I've been instructed to keep off it as much as possible," Sara said. "It was an assassination attempt that mostly missed me, but it certainly killed my luggage. I'm afraid my uniforms were a total loss, including the one I had on at the time. Blood never comes out completely, you understand.

"What I *can* do is present my identification and corroborate everything Commodore Romanoff has said. I personally validated the orders giving him command of the battleship division and promoting him to commodore. He commands this vessel and eleven others just like it in storage here in the cluster. Your information is out of date, Captain Magri."

"That's supposing I believe *your* identification isn't forged as well," the man said, planting his fists on his hips. "I don't know what kind of game you people are playing, but I watched the rear guard being ripped apart and know for a fact that I'm the senior combat commander left in the cluster.

"As such, I'm commandeering this vessel for use by the Confederation Navy. If you resist, the consequences will fall on your heads."

Jack chuckled. "You forget that *I* commanded *Hawkwing* just over a month ago and know *exactly* what forces you have available on your *best* day. And, sadly, this is likely *Hawkwing*'s worst day.

"You can mock *Hunter* and her crew, but we have *five thousand* people aboard this ship, with over a *thousand* Marines and Marine recruits. Exactly how do you intend to enforce your supposed seizure?"

Jack leaned forward before Magri could respond, planted his palms on his desk, and stood. "In any case, while you're blowing hot air that my life support system will have to clear out, your crew is suffering, aren't they?

"You've got injured that need care, yet I haven't heard a single request to use our medical facilities and doctors. Do you care so little about your people that you'd prefer to feed your ego rather than take care of them? That's despicable."

"You don't frighten me," Magri scoffed. "You're a failure. I watched Vice Admiral LaChasse drum you out of the service, so don't peddle your lies to me."

"Vice Admiral LaChasse was arrested for embezzlement and conspiracy to commit murder just before our arrival here," Sara said with no inflection. "I wasn't present when she was taken into custody, but I have zero doubt she's sitting in a cell awaiting trial.

"And it has come to my attention that you or your family paid a significant amount of money in exchange for your promotion. You can rest assured that that type of behavior will also be investigated thoroughly by my office."

"I don't have any idea who you are, but you don't frighten me either," Magri sneered.

Sara dug into her pocket and pulled out an ID wallet. "You're welcome to verify my identification, Captain. Everything is in order, I assure you."

India walked over, took the wallet, and examined the identification behind the laminate. She didn't just give it a cursory glance either. She scrutinized it as though she thought it was a forgery.

After a few moments of doing so, she handed the wallet back and walked back to Magri. "Her identification is in order, sir. She is indeed Commodore Nastasi of the Judge Advocate General's office on Faust."

"And that means nothing," Magri said with a dismissive wave of his hand. "This isn't Faust. This is the Perseus Cluster, and she has no authority here, just like Romanoff."

"Would you care to examine my identification as well, Commander MacKinnon?" Jack asked as he stood, pulled out his own identification, and slid it across the desk for her.

She examined it much more thoroughly than she had Sara's but eventually nodded and slid it back toward him. "His identification is authentic as well, Captain. It indicates that he is indeed a Commodore, and the fact that everyone aboard this ship is behaving as if he were in command is an indication they believe he's their valid superior."

"I have a hard copy of my orders that I'd be happy to share with you, but they're back in my quarters," Jack said. "I can send someone to retrieve them if you'd like. Or you can accept the ones I can print out from the ship's computer. It's your call."

David Chen reached into his jacket and pulled out the somewhat crumpled orders. "I took the precaution of bringing the original, Commodore. I felt it likely someone would request to see them."

Chen laid the parchment on the desk in front of India. "I understand this isn't in the best condition, but Vice Admiral LaChasse felt it necessary to attempt to destroy them. As you can see, they are still in adequate condition to be read.

"If you'd care to note the routing numbers across the top, you should be able to compare them to what's in your computer system and validate that they are authentic."

She'd only begun to look at the orders when Magri stalked forward and swiped them off the desk. "This is outrageous! You're not going to be able to fast-talk your way out of this situation, Romanoff. I command a Navy cruiser. You command a museum."

"You command a *wreck* that will never fly under her own power again, Captain," Jack said. "I'm not sure what the regulations say about a ship that's disabled in a combat zone, but it's obvious your engines are gone, and her structural integrity has failed. *Hawkwing* will never move or fight under her own power again.

"Your ploy to seize command of my vessel is ill-considered and doomed to failure. I'm in command here, and as the senior Navy officer in the Perseus Cluster, I will do whatever I must to save as many people as possible."

"The only reason my ship is wrecked is because *you* rammed her!" Magri sputtered. "You and this ship are *directly* responsible for what happened to *Hawkwing*."

"So, you admit that your ship is disabled?" Sara said. "I took the liberty of reviewing the pertinent regulations. You're not going to like what they say, Captain Magri.

"With your ship being unrepairable, we're required to scuttle her so she doesn't fall into enemy hands. Thankfully, from what I'm given to understand, we have time to evacuate your crew and scavenge any parts and equipment that might be useful in continuing operations before we do so, but the regulations give no leeway as to *Hawkwing's* ultimate fate.

"It's up to the senior officer in the combat area to determine the best disposition of yourself and your crew. As Commodore Romanoff is, so far as we can determine, the *only* combat commander still operating inside the Perseus Cluster, that duty falls to him."

Magri stalked over to Sara and glared down at the unperturbed woman. "Even if that were true, you said he was in command of some battleship division, whatever that is. That's not the same division I and my ship are part of. He has no authority over me or my ship."

Jack sighed. "You'll have to forgive me for not knowing her name, but the rear admiral in command of your fleet before the Locusts destroyed it indicated she was dispatching *Hawkwing* to assist us. I assume you received specific orders on the subject as well. Might I know what they are?"

"They're none of your damned business!"

Jack slapped his hand on his desk. "I've had quite enough of your mouth, Captain. I've allowed you far more leeway than anyone else would have, but I'm at my end. If you continue to behave in this manner, I will have you taken somewhere to cool down while you contemplate your situation.

"Consider your next words *very* carefully. Whatever you'd hoped to gain from this situation is lost to you. If you want to continue to be relevant to the fight against the Locusts, you'll have to take a deep breath and accept the situation as it exists. Which way is it going to be?"

"Sir," India said from beside Jack's desk, where she was holding Jack's orders and her communicator. "I sent the routing number for these orders back to *Hawkwing*, and they confirm they are authentic. Commodore Romanoff is indeed an active-duty Navy officer and in command of the battleship division."

"And let me add that the standing orders of the battleship division are to assume *direct* command of the fight against the Locusts should they ever invade again," Jack added. "I'll be happy to provide you a copy of those orders as well, Commander MacKinnon."

"None of this matters!" Magri snarled. "And you won't talk to my executive officer, Romanoff. You'll talk to me. *I* command *Hawkwing*, no matter what lies you spew.

"We won't stay here and listen to any more of this nonsense. We're returning to my ship. Commander MacKinnon, you're with me."

"Actually, Captain, according to regulations, I'm not. Rear Admiral Hagy ordered us to assist *Delta Orionis* in every way possible and *specifically* detailed us to follow the commodore's orders. Now that we've verified his identity and his orders, we have no option other than to—"

"You're a damned traitor, and I should never have expected anything less," Magri growled, interrupting her. "With all the time you served under Romanoff, it's no surprise you'd back his play. It wouldn't surprise me if the two of you were lovers. That's just the kind of behavior I'd expect from someone like you."

Jack started to respond, but India stepped forward, her face hard. "You're out of line, Captain. You've done nothing but criticize *everyone* aboard *Hawkwing* since you assumed command, and I can't begin to tell you how happy I am to see you finally step in it."

"And I do believe that's my cue to bring this little show to an end," Jack said with just a little bit of a smile. "Major Turner, please take Captain Magri somewhere to cool off before I have to start tossing around phrases like 'insubordination to a flag officer' and 'refusing to obey a direct order.'"

"It'll be my pleasure, sir," the older man said as he stepped forward and grabbed Magri's wrist.

Magri attempted to wrench his hand out of the retired Marine force recon officer's grip but found his arm jammed halfway up his spine. He squeaked in pain as Turner frog marched him out of Jack's office and into the corridor where two Marines joined him in escorting the disgraced officer away.

Almost shockingly, the Marines accompanying Magri didn't raise a single objection. That spoke volumes about the man's character.

Jack shook his head. Not because he was sad, but because this outcome had been almost inevitable. He'd hoped the man would show more cognizance of the situation, but his arrogance wasn't exactly a surprise in the end.

"What are you going to do to him, Jack?" India asked. "As much as I dislike doing so, I'm going to point out that he's been under tremendous strain since the invasion kicked off.

"We've had crew killed in the fighting, and our medical bay is overwhelmed. If we get assistance in transporting our wounded to your medical center, I'd be deeply grateful."

He nodded as he resumed his seat. "Anything and everything *Hawkwing* needs is hers for the asking. David?"

"I'll see to it at once," Chen said as he headed for the hatch, pulling his comm unit from his belt.

"While you could press charges, Jack, it would be impossible to seat a board," Sara said with a grimace. "My advice is to let him cool down and try to have this conversation again later."

"It's true that we don't have very many senior officers," Jack said with a sigh. "Having a trained Navy officer doing *anything* aboard this ship would be a boon. As things sit, I have to trust an untrained midshipman to keep watch because I can't sit in the command chair twenty-four hours a day.

"My next highest-ranking officer is the lieutenant in charge of engineering. We're stretched so thin that it's impossible to keep doing business the way we are and still fight the Locusts."

India blinked at him. "That boy? He's been sitting bridge watches by *himself*? That seems a bit… rash."

"Desperate people do desperate things, India. He's got skills that I don't. I'm a trained helmsman, but these old-style controls are almost impossible to figure out without training. I haven't had time to go over them in any detail, but Calvo has them mastered.

"I don't know how much of the combat operations you saw once *Hawkwing* was disabled, but *Hunter's* maneuvering and fighting were conducted by midshipmen and trainees operating my bridge. I gave the orders, and they executed them."

"We were a bit busy, but it seemed as if you were maneuvering well enough, and your lasers were hitting their targets, so I suppose I'm not in a position to complain," she said, looking a bit shell-shocked. "I just can't imagine how anyone could manage something like that. That boy looks like he's barely competent to tie his own shoes, though I'll warrant he has a spine. He threatened to toss Magri out an airlock if he didn't have our Marines surrender their sidearms."

Jack smiled. "Did he, now? That's an excellent sign of things to come. I'll want to hear the whole story when we have time.

"As for his skills, he's spent uncounted hours playing a game called Locust War Online. He and the rest of my bridge crew have the equivalent of a decade or more of simulated experience flying and fighting a battleship just like this one. They can't do anything *else* very well, but at the moment, that's what we really need."

India stared at him as if she were waiting for him to deliver a punch line. He said nothing, which was, in its way, a great comeback.

"We need to get your people taken care of," he finally said. "Since Captain Magri is… indisposed, I'd like to get your official opinion about *Hawkwing's* condition."

India stared at the floor and shook her head. "Her back is broken, Jack. She's got so much structural damage that the destruction of our engines is irrelevant. She'd collapse like a soap bubble if anyone tried to put thrust to her.

"I understand you had to scoop us up to get us to the jump point. Nevertheless, even though it was a soft impact, you basically rammed us with a kilometer-long asteroid. There was no way *Hawkwing* could have survived that in operable condition. She's done."

She gestured toward the hatch. "I can either head back to *Hawkwing* now and get things in motion or call someone to meet your people as they come over. How do you want to handle this?"

"They're your people, so you should be the one making sure everyone who needs help gets it as quickly as possible. David should have the medical people moving by now. They were on standby waiting for your call.

"I'll send as many of our people as I can to assist with damage control, but in the end, it's the people that matter. Go take care of them, India. We can talk again once that's done."

Tina stepped into the compartment from one of the side hatches. He'd wanted her listening to the meeting, but she'd declined to directly participate. That probably had something to do with her training as a covert agent.

"My name is Tina Chen, and if neither of you has objections, perhaps it might be helpful if I go with the commander and explain our situation. There's a lot of background material you're too busy to explain right now, Jack, but I can bring her up to speed."

Jack snorted in amusement. "If there's anyone *more* plugged in than you are, Tina, I'm not sure who it would be. I'm confident *I* don't know everything that's happening. Hell, I think you have secrets even your husband doesn't know."

She sniffed at him almost playfully. "Of course I do! We're married!"

"You can trust Tina completely," Sara said. "She saved my life, and she's our acting intelligence officer."

"It may be unconventional, but we're having to improvise," Jack said. "Both Tina and her husband David are retired from the Office of Naval Intelligence. Him as an analyst and her as an operative. Underestimate either at your peril."

"He makes it sound so scary," Tina said as she took India's arm and led her toward the hatch. "Now, you've got important work to do, and I've got a lot of things to fill you in on, so let's get moving."

Once they and the Marines from *Hawkwing* were gone, Jack rubbed his face and looked over at Sara. "Well, that could've gone better."

"It could have," she agreed, looking up at him. "It could've gone much worse, too. Look at this way, Jack. There was no way Magri was ever going to support you right off the bat. Maybe he'll come around once he's spent some time cooling off.

"You've been running yourself ragged, and you need to get better at delegating. You've got competent people, and you'll need to rely on them because you can't do everything yourself."

"I'll try," he said. "I'm sorry about your luggage. If you talk to Petty Officer Hutton, I'll wager he can dig up an appropriate uniform.

"I did a little research and discovered that we don't necessarily have to wear the greatcoats and hats all the time. I had Hutton put together some coat racks that we could put inside the bridge and other locations for officers to hang their gear, so maybe it won't be as overwhelming."

She smiled as she stood and limped toward the hatch. "My advice is not to disregard the use of hats and greatcoats entirely. Visual impact can be more important than we'd think, particularly for a commanding officer.

"Now, shall we get something to eat? I'm starving. Besides, we need to talk."

Well, that certainly sounded ominous.

4

TINA STEPPED into the corridor beside Commander MacKinnon with *Hawkwing*'s Marines at her heels. They were joined by a brace of *Hunter*'s Marines.

"Gentlemen," the commander said to her Marines. "No matter your feelings on the subject of Captain Magri's situation, I expect your discretion. We'll keep this information to ourselves for the moment because there are a lot of injured people we need to get ferried over here as quickly as possible, and we don't have time for gossip. Is that clear?"

The Marines speedily indicated their understanding. Tina even saw that both were suppressing smiles as they looked at one another. Apparently, Captain Magri was not popular among the rank and file.

MacKinnon turned her head to face Tina as they walked. "So you're a spy. That must be exciting work."

Tina shrugged, making a show of the gesture. "It has its moments. Thankfully, I'm retired, though I suppose this invasion counts as me being recalled to service. However, Commodore Romanoff wasn't entirely correct when he indicated that I was a spy for ONI.

"While I technically worked for them, my operations were under the direction of Confederation Intelligence. The Navy doesn't have much call to spy on people."

The other woman pursed her lips and nodded. "I can understand that, but it's a difference without any real substance. All that matters is your skillset and your judgment. If Jack says you can be trusted, then I'm going to take that to the bank."

"The two of you served together for several years," Tina said as they entered one of the lifts. "I gather you've built quite a bit of trust. You're going to have to trust him even more now because he's all we've got out here.

"He understates the level of difficulties we're having and how much we have to work around different aspects of this vessel, as well as our shortcomings when it comes to personnel. We have five thousand people, but they're almost universally recruits and officer candidates. Very few of them have any real-world experience whatsoever. All they bring to the job is enthusiasm and extra hands."

"Never discount enthusiasm and extra hands," MacKinnon said. "Without those, you might as well stay in bed."

Tina laughed. "True enough. Still, this ship was—as your captain said—a museum very recently. The problem is that it was supposed to be reactivated if needed. The money to keep it in shape was siphoned off for a long time, so the ship is in terrible condition.

"The only thing working close to specifications is engineering. I'm given to understand the engineering crews have maintained the engines and power plants the entire time the ship has been in orbit around Faust. Unfortunately, that means our combat capability is greatly restricted at the moment."

"*Hunter* seemed to fight pretty damned well when she was fending the drones off and saving our asses," MacKinnon said as they exited the lift. "She might have older weapons, but she's got a lot of them."

"This is probably the time to point out that the lasers are only short-range defensive weapons. And less than five percent of them are operational at this time."

MacKinnon stopped dead in her tracks and turned to stare at her. "Five percent? You're telling me that with just a tiny fraction of her potential firepower, this ship vaporized the Locust drones that almost obliterated *Hawkwing*?"

"That's *exactly* what I'm saying," Tina said. "She doesn't have any of her missile launchers in operation either. I'm given to understand those are the primary offensive weapons, but we have no munitions, and the launchers are likely in worse condition than the lasers.

"We know where the other battleships are stored, and there's a station there that supposedly has what we need to turn *Hunter* into a true offensive platform. We just have to get there."

MacKinnon seemed to mull that over for a moment before starting forward again. "How hard will it be to get there? Your ship pulled ours and two hundred civilian ships into this system. What comes next? What's the impediment?"

"Power. According to our chief engineer, extending the quantum field to cover the extra ships put too much strain on our fusion plants. *Hunter* was built with four large ones, but one was nonfunctional before this mess started. They had to scavenge parts from it to get some of the others working.

"The jump put extreme strain on the three operational plants, and they all came down hard. One of them is back up, and Lieutenant Danek is relatively confident it can be restored to full power. Another is scrap. The third she only trusts with a partial load."

Tina took a deep breath. This wasn't her place to say, but she'd broach the subject anyway.

"To utilize the independent quantum drive, *Hunter* needs the full output of two large fusion plants. Right now, we're trapped in this system, and we have every reason to expect the Locusts will send motherships after us. We need to salvage the fusion plant from *Hawkwing*, or we're going to be trapped here until they come to kill us or we run out of supplies."

That news kept MacKinnon silent as Tina led the group into the small craft bay. When she came through the hatch, the cavernous space was far busier than she'd *ever* seen it.

Cutters and other small craft were coming and going at a furious pace. There were hundreds of people rushing around the bay, making sure everyone cleared out of the ships that were inbound in time for the very limited amount of free deck space to be cleared before someone else needed it.

"There must be hundreds of small craft in here," MacKinnon said in an awed whisper. "*Hawkwing* only had *four*. You could move our entire ship's complement in one trip without straining your resources at all."

"Let's not get carried away," Tina said with a grimace. "You forget this is *Hunter*. All the small craft you see coming and going belong to the civilian ships. Most of ours are nonfunctional.

"The mechanics seem confident they can get a significant number of them working again, but they haven't had time to work on them. Right now, we need to focus on the ones we have working so we can get your people over here as quickly as possible."

She turned toward one of the Marines. "Which one is ours?"

The Marine trotted over to someone with the headset, who pointed toward one of the old pinnaces. Tina followed MacKinnon to the pinnace and saw it was already packed with medical personnel and first responders. Someone must've called ahead and held this flight for them.

Tina had a brief view of the small craft bay flight control area immediately above the personnel hatch and saw half a dozen men and women working at consoles in the lighted compartment overseeing the entire docking bay and the flight control zone around the ship.

She knew none of them had any experience directing traffic in a busy environment. In fact, very few of them had experience directing traffic at all. They were learning as they went, and she only hoped they'd been thoughtful enough to warn everyone to keep an eye out for other traffic because having an accident on the way to rescue the injured aboard *Hawkwing* would be a tragic outcome.

Once they were aboard and strapped in, the pinnace buttoned up and lifted off the deck. She had no way of knowing how fast it was going or what order it was in the traffic leaving the ship, but they were on their way.

"So, you said you knew the entirety of what's going on," MacKinnon said in a low tone. "Give me the abbreviated version. What exactly are we dealing with?"

"Have you ever seen any of those entertainment videos where you've got a critical mission, but all you can find are unqualified people to execute the job? This is that entertainment video writ large.

"I don't want to denigrate anything these people are doing because they're trying their very best, but we have probably fewer than two hundred trained Navy or Marine personnel aboard."

Tina stretched and rubbed her neck. She didn't usually allow herself to show how tired she was, but she was starting to feel it. She'd been doing what she could to make things better for days, and it was catching up with her.

"Jack invited me up to the bridge to pass along some information, and I got a look at his crack bridge crew. They're a perfect example of what I'm talking about. I don't know if you've ever seen a bridge on one of these battleships, but Jack tells me it's significantly more extensive than what's on a cruiser. It literally has dozens of stations.

"Now imagine them filled with people like Derek Calvo. Don't get me wrong, that young man is smart, dedicated, and skilled at what he does, but he's only barely an adult. None of them are older than him, except for a few of the civilians Calvo brought up from Faust at the last minute to help fill their ranks."

MacKinnon held out a hand, frowning. "Hold up? What do you mean civilians?"

"Oh, I forgot to mention that. Some volunteers aren't in the military at all. They just have critical skills someone thought would be helpful to have along. We had very little time to gather a crew, so headquarters and Jack's father grabbed anyone that looked like they might be helpful and stuffed them into cutters.

"The same holds true with our supplies. If someone thought it might be necessary—or even potentially helpful—they sent it up and squirreled it away somewhere aboard *Hunter*."

She shook her head. "I have absolutely no idea what we have, and neither does anyone else. Our quartermaster—Petty Officer Hutton—is busy going through every single compartment and hasn't come close to cataloging what we have available for use. And trust me, that's with him grabbing as many spare hands as he can to help with the task.

"Every department aboard *Hunter* is in something of a similar state. I'd say it was organized chaos, but the organization part is missing. And this is what we have to fight the Locusts with."

MacKinnon pinched the bridge of her nose and closed her eyes. The gesture was so much like Jack's that Tina almost laughed. She'd obviously picked it up from him. Or perhaps, he'd picked it up from her. Same result.

"So, let me see if I've got this right," the other woman finally said. "*Hunter* is falling apart because she wasn't maintained, you're lacking experienced personnel, everybody's having to learn what they're doing while they're doing it, using systems that no one understands, and you're packed to the gills with whatever some supply clerk thought he could write off. Am I far off?"

Tina chuckled. "I suspect you're far closer than I'd prefer. Nevertheless, we'll have to make do. I have to say, having your crew joining ours will be a great help in organizing everything. The academy instructors help keep the recruits and officer candidates on task, but we have very little ship-wide organization.

"I realize that the last month was probably unpleasant for you, but there's a light at the end of the tunnel. Captain Magri seems to have crossed the line of what Jack will tolerate, so your former boss has a few more tools at his disposal to deal with him."

MacKinnon snorted. "The situation isn't as open and shut as I'd wish. Between us, Magri is a slime, but he's a trained and admittedly competent Navy slime. He's likely to find some way to squirm out of the consequences of his actions, so I'm not going to escape him that easily.

"The only thing in my favor is that with *Hawkwing* completely disabled, it's Jack's call on how to best use us aboard *Hunter*. He's not restricted to putting Magri in the executive officer's slot, for example. I have zero doubt that's where I'm bound and thank God for that. I won't have to answer to that ass now."

Tina raised an eyebrow. "Are you ready for something like that? I realize you have quite a bit of experience as an executive officer, but this isn't anything close to what you've done before.

"Jack isn't going to tell you this, but managing five thousand people—and that doesn't even begin to count the civilians coming aboard—is draining him. And there are other factors that you need to be aware of."

"Like what?"

"He's supposed to be wearing a sling on his left arm. He was shot in the shoulder during an assassination attempt three days ago. The medics wanted to keep him under observation and make him rest, but he refused. He's been working himself into a fugue state that isn't very healthy, and he's not nearly as sharp as I think he should be."

"That's Jack," MacKinnon said. "If there's something that needs to be done, he'll sacrifice his health to make it happen if that's what's required. If he makes me his executive officer, I can take some of that off his hands. Interfacing with all those people will be challenging, but I can help carry the load.

"Our bridge officers are going to have to learn from those kids, too. While what they did was sufficient to save our lives, they don't have the depth of experience to do this work in a real fight. A game isn't life."

Tina wasn't sure how easy that would be. She'd heard Jack talking about how radically different the controls were and how unintuitive some of the work could be.

Still, that wasn't her concern. If India MacKinnon believed she could make it work, then she'd have to trust the woman to do it.

She spent the remainder of the flight going over everything she knew about their current situation and the odds stacked against them. If there was an unusual nature to any situation, she tried to pass it along. It was a lot of information for MacKinnon to absorb, but she was a Navy officer, and she'd probably remember it better than most.

Tina wrapped up her overview just as the pinnace docked with what was left of *Hawkwing*. The hatches immediately opened, and the first responders streamed into the crippled ship.

The air was filled with the scent of something burning, and she heard shouted instructions and cries of pain ahead of them. This was a disaster zone, and she needed to set aside the civilized part of her soul and get her hands dirty.

It was like doing a covert operation because she needed to lock her emotions away and do what needed to be done. Now was the time to save people's lives and worry about the nightmares later.

5

WHEN JACK and Sara arrived at the mess hall, they found the compartment packed with people. It was a mixture of Navy and Marine personnel, with a sprinkling of civilians thrown in for good measure. Everyone seemed to be eating as fast as possible, and the conversational volume was extremely high.

He started to mention that to Sara when something extraordinary occurred. In a bubble around them, the conversation ceased. It was almost as if someone had dropped a rock into a small pond, and the silence spread throughout the compartment as everyone stopped what they were doing and stared at him.

As the commanding officer of a Confederation Navy warship, Jack was used to some level of attention, but this was new and spooky.

Then one of the ratings standing nearest him began clapping.

That spread like wildfire throughout the crowd, and soon the entire compartment was filled with cheering, clapping people calling his name.

It was humbling, and he thought, mostly undeserved. He'd done the best he could, but so many people had still lost their lives. They'd been run out of the system with just the ships they could rescue.

That hadn't been a victory. All he'd done was avoid a complete disaster.

Sara poked him in the side with her elbow. "Say something. They need to hear you speak."

That almost intimidated him more than going into combat. He took a deep breath and stepped forward. "Don't clap for me, people. We did this together. Never forget that, but remember we've got a lot of work to do to get *Hunter* in condition to take the cluster away from the Locusts. And make no mistake, we're going to do just that."

His words set the crew off into another set of cheering and clapping. He didn't think his words were all *that* motivational, but these people had been through a lot. They'd needed to hear their work had meant something.

And it had. Everything he'd said was true. Together, they'd saved more than two hundred civilian ships, and while that was only a fraction of the shipping in the cluster, it had been all they could do.

They'd do better next time. Humanity was counting on them.

Sara hobbled over to one of the small tables, and the crew sitting there scrambled to clear it for them. Jack started to tell them not to, that they'd find their own table, but Sara was already thanking them for their courtesy and sitting. He could only do the same.

"I could've said something a bit more motivational if I've been thinking about it," he said, pitching his voice so only she could hear him.

"You didn't do that badly," she argued. "They needed to hear they'd done well, and word of what you've said here will make its way through the ship as fast as people can gossip. The crew has to think what they've done is worthwhile."

He smiled a little. "They've taken an impossible situation and made something magical happen. We made it into the Perseus Cluster and defended the people of the Confederation against these invaders, and we'll do it again."

A rating wearing a white apron came up and took their order. Jack noticed that nobody else was having their orders taken. They were just getting into line and being served, so he almost rejected the offer but remembered that Sara couldn't walk very well.

For her, he'd do this.

He suspected there was an officer's mess somewhere on the ship, but he preferred eating here rather than his quarters or in some other segregated area. He needed the connection with his crew more than anything right now. If he didn't have their full support, there was no way they could save the cluster.

"So, what do we need to talk about?" he asked, feeling more than a bit apprehensive.

"It's really an extension of the conversation we were having earlier," she said as she took a sip of water. "You're not delegating enough of your work, so things aren't getting done, or they're getting done poorly because you're trying to oversee every aspect of what's happening."

"The officers and crew from *Hawkwing* will help," he said. "India has a lot of experience at running a ship, and she'll be able to give me a hand doing the kinds of things I should be delegating to others.

"It's not going to cover everything that needs to be done, but she'll take a lot off my plate. The rest is sorting order from chaos. There are so many tasks that need doing. I can't be sure any of them are being done correctly or even at all. It's frustrating, maddening, and maybe a bit terrifying."

She shook her head and sighed. "Everything is a process, Jack. You start with what you can affect, and you work on getting that in order. That's going to bleed over into the other tasks that need attention.

"Having someone like Commander MacKinnon organizing everything is going to make the work easier. You've got plenty of hands to make things happen, but you don't have anyone to conduct the orchestra. You're too busy with the big picture."

"That's a good place for me to offer you a job. I realize this might be outside your comfort zone, but I need a chief of staff. Someone to do what David Chen is currently doing. We've got a war to fight, and I'm not even sure what the cluster's layout is. Yes, I've seen the map, but that only includes information about systems that had quantum gates.

"I guess what I'm saying is that I can't see the big picture for all of the problems we're dealing with, and that doesn't even include the civilians landing in our lap. You can rest assured they're not going to be happy when I tell them we're not taking their ships with us when we leave."

"I hadn't considered that," she admitted. "Those are going to be unpleasant conversations. What do we tell them?"

"The truth. Our ship got them here but was crippled in the process. We can't risk blowing any more fusion plants because it would leave us trapped and defenseless against the Locusts.

"We can take the people and potentially useful cargoes, though. The Confederation will need to reimburse them for what we take, or they'll need to deal with their insurance companies to recover their losses."

Sara chuckled without amusement. "You know that's not how this is going to work. Those companies will have Act of God clauses, and they'll definitely say an invasion by alien robots qualifies. Those of them that are still in business, anyway."

Jack grunted in acknowledgment. "True enough. The merchants will know that, too, so whoever is dealing with them will get a lot of pushback. That person will need to be something of a peacemaker. Are you willing to lend a hand?"

"I am, but not as your chief of staff," she said. "You need to have an arbiter, as well as someone who can tell you when you've made a mistake. I'll need my independence for that. My advice is to stick with David Chen as your staff officer. He'd be better at it than me anyway."

Once the man with the apron returned and delivered their food, they ate in silence while Jack considered their situation.

They were still in dire straits, but things were beginning to look up, at least a little bit.

So, of course, that was when he spotted Hutton coming into the mess hall, looking around. The petty officer saw him and headed over at a trot.

"Just the man I'm looking for, sir. We've got a problem."

"Of course we do," Jack said as he wiped his lips with his napkin. "What is it?"

"There are a bunch of merchants demanding to speak with you. I've got them squirreled away, but they're getting a bit rowdy if you know what I mean. They want to know what's happening, where they are, and what the hell we're going to do about getting them out of the cluster before the Locusts kill them."

Jack crossed his arms and leaned back in his chair. "I assume you've already told them everything we know. Exactly what will me repeating the information do?"

"Get them off my back? Look, sir, I can talk to them until I'm blue in the face—and believe you me, I love to talk—but that won't slow them down.

"I told them exactly where we are—in the middle of nowhere with no way out other than *Hunter*—and that the ship was damaged and under repair. I wouldn't commit to anything about getting their ships out because I know we're not going to be taking their ships with us when we leave."

He leaned toward Jack and lowered his voice a little. "Let me be the first to clue you in, sir, but that's not going to go over very well. Right now, they're scared. As soon as we tell them we're not taking their ships with us, they're going to get super pissed, super fast, and that's not something a petty officer should be dealing with.

"I hate to dump this in your lap, but this is a *commodore* problem."

Jack looked over at Sara and smiled. She rolled her eyes.

"Well, since I can't eat on a regular schedule, they're just going to have to wait until I finish this meal. Where do you have them stashed?"

The quartermaster rattled off a location tag that Jack was supposed to decipher. He wasn't sure precisely where it was, but he'd learned enough to be able to eventually find what he was looking for. It might take twice as long to get there as it should, but he'd find it.

"I don't want to have to do this all over again," Jack warned. "How many of the ship's captains or owners are we talking about? I know we've got just over two hundred ships out there. Please tell me this is at least a significant percentage of them."

Hutton shook his head. "Only a couple of dozen, but these are some of the ones with the largest freighters. If you want, I can see about getting as many of the other captains and owners aboard for the meeting as possible. If I tell them we're gathering everybody, that'll calm them down long enough, I expect."

"How long do you think gathering them will take?"

"If I tell them you're going to brief them about their situation, discuss the options going forward, and set a time of ninety minutes, I'll wager we can get most of them on board. I figure as long as we have two thirds of them, that'll be sufficient."

Jack laughed. "You are way too optimistic. Absolutely *nothing* we do is going to be sufficient. Those poor bastards are about to lose everything except their lives and what they can carry with them. They're going to be beyond angry, and there's absolutely nothing we can do to change that.

"We'll need to come up with a mechanism of dealing with problems from the civilians once we have more of them aboard. You're too busy doing other tasks, so we'll need to assign someone to be their liaison. Do you know anyone that might be worthwhile?"

"We're not going anywhere for at least a while, right?" Hutton asked. "If that's the case, I suggest Midshipman Calvo as a starting point. He's young but levelheaded. He's also somebody junior enough that he'd be delegated that kind of thing in any case."

"Technically, you should use a real officer," Sara said, pausing with her fork partway to her mouth. "The situation being what it is, you might want to bump him up to ensign so he can deal with this from a position of at least some authority. After all, you're trusting him to fly your ship. Shouldn't you trust him with real rank? That's true of all of your bridge officers."

Jack had avoided doing anything like that, but she wasn't wrong. "That's a big step for people that were just enlisted recruits and a real change for those that were civilians beforehand, but you're right. It makes sense, and it's time.

"I'll handle that before I meet with the captains. Hutton, gather everyone from the bridge crew—on shift and off—and make sure you have rank tabs for them all. If anyone doesn't have a uniform, they're going to need one."

"I'll handle it, sir," the man said. "Even the civilians have uniforms, though we didn't give them rank tabs. They'll be set once you do whatever magic you do to incorporate them into the service."

"Good enough. I'll be on the bridge in forty-five minutes."

"See you there, sir."

After the man had departed, Jack raised an eyebrow and looked at Sara. "I don't suppose you're familiar with any regulation that allows me to conscript civilians into the Confederation Navy, are you? Or promote people without going through the personnel office?"

"No, but I suspect something probably exists. People in combat situations often have to do things that would never fly under normal circumstances.

"Just focus on just doing what you need to do, and I'll see if I can find some regulations to back you up, Jack. We're all behind you."

"Thanks. That's the only way I can make this work. Now, let's see if I can finish this meal before someone else comes running up with a disaster that needs my attention right this very second."

6

DEREK SAT SOMEWHAT self-consciously in the command chair on the bridge, keeping watch over the crew on station while they oversaw the hundreds of ships in the area. It was pretty dull, all told, until some of the off-duty bridge crew sauntered in.

At first, he didn't think anything of it because people generally came and went as required, but when a few more clumps of people arrived and then a whole lot more in a rush, he knew something was up. There were now more people on the bridge than seats, and they just kept coming.

"What's going on?" he asked the latest group.

A young woman shrugged. "I'm not sure. Petty Officer Hutton called us in for a meeting."

That was interesting. No one had told him anything about a meeting, not that a midshipman was usually notified in advance of, well, anything. Still, this had to mean the commodore needed to talk to them all.

That seemed to be the general consensus because the conversations kicked into high gear with speculation about what was going on. Some people wondered if engineering had managed to get another fusion plant online, so the engineering watch officer —a civilian—had to shoot that down.

The next supposition was that they wouldn't be able to get enough power to jump, and they were trapped. That was serious enough that he had to step on it immediately.

"Belay that kind of talk," he said, pitching his voice to discourage argument. "Engineering is still working on the fusion plants, and there's every chance they're going to get them working again, or we'll be able to salvage something from one of the civilian ships or *Hawkwing*.

"Don't start rumors like that because we don't want to cause a panic. Got me?"

A bit abashedly, everyone nodded their agreement.

Before anyone else could come up with another theory about the meeting, Commodore Romanoff strode onto the bridge with Petty Officer Hutton two steps behind him. The latter carried a bag.

Derek started to stand, but the commodore waved him back down. "At ease, everyone. Those of you on watch, keep an eye on your consoles but listen up. Things have been hectic, and I haven't had an opportunity to talk to you as a group, so I apologize for waking those off shift, but this needed to happen now.

"Without your skill and know-how, we wouldn't have been

able to save over two hundred civilian vessels and their crews. The Navy cruiser *Hawkwing* is also in your debt. On behalf of the Confederation Navy and all the survivors of the fight, well done."

That generated a mild round of applause, but Derek suspected most of them weren't sure how to take the compliment. He personally had mixed feelings. Although they'd done everything they could, the Navy had still lost that fight.

All they'd managed to do was protect *Hawkwing* from being destroyed before they retreated from the system. He felt ashamed that they hadn't beaten the attacking drones and saved the other cruisers. They'd done their best, but the ship just wasn't in condition to fight.

That would change. It had to.

"We're not getting reinforcements, so we're going to have to conserve and marshal what we have," the commodore said, slowly looking around the compartment. "That's not going to be easy, and all of us are going to have to step up in ways we might not feel comfortable with. That's true of me, and it's certainly true of you."

Derek felt a sense of foreboding. This was leading to something, but he couldn't figure out what it was.

"Each of you volunteered for this duty and gave it everything you had. That has earned you the gratitude of myself and the Confederation Navy. Unfortunately, the people operating a warship of this caliber need to be Confederation Navy officers.

"The closest some of you come to that is being midshipmen recently bumped up from officer candidates. Many of you are recruits on the enlisted side or even civilians. That's not going to cut it going forward."

Derek's heart froze. Were they about to be sent back to the training units they'd come from, their time serving on the bridge over?

He didn't want that to be true. This opportunity had given him the chance to use skills he'd spent a decade honing, and he still had a lot to offer.

Based on everyone else's expressions, he wasn't the only one with that impression. Everyone in the room looked shocked or stricken.

"Luckily, I've come up with a way to solve that particular problem," the commodore said with a grin. "Everyone still seated, please stand."

Derek stood and faced the commodore, knowing his expression was more than a bit quizzical. What was happening?

"Raise your right hands and repeat after me. I, state your full name, having been appointed an ensign in the Confederation Navy, do solemnly swear that I will support and defend the Confederation against all enemies, foreign and domestic, that I bear true faith and allegiance to the same; that I take this obligation freely, without any mental reservation or purpose of evasion; and that I will well and faithfully discharge the duties of the office upon which I am about to enter."

Stunned, Derek managed to repeat the words, but he felt as if his brain were frozen. Of all the potential outcomes, this one had never occurred to him. He'd been working toward becoming a

Navy officer for years but to have it arrive with such speed made it hard to grasp.

The commodore nodded when he'd finished listening to the crowd recite the words. "For those of you who were not previously members of the Confederation Navy, allow me to be the first to welcome you to our ranks. You've got a lot to learn about military decorum, but I expect your comrades will see you brought up to speed as quickly as possible.

"For those of you who were already in one of the academies, either as an officer candidate or recruit, you've now leapfrogged the entire educational process, and you've got a lot of gaps that you'll need to fill as well."

He grinned. "Particularly for those that were recruits rather than officer candidates. You've gone from working hard to becoming enlisted crewmen to being officers. There will be some behavioral changes that come with that, so I expect you to keep your awesome powers under control. Got it?"

That earned chuckles from everyone. Even the recruits and civilians knew ensigns had virtually no real power or authority. Still, when everybody else crewing the ship were recruits and officer candidates, there would be moments where everyone would have to mind what they were doing and how they were doing it.

The commodore waited until the chuckles had faded before continuing. "Your focus right now is to keep doing exactly what you're doing. The Confederation desperately needs the skills you've brought to the table.

"We're getting some new officers to oversee each of the

departments. They'll be able to provide you with guidance, but they'll be relying on *your* skills. The officers and crew from *Hawkwing* won't know how to operate *Hunter*'s equipment, nor will they know exactly what the limitations and tactics they should be using are. It's your job to tactfully educate them."

Derek had suspected that's what would happen, but he hadn't taken the thought to its logical conclusion. Of course they'd have officers taking over the bridge watch, and frankly, that made him feel a lot better. He was bright enough to know there were holes in his knowledge.

It was going to be his job to work with whoever the new helm officer was and bring them up to speed on how to control the giant battleship. Then he'd have to go through everything he knew about how to use the quantum drive. They'd pushed the ship severely getting here, and he still hadn't had an opportunity to incorporate what they'd learned from the almost disastrous experience.

For example, was it entirely out of the question to take other ships with them when they jumped? Had they extended their quantum field too far, but a shorter distance would've been acceptable? If they'd had more fusion plants, would that have been fine?

No one knew, and it was his job to help figure out the answers. Somehow.

"I won't take up any more of your time," the commodore said. "Those of you that were off shift may return to whatever you were doing once you've picked up your new rank tabs from Petty Officer Hutton.

"Again, you have my congratulations and gratitude for everything you've done and will be doing. Dismissed."

Even as everyone filed out, getting their rank tabs, Derek stood waiting. He had some questions for the commodore if the man had time to answer them.

Once the on-duty bridge crew had their new rank tabs and were busy putting them in place, Commodore Romanoff took a set of ensigns tabs and began putting them on Derek's shoulders in place of the midshipman's tabs.

"I'd imagine this is a confusing time for you, Derek. You've had to step into a leadership role, and now someone else is going to be taking over. At least that's got to be what you're thinking. I'll let you in on a little secret. It's only partially true.

"You're going to have someone as a new department head, true, but the two of you are going to get along just fine. Lieutenant Commander Golousenko is a good officer and a very talented helmsman. He's not going to dismiss your input simply because of your inexperience. Far from it."

The commodore finished his work and clapped Derek on the shoulder. "He can't be on the bridge all the time, and I'm going to have to rely on you to help fill as many blanks as you can while still running herd on the bridge crew during the off shift. There just aren't enough trained personnel to fill every role."

Derek nodded. "Whatever needs to be done, sir, I'm your man. I've already been thinking about how to bring the other helmsmen up to speed, and we've even set up a few simulator consoles in the operations center."

The commodore pursed his lips and nodded. "That's the first

I've heard of this, but it's good news. I'm sure there are a lot of simulations available in *Hunter's* systems. The computers were built back during the war, and they'll be filled with various simulated encounters and situations that can be used.

"We can make it more realistic if we set aside one of the compartments in there as a makeshift training facility once we know which simulations are the best to start off with. That's going to be one of your first tasks after I drop *another* job in your lap."

Derek raised an eyebrow at his commanding officer. "Whatever it is, sir, I can handle it."

"I certainly hope so because it's going to be one of the most challenging jobs you've ever done, and it's an important one. I'll need you to do some liaison work with the civilian captains and owners. They're coming aboard for a meeting right now, and I expect it to be a raucous affair with a lot of finger-pointing and shouting.

"The end result will be that they'll have to leave their ships here when we depart the system. If, of course, we can manage to get the quantum drive functional again."

"That does sound challenging, sir," Derek admitted. "You know I'll do absolutely everything I can to make this work, but I don't expect they're going to take the news very well."

"No, they won't, but you're not going to have to deal with the initial heat. I'll head this meeting, and you'll only be handed over as the liaison after they've had a chance to lose their minds with me first.

"They're going to be in shock—hell, they're already in shock

—and that's going to make them lash out, so you'll need to be very patient with them. I understand this is different than anything you've done before—and the same is true of me—but we're all going to have to do things we've never done before if we hope to beat the Locusts and free the Perseus Cluster. Do you think you can handle this?"

"I'll give it my best shot, sir. If I run into something I can't handle, I'll tag you or one of the new officers coming over from *Hawkwing*. If I might ask, sir, how did that meeting go?"

The commodore grimaced. "About as badly as you'd expect. Captain Magri is cooling off in a set of borrowed quarters. He lost his temper, and I'm afraid he said some things that won't be easy to walk back.

"I've threatened him with charges of insubordination and disobeying a direct order, but I expect to drop the threat once the situation has cooled off. I needed to do that because he wasn't seeing reason."

The commodore smiled again. "By the way, I respect the backbone it took to stand up to a ship's captain and tell him you were going to throw him off this ship if he didn't comply with my instructions. It was the right call, and it shows you've got what it takes to be a good officer. Just keep in mind that he's going to hold a grudge."

Wasn't that just perfect. The man would probably think Derek had been promoted for mouthing off to him.

"Still, you won't have to deal with him for the time being," the commodore continued. "I'll make Commander MacKinnon my executive officer as soon as the rescue operations aboard

Hawkwing are complete, and she'll bring over the existing command structure for us to build on.

"I won't say that's going to make everything easy, but it'll at least give us something we can work with. Whatever happens with Captain Magri, rest assured that I have no intention of putting him in a position of direct authority over any area of the ship."

The man sighed. "It's wrong of me to speak ill of another officer, but he's got too many things going against him for us to trust him. If he wants to do something more constructive aboard *Hunter*, he's going to have to show he's worthy of the opportunity."

The commodore gestured toward the bridge hatch. "Tag one of your compatriots to head the rest of the watch and come with me, Ensign Calvo. It's time for the shouting to begin."

7

JACK FOLLOWED Hutton with Calvo trailing behind them both into a section of the ship he wasn't familiar with. Mac Turner was there with two dozen Marines—a mixture of his people and Laura Dubsky's regular Marines—to keep things from getting out of control.

Not that even they could stop a riot if one broke out, so he hoped there were more Marines standing by just in case.

When they arrived outside the open hatch, Jack could hear quite a bit of loud talking. The crowd seemed riled up, and they wouldn't be happy to hear what he had to say.

"Any clue how many people are in there?" he asked Hutton. "We rescued two hundred and six civilian ships, so what are we looking at? Captains, first officers, owners?"

"All of the above, sir. The last tally I had said we had representatives from almost every ship. I suspect those that aren't here will arrive before you're done. Go get it, sir. You've got this."

Taking a deep breath, Jack stepped into the compartment and found it filled with people. He wasn't sure what its original purpose had been, but there was a small platform off to one side with a lectern on it, so that's where he headed.

He hoped the sound system was functional because there had to be five or six hundred people in the compartment, easy, and none of them were very quiet.

His arrival didn't go unnoticed, and people were already shouting questions at him. The kind of things one would expect. Where are we? What's happening? When are we getting back to the Confederation?

There were variations on the theme, but those would be the big questions. He didn't know everything these people had been through during the invasion, but it had to have been hell.

Up until a few hours ago, they'd been on the run for their lives. All of that fear and panic was still in their systems, and he'd have to stay patient with them when they inevitably lost their tempers.

Jack walked up the short set of stairs onto the platform and waited for Hutton to step up to the lectern before positioning Calvo directly beside him. He wanted the crowd to get a good look at the young man. He'd be fielding their complaints, so they needed to be familiar with what he looked like.

"If I can have your attention," Hutton said through the microphone on the lectern, "Commodore Romanoff is here to give you a briefing and then answer some questions. You'll need to quiet down, or he's not going to be able to talk."

The conversation didn't die down immediately, but it started edging that way as the various participants quieted those around them so they could find out what was going on. Jack didn't wait for total silence because he knew that wasn't going to happen. This wasn't a military crowd, and he couldn't treat it like one.

He stepped up to the lectern as soon as Hutton moved aside and looked out over the crowd. The compartment was filled with men and women of every description, and each of them looked desperate, angry, or terrified. Often all of the above. This wasn't going to be an easy task.

"My name is Jack Romanoff, and I'm the commanding officer of the Confederation battleship *Delta Orionis*. I want to start by saying I know you've been through a lot, and I'm afraid that hardship isn't over yet.

"I'll explain everything in detail and then take questions, but you have to remember the Confederation is in the midst of one of the greatest crises of its existence. We're doing the best we can, but you already know deep in your hearts that what I have to say isn't going to be what you want to hear, and I ask you to try to keep a lid on those feelings for the moment."

That sent a murmur through the crowd, but he could see at least a few of them understood though it didn't make them happy. This crowd would have some smart people in it, and they'd understood the stakes, and how screwed they were.

And then there would be those that only cared about themselves and/or their money. He could sympathize with them, too, but that didn't change the facts.

"The Perseus Cluster has fallen to the Locusts," he started off with. "I haven't read any briefings or spoken to anyone involved in the evacuation, so I have to assume it was like the last invasion, and every ship and station in space was destroyed, and our ships are the only space-going vessels still in existence in the cluster.

"I'm sure many of you lost friends and family, and for that, I am truly, deeply sorry. So did I, when the Navy lost every ship holding the Locusts back while you tried to escape. We're going to do what we can to take the cluster back, but that's not going to be quick or easy. And it's going to require sacrifice."

He took a deep breath and launched into it. "*Hunter*—which is what we call *Delta Orionis*—is probably the only ship in the Confederation with an independent quantum drive. We don't need quantum gates to get from system to system, and that's going to be necessary inside the cluster because the Navy triggered self-destruct devices inside the quantum gates.

"*Hunter* extended her quantum field to take you with us when we jumped to this system, but she wasn't designed to transport other vessels with her like that, and we blew one of our fusion plants. Until we get the power systems repaired, none of us is going anywhere."

That sparked a great deal of shouted questions, but Jack let them wash over him. It wasn't that he ignored them, though. He'd have to answer them eventually.

He raised his hands to quiet them down after a few more seconds, and that prompted them to lower the volume a little.

"We have a plan for restoring power, but it's not going to be good enough to risk taking any other ships with us when we leave this system. I'm afraid you're going to have to bring your crews and passengers aboard *Hunter*, and we're going to leave your ships here."

As expected, that caused pandemonium. He'd only thought the shouted questions earlier had been loud. Now people were screaming denial and demanding that he find other solutions.

Rather than trying to quiet them down, he let them shout. There was no use trying to get louder than they were. That just wasn't going to happen.

He was grateful that Turner and the Marines were between him and the crowd. Tempers were running high, and people might be tempted to do things they otherwise wouldn't.

"I understand you have everything invested in your vessels and cargoes," Jack finally said. "I wish I had better news for you, but without some way of repairing the fusion plants we have, we can't take that kind of risk. How would you feel if we went to a system full of Locusts and were trapped because the power plants failed again?"

"Just take us back to the rest of the Confederation!" someone shouted.

"We can't make a jump that long, and the cluster is isolated from the stars around it," he said.

A large bearded man wearing a red hat and matching jacket stalked to just in front of the Marines and glared up at Jack. "You're asking us to abandon everything we've worked a lifetime to build with no guarantee we'll ever see it again. Hell, if we go with you back into the cluster, there's every chance we're going to die.

"We were promised evacuation by the Navy, you haven't delivered, and we're not going to stand for it! You'll have to come up with a solution if you want any cooperation from us because you can't make us go!"

That earned a lot of shouted support for the man's position, and Jack sympathized, but it didn't change the situation one bit. He'd been afraid things would go this direction, and he'd been mentally preparing himself.

"You're right about that," Jack admitted. "I can't make you abandon everything you've spent a lifetime building. What I *can* do is leave this system and carry out my duty.

"Anyone who doesn't go with me will be trapped here, potentially forever. This system doesn't have anything habitable in it, nor any way for you to do things like grow food or produce oxygen easily. Those who remain would be doomed to a slow death by starvation or asphyxiation. Not a fate I'd wish on my worst enemy, much less the people I'm sworn to protect."

That quieted the crowd right down. He hadn't wanted to put it so bluntly, yet he had to be crystal clear or risk more resistance going forward.

"Look, once we get *Hunter* repaired, there are potential options. Your ships could likely be helpful in the areas of the cluster we take back from the Locusts. In that case, we might come back for your ships once I can be sure the power levels on *Hunter* can support moving your ships. And make no mistake, we're going to be taking this cluster back from them.

"The other option is that once the Confederation kicks the Locusts out of the cluster, they'll rebuild the quantum gates. I'm not saying getting your ships out of here would be a high priority for them, but the case could be made that they owe you that much."

He didn't mention his suspicion that the Locusts would be sending motherships after them. They wouldn't know which system to go to, so it might take them a while to find the right one, but they'd eventually do so and destroy the ships left here. He'd keep that to himself for now.

Jack took a deep breath and laid out a line he knew that no one would be pleased to hear. "Sadly, in the short term—and perhaps the long, too—you're going to have to deal with your insurance companies for the losses."

That didn't *quite* cause the same level of pandemonium as earlier, but not a single person in the compartment believed their insurance company would give them one red cent. In fact, they shouted derision at the idea of insurance companies paying out *anything* during the war, and they couldn't have been clearer and more profane in doing so.

The fact that they were almost certainly right didn't help.

Once again, Jack just let them shout. Nothing he said would make things better, so he didn't even try. He'd laid out the basics of their situation, and they were going to have to get used to it.

In the end, all he could do was offer to save their lives. If they chose to remain here, he couldn't do anything to stop them.

Well, he supposed if push came to shove, he might decide he couldn't let the stupid or stubborn commit suicide. He'd only make that call if he had no choice, though, because that would open up an entirely different can of worms.

And their current mood didn't even reflect the *other* bomb he had to drop on them. Might as well get that out of the way.

"None of you have to make any decisions right now," he said once they'd run down a bit. "I understand that this is hard, and you're going to have to think about it. One other unpleasant thing to be pondering is that it may prove needful for me to commandeer some of your cargoes that would be useful in the war effort. If so, the Confederation will pay for them.

"I'll open the floor to questions, but I suspect they'll revolve around everything I've just said, and I'm not changing my plan of action. We're not leaving immediately, so there will be a few days —maybe as much as a week, but I wouldn't count on that—while we wait for enough power to be restored for *Hunter* to jump. You'll have that long to make up your minds."

"Why did the Confederation trap us in the cluster in the first place?" a woman demanded. "There weren't any damned Locusts anywhere near us when they blew the gate up! They trapped us here when they didn't have to!"

"I don't know," Jack admitted. "We'd only just arrived in the system when that plan was launched, and Vice Admiral LaChasse didn't see fit to pass her reasoning on to me.

"I wish she'd have allowed more time for you to evacuate, but unfortunately, that's not the case. As the old saying goes, there's no use crying over spilled milk. What's done is done, and now we have to live with the consequences."

"Does your ship have enough space for all of us?" someone else asked. "It's big, but there will be a lot of people."

"It might be a tight fit, but we can carry everybody," he confirmed. "If we need to dig out more compartments, so everybody has a place to stretch their elbows, we can do that. Next?"

"I don't know what kind of questions I should even be asking," another man complained. "You've probably got more pressing things on your mind than talking day and night with the likes of us, so who do we talk to?"

"I have someone in mind to make sure your questions are answered."

He turned toward Calvo and opened his mouth to introduce him, but somebody in front of the Marines called out before he could speak.

"And that would be me," a man yelled. "I'll be your point of contact and liaison."

Jack turned back toward the crowd, shocked at the unexpected interruption. What he saw below sent a jolt of rage through him.

Standing there with his arms raised over his head was Ronnie Magri. The troublesome captain had just inserted himself into a volatile situation that Jack had no desire to see him part of.

Yet the man had virtually tied his hands by jumping in the way he had. The mob was already crowding around him, asking questions and making demands. Jack couldn't hear any of his responses, but the damned man was already in the thick of it, and if he yanked him out now, it would damage his own standing since it would look like he couldn't even control Magri.

Which, it seemed, he couldn't.

"Sir?" Calvo asked. "What's going on?"

"I don't know, but it looks like you're off the hook for this particular job," Jack said with a grim sigh. "I'll deal with Captain Magri later, but it looks like he's going to be the new liaison with the civilians. God help us all."

8

Tina followed India MacKinnon through the emergency
airlock into engineering and tried to control her breathing. She
didn't have much experience in vacuum suits, though she'd done
some training. As the other woman had told her, the key was to
take things slowly and make sure she watched out for things that
could damage her suit at all times.

The engineering compartment aboard *Hawkwing* was in
vacuum because the drones had done a tremendous amount of
damage to the engines and blown gaping holes in the engineering
compartment itself. A fair chunk of the fatalities that the warship
suffered had been in the aft portion of the ship because that's
where the drones had focused their attention.

It was astonishing that the ship still had power, yet the lights
were still on. Of course, light and dark had no softness to them in
vacuum. Shadows began as suddenly as a knife fight and were

just as keen as a well-honed blade. Inky blackness stood in sharp relief to the bright light when something blocked the illumination.

The recovery efforts had already ended, and virtually the entire ship's complement had been moved to *Hunter* already. There were probably less than a dozen people still aboard the crippled warship, and they were almost all in engineering.

Lieutenant Commander Charlie Ferrero, the ship's chief engineer, was heading them up. She felt sorry for the man because he'd lost so many people under his command. In a vacuum environment, injuries that might otherwise have been survivable had claimed the lives of anyone whose suit had been compromised.

Nevertheless, he seemed to be holding it together and was laser focused on the tasks that needed doing. He'd no doubt deal with his demons later.

Once she could finally see what MacKinnon and Ferrero were looking at, she understood why the other woman had brought her down here. They were staring at the fusion plant and all of its support equipment.

It was a miracle it hadn't been destroyed outright in the fighting because there was a massive tear in the hull just a few meters away that was bigger than it was. Not only that, but some of the destroyed fusion drives had also sprayed the compartment with fragments and debris, rendering other equipment unusable but only slightly denting the outer containment cylinder of the fusion plant itself.

"So tell me about the fusion plant, Charlie," India said over the radio frequency they were using. "Commodore Romanoff says they need it aboard *Hunter* so they can use their independent quantum drive again. Are we going to be able to safely move this thing?"

The man chuckled without humor. "It's a bloody miracle that it works at all, but even with all the destruction the Locusts wreaked in engineering, it only has a few dings that affect its appearance rather than its function. All of its support systems are still operational, too, so we should be able to salvage everything.

"In fact, with the vast amount of hull damage we've taken back here, we're not even going to have to disassemble it. We can just shut it down, disconnect it from its mounting and support equipment, and then push it out through the hole right over there."

He turned so that his face was visible through the faceplate. "I wish I could argue against us being so generous with our critical equipment, but *Hawkwing* is dead, and that breaks my heart."

India put her hand on the man's shoulder. "I know it's hard, Charlie, but we can't give up the fight. A lot of people are counting on us, and we're just going to have to keep doing what we need to do.

"If you started right now, how long until we can salvage not only the fusion plant but everything else that might be useful? I'm talking weapons and anything else you think we should take before we destroy the ship."

Tina could hear the pain in the other woman's voice as she said that last sentence, and she understood. These people had a lot of emotion and loyalty invested in this ship, and they didn't want to destroy it, but they didn't have a choice. Nothing useful to the Locusts could be left intact.

"If we can get some support from *Hunter's* engineering team, we should be able to get the fusion plant and support equipment out in twelve hours. Things like the primary weapons and other significant pieces of equipment will probably take at least another couple of days.

"All of the ancillary gear and supplies can be gathered at the same time, so we should be able to strip the ship completely in three to four days once we get the assistance we need. I wish I could argue against setting off the self-destruct charges, but sadly, I can't."

The sandy-haired officer grimaced. "Do we have any idea what's going to happen once we transfer to *Hunter*? I've been a little too busy to do more than listen with half an ear to the rumors making their way through the ship, but it sounds like they're in bad shape over there. How do we merge the crews without making that situation worse?"

"That's one of the reasons I brought Tina down here. She has Commodore Romanoff's confidence, and I think she can give you a better idea than I can of what we're looking at."

Recognizing her cue, Tina smiled at the man. "As one of the engineers, you're going to be transferring into a section of the ship that's mostly operational. The drives are in good condition, and so are the general power systems, but that isn't to say there's not some chaos and a lot of work to do.

"*Hunter's* chief engineer, Lieutenant Kelly Danek, has a decent team, though I'll admit all of the original crew members aboard *Hunter* are a little quirky. The Navy used *Hunter* as a dumping ground for the undesirables they couldn't just get rid of, and it sometimes shows."

The man frowned. "Danek. The name seems vaguely familiar. I don't think I've ever met her, but the name is tickling a memory. It is a woman, right? Kelly's one of those ambiguous names, and I want to be sure I've got this right in my head."

"That's right. Brown hair and thin, she's a real go-getter when it comes to keeping things working and getting equipment back online, but *Hunter* is in bad shape in spite of that.

"For example, the ship originally came with four large fusion plants, but one of them hasn't been functional in a long time. She had one running at full power and another at partial power and then got a third one online on the way out here."

Now it was her turn to grimace. "That last one is now trash, leaving us with one and a half fusion plants. Hence the need for *Hawkwing*'s to make up the power differential so we can use the independent quantum drive to get out of here."

The man nodded, his mind obviously still focused on who Danek might be. Then he frowned even more.

"I think I remember her. Like I said, we've never met, but one hears rumors. She used to be a chief engineer aboard a cruiser, but something happened, and she got busted. If she's a lieutenant now, she didn't get run out of the service, but they took some of her rank. Not sure what she did, but it raises some flags for me."

"You've got to stop that kind of thinking right now," Tina said. "All of the original crew aboard *Hunter* were castoffs and rejects, but they've come together to get the ship operational.

Commodore Romanoff said that whatever happened to them before they arrived aboard *Hunter* didn't matter. What matters is what we do now."

"And he's right," India said. "Anyone we run into over there likely has a black mark on their record, or they're a civilian, or they're fresh from the Academy. All of us will have to come together and make this work.

"And here's another thing that's probably going to irritate the hell out of you. Kelly Danek might be a lieutenant, but she's *Hunter*'s chief engineer, and it's going to stay that way. She's been working on that ship for years, and I doubt very seriously that Commodore Romanoff would replace her during a crisis."

The man sighed and nodded. "I get that. Honestly, my ego doesn't mean that I have to be in charge just because I'm a grade higher than she is. If she was a chief engineer, she has as much experience as I do. Hell, on that ship, she's got a lot more experience, and I don't intend to joggle her elbow.

"I'll talk to my people, and we'll do everything possible to integrate smoothly. She's in charge, and I'll back her."

"You're going to have to pass that word to everyone," Tina said. "I'm not sure how Jack intends to handle crew integration, but we can't afford to upset the applecart at a critical moment. We've got a life-and-death fight in front of us, and that has to be our primary focus. This is an all hands on deck kind of thing."

Both of the Navy officers nodded.

"Assuming he makes me his executive officer, you can rest assured I'll make that clear to everyone," India said. "Rank isn't necessarily the driving factor of who's in charge of doing what.

For God's sake, we've got midshipmen flying the ship and firing the weapons. Civilians and basic recruits as well. We can't get hung up on who outranks who."

"We'll figure this out," Ferraro said. "Whatever it takes, my people and I will work with whoever we need to beat the Locusts. The Confederation is counting on us, and I'm not going to let it down. None of my people will.

"Now, if you two could get out of my hair, we've got a lot of work to do, and I'm going to need some help from *Hunter*. If they have anyone that knows anything about fusion plants, that would be helpful."

"As a matter of fact, headquarters sent over a slew of engineers specialized in fusion plants," Tina said. "I have no idea who they are or what they do, but that's supposedly their bag."

"That would be perfect," Ferraro said with the first hint of a smile she'd seen on the man. "Send them my way as quickly as you can, and we'll have this power plant relocated to *Hunter* and back online within twenty-four hours. With specialists, we might even be able to shave some time off of that. No promises, though."

Tina was about to say something else when her suit comm unit chimed for her attention. She looked at the small heads-up display and saw she had an incoming signal from the pinnace that had brought them over.

"Excuse me for a second," she said. "I've got an incoming call that probably means something else has gone wrong."

She switched channels and accepted the call as she turned her back on the others for privacy.

"Tina, this is Jack. We've got a problem."

"Of course we do. Could you be more specific?"

"Magri. The bastard slipped out of confinement—though I suppose that's a bit of a stretch since I didn't have him arrested—and made an appearance when I was talking to the assembled captains and owners of the civilian ships.

"I was going to assign Calvo as their liaison and point of contact, but Magri declared *himself* as my choice for the position. Considering how adamant he was about resisting me just a while ago, this isn't him having a change of heart."

"No, probably not," she said. "What exactly do you want me to do about him? Shove him out an airlock, and make it look like an accident?"

That got a short bark of laughter from Jack. "Hardly. I want to tap into your experience with covert operations. Since you weren't in the room when we met, he doesn't know you, so I wonder if we can mix you into the civilians as one of the shipowners.

"You don't know anything about ship operations, but a lot of owners are relatively ignorant about that sort of thing. I need someone that can make sure he's not playing me false. Rather, I need someone to tell me exactly how and when he plans on sticking a knife into my back."

"Finally," she said with a predatory smile. "Something that's right up my alley. Count me in."

9

Jack put away his communicator and stared at Magri as the crowd shifted and swirled around the man, demanding answers to questions the slick bastard couldn't possibly know the answers to.

Yet somehow, whatever he was saying seemed to reassure them somewhat. As annoying as that was, the man seemed to be able to handle their complaints better than Jack had.

Frankly, if that had been the extent of his concerns about the situation, Jack might've been willing to let things continue as they were, but he didn't believe that was all the irritating officer had in mind.

Not for one single second.

"Excuse me, Commodore? Might I have a word with you? It's quite important."

Jack focused his attention on the older woman standing on the other side of the line of Marines. She was dressed in a basic ship's suit, but it sported a pastel pattern that indicated she had particular tastes that she was more than willing to wear even when working.

Standing behind her were half a dozen young adults of both genders dressed in similar ship suits, though thankfully sporting more pedestrian colors. On balance, they didn't seem to be all that threatening, so he gestured for the Marines to let them pass.

"If you're looking for different answers than I just gave, I'm afraid I don't have any for you," he said. "You'll need to speak with Captain Magri, and don't be afraid to ask him as many questions as you'd like. It's his job to give you answers."

He hoped the crowd wore the man down to a nub.

The older woman smiled but shook her head. "This isn't the type of question that can be answered by anyone else, I'm afraid. I possess information that requires a high level of confidentiality.

"I'm Professor Alice Wilson from the University of Benedict. These fine upstanding young people are my research assistants. We were on an archaeological excavation of some sensitivity when the invasion occurred, and we have something in our possession that may be of critical importance to the war effort, so I felt I should pass that information along to you personally and immediately."

"Well, that does sound suitably mysterious," Jack admitted. "Can you at least clue me in on the general nature of your find?"

"Perhaps an image would be better."

She pulled a comm unit off of her belt and tapped on its screen a few times before handing it up to Jack. One glance at the screen, and he knew exactly what he was looking at. A Locust mothership.

"I see," he said. "I've seen a reconstruction of one in the recent past, as well as fragments of destroyed units. Are you telling me that you found one in a relatively intact condition?"

"Please flip through the other images. I believe they'll tell the full story of what we're looking at more effectively than I can."

He did so and saw that the mothership wasn't completely intact. A high-powered laser had drilled a hole through its center from top to bottom. It seemed in good condition otherwise, but the damage in that one area was total.

"While doing some scavenging work at the outskirts of our system looking for battle debris to study, we came across this mothership drifting on a course that told us it had been there since virtually the beginning of the first invasion," Wilson said. "Our vessel had a hold that was *just* large enough to bring it aboard, so we jettisoned the other scraps we'd found and pulled it in. We had just less than a week to examine it in place before the new invasion started.

"It may not be readily apparent from looking at the images, but the laser shot went directly through the computer core. Commodore, the rest of the vessel is intact. *All* of it."

Jack thought about that for a few moments trying to figure out precisely what she was getting at, and then he caught it. She was talking about the alien hyperdrive.

"If you and your students would come with me, Professor, I think we need to discuss this in a more private setting. And amusingly, I think I have the perfect location to do so."

He gestured for Calvo to accompany them and headed for the exit. Magri was just going to have to handle the civilians for the moment because this was important enough to demand Jack's complete attention.

A group of four Marines peeled off from the rest and bracketed the Navy officers as they continued down the corridor. Jack didn't think he was in any danger from an elderly professor and six grad students. Nevertheless, it hadn't been that long ago that someone had tried to kill him.

Thankfully, he knew where the professor's laboratory—his professor—was located. It only took a short trip in one of the lifts and then journeying farther back in the ship. When they arrived at Prescott's laboratory, he tapped the code into the numeric keypad to open the hatch, and all of them walked in.

Wilson jerked to a halt as soon as she saw the scale of Prescott's collection of equipment and debris. "Stars above! I don't think I've seen a collection of Locust debris like this in my life. Where did you get it?"

"Technically, it's not mine," Jack said. "Doctor Alan Prescott, the head of the Locust War Historical Society and a xenoarchaeologist by trade, has been doing research on the Locusts for quite some time. This is his laboratory.

"Oh, and I'm afraid that everyone here calls him the professor, so you're going to have to come up with some other title, or we're going to get very confused about who we're talking about."

"You can call me Doctor Wilson if you simply must, but Alice works just fine." She walked over to the table holding the functional alien computer core. "This goes to a Locust mothership.

What has he connected it to, and what is he doing? And where is he? If he's aboard, I need to speak with him.

"And by the way, I've read a number of his papers and his warnings about the potential for an invasion. I'll admit I was skeptical, but circumstances have proven him correct and me disastrously wrong. That's a bitter pill to swallow for humanity's sake."

"I can't get into the details, but there was an assassination attempt a few days ago, and he was shot. He's recovering, and I'm sure he's going to want to speak with you. I'm not sure how active he's going to be, but you'll undoubtedly have an advocate aboard saying we need to devote sufficient resources to what you've found to understand it.

"And to be sure that I'm clear, you were hinting that its hyper-drive was intact, yes?"

The woman nodded. "To the best of my ability to determine, yes. We know very little about that sort of thing, but unlike previous units, the self-destruct mechanism on this one wasn't triggered, though it is still present. We possess a fully intact Locust mothership, minus a computer."

Jack nodded. "This compartment is too small to house an intact mothership, even if we could get it here. One of the disused small craft bays might be more suitable. Thankfully, most of them are currently unused, and we should be able to work something out to get the mothership aboard without anyone seeing us do it."

He turned to face the seven educators and researchers. "I'm afraid that everything I said in the other compartment is still true.

We're not going to be able to bring your ship with us, but any research equipment and salvaged debris you have aboard will have a home here.

"I feel confident that Professor Prescott can coordinate with you to get more out of what he was doing, as well. He's been complaining he didn't have enough trained people to do everything that needed doing, and the collaboration between the two of you might be very fruitful."

The woman nodded but gestured back toward the computer core. "Let me reiterate my earlier question. Why is that core hooked up to a bank of regular computers? No one has had any luck in deciphering the contents of one before. Has that situation changed?"

Jack hesitated for a moment, and then he nodded. "It has. A civilian computer engineer—who isn't aboard—cracked the interface and was able to read the core. Working with him, the professor determined that the cores he's been working with were disabled and had their critical contents wiped.

"This core—the one the civilian worked on for years—wasn't wiped. It seemingly has everything it originally did. The professor's hypothesis is that the support equipment that should've wiped it was destroyed before it could perform the task, much like on the ship you found."

Wilson walked around the table, her eyes wide. "So you're saying we potentially have a fully functioning Locust mothership, and you might have the data needed to operate its hyperdrive. All we have to do is come up with some way of bringing the two together without risking the alien intelligence taking possession of

the vessel or damaging the hyperdrive, and we might be able to use it.

"A breakthrough like that would be of unthinkable value. Right now, our ships are limited to quantum gates for their interstellar travel, except for your vessel. Admittedly, the speed at which the hyperdrive functions wouldn't be useful for everyday travel, but understanding how it works would allow us to improve on it."

He nodded his agreement. "And there may be other things hidden aboard that ship that we're not aware of. I agree it's worthwhile, so I'm tasking Ensign Calvo to assist in starting the process of relocating everything to a somewhat isolated location.

"It would probably be best to get that underway before the other ships begin transporting people and goods. The mothership has to come over as soon as possible because I don't want any sightings by the other ships."

The woman grimaced. "I understand the need to abandon our vessel, but the loss of something like that hurts. It took me decades of lobbying and chasing grant money to get that ship put together. Its loss is painful."

"You've got several days to extract as much of the research equipment as you can. I'm willing to delegate some trained engineering personnel to assist you because it sounds like it could be worthwhile to the war effort.

"Strip your ship bare of anything you think might be useful because we need to understand what the locusts are doing and why they're doing it."

He scratched his eyebrow and thought ahead. "I'll let the

professor know what's going on, so don't be surprised if he contacts you shortly. I'm going to sic his minder on him, so he doesn't get himself involved in something that's going to be deleterious to his health, but chains couldn't hold him back from seeing this with his own eyes.

"Set up a meeting when you can, and I'll see he's brought wherever he needs to go. Thank you again for bringing this to my attention, Alice. Now, if you'll excuse me, I need to get things in motion."

He gestured for Calvo to stay with them and headed for the hatch. He spoke to the Marines as they were leaving. "Keep two Marines with our visitors at all times until we get to know them a bit better. Also, see that the professor's lab is locked back up again."

With that done, he headed toward Christine's quarters. He'd made sure the locations of important places were included with the contacts on his comm. Ten minutes later, he was there and pressing the admittance chime.

The hatch slid open, and he found Christine smiling at him. "Jack! Come in. The professor is propped up in the living room, and I'm heading out to get us something cold to drink. Make small talk, and I'll grab three glasses. It should only take me a few minutes."

Jack found her quarters were much more reasonably sized than his own. Whoever had designed this ship had made sure the admiral in command had *way* more space than he needed. The maze of compartments that made up Jack's personal quarters could've housed a dozen people, so it was ludicrous for him to live there by himself.

And that didn't even count the massive dining hall directly next to his quarters for the admiral to host his officers and other guests at the same long table. That was unbelievable. Still, the asteroid had had the space to spare, so no harm, no foul.

Before they'd left Faust, his father had made arrangements to have the original furnishings brought back aboard. David Chen had even gotten the steward's kitchen functional again, though the cook he'd hired for it was busy training other cooks to better prepare food for the enormous number of people aboard the ship.

In contrast, Christine Hooghuis's quarters were filled with cast-off Navy furniture that looked as if it hadn't been used in decades. None of it was in terrible shape, but everything was thoroughly used.

Sprawled on the couch was Alan Prescott. He grinned as Jack came through the hatch and gestured toward one of the nearby seats. "Pull up a chair, dear boy. I understand you've been busy, so it's nice to see you again. How's the shoulder?"

"Sore," Jack admitted. "I should be wearing the sling, but circumstances intervened, and I can't afford to look weak. How about you? Are you actually up and around after your surgery? That seems a little soon."

The professor shrugged. "I was told to take it easy, but some walking is on my list of approved activities. Neither of the shots hit anything critical, but I am sore and tired. My restrictions going forward should last no more than another three or four days, then I can get back to work."

Jack settled himself into the seat and chatted with the professor until Christine returned with three drinks. Jack took the glass she offered him and sipped the reddish liquid. It was sweet and good. He set it down on a beat-up coffee table and launched into his explanation about the visit.

"One of the ships we rescued from the cluster belongs to a Professor Alice Wilson of the University of Benedict. She and a half dozen of her research assistants were in the process of recovering Locust debris for archaeological and research purposes when the invasion interrupted them."

Prescott nodded. "I've read some of her work. She has a brilliant mind and has been doing some excellent research into the drones and motherships. I have to confess that having her on board is a relief because I've had no one to bounce ideas off or assist me in my research. This is great news, Jack. Thank you."

Jack grinned. "Oh, that's not the most interesting part. About a week before the invasion kicked off, she and her people recovered a mostly intact Locust mothership. It looks like someone shot a laser right through its computer core.

"The damage was so devastatingly precise—as well as being instantaneous—that it didn't have a chance to destroy its hyperdrive. They've got it with them in their ship."

The professor sat up abruptly, wincing in pain as he moved. "Dear God, boy! Do you know what that means? We might be able to finally unravel the mystery of the hyperdrives!"

Christine glared at them both. "Don't get him too excited, Jack. If he hurts himself, I'm going to hurt you."

"Sorry," Jack said. "We'll see if we can find someone skilled enough to disable the self-destruct and anti-tampering devices. If you have any data on that, pass it on to Derek Calvo. He's going to assist in getting everything from her ship over to one of the unused small craft bays, so they have a place to work.

"There are a lot of other things going on right now, Professor, but I want you to do what you can in assisting them in this work, so long as Christine signs off on it. By the time we're ready to jump *Hunter* out of this system, they should have their own lab fully set up, and you'll get the helping hands you need."

"You can rest assured that I'll do everything I can to break their secrets free," the older man promised. "And I'll do so judiciously, so Christine doesn't have to cause either of us any pain."

"Smart man," she said. "I'll want to see this once it's all set up to make an official record of it."

Jack turned his attention to Christine. "I've got another problem that you can help me with. Captain Magri of *Hawkwing* has set himself up as the liaison between the civilians and the ship without my leave or consent.

"I want you to keep as much of an eye on him as possible because I suspect he's up to no good. He tried to take command of this ship at our first meeting and accused me of being a fraud right before I had him frog-marched to a quiet place where he could cool off. This is not him seeing reason."

Jack rubbed his face. "I've already tagged Tina Chen to insert herself into the civilians as a shipowner. Still, I don't want to count on her being there whenever he says or does something I need to know about."

Christine nodded, already reaching for the large communicator on her belt. "You can count on me, Jack. I'll make sure there's a drone covertly watching him most of the time.

"I'll also do what I can to help the professor get around so he can see what's going on with the mothership. He's going to do what he wants—no matter what the doctors say—so I might as well make sure he doesn't hurt himself while he's doing so."

She grinned. "Besides, I can't let him sniff around some strange woman when we're just starting our relationship. I've got to keep an eye on him and warn her off."

Jack laughed as the professor made indignant noises. "I think you've got the right of it, Christine. Keep a close eye on this character. He looks like a real womanizer."

He picked up his drink and took another sip. He'd intended to rush right off and do something else, but he'd been running around like a chicken with its head cut off for hours. Sitting here with a few friends and having a drink might be just what the doctor ordered.

There were going to be more problems, for sure, but he'd deal with them after he took a little break.

10

ONCE THE COMMODORE WAS GONE, Derek decided the best use of his time was clearing the area that would receive the new equipment rather than going over to the researcher's ship. They already knew what they had and what they needed to bring back, so he needed to get the space ready to receive it.

Given that the researchers and their equipment needed to be housed out of sight, he decided small craft bay four was probably the best bet. It would allow them to bring the mothership directly into *Hunter*, and the bay wasn't currently in use. His mind made up, he headed down to give it a look.

Its pressure had been restored, but there hadn't been any further need to mess with it. They'd been using it as a storage area for some of the small craft relocated from the operational bay. That meant its landing area was completely packed with inoperable small craft, and that wasn't going to do.

In a way, *Hunter* had a comedy of riches. They had so many small craft that they didn't have places to put them all. He needed to relocate dozens of the potentially useful craft. Somewhere.

To do that, he needed help. Luckily, they had people with experience moving small craft under zero-gravity conditions. Some of the mechanics that had come aboard at Faust had traded twelve of the small craft for spare parts and other needed gear. To get that done, they'd had to move them to another vessel even though they hadn't been flight worthy.

Derek probably needed to relocate three times that number of small craft to open up enough space. Even once they got the researchers and their equipment into their new laboratory, *Hunter* needed every landing zone they could get for the more than two hundred vessels to unload their people and specific cargoes, so the time wouldn't have been wasted.

It also meant that whatever workshop the researchers ended up in had to be secure and secret while people were passing by in large numbers. No one could be allowed to see what they were working on.

The best candidate for that was one of the repair bays off to the side of the small craft bay in question. The biggest was made to house multiple small craft undergoing maintenance simultaneously, which should be large enough for the researchers' needs.

When a ship had as many small craft as *Hunter*, there just wasn't space in the main bay to do all the work. Sometimes you had to pull a craft's engines and inspect its framework. That required overhead lifts and supports that took up some of the deck space, which would've interfered with normal flight operations.

Unlike the small craft bay itself, the largest repair bay was mostly empty. There were some small craft parked there that would have to be moved, but there was enough room to fit the mothership with ease.

Even better, it had internal hatches that connected to several of the surrounding small repair bays, which could be used for sleeping quarters and other purposes. He made a mental note that they needed to move furniture in for the researchers and their ship's crew.

He'd seen seven academics, but a ship of any size was going to have at least a dozen crewmembers. If he wanted to avoid them talking out of school, he needed to put them into the same area as the researchers for now. They might see that as a plus since they could avoid the chaotic crowds that would soon be roaming the ship.

Ready to get started, he called in Richard Klein. He was a Locust War reenactor and mechanic whom Commodore Romanoff met on Faust. He'd more than demonstrated his competence by getting a number of the small craft functional again, and he'd been the one overseeing the relocation of the various inoperative small craft so far. That made him the expert in Derek's book.

"What's going on, Derek?" the man asked once he'd arrived. "I've got a lot of work to do and a short time to do it."

"The commodore has a classified, high priority use for this space. A ship full of academic researchers found a Locust mothership that *might* have a functional hyperdrive. We need to park it in that repair bay over there, which we'll let the researchers turn into a full-fledged lab.

"We'll also need several of the adjacent bays for them to use as quarters for both themselves and their crew. They've probably got a lot of equipment in addition to the mothership, and we've got to clear out enough space for them. We also have to open some space out here so we can use this bay to help get the rest of the civilians and selected cargoes aboard."

Klein put his hands on his hips and looked around the cluttered and dingy bay. "We'll need to get a bunch of these nonfunctional boats out of the way while we're moving things in and out. Hell, we might have to abandon some of them because we're just not going to have space."

Derek shook his head. "You're talking about military small craft that have more redundancy and power than modern versions. Yes, they're in worse condition than the ones the new arrivals are bringing over, but are civilian cutters and cargo shuttles going to be all that helpful in the long run? Maybe it's the civilian boats that need dumping."

"I'm a bit leery of getting rid of any of them," the man grumbled. "You never know what we might need. Maybe we can park the ones we don't need out on the hull for right now. We can sort out a final plan when we have time."

"That sounds good," Derek agreed. "That mothership is going to be here pretty damn quick, so we need to clear out enough space in here now.

"I'll call Petty Officer Hutton to help me get things going inside the repair bay. We can close off most of the hatches leading into it while moving the research equipment and other supplies aboard, but we've got to move the mothership soon. Can you help me?"

Klein sighed and nodded. "I can make it work, kid. We'll shut off the gravity and basically tether as many of the small craft as we can to the tops of the other ones on the far side of the bay for now. That'll allow us to expeditiously clear the space, but we won't be able to turn the gravity back on until we're finished relocating the small craft outside. Otherwise, it'll just be a big wreck and cause a lot of damage."

Klein followed that up by pulling his comm off of his belt and calling Lieutenant Danek. Derek's part in getting that plan in motion was done, so he needed to get his own work underway. Thankfully, they could clear the repair bays without divulging what they'd be used for, so he could get a lot more hands involved.

Knowing the gravity was about to go out in the main bay, Derek went to where the vacuum suits were stored and dug out a pair of magnetic boots. They'd be awkward to use in gravity, but he might have to come back into the main bay to help once the researchers arrived.

He stepped into the repair bay and called Hutton. The petty officer answered almost immediately. "Whatever you need, Ensign, I don't have time for it."

"I hear you, PO, but I'm afraid this is one of the commodore's projects, and he's got a very high priority on it. I need you to come to small craft bay four to handle something classified and time sensitive."

He could hear the other man sigh through the connection. "It's going to take me at least half an hour to wrap up what I'm doing. What are we talking about?"

"Something that I can't talk about over an open channel. Seriously, find someone to handle what you're doing and come down here right away. I promise I wouldn't yank your chain for this unless I had to."

The connection was silent for a couple seconds. "Fine, but this better be worth it. If I have to start thinking up ways to show you how you've made a mistake, that's not going to be pleasant for either one of us.

"Okay. That's a lie. I'd get a kick out of it."

Derek chuckled. "You're going to like it. Now, hurry up."

He killed the connection and put his comm away. He made another pass around the cutters that had been under service, and they looked mostly intact. One of them had had its fusion drives pulled but was still structurally sound. The other had its avionics compartment opened up.

In both cases, they could be pulled out of the repair bay and stacked with the other small craft designated as needing attention later.

Hutton came in while he was eyeing some of the large tool-boxes. "What's going on?"

Derek verified there was no one within earshot. Even the outer compartment seemed to be empty at the moment. Klein must've left to grab extra hands of his own.

He went through the short version of the story. Hutton didn't need to know all the gory details, only what the researchers had found and the fact that the commodore had instructed them to set up a private laboratory.

The older man's expression changed as he listened, and he started nodding. "Okay, this still isn't convenient, but I get the importance. I can get us a bunch of recruits to clear everything out of this repair bay and all the ones around it.

"We'll need to pick one compartment to hold everything. Once Klein gets the larger bay partially cleared, they should be able to bring the mothership right in as long as we've got the gravity turned off. We can turn everything back on as soon as we've got the damned thing strapped to the deck."

"Then let's make the magic happen," Derek said. "The clock is ticking."

While Hutton started making calls, Derek wandered through the various repair bays and found a parts storage area that would hold everything.

He started moving anything that wasn't tied down. He tried to keep the toolboxes off to one side because those might prove useful, but everything else was just piled as carefully as he could. Somebody could go through it later and decide if anything was worth keeping.

Klein's people arrived in the outer compartment at about the same time as a herd of recruits under Hutton's command came in. They quickly swarmed the repair bays like ants, grabbing everything loose and moving it into the parts storage bay.

It was impressive because cleaning the area out only took

twenty minutes. That included the time it took for Derek to wave Klein over and add the two partially disassembled cutters to his list of ones that needed to be moved ASAP.

Even so, that was only just barely enough time because he got a call from one of the flight controllers as they were clearing the area directly in front of the large repair bay. His contact indicated there were two small craft on their way over and that they'd been precleared for entry.

To the man's credit, he confirmed that was indeed the case with Derek. They'd had an assassin sneak aboard once, and people were justifiably more careful these days about who they let onto the ship.

Derek gave the man the green light and told Klein and Hutton that the mothership was almost there. The recruits were finished with their work, but Klein's people would need to come back and finish relocating as many of the small craft in the main compartment as possible when this was done.

The gravity was still off in the main compartment, and they shut it off in the repair bay as soon as all the uncleared workers were gone. When the small craft bay's hatches opened, the mothership floated in under the control of half a dozen people in vacuum suits scattered across its hull, controlling individual thruster units.

They floated it gently across the main compartment and slid it into the repair bay. Even before they'd made it, a cargo shuttle came in, positioning itself perpendicular to the repair bay hatch.

The large side hatch opened, and the researchers and other

people that must be part of the ship's crew floated out and began setting up scaffolding that the mothership could rest on.

Once they had it assembled, they mounted the mothership to it and indicated they were ready for partial gravity. Klein manipulated the controls, and the mothership and its mount settled gently to the deck. The researchers checked it over and gave Klein a thumbs up, indicating the compartment could go to full gravity.

Derek was happy to leave that matter in their hands. He didn't want to be the least bit responsible for inadvertently destroying something as valuable as the mothership.

He spoke with Doctor Wilson, and she indicated the cargo shuttle they'd come in had the first load of their equipment and that they'd begin relocating it into the area he'd prepared for them.

She also indicated it was an eminently satisfactory place to turn into a laboratory, which was a relief.

He warned her they'd have to keep outsiders clear of the repair bays. In fact, he made a call to Lieutenant Dubsky and requested a set of guards for the new research area.

It was somewhat challenging to figure out when he should be dealing with Mac Turner as opposed to Dubsky, but this seemed like an official task, and so it was best to go through the chain of command.

He figured the Marines had come to some kind of informal agreement on incorporating the retired Marines into their number, but nobody had shared that information with him yet.

As soon as he'd finished, his comm unit chimed with an

incoming call from John DiGiorgio, one of his fellow officer candidates back at the Academy. He supposed the man was a midshipman now unless the commodore had decided to promote all of the officer candidates straight to ensign.

"What's going on, John?" Derek asked.

"We got a little bit of trouble down in landing bay two," his friend said. "We found a stowaway. I kicked it up the chain of command, and they said you could handle the situation for us."

Since they were rescuing refugees, Derek wasn't exactly sure how they could have a stowaway, but he supposed he'd figure it out. "I'm on my way."

11

Jack finished his drink and headed back to the compartment where Magri had been speaking with the civilians. He didn't want to have another confrontation with the man, but he couldn't let the situation sit as it was. Whatever Magri was up to, he needed to figure it out and set some boundaries.

To make sure that everything went smoothly, he called Mac Turner to make sure the Marine recon officer and some of his people were on hand. It was possible things were going to go badly enough that he'd arrest Magri on the spot.

He'd rather let him find a niche aboard *Hunter*, but there were limits to how much mouth he'd tolerate.

When he arrived, he was shocked to find the compartment almost empty. Instead of the hundreds of people that had been there earlier, only a few dozen were left, all huddled around

Magri. Jack recognized the man in the red hat that had barked at him earlier, but none of the others seemed familiar.

Rather than interrupt what they were doing, Jack leaned against the bulkhead nearest the hatch and watched. It only took a minute for Magri to note his presence and say something to the group that had them leaving the compartment.

Jack was pleased to note that buried inside the group was Tina Chen. He'd missed her earlier, and she was good at blending in.

She'd changed clothes and now looked more like a spacer than she usually did. She sauntered past him with Red Hat at her side, nodding but not showing any real recognition. That was slick.

Once the last of the civilians had left the compartment, Jack closed the hatch. "You got a lot of explaining to do, Captain. I suggest you do it without drama, or there's going to be a lot more trouble than either of us would want."

Magri smiled. It was probably meant to be reassuring, but the man's personality simply made it look smug. Or maybe it was intended to be smug. Magri didn't seem to understand limits very well.

"You wanted me to be a team player, didn't you? Since I don't have a crew anymore, it seemed prudent to find myself a task to carry out. Do you think I'm incapable of doing the work?"

Jack crossed his arms and shook his head. "No, I'd imagine you're capable of doing it. I'm just not sure I trust you doing it. Why should I, after the way you behaved?"

The other officer pursed his lips. "Let me be clear. I don't like

you, I don't think your ship is up to the task of fighting the Locusts, and I don't think you personally have what it takes."

Before Jack could respond, the man's smile widened. "The thing is, you made it perfectly clear that I don't have any say in what happens now. Not only did you wreck the only modern naval warship left in the cluster, but you also made sure to strip my crew away from me.

"So, if I'm to help make this work, I've got to find a position where I can work around your personal limitations. It just so happens that I have a great deal of skill in working with civilian merchants. Once again, working at my grandfather's corporation gave me a lot of experience that carries over."

Jack wasn't sure that was true, yet the man hadn't started a riot. Yet.

"Tell me what you told them. If I'm satisfied you're doing what you can to make the situation better, maybe I'll let things stand as they are.

"If you don't satisfy me, Major Turner will take you to the brig. I'm not going to tolerate any more of your mouth or subversion of my authority, Captain. Test me at your peril."

"I just took what you said and ran with it," Magri said, toning down his smile somewhat. "I told them we didn't have enough information to make any kind of promises at this point, but that the Navy would do everything possible to save their lives and, if feasible, return for their ships.

"I asked them to become part of the war effort and make this happen. People work better when they work as part of a team, so if we can make these civilians take on our goals, they're going to help us succeed. That's the secret to making a good deal."

Personally, Jack didn't know much about dealmaking, but he thought the best kind of deals were the ones where both sides were satisfied with the exchange. What Magri was talking about was a bit more manipulative. Which did seem in character, now that he thought about it.

He was tempted to order Turner to arrest Magri and toss him in the brig. There had to be a brig aboard this ship somewhere. One more area of the ship he hadn't visited but needed to check out when he had time.

"I'll give you some rope, Captain, but I suggest you don't hang yourself with it," Jack warned. "I've got my eye on you, and if you cross the line, you're going to spend the rest of the war in a cell."

He didn't wait for a response, turning and heading for the hatch. Turner was ready for the move because he hit the switch and opened it so that Jack didn't even have to slow down on his way out of the compartment.

"Thanks for being ready," Jack said as soon as they were out in the corridor. "I'd have looked stupid if I'd had to stop and wait for the hatch to open."

"I've got you covered, sir," the older man said. "If you don't mind a piece of advice, you shouldn't trust that weasel."

"I shouldn't agree with you, but I do," he said with a sigh. "We need to have a plan in place in case he tries something. I understand he's only one man, but we've already dealt with a solo assassin once. I've tagged Christine Hooghuis to keep an eye on him via drone, but he has to be aware of that by now."

"That's not the only way you've got an eye on him," Turner said with a grin. "I saw Mrs. Chen in that group. He's not going to see her coming, and if he drops the wrong word, you can rest assured she'll make sure we get the full story."

Jack snorted. "If he drops the wrong word, he might just vanish. She did mention an airlock-related accident when I was talking to her."

Turner laughed. "She talks a good game, but don't be fooled. She's not an assassin. Or, if she is, she's smart enough not to kill somebody after having said she was going to. Whatever he's up to, we'll figure it out.

"Meanwhile, I'll set up some contingency plans in case he decides to pull a fast one. Do you need me to keep you informed about the details?"

Jack shook his head. "Consult with David Chen and Lieutenant Dubsky and make sure they're read in on the contingencies. If I need to know something, David will make sure I find out about it.

"Right now, I need to find Tina and get an update about what our weasel is up to."

Jack had her comm number, so he gave her a call. Unfortunately, it rolled right over to messages. Considering that she was working undercover, it was possible she didn't have her unit on her.

If that was the case, her husband was the best bet on how to get a hold of her. When Jack called him, he told him he'd have her call him when she had the opportunity.

Apparently, she had the opportunity now because he hadn't disconnected for more than thirty seconds when his comm chimed.

"Romanoff."

"I hear you want to talk," Tina said. "Any particular location? I like to stay out of sight when I'm on the job."

"Wherever works best for you is good for me."

"Meet me at the steward's quarters. I'm fixing lunch, so I'll make enough for two."

"You can cook?"

She laughed. "I'm a woman of many talents. We can eat and have a chat about your little friend."

Jack agreed, disconnected, and put his comm unit away. As soon as they arrived at Jack's quarters, Turner and his men peeled off, leaving two of Dubsky's Marines guarding the hatch.

Inside the massive dining chamber, the long table gleamed in the low light. The damned thing was so ostentatious. He hadn't used it yet, and he wasn't sure he ever would.

He went to the hatch on the right side of the compartment. It opened up into the steward's kitchen, and there was a hatch leading from there into the steward's quarters that David and Tina shared.

The kitchen was big enough to cook meals for large groups, but Tina was standing in front of the stove working with just one corner of the grill, making something much more restrained in size. She was still dressed in the same ship's suit she'd been wearing earlier.

Jack stepped up beside her and looked down at what she was making. It was a stir-fried mixture of vegetables and meat. It smelled delicious.

"You are a woman of many talents," he said with a smile. "If you weren't married, I might just have to seduce you."

She gave him a toothy grin. "You're developing an admirable sense of humor, Jack. I approve. Still, I'm afraid I'll have to pass."

"Your loss," he said with an exaggerated sigh. "I'll hold out hope for being the other man in the culinary relationship, though. How did the meeting with Magri go?"

She used the flat metal scoop she was cooking with to flip the vegetables and meat before stirring them up again. "The man is a rat. I'm not certain what he's up to, but he's got some kind of plan in motion. He's making promises I doubt he intends to keep.

"Oh, it's all very deniable, but he's making general statements about sharing risk and everybody contributing to the potential rewards. All generic commentary, but the theme seems to be that he expects to work closely with the civilian community to direct the war effort. Personally."

"Really?" Jack asked. "That doesn't seem like being a team player."

"He's not one," she said. "Whatever he's working on is going to benefit him rather than everyone aboard this ship. Also, some of the individuals there had the hair on the back of my neck standing up.

"Once you've worked covertly for a while, you start getting a feel for certain kinds of people. Even when they talk nice or seem reasonable, there are subconscious tells you can pick up on. The man in the red hat, for example. I'm not sure what he's up to, but he's off, and so are his associates."

Jack frowned, casting his mind back to the memory of the man. Nothing had struck him as out of place, but he was a Navy officer and not trained to pick up on those types of subtle cues.

"You should probably talk with your husband and see about getting more information on him. I'm not even sure what his name is or what ship he comes from."

"Christopher Dugan, captain of the freighter *Guppy*. I've already asked David to check him out, but I've made overtures of my own as well.

"I managed to insert myself into their little group. They were using low-key challenges, counterchallenges, and secret hand-shakes, which almost certainly means they're up to no good. The fact that Magri knew Dugan means they share some history, and it's not going to be a reading club."

That news was an unpleasant surprise. He'd thought they'd be dealing with Magri, but it seemed he had an unknown number of friends that might help him. He'd need to tag Chris-tine to get the faces of these people and pass them on to Turner.

"How did you know the secret handshakes and challenges?" he asked.

"I didn't before I saw everybody in that last group start using them. If it had only been one pass, I might not have caught them at all, but they were all using them with one another, so it was simple enough to edge in and mimic them. They obviously didn't know one another by sight."

She scooped the stir fry onto a large serving plate. "I've set up the table just inside the quarters for the two of us and made enough for three just in case David can peel away from whatever he's doing. Let's start without him and see what happens."

The two of them went into the quarters, and he found a nice little central seating area with a pitcher of ice water waiting on the table. The two of them sat and he took a bite off his plate. It was a bit spicy, but he liked it.

"If you think Magri is up to something, shouldn't we just lock him up?" Jack asked. "I've got enough to charge him with insubordination, which may not hold in the long run, but I'm the senior military officer in the cluster. I can stretch things out if I like."

"I had Christine send me the video of your last little talk with him, and I think you have the right of it. You've given him some rope. Let's see if he hangs himself.

"Whatever he has in mind, it's going to take a little bit of work to set things up the way he wants them. He can't act too quickly, or he's not going to have all the pieces in place."

She paused to chew a bite of her own food before continuing. "For example, he'll want Commander MacKinnon and her people back on board before he acts. He'll most likely want to have the new fusion plant installed and running, too.

"Frankly, the best time for him to act would be once all of the civilians are aboard, and everybody's looking forward to jumping out of the system. No one will be thinking of him then."

"Even with new friends, we have five thousand naval and Marine recruits," he objected. "Hell, we've got more retired Marine force recon personnel than he's likely to get supporters. What can he do?"

"Never underestimate an enemy, Jack," she said, pointing her fork at him. "That's how you get your ass handed to you. It's far better to think he's much more capable than he likely is just on the off chance you're wrong."

He was still thinking about how that made much of a difference with Magri when Tina's comm signaled. She made a motion for him to be quiet and answered it.

"This is Tina."

Jack couldn't hear what the other person said, but Tina smiled. "Yes, I'd be happy to join you for dinner. Thanks for the invitation. I'll take my cutter over to your ship. What's the name and transponder number?"

She frowned a bit and grimaced. "That works too. I'll shoot you the details at this number shortly."

"Who was that," Jack asked when she disconnected.

"Our friend Dugan. He wants to talk the situation over. On my ship, which is a complication. I may need to talk to Professor Wilson and borrow her ship."

"Isn't that going to be dangerous?"

"Everything is dangerous, Jack. I judge the risk to be within acceptable limits for this, though. I don't know what his game is, but this is our chance to figure it out."

Jack wanted to tell her not to go, but he knew she was right.

They had to get some information before whatever Magri was working on came to fruition.

"We'll insert some of Major Turner's people onto the ship. He can't be in sight since Dugan has seen him, but there are others that can fit in."

"Don't worry so much, Jack. I've got this covered. By bedtime, we might have a better idea about what Magri is up to."

Jack wasn't so convinced. He'd tag Turner and Dubsky to prep a team. He wasn't about to leave one of his people swinging in the wind if it all went to hell.

12

Tina finished her meal with Jack and declined his offer to help clean up so she could have time to consider the implications of what had happened earlier. She'd told Jack the essential parts, but her concerns about what was going on went a bit deeper than she'd shared.

She had her suspicions about precisely who these people were, and if those thoughts were borne out, it was a complication Jack wasn't going to be happy about.

The first thing she needed was firmer identification of exactly who she was dealing with. Sadly, the computer systems aboard *Hunter* were so out of date that they were useless for running a search on anyone with a known criminal history with the Confederation Navy. Luckily for her, there was another source nearby she could call.

With all the ships in close orbit, she was able to utilize her comm to initiate a call to known numbers elsewhere in their little cluster of vessels. *Hunter's* computers might be woefully outdated, but the ones aboard *Hawkwing* were not.

A quick call to India got her agreement to run facial recognition on the people Christine's drone had recorded meeting with Magri. By the time she'd finished cleaning the dishes, Christine had gotten back to her with still images, and she forwarded them to India. Her next task was to arrange for the meeting place where she and Dugan could have dinner while talking about whatever it was that Magri was trying to do.

She had no direct information on how to contact the researchers but was willing to wager Professor Prescott would have their number, so she put in another call to Christine to inquire.

Interestingly, the woman said she and the professor were with the researchers in small craft bay four right then. She thanked her and set out at once to ask about borrowing the researcher's ship and crew.

When she arrived at the small craft bay, she found it a hive of activity as people came and went, and cargo was unloaded. Interestingly, a pair of Marine guards were stationed near the closed-off repair bays. Since she didn't see Christine, the professor, or any of the researchers, she was confident the Marines were the key to her access.

When she presented herself and asked for entrance, they refused. Not surprising, really.

She pulled out her comm and called Christine again.

Moments later, the woman came out and waved her inside. The Marines looked a bit disgruntled at that but didn't argue.

Inside the repair bay was the secret they'd been concealing. She'd never seen one before, but the big craft had to be a Locust mothership. It was simply too large to be a drone. In fact, she could see multiple cavities where the drones had probably rested during their interstellar flight.

The professor was walking around the vessel, with several of the researchers accompanying him. Christine held herself back and watched his movement disapprovingly.

"I don't like it when he stresses himself," her friend complained. "He should be taking it easy. The man was shot just a few days ago."

"Men are going to be men, dear. You just have to accept they don't see bodily limitations as something they need to give way for. All we can do is keep an eye on them and march them off to bed when they wind down.

"So this is obviously something the researchers recovered. What makes it so special? Why the Marine guard?"

Christine raised an eyebrow and smiled slyly. "I'm probably not supposed to say, but since you're a spy, I'll just tell Jack you somehow ferreted the information out of me. You're so tricky.

"According to the researchers, they believe the hyperdrive on this ship is still intact and perhaps recoverable."

Tina felt her eyebrows rising. "Well, that is unexpected. I've done a bit of research on the Locusts and their behavior, and to the best of my knowledge, something like this has never happened before. It must have something to do with the rather large hole blown through the center of this craft."

"That's my assumption, too. I'm told some Marines with explosive ordnance experience will be along shortly to see if they can extract the self-destruct charges without setting them off.

"They don't have any experience in actual bomb disposal, so I don't know how they're going to deal with the anti-tampering features built into the system, but we can only do what we can do."

Tina made a face. She hated bombs.

"Did you ever know something you didn't want to mention because it was going to get you into trouble?" she asked. "Well, part of my training with Confederation Intelligence was in planting explosives and disarming them. I have *some* knowledge of anti-tampering devices and how to bypass them.

"The problem is, these are aliens. How does one know how their minds work? Their idea of an anti-tampering circuit might be something completely different than what I'd expect. If I were to volunteer my services, I might very well blow myself up. David would be very unhappy about that, and so would I."

That revelation turned Christine's expression into one of worry. "Yet you wouldn't volunteer that information if you didn't intend to also volunteer your services. How dangerous do you think it will be?"

"Very dangerous," she assured her friend. "The first trip would be to look at what we're dealing with. There has to be at least some level of similarity in how that kind of equipment works, even if it was designed by aliens. Function drives form.

"When the Marines get here, I'll get into one of the explosive protection suits and go in with them. At the very least, I'll know if my experience is useless pretty quickly. I'll withdraw if I don't feel comfortable committing to the process. I've got other things to risk my life on, and I can't afford to be blown up right now."

"You mean those people that Captain Magri was talking to. Who are they?"

Tina shrugged. "I don't know, specifically, but I suspect they belong to some type of criminal organization. Magri used to work for his grandfather at a shipbuilding corporation, and there's circumstantial evidence he and at least one of those people know one another.

"That connection was good enough to have the other person draw some of his friends in for a private conversation. Tell me, were you able to pick up any of what they said before I got there?"

Christine shook her head. "Unfortunately not. There are limits to how close I get with my drones without being obvious. Magri knew they were there, and so did the people he was talking to, though they couldn't be sure it was explicitly watching them.

"He had his head turned in a way that I couldn't see his mouth when he spoke most of the time and obscured what he was saying when he wasn't. The people with him also seemed to be worried that they were being recorded. The only parts I caught were about cooperation and working together to achieve their goal, whatever it was."

"That's even hinkier than secret handshakes and passwords,"

Tina complained. "It's like they're in a secret society and not a benign one. If they aren't pirates, I'll eat that mothership."

Christine pursed her lips and considered her statement. "If that's true, there were a dozen people in that final huddle. We need to figure out who belongs to what ship and get a handle on what we're dealing with."

Tina agreed. "I'll see if I can get some video of them arriving and try to peg what ships they came from. My husband has a list of the ship names, but I suspect they probably gave him some false information. Why make it easy, after all?"

The personnel hatch opened before Christine could respond, and two Marines came in with large packs. Those would be the people with specific knowledge of explosive ordnance.

"Do me a solid and talk to the researchers for me," Tina said. "I need to borrow their ship for a meeting with one of the suspicious people. If they're pirates, I'll probably have to talk to Major Turner and see about getting a force of people stashed aboard for my safety, but as a pretend pirate, I need a ship."

Her friend nodded. "I'll take care of it. Be careful."

Tina gave her a breezy half salute and headed toward the new Marines. Surprisingly, both were women. She'd have expected boys to be more prone to playing with things that went boom. It looked like she was just as guilty of making assumptions about gender roles as other people.

"Ladies," she said as she walked up. "My name is Tina Chen, and I used to work for Confederation Intelligence. I have some experience with planting explosives and creating anti-tampering circuits. I also have a little bit of experience of bypassing them. I don't want to insert myself into your business, but can I lend my expertise?"

The two glanced at one another, and one of them nodded. "I'm Sergeant Christa Tazzeo, and this is my friend Sergeant Stefanie Barbato. We're instructors at the Marine Academy dealing with explosive ordnance. We'd be happy to have your assistance, but I don't have another suit for you. Maybe you should do this by video."

Tina shook her head. "That's a bad call, and you know it. I have to see this with my own eyes, and if it's something I can deal with, I'll need to be there."

The woman pursed her lips and narrowed her eyes in consideration. "Are you any good with this sort of stuff?"

Tina waved her hands with all of her fingers still attached. "Good enough to avoid getting my hands blown off."

That made the woman smile. "Then I think we can work with this. We'll get you into the second suit, and Stefanie will stay out here for now. We'll let you take a look at what's in there, and then we'll make the call.

"If it seems straightforward, we'll see about bypassing the anti-tampering circuit before I send you back out and call my friend in to help me remove the explosives."

Her expression grew hard. "When we get in there, my word is law, you got that? You don't do *anything* without my explicit permission. If you can't live by that rule, then you're not going in because my life depends on your actions."

"When it comes to high explosives, I *always* play by the rules,"

Tina assured her. "You're in charge, and I won't do anything unless you tell me to do it."

Satisfied, the Marines began unpacking their explosive protection suits. They were hefty, thick, and just as uncomfortable as they looked, she discovered once she was fully dressed in the bulky suit with the thick faceplate.

They were vacuum rated, so at least they had environmental controls. Sweating would be bad when working on bombs.

Thankfully, the long arms allowed her to manipulate finger-like appendages as delicately as she might her own fingers, though she'd obviously have to be very careful to work slowly since she wasn't used to working with mechanical linkages like that.

Once they were set, the older woman that had been walking with the professor came and escorted them to the scaffolding underneath the mothership. She pointed toward the rear of the craft.

"There's a passage big enough for you to go all the way back from the hole. The fusion plant, fusion drives, and the hyperdrive are all packed together back there, though everything is shut down. Our people went in without suits, and they had plenty of room.

"You're going to be in some tight spaces, but I think you'll probably fit. Do me a favor and try not to blow up my find."

"If I blow it up, you can take it out of my pay," Tazzeo said in a deadpan voice. "I want everybody out of this compartment. You can go to one of the other repair bays or out into the main bay, but you can't stay here.

"When this is all over, we'll come out and let you know how it went. Or there'll be a massive explosion, and you can figure it out for yourselves."

"Thanks for *that* reassuring thought," the woman said. "I know you're going to be careful, but if you're not certain you can do the work, don't push it. Back away, and we'll figure something else out. We've only got one shot at this, and if you blow up that hyperdrive, it's gone forever."

"No pressure."

The older woman gave her a dark chuckle and gestured for everyone to follow her out of the repair bay.

Tina noted the other Marine didn't leave. She was going to stay there and see how this played out. That was kind of stupid but very loyal.

The two climbed into the mothership, with the Marine going first. The lights situated to either side of their faceplates provided them more than enough illumination to find their way through the alien craft.

It was cramped, and they had to move on their elbows and knees. Either the aliens were tiny, or these passages were made for robotic repair units. Wouldn't it be perfect if they looked like mechanical spiders?

Perfectly ghastly. She shuddered and forced herself to continue on.

Tina had some familiarity with equipment common in engineering spaces, and the fusion plants and fusion thrusters seemed similar to those used by humans.

"It's weird how close these look to the ones we use," she said over the external speakers. "I guess they have to be of somewhat the same form to have the same function."

"I suppose so," the other woman said. "This thing right in front of us must be the hyperdrive. Let's approach it carefully and get a good look before we decide what to do next."

The hyperdrive was unlike anything she'd seen before. It was part black box, yet covered with a forest of what looked like small antennas.

They weren't very tall, nor were they consistent in length or thickness. Some of them were half a dozen centimeters tall, others were a dozen, while still others fell somewhere in between. They ranged from wire thin to as thick as her thumb.

Wrapped around the case was what certainly looked like a conduit. It stopped at little boxes along the way and then encircled the device completely. It was also along the top among the antennas.

"I guess that's the explosives," Tazzeo said. "They must've used sensors to figure that out because it doesn't look like anyone opened any of the conduits or boxes. Good call on their part. That would probably have set the explosives off.

"How are you going to check for the anti-tampering circuit without risking everything?"

"I'm going to look very closely and let you know what I find," Tina said. "Trust me, I'm going to look with my eyes, not my hands."

Tina circled around the hyperdrive as much as possible and examined the supposed explosives. There didn't seem to be any external connection until she got to almost the very rear of the hyperdrive. At that point, she saw something attached to one of the boxes and wedged herself in as close as she could to get the best look possible.

After considering the possibilities, she decided there was likely a detector built into the explosive circuit. Maybe pressure, or even atmospheric mixture.

It was probably looking for a change in pressure inside the conduit. This was a robotic ship, so there was no need for an atmosphere. Why make things complicated?

If the explosives were sealed, and someone opened one of the boxes or conduits and let the atmosphere in or out, it would note the difference in pressure and set off the explosives.

She passed her thoughts and verbal findings on to the Marine.

"Do you think there's anything in there to detect transmissions or sensor scans?" Tazzeo asked.

"I'd wager not. We can be sure those researchers were chattering to each the entire time they were looking through this ship in their suits. If there was anything to detect comm transmissions, living beings, or sensor scans, it would've already gone off."

"Let me back out and talk to Barbato. I'll confirm that with the researchers and come back in with something to keep the pressure steady while working on it. I'll also have them clear the bay until we're done. When that's done, we'll see about disconnecting the anti-tampering device. Is that something you think you can manage?"

Tina took a few moments to study the anti-tampering device.

"I believe so. It looks like a straightforward detonator attached to a pressure detector, but I can confirm that with a sensor scan."

Of course, if she was wrong, she was probably dead.

Clearing out the small craft bay took about forty-five minutes. Once Barbato gave them the all-clear, the other Marine returned with more equipment.

A sensor scan was a calculated risk, but she needed to know for sure what she was dealing with. To her relief, it didn't set off the explosives.

It also gave her a much better idea of what she was looking at. The interior of the hyperdrive and conduits were filled with nitrogen under pressure. She suspected there was some leeway in the explosive threshold, so sealing off the area she was working on would only cause a minute drop in pressure and would probably be safe.

Probably.

Well, the only way to be sure was to do it. At her companion's signal, Tina enclosed the pressure sensor/detonator in a small bag she could seal around it. Once it was secure, she filled it with nitrogen to match the internal pressure.

Then a hair more just to be on the safe side.

Finally, she used the manipulators built into the suit to slowly cut the device from the box. She held her breath when she punctured the conduit, but nothing happened.

With more confidence, she used a cutting tool to separate the sensor and detonator from the explosives themselves. It was like a saw, only it moved very slowly because the explosive might be heat sensitive. Once again, best to take things slowly.

Ten minutes later, she had the detonator completely off and had sealed the conduit to maintain the internal pressure. She got the detonator to the corner of the bag and twisted it off before cutting the bag and separating the bubble with the sensor/detonator from everything else.

The bag was made to self-seal, so the detonator should be safe enough at this point. Still, she wanted it out of her hands and passed it to the Marine.

"Time to scan this thing a little more deeply," she said. "If I was a paranoid alien, I'd have a backup detonator."

Again, it was a risk upping the power of her sensor scan, but she had to know. She scanned the exterior and found nothing. Then she scanned the hyperdrive itself.

A lot of it was alien machinery, but it didn't take long to find a second pressure sensor/detonator deep inside the drive, along with more explosives. That meant she'd need to drill a hole in the drive and insert a tool to do what she'd just done.

That was a lot more ticklish, but it was only a matter of scale. She cut a hole large enough to get the detonator out, which gave her room to see what she was doing and do the work itself.

This time it took almost twenty minutes, but she had the second detonator extracted safely. A final scan showed no more detonators, but that didn't mean she couldn't have missed one.

"I *think* I've gotten them all. The real trick now is opening this thing up and removing the explosives."

"And that's your cue to head back out," Tazzeo said. "You've done a great job, but my partner has a lot more experience than you do at this sort of thing. Besides, if I'm going to die, I'd rather she die with me. She's borrowed too many of my dresses without returning them to be allowed to live."

Tina was half inclined to argue but decided she needed to abide by the agreement she'd made. "I'll take the detonators with me just to be sure they make it out. There may be some other kind of tripwire in these, so do a girl a favor and stay in one piece. If you do that, dinner is on me."

"I'll hold you to that," the Marine said with a hint of amusement in her tone. "Now, get out of here."

Once Tina had extracted herself from the mothership, the Marine in the bay gestured toward the personnel hatch once she'd taken the suit.

Deciding that discretion was indeed the better part of valor, Tina made her way out into the small craft bay, where she found the rest of the research team waiting in vacuum suits. They had one for her, so she climbed into it quickly.

"How did it go?" the woman in charge of the researchers asked.

"I extracted two anti-tampering devices, and I think they're going to be okay. I don't think we've met. My name is Tina Chen."

"Doctor Alice Wilson. As I told Christine, you're more than welcome to use my ship. Might I ask why you need it?"

"This is one of those sets of circumstances where it might be best if you don't know. I'm not anticipating anything terrible happening, but the chances of the interior getting shot up aren't *entirely* out of the question."

The woman shook her head. "It's not like I'm going to be

able to take her with us, so if something terrible happens, I'll just make sure the Navy pays for her. Keep yourself safe."

The two of them chatted about the discovery of the mothership while Tina listened in on the Marines' conversation over their channel. The Marines worked their way around at the hyperdrive until they'd scoured it of explosives, both internal and external.

Eventually, the Marines declared the hyperdrive clear and began extracting themselves from the mothership. That was a huge relief and an incredible success. It made Tina happy to have played a small role in their success.

She was still smiling when her comm signaled. She'd taken the precaution of linking it to the suit she was now wearing, so she was able to answer the call.

It was Commander MacKinnon. "I finally got a chance to run those images you sent me through our system. About half of them showed up in the criminal database, but not in a way that was of interest to the Navy.

"That changed when we got to the guy in the red hat. It seems he's a suspected pirate. You said these people seem so chummy, so I suspect they're all pirates. I've talked with the flight controllers aboard *Hunter*, and they've indicated the small craft carrying these people came from six different ships, all freighters."

"Don't pirate ships mostly look like freighters?" Tina asked.

"Pretty much. The only thing that separates them is their weapons, and we can't see those unless we turn active sensors on to look at these folks more closely, which they would definitely notice.

"It's a good thing *Hunter* was running active sensors right up until she jumped to this system. She was looking for Locusts, but she saw each of those ships at point-blank range. All of them are armed. None of the other Navy ships were looking for that kind of thing, so they managed to slip in among the rest of the refugees."

"Keep that under your hat," Tina said. "I'll brief Jack, but I don't want that to become general knowledge. All it would take is for one person to tip off Captain Magri or the pirates, and this situation would spin completely out of control. This has just become need to know."

There was a brief pause before MacKinnon said anything else. "Do you think Magri is in league with pirates? I realize he's got his flaws, but that's a terrible accusation."

"I saw him being all chummy with the guy in the red hat, so I can only assume he's worked with him before. I'll be generous and say it might have been before he joined the Navy. Maybe the guy was a low-level crook back then, and part of Magri's job at his grandfather's corporation involved interfacing with him. We can always ask later, but I think the evidence that Magri's hands are dirty is pretty strong."

"Okay, I'll follow your lead, but I'm coming over shortly. If Jack doesn't know by then, I'll tell him. Good luck."

"Thanks, I think I'll need it."

She turned her attention to Doctor Wilson. "Good news. The Marines have finished extracting the explosives and are on their way back out. I'll leave you to deal with getting things back on track here because I've got to go prepare for a dinner date."

"Remember to take a breath mint, dear. Hygiene is very important when making first impressions."

Tina laughed, stripped off the vacuum suit, and headed for the exit. She left the anti-tampering devices with the Marines on guard duty with a fair warning about what they were.

She should've handled it personally, but she had things to get set up, including sending an update to Jack and David. She also needed to get a crew that could fight aboard the research ship, make sure she had complete access to the ship's systems, stash a few Marines to deal with any problems, and find some way to make an academic research vessel look like a pirate ship.

All before dinner.

13

Jack sat in his office, going over the information Tina had forwarded to him. Her hunch had paid off, and they had at least six ships full of pirates on their hands. That was definitely not what he'd wanted to hear, yet it was a problem that could be solved.

For once, he was ahead of the curve and could take steps to deal with both Magri and his new friends. The trick was going to be making it happen in a way that allowed Magri to incriminate himself and didn't put any of Jack's people at needless risk.

Dealing with six ships full of pirates wasn't exactly that complicated, with them sitting right next to *Hunter*. The pirates could either surrender or die.

Or they could run away and eventually die in this inhospitable system.

Hunter was effectively invulnerable to their threats. There would be some risk to the other ships around them, but those were being evacuated as quickly as possible. The danger to the civilians went down with every cutter and cargo shuttle that made a pass through his ship.

Still, low risk wasn't no risk.

He called Christine. "Where do your drones show Magri is right now?"

"He's in the quarters assigned to him," the videographer said. "I have no way of monitoring him in there, but he's been in place for about an hour. Why? What's up?"

"Nothing I'm ready to talk about just yet. Thanks for the update."

Jack called Dubsky and asked her to come to his office. She showed up promptly, and he got right down to brass tacks.

"I want a guard on Captain Magri around the clock. You can make up whatever excuse you like when he complains about it, but I want eyes on him at all times when he's out of his quarters. It's come to my attention that he may be working with a known pirate, and I'm very much afraid he's trying to make a deal to stage a mutiny."

The woman's eyes narrowed. "Where is he at, sir? I'll go inform him of the change immediately. I'll just say that somebody in the civilian group started making threats against him and the security detail is for his own protection. Better safe than sorry, right, sir?"

"His safety is, of course, our greatest concern," Jack said with a slight smile. "You can't be in his quarters with him, but you can scan it for dangers. You know, like unauthorized weapons and the like."

"I'll make it happen right away, sir."

The Marine lieutenant exited his office with her comm in hand, undoubtedly calling for backup. Hopefully, her intervention would spike any attempts by Magri to interfere in what was about to happen.

The next thing he did was call Turner, read the man in on what was happening, and instruct him to link up with Tina to get his people aboard the research vessel before anyone else came to visit. He made sure to warn him that the visible part of the protection detail needed to be people the pirates couldn't have seen.

With that accomplished, he'd done as much as he could. Tina was responsible for making sure her operation went off as cleanly as possible, and he'd be ready to back her up when the time came.

If the pirates proved to be a threat to the safety of the civilian vessels, he'd destroy them without a second thought. Still, he'd much rather have them surrender, find out exactly what they'd been up to, and if they had resources they hadn't told anyone about.

He checked the time and was annoyed to find he had about an hour before India was supposed to board. He needed to meet with her and finalize the transition of *Hawkwing*'s crew to *Hunter*. Only once that was done could he be sure he had Magri completely isolated.

Of course, he also needed to read Sara in on the situation. If

Magri was working with the pirates, dealing with them was going to fall squarely inside her purview.

He was about to call her when his comm chimed for his attention. A quick check revealed that it was Kelly Danek. It seemed a little early for good news, so odds were he was about to get another complication tossed into his lap.

"Romanoff."

"Sir, if you could come down for a bit, I believe I might have some good news."

Jack stood and smiled. "I can *always* use good news, Kelly. I'm on my way."

He picked up his Marine guards just outside his office and headed directly to engineering. Fifteen minutes later, he was striding off the lift and into the cathedral-like engineering space. Kelly was standing next to her office and waved at him.

He followed her inside and was once again amazed that she could get anything done in there. Every flat surface was piled high with printouts and manuals. Her desk was literally groaning under the weight she'd piled upon it, and he still wasn't sure if she had a seat behind the stack.

The walls were covered with boards holding diagrams of all kinds, including power conduits and life-support systems. Innumerable stick pins were placed across the maps indicating various statuses, mostly red or yellow, though there were many more green pins than the last time he'd been in here.

He closed the door behind him and raised an eyebrow. "What kind of good news are we talking about?"

She grinned. "A theoretical set of good news. I've been going over everything I could about the independent quantum drive. There's a ton of math in there and all kinds of theory that I never took the time to dive into.

"Turns out, that was a mistake. It seems there may be a solution to moving the civilian ships. We can seemingly have our cake and eat it too."

"I've heard the saying," he said as he gingerly leaned against one of the walls. "What does it mean in this case?"

"On the trip here, we expanded the quantum bubble to encompass the ships scattered in a globe around us. That caused a massive power draw that screwed up our fusion plants. In theory, there's another way we could've done it that wouldn't have had nearly as much effect on our power consumption.

"The quantum drive is located in engineering, so it has to generate a quantum bubble all the way forward to encompass the entire ship when we jump. The hull is an excellent physical boundary and the energy flowing along its surface is what allows us to make the magic happen without those huge power spikes, but it turns out there's another solution to the problem that might allow us to manipulate the quantum bubble in a completely different way than we have in the past."

She walked over to one of the boards and began cleaning it off. She quickly drew a cigar shape that he assumed was meant to represent *Hunter* and drew a smaller bubble just behind the ship.

"The math shows we might be able to position ships *behind* us where our fusion drives would typically make everything far too dangerous for any other ships to be. Again, according to theory, we should be able to encompass about a quarter of the area that

Hunter occupies with only a minimal spike to our power consumption during jump. It would require us not to be under thrust, of course.

"If we can get the ships to fit inside that area, it's possible we can jump them safely once we have the fusion plant from *Hawkwing* installed."

He walked forward and considered her drawing. "And what happens if the theory is wrong?"

"Then we might just blow another fusion plant," she said. "Though I think the odds of that happening are much lower now that we've weeded out the worst offender among the fusion plants. Everything I've seen for the unit coming over from *Hawkwing* indicates it's solid.

"It's smaller than our plants, but it's much more modern too, so the power output is about two-thirds what one of our bigger plants would generate in a high demand situation like a quantum jump. As long as we can keep the questionable third fusion plant operating at least half power, we've got enough for regular jump and enough of an edge to give this a test."

He considered her skeptically. "And exactly how do you intend to test this theory without causing irreparable damage to our ship?"

"We only take a couple of ships with us on this next jump in a very small bubble aft of the ship. We'll be able to see how much of a power draw that causes. If it's within acceptable limits, we can jump back and grab more ships and test it again with a larger bubble.

"I'm no math genius, but I've had some of the engineers from

Hawkwing double-check my assumptions, and I believe it should be possible to take all the ships we've got with us if they're willing to pack themselves closely enough together. After all, it's not their mass that's the problem. It's the volume of space they occupy."

Jack shook his head. "I hear what you're saying, but this sounds like a dangerous stunt. We're working with technology we don't fully understand. If we make a mistake, we could doom the cluster and perhaps even the Confederation. That's not a chance I'm willing to take lightly."

She smiled a little, putting down the marker she'd been holding. "But it's a chance you'd be willing to take as long as there's a sufficient safety buffer, I'd wager. We both know having these other ships with us might prove useful, and if we leave them here, they're undoubtedly going to be picked off by the Locusts at some point soon.

"We both know they've probably made a guess at our destination—though they'll have to check multiple systems to verify where we went—and they're going to come looking. Within four months—six months at most—they'll be here. If we don't take these ships with us, we're abandoning the resources they represent."

She took a deep breath and pressed on before he could say anything. "I realize their quantum drives aren't going to be useful to us, but we need to consider that just having extra ships in space could make for great listening posts we could drop off in various systems to keep an eye on what's going on from a safe distance."

Jack didn't want to agree with her, yet there was some logic to what she was saying.

"I'll have to think about this before I authorize anything. When I make a decision, I'll let you know. Until then, work from a plan where we don't take any of the ships with us.

"And under no circumstances should anyone mention this to anyone not directly involved. If the civilians get wind of this possibility before I make a decision, they're going to lose their little minds should I decide not to chance it."

He checked the time. "I need to go find Commander MacKinnon. She and I have a long conversation ahead of us, and she should be aboard by now. Keep doing the theoretical work, but implement nothing to change the hardware configuration we need to go with our original plan. Understood?"

Kelly nodded, a little crestfallen. "Understood, Commodore. At this point, it's all theoretical anyway. We shouldn't have to make any hardware changes if you approve the plan. Everything should work just fine with a tweak to the software. That's all we had to do on the last jump."

"Thanks for looking into this, Kelly. Keep doing a job like this, and I'll have to find a way to promote you."

Her expression soured. "As if I need that headache."

He chuckled, headed out of her office, and made a beeline for the lift, picking up his Marines along the way. If he knew India as well as he thought he did, she'd be making her way to the bridge. Just like him, she'd want to see where all the magic happened.

Well, she might just get more magic than she'd bargained for once he executed his full plan for her.

14

DEREK MADE his way to small craft bay two and found the place a hive of activity. Someone had moved several defective and nonfunctional small craft out of the way in a manner similar to what Klein was doing in small craft bay four, and now there was a steady stream of cargo shuttles pulling in and unloading their crates and boxes.

A swarm of Navy and Marine recruits were sorting everything under Petty Officer Hutton's direction. This must've been what he'd been preparing for when Derek had co-opted him. Still, it looked like the work was going just fine, even with the interruption.

Derek spotted DiGiorgio standing off to the side of the unloading area with his arms crossed, staring at the crates stacked on that side of the bay. They were larger and didn't seem to be in danger of being moved just yet.

He walked up to his friend and made a mental note of the midshipman's tabs he wore. The commodore hadn't gotten around to promoting all the midshipmen to ensigns. That might still come, but it wasn't the case yet.

"What's going on, buddy?" he asked.

John turned and started to say something to him and then smiled. "Congratulations on the promotion, Ensign. You're moving up fast."

"I wouldn't be shocked if you got bumped before much longer. My impression is that the commodore doesn't want people sitting in that zone of rank where they're neither fish nor fowl.

"Unless I'm terribly mistaken, midshipmen are going to be bumped up to ensigns, and recruits are going to become privates or spacers. We're in the middle of a war, and we don't have time to stand around learning. We've got to figure it out as we go."

John nodded. "Makes sense. That'll make things a bit easier, I hope."

"It will. Now, what's this I hear about a stowaway? How exactly did that happen?"

His friend grinned at him. "It's not your usual sort of thing, but it's the kind of situation that's right up your alley. You've always been a problem solver, and this one will be a real head-scratcher."

He gestured up at the top of the pile of crates. Confused, Derek followed his gaze and spotted the stowaway. Perched on top of the stack of crates watching over all of the activity in the small craft bay was a large orange cat.

Just based on its appearance, it didn't seem that it had been starving because it still had an excellent color to its coat and didn't seem undernourished. There was a kind of serenity or maybe lordly disdain as it stared out over the activity. It didn't seem frightened of the human presence, and it had a collar, so it wasn't feral.

"A cat?" Derek asked. "You called me down here to take care of a cat?"

"Of course I did. We can't just let it wander off into the ship. It would starve. Is that what we want?"

Derek grimaced. "Of course not. You did the right thing. I'm not sure how, but I'll take care of this. I may need to recruit some help in getting him down."

"My crack team of cat wranglers and I are standing by to assist you, sir."

He shot his friend a sour look. In this case, the team of cat wranglers was half a dozen Navy recruits who were watching the situation with poorly concealed amusement.

Derek considered the ramifications of simply chasing after the cat and realized that was the worst possible outcome. They needed to restrict where it could flee in order to get their hands on it. Even if they managed to catch it, somebody would get scratched or bitten if things went badly.

"Seal the main hatch for now. I may be able to catch it without chasing, but if it runs, I'd rather it not get out of the small craft bay. I'll also need something to stash it in until I can relocate it somewhere safe. Something either one person or just a couple can carry."

This would disrupt the flow of cargo, but he needed to give

this a try. He'd have a hard time forgiving himself if he missed the chance to save an innocent creature. He'd never had pets of his own growing up, but he'd known people with cats, and he had a soft spot for them.

Ready for the cat to run, Derek climbed onto the first crate and moved slowly toward it while making clicking noises with his tongue and holding his hand out.

The creature considered him with dark green eyes. Then it rose to its feet and sauntered over with its tail high in the air, brushing against his hand with its head.

Gingerly, Derek picked it up and petted it. It was purring and seemed to have accepted his attention, so this wouldn't be nearly as challenging as he'd feared. He still had no idea whether the cat was male or female, but it seemed friendly enough.

"So, who are you?" he asked the cat as he looked at the collar. There wasn't a tag, but it was probably chipped.

Derek held the purring creature to his chest and stroked him. "You slipped into somebody's cargo shuttle, and now you're aboard our ship—and maybe other ships if you came from a planet—so you're a traveler.

"Well, don't worry, buddy. We'll take care of you, and if we can figure out who owns you, we'll get you back to them."

He looked over to John. "Hold the crate up so I can get it in."

Derek slid the cat inside the container and swung the lid shut. It would be dark in there for a bit, but they needed to get the cat into a more restricted area.

With the cat safely secured, Derek climbed down. "I doubt we have any veterinarians aboard, but let's take our little friend to the medical center and have them ask around.

"We need to find something safe for him to eat and drink and make up a litter box. Sand isn't the best option, but we may have something else on hand. See what you can find."

John gestured toward the work going on in the small craft bay. "I'm supposed to be watching this."

"Then tag someone to take it. Until he's used to us, we'd best find a room for him to adjust to his new situation. We'll try to find his owner, but if we can't, we have a ship's cat."

"You're the boss," John said, gesturing for two of the recruits to grab the crate. "I'll take off long enough to make sure this gets started the right way. Thanks for coming down and giving us a hand."

"It's what ensigns are for. Rescuing cats."

He watched the men carry the crate through the once again opened hatch and shook his head. What was the world coming to?

"Ensign Calvo."

Derek turned to find Commander MacKinnon standing nearby.

"Sorry, ma'am, I didn't hear you come up. Is there anything I can do to assist you?"

"There is, actually. I've heard a lot about your bridge, and if you've got a few minutes, I'd like to see it. I'd also like to get an idea of exactly what kind of challenges those of us not trained in using your equipment face, and I hear you're a good source of information about that."

He nodded and gestured toward the hatch. "I can do that, but I'm afraid the learning curve is steep. The control systems have changed a lot over the last two hundred years. What are you trained in? Helm operation? Weapons? Something else?"

She walked out into the corridor, and he had to lengthen his stride to keep up. She was a tall woman with long legs, and she didn't dawdle.

"I came up the tactical track, so weapons are my specialty. I understand you're the helm officer, so do you know much about the weapons on this ship?"

"Since I learned how to fly the ship by playing a game my friends and I were deeply involved with for more than a decade, I had more than my fair share of time sitting tactical. I wouldn't say I'm nearly as good as some of the others, but I understand how the controls for the tactical stations work well enough to run them in a pinch."

"That's good to know," she said. "You were playing this game for more than a decade? Exactly how much time did you spend on it, relatively speaking?"

"A lot," he said with a shrug. "It was kind of an obsession, and I spent every free minute improving myself to get into the tournaments. By the time I'd joined the Navy, the team I'd been part of was competing at the highest levels. I know that that doesn't translate directly to experience, but the time wasn't wasted, either."

She nodded and followed him into a lift. The two of them turned and faced the doors as they slid closed, and it started moving between decks when he pressed a button.

"I wouldn't expect it would, but there's an old saying. Quantity has a quality all its own. In this case, the sheer number of hours you spent learning the systems and the expected behaviors of a ship like this—even if it doesn't translate cleanly to real-world experience—gives you an edge in understanding how systems like this work.

"Say what you want about only playing a game, but that meant you and your friends had what it took to take this ship into combat and blow the living hell out of a bunch of Locust drones, so don't sell yourself short."

The two exited the lift, and Derek led her to the bridge. Two Marines bracketed the hatch, stiffening to attention as they approached. He half expected them to object to his guest, but they stepped aside and allowed the commander and him to enter the bridge.

The sight of the grand space had become routine for him over the last week. He'd spent so many hours here getting the ship to the cluster and fighting the Locusts once they'd arrived that everything sort of felt ordinary at this point. People could get used to the strangest things.

The same was not true of Commander MacKinnon. She stopped dead in her tracks as soon as they stepped inside, her eyes sweeping over the dozens of consoles in the expansive space.

"Holy crap," she said under her breath. "They told me the bridge was bigger than what was available on a cruiser, but this is orders of magnitude more than I'd expected. I suppose the scale of the ship should've given me my first clue about what was waiting for me, but it didn't.

"Does this ship really require so many people to run it? I suppose it does, but what are all the bridge stations for?"

The ensign sitting watch in the captain's chair made to rise, but Derek waved her back down. "I'm just giving Commander MacKinnon a tour. Ignore us."

He pulled the senior officer off to the side of the bridge and started gesturing at sections of the consoles. "Almost all of the consoles here are related to gunnery. We have a tactical officer and an assistant, but there are so many weapons that we need multiple subordinates to control them.

"For example, if we're just looking at the laser systems, this ship has something like ten thousand laser batteries. Right now, almost all of them are nonfunctional. That's why that large cluster of consoles is empty. If they and the missile batteries were fully online, each of the sub gunners would be responsible for clusters of the weapons and carrying out the general instructions of the tactical officer."

He gestured toward the helm console. "That's the helm. On the other side of that are engineering, communications, and a few other consoles that give the watch officer oversight of specific departments.

"Sitting in this system like we are, we could technically do away with almost everybody on the bridge, but it's useful to have a partial crew here at all times so we can start learning what we need to do to keep watch. Also, with so many ships around us, the chance of a collision is higher than normal, and we want someone keeping an eye on everything."

MacKinnon nodded. "That's a lot more intensive than I

expected. I guess I thought there'd be more automation of the weapon systems."

He shook his head. "That doesn't make sense in this case. When the ship was designed, space was full of Locust drones, and they were always coming in from unexpected directions. It makes sense to have a human trained in the use of the specific weapons watching a particular sector for them.

"The person at tactical is responsible for the overall combat situation and gives specific guidance to each of the sub gunners so they can manage their combat inventory effectively. We don't want someone to get tunnel vision on one particular threat when another can just come out of the black."

MacKinnon walked around the bridge, looking over people's shoulders but not interrupting them. If anyone made to engage her, she waved them off and murmured that she was just looking.

After a couple of minutes, she moved to one of the empty consoles and sat. He walked over and reached down to activate the console through the switch on the side.

"What system are you looking at?" he asked once it had booted up.

"You mean which one do I want to look at? Gunnery."

"You're looking at gunnery. My question, Commander, is which subsystem is this console configured to control?"

The woman scrutinized the layout of the console. "It must be the lasers because everything is grouped into subgroups that can be individually controlled."

He nodded and reconfigured the console into a different setup that looked superficially the same. "And now?"

She pursed her lips and narrowed her eyes. "I can see that it's different, but I'm not sure what the changes mean."

"What you're looking at now are the missile launchers. These would only be a portion of what would be displayed if we configured the console to a full combat simulation. You'd be responsible for firing the missiles and long-range targeting in your assigned sector.

"Thankfully, they split up control of the laser systems and missiles back in the old days, so you're not expected to be running self-defense while you're on offense. As a missile control officer, you're responsible for categorizing targets in your zone before launching salvos of missiles on command."

She leaned back and crossed her arms, still considering the controls. "And this is only the beginning. Someone is responsible for electronic countermeasures and scanning for threats.

"I can see why Jack said my officers and I just didn't have the experience to understand what we didn't know. The sheer scale of this is mind-blowing. Tunnel vision will be a serious obstacle to taking this all in."

She turned to face him. "No matter what happens going forward, Derek, I want you to realize that just because someone else is appointed as the senior helm officer doesn't negate your experience at doing this work. My people and I will be woefully underprepared to operate this ship on a routine basis, much less in a crisis.

"After working as a tactical officer for over a decade, it's a bit humbling to realize I'm in a situation where I'm not capable of performing those duties aboard this ship. Not yet, anyway. That's going to be true of everyone that comes aboard."

She stood. "This ship and the people aboard her are far too important to count on us knowing what we can do and what we can't. You and your friends will need to guide and educate us, even if we get cranky."

"We'll do our very best, Commander," he said. "Do you have any idea when your people will be aboard and officially assigned? We have some consoles in the operations center to run simulations that will get them comfortable with how the controls function. We've got enough people to make that happen without impacting bridge operations, too."

She smiled a little bit sadly. "Our engineering team is just about finished getting the fusion plant extracted from *Hawkwing*. Once that's done, they've got a lot of other systems to pull, so it's going to be a while before we have any engineers aboard *Hunter*.

"Everyone else is already here. Someone is assigning us quarters, and they're getting settled in, so I'd imagine we'll be ready to start as soon as Commodore Romanoff makes us part of the team."

"So, would this be a good time for me to ask you to come to my office so we can get things in motion, India?" Derek heard the commodore say from behind him.

"You can carry on, Mister Calvo," the man said when Derek turned. "I understand you've got a few high-priority projects already in motion, and I'd rather not keep you from them. Thank you for taking the time to give Commander MacKinnon a tour. Both she and I appreciate it."

MacKinnon nodded and extended her hand to Derek. "We'll be working together closely, and I appreciate your willingness to do whatever it takes to achieve success. You're a credit to the Confederation Navy."

"Thank you, ma'am, sir. I appreciate that. Now, if you'll excuse me, I do have something I need to see to."

And with that, he walked off the bridge, already pulling out his comm unit to call John and ask where the cat had ended up. It might not be as pressing as dealing with some of the other tasks at hand, but this was something he'd started and wanted to see through.

15

JACK LED India to his office and closed the hatch behind them. She looked around and grinned. "I could get used to something like this, Jack. You remember how small my office was on *Hawk-wing*, right? If yours has a closet, mine would be about that size."

"Let's not start getting all possessive. You'll have one of your own. While it's not quite as lordly as this, trust me when I say it's not very far behind.

"The executive officer on this ship back during the first invasion would've been a flag officer too. Probably a rear admiral, or maybe even a vice admiral. You can rest assured they worked in as much comfort as somebody of that rank was used to."

Before she could respond, the chime on his hatch sounded, and he called for their visitor to enter. As expected, Sara limped in. She'd exchanged her civilian clothes for an old-style naval uniform very much like his own.

In fact, it was exactly like his, except missing the ship's emblem on her hat, belt, and uniform.

"This thing is quite the bother getting used to," she complained as she removed her cap and shrugged out of her greatcoat at the stand beside the door. "I don't see how you can wear this all the time, Jack. It weighs a ton."

"You get used to it," he said with a smile. "Besides, I'm told it adds gravitas."

He swiveled his attention back to India as Sara settled into one of the guest seats. "You might as well take a seat too, India. We've got a lot to go over."

Once they'd both settled, Jack focused his attention on Sara. "I assume the lack of an emblem on your uniform means you're still standing aside from my chain of command to provide a neutral voice."

She nodded. "The only reason I'm wearing one of the old-style uniforms is that I stand out when I don't. It's my concession to fitting in. Otherwise, I intend to provide a neutral point of view and continue to perform my duties as the senior officer in the Judge Advocate General's office in the cluster.

"You said there was something I needed to be here for. What is it?"

Jack sat behind his desk. Normally, he'd have taken one of the seats out among the visitors, but this was already going to be difficult, and he didn't need to complicate matters by treating it less seriously than it deserved.

"I'll be forwarding information to you that strongly suggests

Captain Magri is collaborating with pirates seeded among the civilians we rescued. I'm not sure how he knew the man we've identified as a pirate, but the two seem familiar with one another, and it seems they're working together to carry out some common goal."

Her lips pinched together. "That's a grave allegation, Jack. Depending on what you've got, it's almost certainly not going to be enough to bring charges. You know that, right?"

He nodded. "Tina is working on getting a clearer picture of exactly who's involved and what their plans are. If the information implicates Captain Magri, I'm going to arrest him. If I do so, I need to know what kind of procedures we're going to follow."

Sara closed her eyes a moment and sighed. "Under normal circumstances, we'd seat a board to consider the charges brought against him. As the senior officer with the Judge Advocate General's office, it would be my duty to head that panel.

"Regulations call for a total of three officers to sit in judgment. They need to be of the same rank as the accused or more senior. Someone would need to provide legal counsel to the accused, and we'd need a prosecutor."

Jack grimaced. "We've only got two people of the same rank or higher than Magri. You brought a staff of people with you when you came to arrest Vice Admiral LaChasse, but you weren't going to put her in front of a board right then. Is there anyone on your staff that could operate as either the prosecutor or the defense?"

"Yes," Sara said. "I've got people who are excellent in those specific roles. That clears away one aspect of the problem, but it still leaves us with a wall between charging him and trying him. We need a third officer ranked captain or above."

Jack turned his gaze toward India. "I'm about to incorporate *Hawkwing's* crew into *Hunter's* and appoint Commander MacKinnon as the executive officer. Since we're in the middle of an invasion, I need to know precisely what the regulations say about battlefield commissions and promotions.

"We're not going to get any kind of support from the Confederation for the duration, and I need some leeway. Is it within my authority to promote an officer or commission a noncommissioned officer?"

He watched India's eyes widen. She didn't say anything, but she knew exactly where he was going with this.

"Aren't you a little late bringing this up?" Sara asked. "I seem to remember you promoting every midshipman on your bridge to ensign and even bumping the recruits with the bridge skills up to the same rank.

"In fact, the original midshipmen were just officer candidates. Isn't that doing *exactly* what you've just asked me if you could do?"

"It is," he said with a smile as he leaned back in his chair, considering the other flag officer. "Only when I did it for officer candidates and recruits, nobody would care until the invasion was over. If I'm doing it to seat a board to try a Confederation Navy captain, it's going to matter."

"True. I did look everything up once I heard about you

promoting so many people, and as it happens, as a ship's commander during a time of war, you have that authority."

Then she waggled a finger at him. "I wouldn't get carried away, though, because all of these promotions are considered provisional until confirmed by a Navy promotions board. Taking a recruit up to ensign is a pretty big step, but I don't think anyone would raise an objection considering the importance of being able to man and control this ship.

"Bumping Commander MacKinnon to the rank of captain is only one grade and should be fine to fill a need in your command. It might even be acceptable to bump somebody two grades if they're in a position of particular need, but I wouldn't be looking to make ensigns into captains anytime soon."

Jack nodded. "I can work with that. I don't need to promote everybody in sight, but there are a few key positions that have to be filled by someone of sufficient rank."

He stood. "Commander MacKinnon, stand, please."

Once she'd done so, he continued. "Pursuant to orders I signed earlier this morning, the entire crew of the disabled Confederation naval vessel *Hawkwing* are hereby incorporated into the crew of *Delta Orionis*.

"You are furthermore assigned the position of executive officer and are promoted to the rank of captain. We'll see about getting you and your people uniforms as soon as possible. I'm damned glad to have you all."

She smiled a little bit. "Thank you, sir. We'll make this work."

"I know we will, but we're going to have to work hard to integrate both crews effectively. There are a number of individuals aboard that have low grades for the positions they currently occupy, yet I intend for them to continue their critical work. I realize that might cause problems with your people, and we need to settle this now."

India nodded. "You're primarily talking about Lieutenant Danek, I presume. She's got all of the skills necessary to be the chief engineer of this ship, and from what I understand, she might have been a chief engineer at some point in the past but was busted in grade.

"I don't know the reasons behind that, and I understand and agree with your assessment that it's better not to ask. I've already spoken with my chief engineer—my former chief engineer—and he's agreed to work under her as the chief even with their difference in grade. Still, you're probably right that it's best to make sure there's no confusion."

"That's good because we're all going to have to make allowances," he said. "Kelly has a lot of in-depth knowledge about this ship and has been working as the chief engineer here for years.

"She's not going to be happy about being bumped back up in grade, but she understands how critical it is for us to find a way to make this all work."

He grinned. "I told her just a little while ago that I might find a way to promote her. The idea didn't please her, yet I find myself looking forward to seeing her face when I show up and present her with new rank tabs.

"The other big spot I see needing filling is in logistics. Right now, Petty Officer Hutton is filling that role. He's swamped, and with all the people now under his command trying to keep all of this in order, I need to get him back to a rank suitable for commanding that number of bodies."

"What rank was he before?" India asked.

"He was a lieutenant commander," Sara said before Jack could respond. "And before you start wondering exactly what happened to get an officer of that rank busted down to enlisted, let's just say he has a way of picking up women he shouldn't, even when they're married to people that outrank him. And he's not shy about defending himself by punching the offended husband in the face either."

India's expression turned wry. "I'm not certain whether I should be amused or horrified. I suppose a womanizer is the least of our problems right now. If he's got the skills needed to make this work, we have to use him. What have you got in mind, Jack?"

"As the head of the logistics department on a ship this large, I think his old rank is appropriate, but that's quite a jump from Petty Officer. Maybe too much of a jump."

India pursed her lips and then shook her head. "Probably, but even a lieutenant would be better placed to handle this than a petty officer. What do you think, Commodore Nastasi?"

"He's acting as the head of a department on a ship with five thousand people," she said. "We literally have no one else with his skills. I understand *Hawkwing* has a supply department and logistics officer, but she was nothing like the scale of a battleship.

"Even considering my warning to Jack about not overdoing it, this might be a case where he may not have much choice. What's the rank of the logistics officer aboard *Hawkwing*?"

"Lieutenant Collins didn't survive the battle," India said, shaking her head. "Our next highest-ranking person in logistics is Senior Chief Petty Officer Doyle. She's a very competent person, but she doesn't have the skills to handle everything you must have aboard the ship."

Jack shook his head in sympathy. "I'm sorry to hear about Collins, but Doyle would be lost inside five minutes. This ship is a maze of compartments that we've literally packed full of everything we could get our hands on before we left Faust.

"It's more than Hutton can handle, to be honest. I'm sure we have a lot of supplies that haven't been cataloged, including important things we desperately need to know about. And that doesn't even count all of the cargoes being brought over from the civilian ships."

Sara chuckled. "Are you ready to get a laugh, Jack? You probably had no idea about this, but all the enlisted personnel from the supply depot were added to your personnel roster during that last surge of personnel sent over from headquarters.

"I'm sure Hutton doesn't trust them any farther than he could throw them, but they're trained in this type of scale, at least."

Jack did laugh. "You don't have time for the full story, India, but let's just say I had to prove the supply depot was selling things they shouldn't sell and performing other criminal acts to get what I needed to get *Hunter*'s spare parts."

He crossed his arms. "I honestly didn't expect to hear that bunch of dirty dealers were here, but I'll even accept them at this point. I'm pretty sure they're not happy being under my command, but as long as I don't have to personally deal with them, maybe this can work.

"Hutton won't be popular with them either, but he's the man on the scene, and they'll just have to accept it. So you're suggesting I should bump him to lieutenant commander again?"

"I think so," Sara said. "It's not going to stand up over the long haul, but many of the promotions you make won't. That's the nature of battlefield commissions and promotions. Once the fight is over, people get dropped in rank or leave the service.

"The process hasn't been used since the last invasion, but it's well documented. Until someone starts yelling at you about it, you might as well take advantage of your isolation."

His hatch signaled. Jack frowned because he wasn't expecting any other visitors right now. In fact, he'd blocked off the time to take care of these necessary discussions.

"Enter."

The hatch slid open, and Dubsky stalked in. She looked furious.

"What's wrong?" he asked with a sinking feeling.

"The little rat isn't in his quarters," she growled. "I tagged up with Christine, and she indicated there was a short break where she had to swap out drones, and he must've left during that."

Jack grimaced. "I want every critical area of the ship on lockdown right away. Form search parties to go through every compartment and find him as quickly as possible.

"We don't have enough information to arrest him at this

point, but I want eyes on him. As soon as you locate him, I want to hear about it."

"Yes, sir," she said through clenched teeth. "We'll find him."

Jack knew she would. The only question was what kind of mischief he'd get into while he was out of sight.

16

TINA WAS RELIEVED to find the research ship was a converted freighter. She'd been afraid it was a specialty ship, and that would've been a lot more difficult to explain to Dugan. The exterior wouldn't raise any eyebrows, and they only needed to do a bit of interior decorating to make things look more realistic for her purposes.

Even pirate ships were boarded by the authorities once in a while, so it wasn't like there was a lot of conspicuous evidence left lying around. Still, a few things needed to be done to set the stage.

The first of those was making sure they had enough bodies aboard. Pirates needed people to board other ships, and they needed things like body armor and weapons to do so. Those wouldn't be in plain sight, but they'd be readily accessible. Pirates would see the signs of that sort of thing and would miss them if they weren't there.

The retired Marine recon folks were responsible for setting everything up, and they'd packed the cargo shuttle belonging to the research ship full of weapons and armor. Those were also the weapons they preferred to use, which was a nice bonus.

The weapons might be a little high-end for a pirate group, but there was only so much that could be done on short notice. This was supposed to be a dinner date with one man, so she didn't need to have a hundred people on standby. She just needed enough people to give the appearance of a fully crewed ship and to have a small group ready to respond instantly if there was trouble.

When they docked, the Marine force recon personnel spread throughout the ship, checking to make sure there were no surprises. They weren't rude to the regular crew about it, but they wouldn't take no for an answer.

Many of these folks were on the older, grizzled side, and she watched with approval as they moved down the corridors with their weapons at the ready, calling out to one another as they did their work.

They politely herded the remaining crew into the cargo shuttle to be taken back to *Hunter*. The pilot would bring the second tranche of force recon personnel on his return trip. Most of Turner's personnel would be on the research vessel for this operation, so she hoped she wasn't pulling them away from other tasks that needed their attention.

While they focused on their search, she went to the galley and began preparing dinner. She'd brought everything she'd need, though she suspected the ship had the raw ingredients already. Best to be ready for anything.

The real question was how many people Dugan would bring with him. Pirates weren't known for being trusting sorts, so she didn't expect him to come alone. He'd have a handful of guards, and so would she, for that matter.

He might also bring along several of his officers. Hell, he might surprise her and show up with one or two of the other captains as well. She couldn't count anything out at this point, so she needed to be prepared for whatever came.

That being the case, she cooked as if she was expecting two dozen people. It was more challenging than her normal meal prep. Still, surprisingly, some of the Marine force recon personnel were adept in the kitchen and assisted her in getting everything ready. At the same time, their compatriots finished securing the ship and setting up the props they'd need.

"Don't you have something to do in the dining room or the office?" the woman that was helping her chop vegetables asked.

"I do, but it's only going to take me a few minutes to make that happen," Tina said as she minced leeks. "We've got someone on the bridge keeping an eye on the sensors, so as soon as someone looks like they're headed our way, I can plant the listening devices.

"I took a look around the office earlier. There are plenty of places to hide things."

The older woman raised an eyebrow. "Not to be judgmental, but you should probably do that now rather than rushing around when the pressure is on. I've got the skills to keep all of this simmering until you get back.

"Seriously, no offense, but I've almost certainly got more experience in the kitchen than you do. Go take care of what you need to do and let me focus on the food preparation."

Tina considered that and decided the woman was probably right. She did have enough on her plate, so to speak.

"Okay," she said as she pulled off her apron. "Thank you."

She headed for the dining room and placed tiny devices to catch everything said in the room and record video from multiple angles. The devices were ridiculously small and designed for use by Confederation Intelligence. If the pirates brought something to scan for them, they'd almost certainly come up empty-handed.

At least she hoped they wouldn't detect them. If they did, that would make for some interesting predinner conversation, for sure.

The dining room was utilitarian and wouldn't cause any comment, but if Dugan wanted to go to Tina's supposed office, that would be a bit more challenging.

The space was set up as a working environment for someone with a great deal of knowledge about the Locusts. There were books about the first invasion and technical treatises on Locust equipment. Everything was very highbrow, and frankly, it looked like an academic's office.

Tina couldn't do anything to change the professor's office in the time she had, so she needed to incorporate everything there into her new persona. Who was she? No doubt the pirate captains in the cluster knew of one another—at least generally— but she was an anomaly.

She knew the signs, handshakes, and passphrases because she'd been literally standing right there when they'd executed them. If they'd only had two people meeting, she probably would've missed what was going on, but they'd had to go through the process several times to make sure that all of them were really part of their secretive little club. That gave her the repetition she'd needed to recognize the patterns and the importance of the gestures and words.

Tina had been able to get into that meeting, but once they had a moment to speak with her alone, they'd ask more questions. Who was she, and how had she come into the cluster without any of them being aware of her presence or identity? It didn't take a genius to figure that would come.

Her cover story had to be something straightforward, simple, and believable. She'd come from outside the cluster and only arrived just before the invasion. That's the reason none of them had met her.

As for her obvious academic paraphernalia, that was her cover story for taking her ship wherever she wanted inside the cluster. She was doing research on Locust debris and wreckage. After all, why hide the obvious nature of what Wilson had been doing? Tina could incorporate the existing details into her cover story easily enough.

In fact, she'd become Wilson. There were some pictures on display in the office, so she immediately took them to another compartment and stashed them. There was no need to have anything present that indicated another person used this office.

That done, she bugged the office thoroughly. If the pirate

wanted to talk privately, the office was an excellent place to make that happen. It was roomy—comparatively speaking—so there would be no problem if he wanted to bring a few of his people with him.

In fact, if more of the captains were involved in this meeting, it was even more likely they'd spill important information. More people also made it easier to let others do the talking. After all, some people loved to talk, and given a little encouragement, they'd chatter right along. Hopefully, someone in this group would fit the bill.

The final thing she did was track down Turner. He'd come across with the second wave of people and led a ready reaction squad out of sight somewhere.

When she found him, he was in one of the small cargo areas with a dozen other people. All of them were festooned with weapons and armor. They definitely didn't look like pirates. These men and women were Marine special operators. If they had to come out to play, the time for deception would have passed.

He walked over to her as she came in. "Are you all set up?"

"I'm ready. Take this."

Tina handed him a comm unit that was tapped into her bugs. "I've got a camera in my blouse that will record both video and audio. You'll be able to see and hear what I do. If you want to bring up other channels to see what's happening with them, you can do that as well.

"I'm not anticipating trouble, but you need to have a way of knowing if I need you to intervene. If I say the word artichoke, that's your cue to come running."

"Artichoke?" he asked with a hint of amusement. "That's the best you can come up with?"

"This isn't a contest to see who can come up with the cleverest word," she said with mock severity. "It's selecting a word that's not going to come up in normal conversation but that I can somehow find a way to weave in if I choose."

"Now I'm almost hoping you run into trouble so I can hear how you work artichoke into *any* normal conversation with pirates."

"You're a funny man. What's our communication status with *Hunter?*"

"We don't have a continuous feed if that's what you're asking. We've sent them some burst updates, but we'll stop doing even that once we have our visitors aboard. There's too great a chance their small craft would detect the transmission, and that would raise questions you can't answer. The commodore will have to wait until they've left for a report."

"Or until things go pear shaped."

"Let's hope it doesn't come to that," she said with a sigh. "I'm a spy, not a Marine, so I'd like them all to walk out of here fat, dumb, and happy."

She turned and headed for the hatch. "I'll leave you to your prep and get back to my own. I hope I don't need you, but if I do, come running."

"Will do. If we come in guns up, hit the deck."

As if she wouldn't have the sense to get out of the way if it came to shooting.

It turned out dinner was coming along just fine. Her impromptu cooking team seemed to have everything well in hand when she returned to the kitchen, so she supervised while plotting out the potential complications for this meeting.

She had a lot of experience with undercover work, and she wasn't worried things would spin out of control because of something she either said or did, but it was always possible there would be blind spots in her knowledge. It was always best to think about answers to questions before they were asked.

Tina was a great extemporaneous speaker, but when people had guns and took a very dim view of being fooled around with, it was never good to just wing it.

The woman helping her cook stopped stirring the dish she was preparing and pressed something deeper into her ear. "Copy that."

She turned toward Tina. "We've got a cutter on approach to the forward docking port, starboard side. Since we're not running active sensors, we're not sure where it came from, but the odds of it being anybody but your dinner date are pretty low. You'd best go welcome him aboard."

"I'll leave getting dinner set up in your hands, then," she said as she pulled off her apron. "If you hear any shooting, you can safely assume we're skipping straight to dessert."

The woman laughed. "I'll be listening over the tacnet, and if there's any trouble, you can be sure I'll come running with pudding in hand."

Tina was still smiling as she walked down the corridor toward the indicated docking port. Along the way, she picked up a pair of burly Marine force recon troops wearing leather jackets over their holstered pistols. They had what might be charitably called plausible deniability because they weren't openly armed, but they certainly looked like pirates pretending to be something else, which suited her plans perfectly.

As for herself, she had two concealed pistols she was well and thoroughly trained to use. If need be, she'd be more than capable of defending herself.

She only needed to cool her heels at the docking port for about a minute before she heard the cutter connect with her ship and the grappling locks engage. Once that was done, the flexible port sealed to the cutter and equalized the air pressure.

"I think you should take a step back," one of her guards said. "If they come in hot, it's our job to handle it."

"I'm not going into this with the assumption that I'm screwed before we even start," she retorted. "We have to present a façade of strength, so you can be one step behind me, but I have to be front and center."

As soon as the hatch chimed, indicating someone wanted entrance, she pressed the switch to open the hatch, smiling as it slid to one side. Christopher Dugan stood on the other side with a smile that made her skin crawl.

"Thank you for inviting me aboard, Captain. It's rare for people in our line of work to have an opportunity to get to know one another.

"Unfortunately for my intimate dinner plans, the other

captains and I decided it was best to gather for a candid chat. I hope you don't mind, but I've brought guests."

Tina raised one shoulder and gave him a slight shrug. "I thought this might happen, so I've prepared enough food for everyone. Come in."

Dugan came out of the airlock, and as soon as he stepped aside, she noted the other captains were lined up behind him. One by one, each of them stepped aboard her borrowed ship, and she shook their hands.

Everything was going as expected, right up until Captain Ronnie Magri stepped out of the cutter.

He no longer wore a Confederation Navy uniform, but he still had that same smug air about him. She'd known he was a snake, but this proved it.

She smiled at the traitorous officer. "Well, well. I didn't expect to see you off that big ship of yours, Captain Magri. Welcome aboard. I hope you came hungry."

He gave her a toothy grin. "I'm always hungry. I hope you have some decent alcohol because we're going to have a lot of celebrating to do. I couldn't speak clearly aboard that museum, but I think you picked up the gist of what I intended. Now it's time to spell it out."

She matched his grin and gestured for them to head toward the dining room. "I'm ready to hear all the gory details, but I want some food while we talk. Conspiracy gives me an appetite.

It was a good thing she'd prepared for a few dozen visitors. With all six captains, a pair of guards each, and Captain Magri, that was right at twenty-two people, counting her own guards.

If someone was a little hungry, they wouldn't even have leftovers.

Not that the food situation was her primary concern, but still, she'd nailed it.

As they arrived at the dining room, several of the accompanying pirates pulled out equipment and began scanning the room for bugs. She'd been right, and this was the first big test. Either Confederation Intelligence's brag about their stuff being undetectable would hold up, or the shooting was about to start with her trapped in the dining room with a lot of pissed-off people between her and any actual cover.

To her relief, no one found anything objectionable, and everyone sat down. They also smiled at the selection of food her ersatz servers brought in. There was surprisingly little meaningful conversation as they ate, but near the end of the meal, Dugan—who was seated to her right—engaged her.

He leaned back from his cleaned plate, crossed his arms over his chest, and considered her. "I've been working the cluster for more than a dozen years, and I know everybody that works here by reputation, if not sight. I don't know your full name. Why is that?"

Tina smiled without showing teeth. "That's because I've just arrived. I'm going by Tina Wilson, and my cover identity isn't a merchant. I'm pretending to be an academic studying Locust debris.

"I figured that would allow me to go from system to system without raising too many eyebrows or getting boarding parties that wanted to inspect my ship."

He didn't say anything for a bit, simply studying her with an expression that said he wasn't necessarily buying what she was selling. She, for her part, stared back with guileless eyes.

"Well, I suppose that has the benefit of being new and unexpected," he finally admitted. "You know all the signs and signals, so I can't outright say I don't believe you, but I'm still more than a little skeptical. That's why all of us are here to verify your bona fides."

"And exactly how do you intend to do that?" she asked.

"Where did you come from?" he asked. "Who sponsored you into the profession?"

Tina laughed. "If you mean who made enough threats that if I didn't join the loose organization of pirates rather than being independent, that would be Michael Cioni. If the name doesn't sound familiar, that's because he preferred going by The Claw."

She'd done her research, figured out where she might have come from, and who the other pirates operating in that sector had been. The Claw had been a big name in the pirate organization before the Confederation Navy found his base and broke it up. They'd identified his real name by running his corpse's prints once they'd retrieved it from the wreckage of his ship. He wouldn't be disputing her claims, nor would anyone in his crew.

"I've heard of The Claw," Dugan admitted, "but so have a lot of people. Tell me, why did he go by that name? It wasn't like he had a mechanical hand, after all."

This was a bit more hypothetical, and she was doing a fair bit of guessing, but the information Confederation Intelligence had pulled out of the man's computer had given them some insights into his personality and his preferred entertainment material. It hadn't taken much digging to find out where he'd probably acquired the name.

Now she'd find out if her guess was correct.

"He loved old superhero videos from pre-spaceflight Earth. There was a villain who'd been transformed into pure sound if you can believe that. He wore some kind of sonic emitter on his right wrist. That's where the character picked his name, and so did the pirate."

Dugan's eyes narrowed even further, and then he smiled. "I've been wondering where he got that stupid name for years, so thanks for sharing the information. I can't say I was sorry when I heard the Navy had caught up with him. He was kind of an ass."

She smiled back, hiding her relief. "He was *definitely* that. If we're finished playing twenty questions, I'm curious about what we're doing next. Why don't we have some dessert while you fill me in?"

The woman from the kitchen brought in the pudding when Tina called and made sure everybody got a good-sized serving before she left the room.

Once she was gone, Magri ate a heaping spoonful of chocolate pudding and smiled. "This is quite good. We might want to start gathering some of your best liquor now. Things came together far better than I'd expected when I reconnected with Dugan.

"He and I met back when I was working at my grandfather's company, though he had a different name back then. He was smuggling, and the two of us came to a few mutually beneficial agreements that made us both a lot of money."

Magri smiled a bit, though the expression never reached his eyes. "I'd heard after I'd joined the Navy that he'd moved into piracy and thought we'd never see one another again.

"It's fortuitous to come together this way. I suppose we can finish our dessert and then move on to the liquor. It won't change the timing, after all."

He grinned at Tina. "We didn't trust you enough to share our plan without vetting you first. Now that we're sure who you are, you'll get to play clean up rather than being involved in the primary operation.

"You see, Dugan and the rest have already positioned their people and weapons aboard that relic of a ship. They're just waiting for the right moment to seize control of the critical areas."

Tina's heart leaped into her throat.

"Once they do," he continued, "I'll install myself as the commanding officer, and we'll continue on with our mission of driving the Locusts out of the more lucrative systems. Not all of the cluster, you understand. Just the systems where we can set up shop and make our own pocket empire."

Dugan smiled coldly. "Why be a pirate when you can become a noble in some new political organization? As long as we leave the rest of the Locusts alone, they can form a buffer between the Confederation and us.

"We'll have that big ship to beat them back once we get it repaired, and I think I know just the place where that needs to happen. We'll need the ship's firepower to take it over, but we can make it work."

"It seems you've fallen in with us at a good time, Wilson," Magri said. "Your crew can act as our reserve, so you'll want to get them to armoring up shortly. Once this is all over, we'll live like kings and queens."

That was probably the worst possible news she could've heard, and she was glad Turner was monitoring everything. She wasn't sure how—or even if—he could get word back to *Hunter*, but they had to act now.

She needed to take them into custody or kill them without getting word back to their ships. Turner undoubtedly had a plan to take their cutter, but there had to be serious risks involved with that.

Hell, there were risks involved with *everything* they were about to do, but the stakes had just gotten far too high to let things sit.

"How soon are we talking about?" she asked, inserting the appropriate amount of eagerness into her tone.

Magri glanced at his watch. "Any time now, I suspect. Dugan?"

The pirate nodded. "The window is already open. Once they have enough weapons from the stashes we sent aboard as cargo, they'll move on the bridge, engineering, and the Marine barracks. Once they bottle up the real fighters, the ship will be ours very quickly."

Oh, hell. They were *completely* out of time. She'd have rather avoided going this route, but she was out of options.

"I hope everyone is thirsty," she said with a smile. "I think it's time to break out a few bottles of an exceptionally rare liquor I have stashed away to celebrate. Have any of you ever tried artichoke brandy?"

"Artichoke brandy?" Dugan asked with a stunned expression. "Are you serious?"

"Don't knock it until you've tried it," she assured him as she covertly reached for her concealed pistols and prepared to throw herself to the deck. "It packs a much stronger kick than one might imagine."

17

Jack was still working out the details about how India and her people would fit aboard *Hunter* when he got the call from Turner. The pirate had shown up as expected, only he'd brought guests. It seemed all the rest of the captains were aboard the research ship, and their missing Navy officer was with them.

He wished they could tap into the feed and see what was going on for themselves, but that was just asking for trouble. Turner had taken a risk sending them as much warning as he had. He wouldn't risk operational security further, and Jack didn't want him to. They'd have to wait until things wrapped up to get the play by play.

"I can't believe the balls on that man," India growled. "He's trying to commit mutiny and treason and acts as if no one is paying any attention at all."

Sara chuckled. "Well, one thing is for sure. This meeting will provide a lot more evidence for his court-martial than I'd expected. If he participates in the conversation about usurping command of this vessel, it's pretty much an open and shut case."

"I want enough to nail him to the wall," Jack said through clenched teeth. "I don't want him weaseling his way out of this, so we need to have such overwhelming proof that the board is merely a perfunctory affair.

"Now, if you will excuse me, I need to head to the bridge and make sure we're ready for what comes next."

"Are you sure going to the bridge is the best option?" Sara asked. "Those pirate ships aren't a threat to us. Captain MacKinnon is more than capable of handling the bridge.

"I think you should slip aboard the research vessel. When the time comes to arrest Captain Magri, you should be the one putting the cuffs on him."

"That's a bad call," Jack said with a shake of his head. "With all the pirate captains on board, their ships are undoubtedly watching the research ship closely. If anybody tries to take a cutter over there right now, it will raise the alarm. No, we need to let Tina and Major Turner handle the situation there on their own.

"What we need to do is prepare *Hunter* for trouble. If they're meeting as a group, odds are they're going to set up whatever their final plan is. Once we have the details, we can counter it. Until then, we need to take precautions to make sure we're not surprised."

He pulled out his comm and called Dubsky. "If you could come to my office, we need to set a few more plans in motion."

"On my way, sir."

"What exactly do you have in mind, Jack?" India asked. "The idea that six pirate ships are going to cause you heartache seems a bit of a stretch. How many Marines and Marine recruits do you have? More than a thousand, if memory serves. How many pirates are you expecting?"

"Maybe half that, at most," he admitted. "The thing is, they're going to be trained—sort of—and most of our people aren't. If the fecal matter hits the rotary impeller, most of them will be scrambling, and leadership will be thin on the ground.

"Our best bet is to prepare before the pirates make their move. The only thing we need to do for sure is to make certain they don't recognize what we're doing before we're ready for them to see the trap close. To do that, we need Dubsky's input."

It took a few minutes for the Marine lieutenant to get to his office, but as soon as she made her appearance, Jack got right down to business. "You can suspend the search for Captain Magri. He somehow got off *Hunter* and is now aboard the research ship, meeting with all of the pirate captains and Tina Chen."

"Dammit," the Marine officer muttered. "What do we do now, sir?"

"We plan for an attack. If the pirate captains are meeting, they're finalizing their plans, and we need to be ready. If they get their people aboard *Hunter*, it's going to be one hell of a fight.

"We have the edge when it comes to bodies, but our people are woefully untrained for this kind of thing. Also, we're not going to be as heavily armed as them unless we get something set up in advance."

He stood and began to pace. "I assume you have contingency plans for something like this in place. Brief us."

"We do, but we haven't gotten everything ready to move," she admitted. "If things look imminent, I should probably be moving my people into position now and making sure everyone has the weapons they need.

"All of our plans involve having several regional armories that the Marine personnel can draw weapons and armor from. Right now, everything is centrally located in the Marine barracks because we didn't have time to prepare for an armed attack inside the vessel. That's going to have to change."

"What about naval personnel?" India asked. "Shouldn't we be armed as well?"

The lieutenant started to shake her head but stopped and frowned. "I have this vague memory of watching some old Locust War movie, and I seem to recall the officers were armed. Was that really the order of the day or just creative license?"

"I don't know, but I'm going to make a snap judgment right now that all officers need to be armed," Jack said. "If it's not in the standard rules, we're going to run with it anyway. All of us are trained in using sidearms, except for the newly promoted ensigns and midshipmen.

"Technically, the midshipmen aren't officers yet, but I'm making the call to promote all of them to the rank of ensign. This isn't the time for half measures, so we need to quietly get our officers into the correct uniforms with the right rank tabs and see that they're issued sidearms. Since we're wearing greatcoats, no one other than us needs to know we're armed."

India stood. "I'll see about getting a new uniform right now. If things fall into the crapper, I don't need to be rushing around trying to find one. I'll make sure *Hawkwing*'s people meet me in the logistics area so we can get this sorted out ASAP. If someone would bring us weapons, I'd appreciate it. With your permission, Commodore?"

Jack gestured toward the hatch. "Make that happen, and then assume command of the bridge. I'll keep an eye on the bigger picture for right now.

"We're not going to be attacked by those pirates in a ship-to-ship exchange, in any case. They could open fire on us right now, and we'd still be okay. They don't have the firepower to endanger this vessel. If they go for the engines—which are our weakest vulnerability—they risk being trapped here forever, so that's unlikely."

"Understood," she said as she exited the compartment.

Jack's comm went off before he could continue giving instructions to Dubsky. It indicated the incoming call was from Calvo.

"Romanoff."

"Sir, I'm down in the medical center, and I've found something you need to see. I'd rather not go into the details over an open channel, but it's urgent. It might be appropriate to have Commodore Nastasi and Lieutenant Dubsky here, too."

Jack couldn't imagine what the ensign might have found, but he wasn't going to second guess the young man's judgment. "We're on our way."

He shut off his communicator and hung it back on his belt. "Have someone bring us sidearms, Lieutenant. I hope we don't need them, but it's better to be safe than sorry."

"I'll see to it, sir," she said as she pulled out her comm.

"Then let's go see what Calvo has found for us."

The three of them made their way to the medical center. Dubsky talked on her comm the entire time and only put it back on her belt as they arrived. Her nod most likely indicated she'd gotten everything he'd ordered in motion. He hoped none of the precautions were needed.

When they came into the medical center, he stopped and smiled. It hadn't been operational when they'd left Faust, but the doctors had put a lot of work into the place, and it looked good. Right now, they were dealing with survivors from *Hawkwing*.

His medical crew had been bolstered by the medical team from the cruiser as well, and they seemed to be getting along just fine. The fact that his mother had recruited the vast majority of the doctoral staff meant they were very experienced, though older in years.

He spotted Duncan McRae working on the far side of the room. That reminded him that the medic had once been a general practitioner before he'd gotten shipped to *Hunter*.

That was another battlefield commission he'd make because he wasn't going to ignore the man's obvious proficiency. Whatever he'd done in the past, the man had saved Sara's life. That deserved to be rewarded.

Before he did that, though, he needed to find out what Calvo wanted. He didn't see the boy, but one of the nursing staff came over and directed the three of them to an examination room.

When they went in, he was utterly stunned to see the patient on the bed was an orange cat who sat there placidly considering them as Calvo petted it. Jack opened his mouth to say something but discovered he wasn't sure *what* to say. This felt so far outside his expectations that it left him bemused.

"I know this looks strange, sir, but trust me, there's a serious point to it," Calvo said, defending himself from the obviously incredulous expressions the three of them were sending his way. "I helped rescue this cat in one of the cargo bays and brought it here to make sure it could be checked out. That, in and of itself, wouldn't be cause for you to come, but we found something disturbing."

The young man grabbed the cat's collar from a small rollable table nearby. He held it up for them to examine.

"This looks like a regular collar, but it's not. It seems our friend's owner wanted to keep an eye on his crew and stashed a hidden camera in it. We just happened to find it when scanning the cat to see if it had any injuries. It's a he, by the way.

"When I asked one of my friends with experience in electronics to check it out, he was able to pull what was currently recorded off. That's what you need to see because it's bad."

The young man pulled his comm off of his belt and held it out to Jack.

Jack took the unit and began playing the keyed-up video. Sara and Dubsky leaned in to observe over his shoulder.

He wasn't sure if this was the only information recorded, but obviously, Calvo had queued it up to this location because it was something he thought was important.

The cat was obviously perched somewhere out of sight. Jack was certain it wasn't supposed to be inside a cargo shuttle, but that's what he was looking at. The crates stacked all around seemed mundane, and two men that looked like cargo handlers were busy sealing one.

"Get that lid down tight," the older one said. "This isn't the kind of cargo one wants tumbling out on the deck if there's an accident. If Dugan knew you'd been this sloppy, he'd space you, so you'd best remember the favor I'm doing you."

"Sorry, Ray. It was an accident, and it won't happen again."

"See that it doesn't."

The conversation was interesting, but then the cat climbed higher on the stack of crates he was perched on, and Jack got a look into the crate itself. It was filled with weapons. Lots and lots of weapons.

If the other crates were equally full, there were enough weapons on that shuttle to arm a thousand people. He doubted most were filled with weapons because they had to expect some of the containers might be checked. Still, the fact they were bringing weapons aboard *Hunter* at all was a very, very bad sign.

"How long after we get aboard do we rendezvous with the other crews and get the weapons?" the younger man asked.

"Did you listen to the plan at all?" the older man complained. "By now, all six crews are aboard that warship, and they'll be getting into the crates they brought as quickly as they can. By

1500 hours ship time, everyone should have their gear and be moving on their primary attack locations."

Jack froze the video and glanced at his chronometer. They had less than ten minutes before this supposedly kicked off.

"Dubsky, go do what you need to do," he ordered. The Marine lieutenant raced off without bothering to answer.

"Calvo, get to your station on the bridge. I'll be right behind you, but don't wait for me if the attack starts before I get there. Seal the hatch and do whatever needs doing. Do you understand?"

"Understood, sir." The young man sprinted out of the medical center. At that speed, he'd definitely beat Jack to the bridge even though Jack was going to be running too.

"Stay here," he ordered Sara as he headed for the hatch. "Watch the cat. It's evidence."

"Transparent, but I've been shot and stabbed too many times to complain. Get moving, Jack, and be careful."

A Marine with a befuddled expression came through the hatch with a bag that likely contained the sidearms Jack had ordered. He was willing to stop for that, so he dug into the bag, took a weapons belt, and slid it around his waist underneath his greatcoat.

The bag only had one other sidearm, so Calvo had already grabbed the one intended for him. That must explain the Marine's expression.

Jack headed off at a fast trot, bringing up his comm unit, and called the bridge. Calvo was probably halfway there, but this couldn't wait.

"Bridge," a woman answered.

"This is Romanoff. Go to general quarters. Seal all sensitive areas of the ship and notify the Marines to deploy to repel boarders already on board. This is not a drill.

"I'm on my way, but until I get there, Ensign Calvo has the conn. When either Captain MacKinnon or I arrive, we'll take charge from there."

"Aye, sir."

The overhead alarm began hooting, and the woman's voice rang out over the speakers. "General quarters, general quarters. This is not a drill. All hands to battle stations. Prepare to repel boarders already aboard. I repeat, prepare to repel boarders already aboard."

Jack skidded around the corner where the lift was and saw that he was already too late. A dozen men and women in mixed body armor were already there. They saw him coming, and two of them raised their weapons, opening fire.

18

Derek ignored the lifts and headed straight for the stairwell. There was no time to stand around waiting. He'd taken a few moments to strap the pistol the Marine had brought for him around his waist, but he had no time to waste.

When he reached the correct deck, he turned and raced down the corridor for the bridge. That's when the overhead speakers came to life, calling for general quarters at the same time the alarm began sounding. Somehow, that made this seem even more real.

The Marines standing guard outside the bridge had their weapons out and covered both directions as he raced toward them. They were both known to him, and they obviously recognized him because they diverted their aim and didn't stop him as he ran past.

He half expected to find the bridge in pandemonium, but

everyone was focused on their consoles already bringing the combat systems to life and preparing the ship to maneuver. Carrie Sandgren, an engineering watch officer, was sitting in the command chair. She leaped to her feet as he approached, and he took the chair.

"What are the statuses of the ships around us," he demanded.

One of the tactical officers half-turned in his seat. "No ships are maneuvering at this time, and we're not detecting any kind of unusual activity. What's going on?"

"Pirates put armed boarders on the ship, and an attack is imminent. We have to assume the bridge is a primary target."

There was a shout in the corridor, and someone opened fire at a distance. He turned his head and saw the Marines pull back into the bridge, returning firing down the corridor.

"Seal the hatch, Marines," he ordered. "No one gets in or out until this is over."

A few bullets ricocheted off the massive hatch as it smoothly slid shut, but he didn't see any of the pirates before the slab of thick metal closed and latched with a loud clank. One of the Marines activated the manual lock and disconnected the hatch from the automatic controls, sealing them in.

The damned thing was built like a bank vault door, so there was no way short of blowing it up that the pirates were getting in. Unfortunately, that also meant they couldn't expect any support until this was settled.

That meant all of this was on him and his friends.

"Active sensors," he commanded. "Light up everyone in the

vicinity. If anyone has weapons—especially powered weapons—I want to know about it. What's the status of our lasers?"

"All lasers are online and ready to go," the tactical officer responded.

"Engineering status?"

"They're locked down and report all systems operating at standard levels," Sandgren said from her console. "They'd just gotten the new fusion plant through the airlock, so they've got the engineering staff preparing to repel boarders and keep the systems operational."

"Derek, I've got six ships with weapons scattered all around us," the tactical officer said, his voice rising a bit. "Looks like they're powering them up."

"Communications, take me live on the general channel."

"You're on."

Derek knew he wasn't all that threatening, so *Hunter* would have to do the intimidating for him. He leaned forward and scowled toward the camera anyway, but he probably looked ridiculous.

"All civilian vessels, this is *Delta Orionis*. There has been an armed incursion aboard our vessel, and some of the freighters in your midst are pirates. Do not maneuver. I repeat, do not move your ships one meter. Whatever happens, this is not going to affect you. We'll let you know once the situation has been dealt with.

"Pirate vessels, power down your weapons and do not maneuver. If you disregard my orders, we will have no choice but to consider you hostile and respond accordingly. There will be no warning shots, so do not test me."

"One of the pirate vessels is maneuvering," the tactical officer said. "They're already at the rear of the convoy, and they seem to be reversing course to bring our engines into their cone of fire."

"Pirate vessel, cease maneuvering now, or you will be fired upon," he warned since the channel was still open. "This is your only warning. End transmission."

After a few seconds, the tactical officer shook his head. "They've increased speed."

"Target that ship with every laser cluster that does not endanger any other vessel when firing," he said coldly.

"Derek, not only is that overkill, but we also don't have the authority to fire on civilian vessels," the tactical officer said quietly, visibly sweating. "This isn't like fighting the Locusts. Those ships are filled with human beings."

"I don't like it, but we have an obligation to defend ourselves and those under our care. If they fire on our engines, they're dooming all of us to death. Fire."

The young man hesitated for just a single moment, turned, and stabbed his finger down on the button.

There wasn't anything dramatic about firing lasers on a ship this size. The lights didn't dim, and there was no noise. Everything happened as if this were just a simulation, only it wasn't. Real lives ended because of his orders.

"Volley complete," the tactical officer said, his voice somewhat hollow. "Target destroyed. Scratch that. Target obliterated."

The full weight of what he'd just ordered felt like a hydraulic press crushing Derek into the command chair. Had he been right to order their destruction? Had he made a mistake in using such overpowering force with the hopes of cowing other pirates into surrendering?

He didn't know, and he didn't have time to think about it.

"What's the status of the other pirate ships?"

"None of them have moved yet," the helm officer said. "Hold it. One of them has begun accelerating, but not towards our rear. It looks like they're getting behind another freighter, and they've managed it."

"Put me back on a general transmission."

The communications officer pointed at him.

"All pirate vessels, you've seen the results of trying to fight us. Surrender and power down your weapons, or we will be forced to destroy you. You will not be given another chance."

He made a gesture to cut off the transmission.

"Are we really going to destroy them all?" Sandgren asked. Her voice sounded a bit strangled. "They can't hurt us."

"They could hurt the civilians," Derek said. "They could take hostages on the other ships, and we'd have to risk innocent lives stopping them. They've put armed fighters aboard *Hunter* who are wounding and killing our crewmates right now.

"There's a time and place for mercy. This isn't it."

"We have an incoming transmission from the pirate ship behind the freighter. We have it tagged as *Guppy*."

"Put them on the main screen," Derek said. "Retransmit their signal and our reply to everyone on the general channel. Be ready to engage. If I give the order, just do it. If they fire on any civilian ships, don't wait on me. You'll be weapons-free at that point."

The primary display changed to a visual of a freighter's bridge. The man sitting in the captain's chair had more beard than he had face, but his eyes shone out cold blue. His expression was one of snarling fury.

"You'll damned well stand down, boy, unless you'd like to see a lot of ships shot to pieces. Don't think we won't. Do yourself and your friends a favor and give up now."

Derek leaned forward, focusing on the man's eyes. "The Navy does not run, and it does not cower from scum like you. You've made a tactical error, in addition to the strategic one of attacking us in the first place. Would you like to know what it is, pirate?"

The man didn't say anything, so Derek pressed on. "*Delta Orionis* is more than a kilometer long. Geometry might not have been your strongest class in school, so let me spell it out for you. The laser clusters at the front and back of my ship can shoot you to pieces even though you think you're hiding behind that other ship.

"I've already proven I'm more than willing to burn pirates just like you down, so don't test me. Strike your weapons and surrender, or I'll do it again. You have five seconds."

The silence hung heavy in the air as the man hesitated. Then the man snarled at one of his subordinates. "Shoot the freighter."

The tactical officer instantly pressed the button, and dozens of laser clusters at *Hunter*'s prow and stern opened fire. Designed to kill armored Locust drones and motherships, the pirate vessel came apart, never having a chance to follow its commander's order. The view of the enemy bridge was wiped away in flames as the transmission ended.

"What's the status of the other pirates?" Derek demanded, feeling a little empty inside.

"Two of them have struck their weapons and are signaling surrender. Make that three, no four. All remaining pirate ships have killed their weapons and are signaling surrender."

Derek felt an immediate sense of relief. He wasn't going to have to kill anyone else today. At least he hoped not.

"Order all civilian ships to get clear of those pirates. I want unrestricted lines of sight on them and our weapons ready to fire if they look like they're reconsidering.

"Make that clear to them, Comm. Make sure they know that if they twitch, we're going to blow them out of space without any further discussion."

Almost as soon as the communications officer had made those transmissions, and Derek could see the rest of the civilian ships putting as much distance between themselves and the pirates as they could, there was a tremendous explosion outside the main hatch. It didn't open, but it looked like it might've buckled a bit.

"Looks like we've got a little bit of company outside," Derek said. "Let's see if we can get them to lay down their arms."

He activated the all-hands channel from the command seat. "Attention all pirates aboard *Delta Orionis*. Your ships have either surrendered or been destroyed. Lay down your weapons, or our Marines will hunt you down. Anyone with a weapon in their hand will be shot. Surrender, and at least you'll still be alive."

He had no way of knowing whether they'd follow his orders,

but he'd done what he could. Now other people would handle the fighting. All he had to do was make sure the space around them stayed clear of traitorous enemies.

A second explosion went off in the corridor, and the hatch did buckle this time. It looked like the pirates weren't going to give up so easily.

He drew his pistol, crouched in front of the command chair, and leveled it at the hatch. One more explosion would probably bring the hatch down, and then they'd be fighting for their lives.

"Does anybody have the code to open the arms locker?" he asked.

The answer was, of course, no.

"One of you Marines, blow that arms locker open so that we can defend ourselves. Move it! Everyone else take cover. You don't want to be hit by a stray bullet."

The Marine opened fire on the locking mechanism. It held up longer than Derek would have credited, but it did give out. There were some ricochets, but it seemed as if everyone had been behind their consoles, and no one was injured.

The Marine quickly returned to his position, watching the hatch as the bridge crew swarmed the arms locker and grabbed pistols and magazines. They then returned to their consoles and got behind them, covering the damaged hatch with their weapons.

The third explosion did indeed cause the hatch to fall inward with a tremendous clang. It was too heavy to be moved very far, but the way into the ruined corridor was now open. Screaming pirates charged through the smoke, firing in an almost random manner.

Derek's vision narrowed to almost a tunnel. Thankfully, he was able to see everything he needed to. He shot the first person he saw, shifting his aim to the next when that one fell. Then everyone else in the bridge opened fire, and a fusillade of shots went back and forth.

The Marines had automatic weapons, and so did the pirates. That meant the bridge crew was under intense fire, but the pirates had to expose themselves to fire. They'd pay in blood for every single centimeter they took.

Someone behind Derek screamed. They'd obviously been hit. His friends were bleeding and likely dying, but all he could do was keep firing at the pirates as they presented themselves. It was like a first-person shooter, and it felt unreal.

A pirate emptied her magazine directly into the command chair, and Derek was pleased to discover its back was armored. That allowed him to put two bullets into her face, killing her before he ejected his empty magazine, pulled another from his belt, and fumbled it into the pistol.

It took him a second to find the slide release and put a bullet into the chamber, and the pirates seemed to surge forward in just that short time. He resumed fire at anyone he could see charging them.

Derek didn't think they were going to hold out. There had to be more pirates out there than defenders. This was a last stand.

Then a grenade went off in the corridor, throwing body parts and blood onto the bridge. More screaming and the firing of additional weapons announced the arrival of the cavalry. Or, in this case, the Marines.

It took a minute for the fighting in the corridor to die down and the shooting to stop. Weirdly, now that the fighting seemed to have ended, he could smell the burnt gunpowder and the iron scent of spilled blood and hear the moans of the wounded. Those had to have been there the entire time, but he hadn't noticed them.

"Ahoy on the bridge! This is Captain India MacKinnon. I'm coming out with empty hands, and I ask most sincerely that you don't shoot me."

"Step forward and be recognized, Captain," Derek called out, astonished that his voice was cold and even. "Everyone, hold fire."

Derek recognized MacKinnon—in an old-style uniform—as she came out with her hands in the air. That still didn't mean she was doing this of her own volition, though.

"What was the last thing you saw me with, Captain?" he asked. "I need to make sure you're not being pressured by pirates."

She smiled a little. "A cat."

"Weapons down, everyone."

He rose from where he crouched in front of the command chair as she strode onto the bridge, and he saw Marines behind her. They were safe, at least for the moment.

"What's our status?" she asked as she took the command seat.

He ignored her question for just a moment as he ordered the

other ensigns to see to the wounded. Then he turned toward her. It was time to face the music.

"I ordered the pirates to surrender, and one of them made a break toward the rear of our ship. I ordered it destroyed. Another one tried to threaten a freighter, and I gave them the opportunity to change their minds. They didn't, so I killed them too.

"The other four pirates have struck their weapons and are signaling surrender. I had the rest of the civilians get as far away from them as possible. That's the situation, Captain. If it was the wrong call, that's on me."

She shook her head. "You did what was necessary to protect this ship and the lives of civilians under our care, Ensign. There will be an after-action review to go over everything once we've regained control of the ship, but I'd have given the exact same orders without a single second's hesitation.

"I wouldn't have given them the chance to surrender if they'd had their weapons armed when I started shooting. That might have gone badly, but you did the best you could, and I'm not going to second guess you. Well done."

He nodded, his throat tight enough that he had no idea if he could manage to speak.

"I have the conn," MacKinnon said. "See to your fellow officers. I'm not sure if we have a clear path to the medical center, but I'll request assistance for those that need it. We've got enough Marines in the corridor to hold the bridge if more of them are on their way.

"Your warning about the impending attack and Lieutenant Dubsky's preparations turned the trick. I think we're going to win this fight. Now, let's get the bridge back into order and see if any of the consoles are nonfunctional."

Derek nodded once and made the rounds to see how everyone was. The news was better than he'd expected and worse than he'd hoped. Two of his friends were dead, and four others were wounded, two of them seriously.

Once he had people caring for the wounded, he got everyone else back to their consoles or to other consoles if theirs were no longer working. Even with all of the chaos, blood, and death, he had to make sure the ship could fight.

To his shock, the tactical officer had never left his post. He'd kept his eyes on the pirates in space even as the ones behind him were shooting up the bridge. It was the bravest—and possibly the stupidest—thing he'd ever seen.

He reported back to MacKinnon. "We're able to operate, Captain. The pirate ships have maintained their position, and their weapons are powered down. What about the commodore? Is he okay?"

She grimaced. "I haven't heard anything, so we're just going to have to hope so until we hear differently. Take over one of the consoles and keep a general watch on the situation. If anything changes around us, I want you to tell me about it immediately."

He nodded. "Yes, Captain."

"And Derek? I wasn't kidding. You did one hell of a job, and I'm proud of you. I'm proud of all of you, and you can bet your last dollar that the commodore is going to feel exactly the same way."

Derek nodded, taking a seat at one of the abandoned

consoles. A check showed it was functional, but getting it in order took twice as long as it should have because his hands were shaking.

The fear and terror had ended, and now his body was coming down from an adrenaline high, unlike anything he'd ever experienced before in his life.

He hoped he never had to do anything like this ever again, but this war was only getting started. He forced himself to breathe and did the job. His reaction to the violence would just have to wait until he had time to deal with it.

19

Jack ducked back out of sight and ran. He didn't have the kind of firepower he'd need to fight that many people, so his only option was to be somewhere else.

He half expected them to give chase, but they obviously had a goal in mind and didn't recognize the significance of his rank tabs. They thought he was just another Navy guy and took potshots at him while continuing on to their target.

And that was fine with him.

Since he couldn't make it to the bridge, Jack headed for operations. Among other things, it contained auxiliary control, and he'd be able to influence events from there. Of course, if the bridge and engineering were targets, so was the operations center.

Dubsky would have a contingency plan to protect all of those locations, but there was no telling if she'd gotten it fully implemented yet. He wasn't sure whether he'd find the area under the control of pirates or Marines.

The operations center was buried in the ship's depths—like the bridge—only toward the ship's bow. It took up significantly more space than the bridge itself, but its stated purpose was to provide additional insight to the officers serving on the bridge.

Under ideal circumstances, they'd have teams of specialists to interpret data and give the bridge officers exactly what they needed to perform their duties. Auxiliary control would've been manned with a backup team to replace the bridge if called on. Unlike operations, it was currently staffed.

He didn't make it there before he ran into pirates. Thankfully, they didn't see him before he dodged into a side corridor. They hadn't been able to get into auxiliary control because someone was ordering up a breaching charge. The crew must've sealed the hatch.

The area was a warren of small compartments, and Jack was able to slide into one of those. Some of the consoles had been used for flight control when they'd first brought the battleship online, but those personnel had moved, and the space was now empty.

Or it should've been.

To his surprise, he found a dozen Marines in unpowered combat armor there. The Marines slowly lowered their weapons and allowed him to advance. Obviously, his face was recognizable enough that they knew who he was. Thank goodness for small favors.

When he reached the noncommissioned officer in charge of

the group, the man gestured for Jack to put his ear next to his mouth and spoke softly. "You about got yourself shot there, sir. Why don't you stay behind us for now? We're waiting for reinforcements, and then we'll attack the pirates outside auxiliary control."

Jack nodded. When he spoke, he made sure to pitch his voice just as low as the man had. He didn't want to attract the pirates' attention.

"Where is Dubsky?"

"She's nearby, sir. When this kicks off, she'll be in the thick of it."

The Marine tilted his head and nodded to himself. "She just gave the call to move into attack positions, so it's game on. You stay here, sir, and we'll take care of the pirates for you."

It had been a long time since Jack had been in a fight like this. Back when he was a lieutenant, he'd led a fireteam of Marines to secure a freighter. It turned out the situation was significantly more complex than he'd expected, and the Marines had needed to go into combat against pirates.

Pirates seemed to be a recurring theme with him.

He'd had a weapon then, too, but he hadn't had to use it. He probably should have. If he had, the smugglers that had been playing them might not have gotten away.

Or, he could've been shot. At this late date, there was no telling.

There was a loud explosion down the corridor, and he wondered if they'd breached auxiliary control. The lack of gunfire likely indicated they hadn't, but one never knew.

The Marine NCO gestured for his people to precede him out. It looked like the counter-attack was underway. Jack fell in at the back of the group and drew his pistol. Whatever happened next, he'd be there.

The Marines moved down the corridor to the major junction, and Jack could see another team of Marines on the other side of the large corridor, also waiting to move into position. At some unheard signal, both groups poured out into the main corridor and opened fire as they advanced.

Jack stayed to the rear because getting into the firefight was stupid. That didn't mean he wasn't in danger because he could hear bullets flying down the corridor from where the pirates were firing at them. Some Marines cried out and fell while their compatriots advanced and continued shooting.

In one of those odd moments that happen in combat, a gap opened in front of him, and he saw the pirates. He only had a few seconds, but he emptied his pistol at them. He wasn't sure if he hit anyone, but he'd done his part.

The gap had closed just after he'd finished emptying his pistol, so he pocketed the empty magazine, grabbed one of the replacements off his belt, fed it into his pistol, and released the slide to chamber a fresh round.

Resistance had faded away to nothing as the Marines exterminated the pirates. That was a pity. He'd have liked to have had some prisoners to question.

Once he was sure the shooting was over, he holstered his pistol. The hatch to auxiliary control hadn't been damaged by the explosion, though the corridor around it had.

Sadly, the Marines were definitely more damaged than their surroundings. He could see some Marines sprawled on the deck unmoving, likely dead. Others writhed in pain as their compatriots worked on them and called for medics.

The smell of gunpowder and blood turned his stomach, but he put it aside. He had things to do.

He advanced on the hatch but was intercepted by that same Marine NCO. "Dammit, sir, you should've stayed back."

"There's a lot of things I should've done over my life, Sergeant. You'll just have to accept this is what I did this time. Where's Dubsky?"

The man grimaced and gestured back to the other side of the fight. "I'm sorry, sir. She took a round while charging the pirates. She's gone, sir."

That was a blow he hadn't seen coming. He'd known that in combat, chance always played a role, and even the most skilled and careful person could still be taken out by a random bullet. Now his senior Marine officer was dead.

"I'm damned sorry to hear that," he said.

He'd only known Dubsky for about a month, but in that time, she'd been nothing but loyal and efficient. He was going to miss her calm and steady presence, and the vacuum created by her loss would be substantial.

Yet that was something he'd have to focus on when he had time. He had more pressing matters to deal with right now.

Surprisingly, the communication system built into the auxiliary control hatch still worked. He pressed the button to open a channel.

"This is Commodore Romanoff. The situation in the corridor has been resolved. You can let us in."

There was a pause of several seconds, and then a young woman with a familiar voice responded. "Forgive me for being skeptical, but can you prove that?"

More than a bit nonplussed, Jack could see her point of view. If they'd lost video into the corridor, this could all be a trick. Hell, in the pirates' shoes, he might have tried something similar.

"Is that you Ensign Harris? If so, would the pirates know your first name is Amanda? I'm sure I could dredge up some other memory about the first time we met on the bridge, but it might be a little tough to get much more than that. From what I'm told, you're an outstanding gunnery officer. Would a pirate know that?"

The only answer was the hatch unlocking and sliding to the side. He saw the auxiliary control crew and the Marines that had been guarding them had breached the arms locker, and everyone was armed. Good for them.

He should've made arrangements for whoever was in charge of the watch to have the codes to the arms locker. He hadn't trusted anyone because they'd been so young and inexperienced. That was an oversight he'd make certain didn't happen again.

Jack strode into auxiliary control and nodded at the young ensign. "We've got enough Marines outside to maintain security, but I need to know what's happening on the bridge. Did they manage to keep the pirates out?"

She gestured toward the command seat. "The bridge was breached, but the Marines arrived in time to keep it from falling.

I understand there have been some casualties. Captain MacKinnon is there now."

Jack settled in the command seat. "What about the rest of the ship? Is engineering still secure?"

"Yes, sir. The pirates tried to pin the Marine forces down in their barracks as well, but they'd already begun dispersing. The Marines would have a better idea what their current status is."

"Do me a favor and connect me with the bridge. I need to get this sorted out."

Harris reached over and pressed a button on the arm of his chair. He would have to learn what all of those buttons did very soon.

"Bridge, MacKinnon here."

"Auxiliary control, Romanoff here. We're secure. What's your status?"

"The pirates breached the hatch, but they didn't take the bridge. We have two dead and four injured, two critically. We have a medical team preparing them for transport to the medical center.

"Two pirate ships have been destroyed, and four have surrendered. We have them under our guns, and if they try to move or power weapons, we'll blow them out of space. The civilian ships have relocated to *Hunter*'s other side and should be safe. Honestly, Jack, it was a bit hairy, but I think we've got our boot on the problem."

"Stand by." Jack turned toward the Marine noncommissioned officer who'd followed him in. "What's your name?"

"Sergeant Robert Nagle, sir."

"I don't know what the existing command structure is like on the Marine side right now, so I'm going to rely on you to relay my instructions to your people. I want Marines on all surviving pirate ships as soon as possible. We don't know how many pirates are still aboard those ships, and they need to be neutralized as quickly as possible."

"I'll take care of it, sir."

The Marine turned and jogged out of the compartment.

"Great job," Jack told India.

"Wasn't me," his friend said. "Calvo handled this all on his own. I'm sure everything was recorded, so you'll have a chance to review it, but I fully endorse every action he took. Like I told him, I wouldn't have hesitated one second before giving the exact same orders.

"And based on conditions when we finally overran the pirates, he was hip deep in a gunfight for control of the bridge. The young man has spine, Jack. It might not be my place to suggest this, but if you're looking for a protégé, you don't have to look far."

Jack had already known Derek had hidden depths, but reacting so well under pressure was definitely a good sign. When he had time, he'd take Calvo under his wing and speed up his education. They needed steady officers.

"I've ordered the Marines to secure the pirate ships," he said. "I'm not sure exactly how and when they're going to make that happen, but if they don't coordinate with you, just be advised that they're moving.

"Lieutenant Dubsky didn't make it through the attack on

auxiliary control. I'm not even sure what officers we have on the Marine side. I know a lot of the people from the Marine Academy were NCOs. Mac Turner is going to have to take a hand. He's the most experienced Marine officer we have left, retired or not."

He rubbed his face and stared at the tactical display. "Do we have any word on what's going on with the research ship and Tina Chen?"

"Not yet."

Well, if the pirates aboard that ship didn't already know things were going badly, it wouldn't be long now. He hoped Tina and the force recon Marines supporting her could handle the situation when the pirates lashed out.

"I'll stay down here until the situation aboard *Hunter* is fully under control," Jack said. "I'll focus on the interior fight. You take care of the exterior. Between the two of us, we'll get this settled."

"You've got it, Jack. Bridge out."

With that done, Jack turned his attention to getting the auxiliary control crew focused on their new tasks. They needed statuses from various parts of the ship and had to interface with whatever command infrastructure was still in place on the Marine side. This fight wasn't over yet.

20

To be honest, Tina wasn't sure exactly how Turner and his people would intervene. The guards sitting next to her didn't seem the least bit perturbed, even though she knew they were aware she'd used the trigger word.

Whatever was about to happen, she had to assume they were in on the plan and would let her know what she needed to do when the time was right.

Turner was listening in, so he knew she wasn't in immediate danger, only that she'd decided the situation couldn't be allowed to proceed. He wasn't going to come busting in without at least attempting to extract her, she suspected.

The woman that had been preparing the food stepped to the hatch with a bottle of what looked like wine in her hand. "Excuse me, ma'am. I'm not sure if this is the brandy you wanted. Could you confirm it for me so I can get the other bottles?"

"Of course," Tina said as she stood without rushing and smoothed her clothes where she'd been reaching for her concealed pistols. She sauntered over to the door so casually that no one seemed the least bit perturbed by what she was doing. That was good for her, though she noted her guards hadn't moved, which worried her.

When she arrived at the hatch, she started to look at the bottle, but rough hands yanked her out of the hatchway right before a line of Marine force recon personnel that had been stacked up just outside the hatch, their weapons up and ready, poured into the dining room, shouting for everyone to put their hands where they could see them.

It was far too sudden a surprise for the pirates to overcome, but that didn't stop them from trying. There were shouts and then several bursts of automatic weapon fire. Then a couple of pistol shots, and then the Marines opened up. Within ten seconds, the fight was over.

The man who'd grabbed her ended up being Mac Turner. He was listening closely to his headset and nodded. "The situation is under control, but we need to make certain everybody's accounted for. Stay with me while they sort it out. There's no need for you to see that kind of thing."

She felt the corner of her mouth quirking upward. "Do you remember when we met? I'd just carted Commodore Nastasi into my cutter after Selter tried to murder her and was covered in her blood. No offense, Major, but I've seen my fair share of death and injury."

"Be that as it may, it's my judgment that you don't need to

see this particular brand of death. It's hard enough for the people that have to deal with it. Perhaps it's just an instance of me being a bit more protective than I needed to be, yet here we are."

She supposed he wasn't wrong. People had just been shot to death, and she already had enough nightmares to deal with. Perhaps she should leave this one for them, even though she'd given the order.

"We've got to get word to *Hunter* immediately," she said. "If the pirates are ready to strike, they've got to prepare."

"Already done. My other team is breaching the pirate shuttle right now. What happens aboard *Hunter* is out of our hands, so we need to focus on our tasks here."

"Were any of your people hurt?"

He shook his head. "Surprise was total. I guess you were right in assuming the word artichoke wouldn't trigger any kind of response. Score one for the Intel weenies."

There were several long bursts of gunfire from the other side of the ship, and Turner listened to his headset. "The shuttle is secure. Also, *Hunter* has indicated they're aware of the incursion and are moving to counter it.

"I'm not sure how many pirates they're dealing with over there, but I need to head back right now. My people and I can make a real difference there."

"Leave a handful with me to deal with any survivors, and go take care of business."

The Marine force recon major nodded, said something into his headset, and jogged off as his people started pouring out of the dining room. The woman who'd been holding the wine stopped beside her. She still didn't know her name.

"Who are you?" Tina asked.

"Beth Cassidy, retired Marine force recon master sergeant. I've got to say, you were as cool as a cucumber in there. They didn't suspect a thing."

"It's the training. When they make you a spy, you have to stay cool no matter what happens. Did we get our main targets alive?"

"Depends on who you count our main targets as," the woman said with a shrug. "The ones that went for weapons got shot. That was most of the pirates because they're the kind of people that won't go down without a fight.

"If you mean our Navy weasel, he's down on the ground with zip ties around his wrists right now. The only reason he isn't shouting his fool head off is that somebody has a pistol screwed into the back of his head to make sure he keeps quiet."

"I'm going to my office—or rather, to Doctor Wilson's office —and I'd like you to bring Magri to me. If any of the pirate captains survived this, I need to know about it."

"The one that called himself Dugan is still alive, but he got shot up pretty good. He might make it, but I wouldn't hold my breath if I were you. The rest are dead."

Tina wasn't going to lose any sleep over people like that. They'd more than earned the worst life could deal them.

Once she'd arrived at the office, she sat with one of her pistols on the desk. Two brawny men that looked more piratical than the actual pirates dragged the disgraced Navy captain in and stuffed him into the seat in front of the desk. They then stood on either side of the man with hands on his shoulders to make sure he didn't move.

His hands were still secured behind his back, so that couldn't have been very comfortable, yet he was so terrified that he didn't say a word. It was kind of refreshing.

She leaned forward and smiled without any humor. "I'm afraid we're going to have to put the after-dinner drinks on hold, Captain Magri. You see, I've got a real problem with you attacking the only functioning warship we have in the cluster.

"Oh, I suppose I should introduce myself. My name is Tina Chen, and I'm a former operative with Confederation Intelligence. You've met my husband, David. He's Commodore Romanoff's chief of staff."

"There's been a terrible misunderstanding," he said, stuttering with terror. "I was getting the pirates to confess to what they were doing. I'm innocent!"

"Hardly. Everything was recorded, so there's no doubt exactly what you intended. The attack on *Hunter* has already begun, but we were able to warn them in time."

She put her hand on her pistol. "Not that that will save you in the end. You're a traitor, and I certainly hope the penalty for that during a time of war is death because I'll cheerfully put a bullet in your brain myself if they ask me to."

The man didn't say anything.

"Find someplace to lock him up," she ordered. "Make sure he doesn't have anything stashed on him he could harm himself with. You can leave him his underwear, but nothing more. It's undignified, but he doesn't deserve any dignity."

Once the men had hustled Magri out, Cassidy walked in and leaned against the bulkhead. "Do you really think he'll get put to death? His kind always seems to get off lightly. Even if he does, you won't have to do it yourself, you know. We can start a lottery, and there'll be plenty of Marines happy to put a bullet right between his eyes."

"If called upon, I shall serve," Tina said, hoping her help wasn't needed. "The Navy takes a very dim view of mutiny under the best of circumstances, I'd wager. During wartime? I suspect Jack has carte blanche. The surviving pirates and Magri could probably be tried on the spot and spaced."

The woman nodded. "You're not going to have to worry about Dugan. He didn't make it. That's a clean sweep of pirates aboard this ship. We've decapitated their leadership, and I've been listening to some of the comm traffic in space. It sounds like two of the pirate ships decided to make nuisances of themselves, and *Hunter* vaporized them.

"The other four are waiting for Marines to board them. At this point, it's not like they have a choice. If they try to bring their weapons online, they'll be blown to little bitty pieces. The only part of the fight still undecided is aboard *Hunter*, and with the loss of surprise, that's not going to go their way either."

"This entire situation was so stupid," Tina said in an irritated tone as she stood and holstered her pistol. "Did they think they could set up a pocket empire and the Locusts would just leave them alone? Surely not even the pirates bought into that fairytale."

The retired Marine force recon NCO shrugged. "Who

knows? What I find laughable is the idea that Magri thought they'd leave him alive and in charge when this was all over. As soon as they'd secured control of *Hunter*, they'd have spaced him for sure. People like that have no honor.

"What do we do now?"

"Even though we're not taking the ship with us, we can't just leave the pirate bodies here to rot. We need to load them aboard their shuttle and clean up the dining room."

Cassidy shuddered. "Are you sure we can't just close it off and pretend nothing happened? Or maybe set fire to it?"

"I'd settle for hosing it down," Tina agreed. "Still, we don't want to leave an ugly surprise for Wilson if she ever gets the ship back. I'll get her office back into shape while you start moving the bodies. Then I need to clean the kitchen while you have the unenviable task of mopping up the blood."

She stopped and put a hand on the woman's arm. "Thanks for having my back."

"It's our pleasure. You can thank us with a real dinner sometime. Just no artichoke brandy."

The two of them laughed as they headed out to start their respective tasks. Tina prayed things worked out on the battleship. Her husband was first in her thoughts, but she was making a lot of new friends, and she was worried about them all.

21

THE FIGHTING aboard *Hunter* wrapped up in less than an hour. Jack spent the entire time monitoring the situation and ordering forces from one location to another to reinforce weak spots.

When the last major group of pirates was overwhelmed, the Marines began going through the ship compartment by compartment. They made their way from the furthest aft all the way to the tip of the bow.

No place was left unexamined, which turned out to be a good thing because they found some pirates scattered throughout the ship. Each of them was hidden away and ready to pretend they were nothing but cowering civilians.

Unfortunately for them, his people had video of every person coming off the pirate cutters and shuttles. Faces were easily compared, and when one of the supposed civilians was discovered to be a pirate, they were taken into custody and put with the rest.

Not that there were very many of those. The pirates had known the consequences of their actions, so they'd mostly chosen to fight to the death.

It was stupid. If they hadn't tried to take over the ship, they could've pretended to be civilians and no one would've known any better with an invasion going on. It hadn't been like anyone was checking to see if any of the refugees had criminal records.

Word from the research ship indicated the pirate leadership had all been killed. The Marines' final tally of captured pirates was fifty-seven, mainly from the surviving ships.

Then there was Magri. Tina had captured him alive, and she'd even recorded him bragging he was in full collaboration with the pirates to seize control of *Hunter* and found his own empire. It was damning evidence.

As much as Jack wanted to focus on the specifics of what was happening aboard *Hunter*, he had to deal with the biggest crisis first. He made his way back to his office, surrounded by a fireteam of Marines in combat armor. It seemed they weren't willing to count on the ship being completely secured just yet, and he approved of their paranoia.

A few moments after he arrived, Sara showed up with an escort of her own. When the two went into his office, some of the Marines made to follow, but Jack shook his head.

"You can search the compartment, but I need to speak with Commodore Nastasi privately. You'll have to stay out in the corridor. Sorry."

He didn't need to apologize for keeping the Marines out of his office, but it felt like the right thing to do. They'd given so much for him and his ship. He didn't have a full count of the dead and wounded yet, but he was certain they'd paid dearly.

The Marines moved through the compartment and searched the adjoining head. Once they'd verified no one was hiding there, they withdrew to the corridor and sealed the hatch behind them.

Sara settled into the chair she'd been in earlier and shook her head. "I don't think I've ever seen anything so terrible my entire life. The medical center was well protected, but they brought in so many badly wounded young people. Not all of them made it, and I'm not sure I'll ever get the images out of my mind."

"I'm not sure we should," he admitted. "They sacrificed everything for the Confederation and for us. Now it's up to us to pick up the pieces, and that starts with Magri.

"I don't know if you've had a chance to review the video of him bragging to Tina, but there's no doubt he was involved in planning this attack and seeing it executed to seize control of *Delta Orionis*. This was a mutiny on his part."

"In a time of war," she added. "I've checked the regulations, and that puts the ultimate penalty on the table. The pirates that survived are also subject to summary trial and execution should you find them guilty.

"You don't need a tribunal for them, by the way. As the ship's commanding officer, you can sit in judgment over them yourself. A warship commander in a time of war has wide discretion and authority. Almost frighteningly so. I'm glad it's you instead of Magri."

Jack wasn't sure he appreciated the responsibility, but he was grateful it gave him options. He wanted to close this sorry chapter as soon as possible.

"What's next if we want to proceed with a tribunal for Magri?" he asked.

"My officer with a flair for defense is speaking with him now, but his skill isn't going to be enough. The evidence is too damning. He'll try, but he has to know his client is doomed."

Jack walked over to the sideboard that David Chen had set up and poured them both a little whiskey. Once he'd handed her a glass, he sat down and sipped at his own.

"When does it happen?"

"We can do it at any time," she said, tossing hers back all in one gulp, a gross injustice to the quality of the whisky. "It's like I said before, this will be an expedited affair with the evidence being so overwhelmingly stacked against him. We need to decide ahead of time just how far we're willing to go with our ruling during the punishment phase.

"According to regulations, the penalty for mutiny during a time of war is death. If we choose to commit to that, we need to make that decision ahead of time. Then we need to carry out the sentence expeditiously."

He waved his glass around a bit. "Isn't deciding his fate before we decide his guilt a bit hinky? I've always thought justice was a little more blind."

"Have you seen the recording?" she demanded. "Do you doubt for one second he did exactly what he said? The pirates were all sitting there, and no one said one word against him.

"There are plenty of things in life to feel guilty about, Jack. Finding Magri guilty shouldn't be one of them. If you don't think he deserves death for what he's done, I'm not going to tell you how to vote. Personally, I hold him responsible for every death and injury those people caused. He's more than earned the ultimate punishment."

Jack sat back and sipped his whiskey, thinking about the fighting outside auxiliary control. Thinking about the dead and gravely wounded he'd seen there. Thinking about Dubsky. He hadn't seen her corpse, but she was gone, too.

"I agree," he said. "We should speak with India and see what she's got to say.

"I told her where we'd be, and she should be along shortly," Sara said as she set her glass down on the small table next to her. "You can't let this get to you, Jack. We've got more than enough things to worry about, and you don't need to lose sleep over Magri. He brought this down on himself."

The chime at the hatch signaled, and since Jack knew the Marines wouldn't let just anyone in, he called out for India to enter. Once it slid aside, she stepped inside and closed it behind her.

"Is that whiskey?" she asked. "If so, I could use a double."

He gestured toward the sideboard, and she quickly poured herself a drink smaller than the threatened double.

"Is everything settled?" he asked as she sat.

"The fighting is done, and it's time to sort out the pieces. What do we do about Magri? It seems like he's the only surviving leader out of the group."

"We were just discussing the matter," Sara said. "With the evidence against him, the defense isn't going to save him. Jack and I agree that the ultimate penalty should be in play, but if you disagree, I'm willing to hear you out."

India snorted. "Oh, don't worry about moderating your response for me. I saw the death and destruction he was responsible for, and I've seen the video. He's guilty as hell, and we need to settle him as quickly as we can. Where will we do this?"

"The chamber I used to talk to the captains," Jack said. "We could put a few seats in for observers, but I don't want to bog the proceedings down with too large an audience. The crew needs to see what's happening, but I don't want a packed room that might get violent."

"Then we should see about getting it set up," India said, tossing back the rest of her drink as she stood. "We can settle Magri first and then deal with the pirates."

She smiled sourly. "What was that old quote? 'You shall have a fair trial after which you shall be hanged by the neck until dead?' I always thought that sounded a little draconian, but now I get it. Sometimes, there's no doubt of the outcome."

The three of them put their glasses where David could wash them later and made their way to the makeshift courtroom.

It only took a few minutes to get a table and chairs on the platform. It was followed by two tables arrayed in front of the platform, one for the defense and the other for the prosecution. Toward the back of the compartment, they put in six rows of seats where observers could watch the proceedings.

Things were moving quickly, and Jack felt a little uneasy. Was this a kangaroo court or justice? It felt like he was rushing in to judge, even though he knew Magri was guilty as hell. Was he making a mistake?

"It looks like we're ready, so let's get the proceedings moving," Sara said, pulling out her comm and calling someone. "Court gavels into session in ten minutes. The guards know where you're going."

Once she'd made that call, she made another one with almost the same wording, minus the word guards. Jack supposed the first was to the defense, and the second was to the prosecution.

While that was taking place, he climbed onto the platform and took the far left-hand seat. India taking his cue, took the one to the far right. Sara put her comm away and sat in the center.

Someone must've notified the crew because the compartment's rear filled quickly. The sides of the room held Marines. Those young men and women still wore combat armor. Some of them still had blood on them.

No, Jack decided. He wasn't rushing things. Sometimes justice needed to happen swiftly. His crew deserved that.

A single officer wearing lieutenant commander's tabs arrived first. She walked to the left-hand table and set down several print-outs before approaching the platform.

Sara smiled. "Commodore Jack Romanoff, Captain India MacKinnon, this is Lieutenant Commander Katie Valovcin, my specialist in prosecution."

The dark-skinned woman bowed. "Commodore, Captain, I'm sorry to meet you under these circumstances. Commodore Nastasi, I've reviewed the relevant regulations and the evidence. I don't anticipate this being a long proceeding, but I'm curious how hard you want me to push during the punishment phase."

"You don't need to worry about making a recommendation, Katie. The tribunal will handle that."

The woman nodded and returned to sit at her table. Jack suspected the woman knew exactly what that pronouncement meant.

A few minutes later, a man wearing lieutenant commander's tabs stepped into the compartment. He walked straight to the platform and bowed before speaking.

"Commodore Nastasi, Commodore Romanoff, Captain MacKinnon."

"Everyone, this is Lieutenant Commander Kyle Valovcin, my defense specialist. He's Katie's twin brother.

"Don't let the fact that the two of them are related make you feel like they won't give everything they have to this proceeding. They're each quite good at what they do."

This was pretty unusual, and Jack couldn't wait to see how it played out.

The hatch slid open, and Magri came in. He was dressed in his modern Navy uniform, but his hands were bound in front of him. Mac Turner, dressed in an old-style Marine uniform, and an older woman in the same uniform manhandled the prisoner to the front of the compartment where they sat him hard in the seat next to the defense counsel.

"May it please the court," Kyle Valovcin said as he stood, "but I request that my client's restraints be removed."

Sara made a gesture, and Turner removed the restraints, though he and his companion didn't leave Magri's side.

"This proceeding will now come to order," Sara intoned. "All rise."

Jack found himself almost standing but stopped himself just in time. As he was sitting in judgment, he had to stay, well, seated.

Once everyone else was standing—including Magri, Jack noted—Sara continued. "Captain Ronnie Magri, you stand accused of mutiny. How do you plead?"

"My client—"

"The tribunal will hear the plea from the accused's own mouth," Sara interrupted. "This is a case with capital implications, and I want there to be no misunderstandings."

"This is outrageous!" Magri snarled. "I will not be party to this nonsense. I am a Navy officer!"

"And as such, you will be judged by your peers," Sara said. "Lacking a formal plea, the court will enter a plea of not guilty on behalf of the accused. Everyone may sit, and the prosecutor may proceed."

"I object!" Magri shouted as Turner forced him down into his seat.

"The defense will inform his client that he will not be allowed to disrupt these proceedings."

"My client objects to the presence of Commander MacKinnon. She is of insufficient rank to sit in judgment over him."

"Your objection is overruled. Under the general orders applicable during wartime, it is within Commodore Romanoff's authority to issue battlefield promotions and commissions. Does your client have any further objections as to the makeup of the tribunal?"

The commander cleared his throat. "My client further declares that Jack Romanoff is not a naval officer. He indicates his belief that the former captain was discharged from the service. As such, he's not entitled to a place on the tribunal, and it is thus improperly formed. That also means that he cannot promote Commander MacKinnon."

"That matter has been previously adjudicated," Sara said in a tone that brooked no disagreement. "Commodore Romanoff's orders to command this vessel and the battleship division are lawful, as is his promotion to commodore. Thus, it follows that he has the authority to promote Captain MacKinnon. Your objection is overruled.

"Does your client have any further objections about this tribunal?"

"Not at this time, Your Honor," the man said before returning to his seat.

"The prosecution may proceed."

The woman stood and smiled coldly at her brother and Magri. "At this time, I would like to introduce into evidence the video recording of the meeting where Captain Magri declared he was colluding with six pirate captains to execute a mutiny and seize control of *Delta Orionis* for himself."

"Objection," her brother said as he once again stood. "My client does not concede he was executing a mutiny. He contends the current command structure was illegitimate, and he was merely assuming command."

"By having pirates shoot naval personnel and civilians at random?" his sister asked. "Surely your client doesn't believe *that* was lawful."

"My client was unaware of the methods the others were using to secure control of this vessel," he fired back. "He was duped into believing they had nonviolent means to capture this ship. He is, of course, horrified and disgusted at what they chose to do on their own."

"This would be the very same meeting where your client indicated he knew one of the captains was a pirate and had previously worked with him?" the man's sister asked, her voice dripping with disdain. "I find it impossible to believe your client was so credulous."

"My client also objects to the introduction of this video because it was illegally obtained. This is clearly entrapment."

"Overruled on all counts," Sara intoned. "The evidence is hereby entered into the record. Does the defense agree that their client was shown the video in full and is aware of its contents? If not, we can play it again for everyone."

"That won't be necessary, Your Honor."

"Very well. With the introduction of that evidence, does the prosecution have anything further to present?"

"Yes, Your Honor. The shore patrol searched Captain Magri's quarters and found an encrypted data pad. The prosecution would like to thank the scientific visitors to this vessel for assisting in cracking said encryption in an *exceptionally* expeditious manner.

"It contained the locations and probable defenses of all critical areas of the ship and held detailed notes about the strategies needed to seize this vessel, including the fact that Captain Magri estimated there would probably be at least a fifteen percent loss of life. With five thousand crew aboard, that comes out to a total of seven hundred and fifty people."

She shot Magri a withering stare. "If we add in the civilian refugees, we're up to a thousand people. By his own hand, Captain Magri indicated he was willing to kill a thousand Navy personnel and civilians in the pursuit of this mutiny. The evidence is overwhelming."

"Objection," her brother declared as he rose, scowling at his sister. "None of these so-called notes were presented to my client or me before these proceedings. On that basis, I ask that they be thrown out."

"They were only made available to me just a few minutes before my arrival, Your Honor," the woman said. "I've brought printouts for the defense to review. It won't take more than five minutes. Should we take a recess?"

"For five minutes?" Sara asked. "I don't think that will be necessary. The defense may go over this with their client while we wait."

Katie Valovcin handed several printouts to her brother and the tribunal before resuming her seat.

Jack read over the notes, and they sickened him. The fact that Magri was so blasé about the fact he was going to kill so many people disgusted him. The man didn't just lack honor. He lacked any sense of morality at all. He was a monster, and the last of Jack's unease evaporated.

After reading the notes, Magri and his defense attorney

exchanged hurried whispers before Kyle Valovcin stood. "Again, my client objects to how these were obtained without a warrant."

"Because of exigent circumstances and the fact that your client was found in the presence of known pirates, his quarters were subject to search," Sara said. "In point of fact, the commanding officer of this vessel can order the search of any compartment for any reason during wartime, so there was no call for a warrant.

"The tribunal finds this new information quite troubling. Combined with what we already knew, it presents a bleak picture. Does the prosecutor have anything further to add?"

"No, Your Honor," she said. "The prosecution rests."

"Does the defense have any witnesses or evidence they would like to present?" Sara inquired.

"I'd like to present some of the pirate captains, but those maniacs already killed them all," Magri muttered loud enough for everyone to hear.

"I again remind the accused that his outbursts will not be tolerated," Sara said. "Does the defense have any witnesses to call or mitigating evidence to present?"

Kyle Valovcin grimaced. "No, Your Honor. The defense rests."

"The accused will stand." Sara looked to India as Turner and the other woman with him hauled Magri to his feet. "Do you have enough information to reach a verdict, Captain?"

"I find the defendant guilty of mutiny during a time of war," India said in a harsh tone.

Sara turned toward Jack. "Do you have enough information to reach a verdict, Commodore?"

"I also find the defendant guilty of mutiny during a time of war," Jack said, keeping his voice flat.

Sara looked down at Magri. "This tribunal is unanimous in finding the accused guilty of mutiny during a time of war. It is hereby ordered that he be stripped of all rank and insignia."

Turner and the unknown woman quickly tore the insignia and rank tabs off Magri's uniform. They had to rip the underlying fabric, but everything came off.

"Do you have a recommendation as to the punishment for mutiny, Captain MacKinnon?" Sara asked as she turned toward the other woman.

"Death," she answered.

"Do you have a recommendation as to the punishment for mutiny, Commodore Romanoff?" Sara asked, turning toward him.

"Death," he confirmed.

"Then under the applicable general orders, this tribunal sentences Ronnie Magri to death," she intoned. "May God have mercy on his soul."

"You can't do this!" Magri shouted, trying to lunge forward before being yanked up short by Turner and the woman with him. They jerked his arms behind him and secured them.

"I have rights," Magri raved. "This entire proceeding is illegal. I appeal!"

"During a time of war, your appeals are limited to your creator if you believe in one," Sara said. "You may discuss the situation with said creator at your leisure once the sentence has been carried out. You may select the option of death by firing squad or spacing. Which do you choose?"

"I choose neither! This is insane!"

"If you do not choose one or the other, this tribunal will choose for you. This is your final opportunity to have any say in how dignified your ending is."

All Magri did was struggle with the Marines, which did him no good whatsoever.

Jack cleared his throat. "If I may?"

Sara nodded. "Please proceed, Commodore Romanoff."

"Once the engineering staff has stripped *Hawkwing*'s wreck, we will detonate the scuttling charges. Rather than burden anyone with executing this man, he should be placed aboard, and the sentence can be carried out remotely. If we strip the ship of vacuum suits and computers, he will have no way to interfere, and the execution will be swift."

Sara considered his words and nodded. "I find your suggestion holds merit and order the prisoner to be held in isolation awaiting the execution of his sentence. These proceedings are concluded."

The force recon personnel manhandled a shouting Magri out of the compartment.

Jack had just ordered a man's death. No matter how much Magri had deserved it, this would weigh on him.

Sara turned to him. "I believe you have a judgment to render on the pirates. Since they aren't naval personnel, you can do that without us being present, but if you wish to have them brought in and render that judgment now, I'd be pleased to see the results with my own eyes."

Jack glanced at India and saw her nod.

"You can both stay," Jack said, sagging a little. "This won't take long."

He made a gesture toward one of the Marines standing near the hatch. "Have the pirates brought in to hear their judgment."

The young woman brought her comm to her mouth and spoke into it briefly. Less than sixty seconds later, the Marines began bringing the pirates in. Each of them was bound and all were chained together.

Not all of them were present. He knew a few were still in the medical center receiving treatment. That was all going to be rendered moot in very short order.

Once the pirates were lined up in front of the platform—some in bandages—he swept his gaze down the length of the line. Interestingly, he saw the young one from the cat's video. His arm was in a sling, but he was on his feet and terrified.

Good.

"You attacked this vessel," Jack said without emotion. "Under Confederation law and Navy regulations, I hereby find you guilty of piracy during a time of war.

"I'm not going to ask you if you have any defense because what you've done is indefensible. Instead, I condemn each of you to death aboard the wrecked Navy vessel *Hawkwing* when we set off her scuttling charges. May God have mercy on your souls."

There was even more pandemonium at that announcement than there had been from Magri. The Marines had the pirates well in hand, though, and they were all gone within minutes. The crew observing the proceedings trailed out after them, leaving him alone with Sara and India.

"Did we just do the right thing?" he asked. "Or did we slake our thirst for vengeance?"

"Sometimes, you can get both for the price of one," Sara said as she stood, sounding exhausted. "I'm not going to lose any sleep over these people, and you shouldn't either. These evil bastards deserve everything that's going to happen to them."

India stood and put a hand on Jack's shoulder. "They made the decisions that earned the punishment you handed out, Jack. I know I can't tell you not to let this eat at you, but you need to focus on the people that deserve your compassion."

He took a deep breath and nodded as he stood. "I suppose you're both right, but I'm still going to have nightmares. Let's get something to eat—even though the last thing I want to do is eat —before we try to figure out how badly they've hurt us."

22

DEREK WASN'T EVEN sure what time it was when he got off duty. It honestly felt as if he'd been sleepwalking his way through the day, checking things off and making sure that everything needed to secure the ship had been done.

The death toll had been ghastly. Barring any further deaths, they'd lost eighty-one Marines, including Lieutenant Dubsky. Deaths on the civilian side had been twenty-three. The Navy had lost thirty-nine personnel. That number might still rise because there were people that weren't out of the woods yet.

He supposed that was light considering the kind of attack they'd suffered. The pirates had gotten past their defenses, which had been his fault. Deep inside, he knew if he'd been faster to find the video in the cat's collar, all of this could've been avoided.

He'd had an opportunity to stop them, and he'd squandered

it. If he'd only gone to the medical center with the cat in the first place, he could have saved so many lives.

Intellectually, he knew he hadn't had a choice about accompanying MacKinnon to the bridge, but he couldn't turn off the part of his brain that just kept asking what if. What if he'd demurred and taken care of the task he'd already had in hand? Would that have changed anything?

He'd been going over things for half an hour, and he hadn't come to any conclusion. He doubted he ever would. The bottom line was that he'd had a chance to change the dynamics of this fight, and he hadn't been up to the task.

That was going to be hard to live with.

The chime at his hatch sounded. He frowned, unsure who could've been looking for him this late in the evening. His friends were just as exhausted as he was, so they'd have gone to bed as quickly as possible. Morning was going to come unforgivably early.

He stood, made his way over to the hatch, and triggered it to open. Standing in the corridor was Commodore Romanoff.

Oh, crap.

"I'm sorry for disturbing you so late, Derek, but our schedules have been so packed that I couldn't find time to see you any sooner. I apologize for disturbing your rest. May I come in?"

He gestured for the ship's commander to enter his compact set of quarters. Of course, on a ship as big as *Hunter*, even the lowest ranking officers had a room by themselves and enough space to make it feel like they were living in a small apartment.

"It's no disturbance, sir. I was still going over everything, and I wasn't resting."

The older man nodded and looked around the compartment with a smile. "I remember when I first became an ensign and was assigned my own quarters. I had to share them with another ensign, and it was roughly a quarter of this size. It still boggles my mind that we have so much space."

He gestured toward the worn furniture in what amounted to a miniature living room. "Do you mind if we sit? There are some important things we need to discuss, and there's no need to be uncomfortable while we do it."

"Of course, sir. Would you like something to drink? I have some water or could make coffee."

"I'll pass, but thank you. As soon as we're done talking, I'm going to find my bed. Coffee—as good as that sounds—would be a terrible idea. I promise that I won't take up much of your time. We need to go over what happened and what's going to happen next."

Derek felt his stomach do a slow roll as he took his seat. This was going to be bad.

The commodore considered him for a few moments. "If you're anything like me, you've been sitting here considering all the ways you've screwed up. If only I had done this thing, everything would be better. I failed my friends and my ship. Were those the kind of things you were thinking?"

He swallowed heavily and nodded. "All of those and more, sir."

"I figured. It's all bullshit."

Derek blinked. That wasn't the response he was expecting. "Sir?"

The commodore leaned forward, taking off his hat and setting it on the seat beside him. "Nothing you could've done would've changed the outcome in the slightest. Or if it did, it would've been by failing to discover the video at all and us being caught completely unawares. Sometimes you can do everything right and still come up short, particularly in your own self-estimation."

"That doesn't help the people who lost their lives today," Derek said quietly.

"No, it doesn't. When someone is taken from us, it's going to hurt, and there's nothing we can do about it except grieve. Your actions or inactions were not responsible for their deaths. The pirates were, and they will pay the ultimate price for what they've done.

"Some of the training we go through as officers—training you haven't had yet—teaches us that sometimes you lose no matter what you do. Learning how to handle that while maximizing the chances of people surviving is perhaps one of the hardest lessons an officer has to learn."

He started to say something, but the commodore held up a hand. "Let me run through what happened. You got a call to retrieve a stray cat from one of the small craft bays. You managed that in short order rather than ignoring the call. You made sure it was taken to the medical center to be checked. That's a plus in your column. That kind of consideration is to be commended.

"When MacKinnon asked you to take her to the bridge, you

had no reason to expect the cat was more than a stray animal. You're not psychic, Derek. You had no reason to suspect there were pirates already infiltrating the ship."

Jack grimaced. "That's a failure in my column. I was too trusting, and Magri and his associates played me. Hell, they played all of us. In the end, I suspect they wouldn't have been able to win this fight no matter how they went about it, but people sometimes do the craziest things simply because they're wired wrong in the head."

The man sighed. "In any case, as soon as you got back to the medical center, you found that video and called me immediately. Then, when I sent you to the bridge, you took command and secured it against the pirates before they arrived. You took action to arm the bridge crew, and when the pirates finally breached the hatch, you fought them off until the Marines relieved you.

"As someone that was just an officer candidate a few short weeks ago, I have to say that my expectations for you were fairly low. That's not meant to be an insult, just the fact that you didn't have the experience or training to know what to do."

He smiled. "Your actions fighting the pirates proved me well and thoroughly wrong. You know what Captain MacKinnon said about you? She said you had spine. For her, that's a high compliment.

"You made the hard calls, and you didn't flinch from the results of those decisions. That's the kind of behavior I'd expect from an officer with far more experience and training. In all, you've done exceptionally well."

"Then why don't I feel like I did the right things, sir? Why do I feel like I let everyone down?"

"Because you're a good person. When things settle down, you'll need to speak with one of the doctors to help sort this out. My mother's a good listener, by the way. She can give you sound advice and steer you in the right direction. Consider that an order.

"Let me say this as plainly as I can. You've far exceeded my expectations. Hell, everyone has. I'm so damned proud of all of you."

His smile turned into a tired grin. "And you know what they say the reward for doing a good job is, don't you? Another, a more difficult job."

He reached inside his greatcoat and pulled out something that he set on the small table between them. They were lieutenant's tabs.

Derek blinked, certain he was hallucinating. This was not the conversation he'd been expecting. He deserved to be raked over the coals and punished, not rewarded.

"Sir?" he said, having to clear his suddenly dry throat. "I'm not ready for that. A month ago, I was just an officer candidate. I don't have what it takes to wear those tabs. Hell, I don't think I have what it takes to be an ensign."

"The funny thing about competence is that people often have difficulty seeing it in themselves. That's one of the reasons the Navy has after-action reviews.

"Sometime over the next few days, we're going to have one that covers everything that took place, and you'll get to hear where things went right and where they went wrong. My judgment—and that of Captain MacKinnon—is that you did everything humanly possible."

He reached out, picked up the tabs, and held them out to Derek. "Everything you said about your lack of experience is true. Even so, you're the best we've got, and the Confederation is counting on us, so you're going to have to suck it up. Take the tabs, Lieutenant Calvo, and help us do the impossible."

Though he was certain his commanding officer was making a terrible mistake, Derek took the tabs.

Commodore Romanoff stood. "As a lieutenant, you'll find yourself stretched in ways you've never imagined. We're going to call on you to do things you think you can't manage, but I'm here to tell you that you can do what needs to be done.

"And in that theme, I've got your first job lined up. It's going to be a thankless task in many ways, but you're the one man I know will give it everything he has. Are you ready, Lieutenant?"

Derek nodded though he wasn't sure, and stood. "Yes, sir."

"Excellent," the commodore said as he walked over to the hatch and opened it. As soon as he did so, several ratings came in with containers and a box.

Derek frowned, unsure of what was happening until a third person came in holding the cat. Suddenly, he realized what this meant.

"It turns out that we've got a total of two dozen cats from the various ships we've rescued," Romanoff said with a grin. "Most of them already have human servants, but since the pirates aren't going to be taking care of this boy, I believe you're best suited to make sure he fits in here.

"All the other cats have names, and we're going to be learning who everybody is as things proceed, but this young man is nameless. Your first duty—along with taking care of him—is to make sure he gets an appropriate name. He started off life in a bad place, so it will be your job to welcome him on behalf of *Delta Orionis*. Good luck."

And with that, the commodore gestured for the ratings to leave and followed them out, closing the hatch behind him. Derek stood in the center of his small living room, dumbfounded as he held the cat.

Unsure of what to do, he set the cat on the small table, and it immediately began exploring the compartment. If the cat was frightened by his new circumstances, it didn't show.

Derek stared at the rank tabs in his hands. This wasn't a good idea, but the commodore was right. What choice did they have? This was a ship filled with inexperienced people, and *someone* had to do the job.

He wasn't sure how he'd ended up where he was, but he'd do the best he could.

The ratings had brought in containers of cat food in bags, cat litter, a cat bed, and a litter box. There were even some toys. It looked like he had everything he needed to take care of this cat, except for one thing.

His new friend needed a name.

While he was thinking about it, he tossed a cat toy out to see if it got the cat's interest. Oh, it certainly did. The orange boy crouched, wiggling his butt slightly, and then pounced. He proceeded to chew and kick the toy as if he didn't have a care in the world.

Derek knew cats on ships were there to hunt things like rats and mice that always seemed to somehow get aboard. Even *Hunter* had that problem. Since they hadn't had any cats aboard, it had occasionally become problematic. Now it was going to be their job to hunt down the vermin.

And that was what led Derek to the obvious name for his new cat.

He reached over and scratched the cat's head as it played with the toy, causing it to turn and nip at him just before rubbing his chin along Derek's hand and purring.

"You're going to be the lead hunter on this ship, boy, so it's only fitting that you be called Orion," he told the cat. "Welcome aboard, buddy. You keep playing with that, and I'll get you set up."

He'd never been responsible for an animal before, which was somewhat daunting. Still, compared to some of the things he'd already done, this was just making sure his new friend had everything he needed to have a happy and productive life.

And honestly, wasn't that his job as a lieutenant as well? An interesting insight and one that he'd have to ponder once he'd gotten some sleep. He was exhausted, and he knew the next day wouldn't be any easier. None of them would get much rest until *Hunter* was on the move again.

23

Jack expected to hold the memorial service the next day, but he got surprising pushback from David Chen and the newly promoted Lieutenant Commander Hutton. They insisted they needed more time to prepare, insisting the ceremony should take place three days after the attack.

Jack bowed to their request as this was the first time he'd ever dealt with anything like this. He wasn't sure what would take so long, but it had to be important. They wouldn't have been so insistent otherwise.

On the morning of the service, he spent a fair chunk of time in his office going over reports dealing with the aftermath of the battle and the incorporation of the new fusion plant into engineering. It wasn't completely installed, but they were now working on subsidiary systems. It was only a matter of hours until the work was complete, and it could be brought online for testing.

The transfer of all of the cargoes that seemed like they might be helpful had been completed. They had plenty of space to store everything, but Hutton's people would still be spending a lot of time organizing everything so they could access what they needed in a timely manner.

About an hour and a half before the memorial service was scheduled to begin, he'd managed to create a rough draft of what he was going to say in his head. It was different from what he'd heard at previous memorials, but his crew needed to hear something different.

Jack dreaded what was to come. This was his first time performing a memorial service, and instead of it being simply one person who'd died in the course of duty, they'd ended up losing almost a hundred and fifty people, including civilians.

He wasn't going to be able to spend time talking about specific people, so he'd focus on them as a whole. That was going to be challenging, and he would have to improvise.

The hatch to his office slid open while he was still considering how he would do that, and David Chen came in. Joby Hutton pushed a small trolley in with some boxes and a garment bag right behind him.

Jack frowned. "What's this?"

"It's your dress uniform," David said. "I've already made certain it's the correct size and has all the appropriate accouterments. All you have to do is get dressed."

Jack hadn't considered there would be a different uniform involved, though, on reflection, he knew that would've been the case in the regular Navy. The standard duty uniform was far fancier than even a traditional Navy dress uniform, so he'd thought it was good enough.

Apparently not.

He considered fighting this but decided it wasn't worth the trouble. Dress uniforms were something one wore when the utmost formality was required. This was one of those moments.

"How bad is it going to be?" he asked.

Chen smiled. "Far worse than you'd expect, I'm sure. I spoke with the professor to make certain we had the uniform prepared correctly, and he indicated, based on how much you detested the standard duty uniform, you'd absolutely loathe the dress uniform."

Perfect.

Jack sighed, hung his hat and greatcoat on the stand by the hatch, and gestured for them to proceed.

"Strip down to your underwear and put your regular duty uniform into one of the boxes," Chen said. "You can put it back on as soon as you're done. Don't worry, I'm a professional, and I've seen it all."

Jack chuckled and began stripping. He'd had reservations about doing so with the professor, but he just couldn't afford to spend the emotion to fight this time.

Hutton opened the garment bag and pulled out the jacket. It was black and had golden shoulder boards with a golden fringe. The right shoulder had braided golden cords that came down from underneath the shoulder board and went both in front of the uniform and underneath his arm to the back. He had no idea what purpose they served, if any.

Then his eyes went to the high-necked collar that looked dreadfully uncomfortable. Far more so than just wearing a tie. It was covered with gold embroidery that made it look fancy and even stiffer than it undoubtedly was.

The left side of the chest held ribbons with medals on them. He didn't recognize the large metallic starbursts in silver and gold that sat below the medals, though.

To top it off, there were wide gold rings around the ends of his sleeves denoting his rank. That was *very* old school. There were also the two rows of gold buttons that ran down the front of the jacket. They weren't decorations but the actual closures of the jacket.

"You've got to be kidding," Jack muttered "If I wear this, I'll look like a peacock."

"If it's any consolation, the enlisted uniform is almost identical, sir," Hutton said with a grin. "You're not going to look out of place."

"I am not reassured. I don't suppose there's time to just wave off this entire dress uniform thing and go with the standard duty uniform."

"Afraid not, sir. We spent the last few days making certain everybody had a dress uniform. By now, they're all dressed. We saved you for last, so you couldn't bolt."

"This sounds like a waste of time."

"That's where you'd be wrong," Chen said. "At times like these, formality shows everyone just how important what you're doing is. This uniform isn't for you, Jack. It's for your people."

As much as he wanted to argue, Jack knew the man was right. He'd just have to put up with this for the ceremony.

Once he had the dress shirt on, Chen held out the jacket, and Jack slid his arms into the sleeves. They quickly buttoned it tight, and he was relieved to find he could breathe and that the collar sat just a little bit away from his neck.

The next thing was a belt across the outside of the jacket. It was black leather with a golden band taking up most of its center. The circular buckle was smaller than the one on his regular duty uniform, but it also held the ship's emblem.

"What are these big, gaudy metal things?" he asked, gesturing toward the emblems below his medals.

"Those are awards won by this ship over the course of the first invasion," Chen said. "Everyone is going to have them."

Jack winced as Chen opened a box and pulled out an old-style naval hat that looked to be of an even older style than the one on the standard duty uniform. It had no brim, instead coming to a point far forward and behind his head. It rose to a high curved peak with a gold band along the top edge. The center of the sides held a fancy gold twist surrounded by two additional gold bands.

Chen firmly seated it on his head, then he stepped back and considered Jack. "Hmmm. It's rather rakish, but I think it works."

"You forgot the sash," Hutton said, holding up a white sash with two thin gold lines down the outsides. "It goes under the right shoulder board and then tucks underneath the left side of the belt."

"This is out of control," Jack complained. "I look utterly ridiculous."

"I wouldn't say that, sir," Hutton said with a lopsided smile. "Besides, we haven't gotten to the best part yet."

Jack tolerated them putting the sash on him and then breathed a sigh of relief when the next thing they opened was a box holding a pair of polished shoes. No boots this time. That wasn't nearly as bad as he'd expected.

Once he'd gotten his shoes on and walked around to make sure they'd be comfortable, he held up his arms. "I survived."

"Oh, we're not done yet," Hutton said as he hefted a long box.

Jack felt his eyes widen when they opened it and pulled out a sword in a golden scabbard. "Is this some kind of joke? A sword?"

He had to submit while they attached straps to the belt on his left side and then clipped the sheathed sword to it. It was a thin rapier with a curved golden guard at the hilt. A tassel of the same color was wrapped around the guard and hung a quarter of the sheath's length. A dagger in a similar sheath went on his right side.

He made sure to step clear of the two men and drew the sword. Its blade was made of a wavy metal that he immediately recognized as Damascus. It might be a ceremonial blade, but it was well made and razor-sharp.

"Who came up with this thing?" he complained as he sheathed the sword.

"The Navy," Hutton said in a matter-of-fact tone. "We're just lucky we had enough in storage for everyone."

The chime on the hatch sounded, and he called for whoever

it was to enter. When it slid aside, India walked in wearing a uniform identical to his own, though with a different selection of medals.

Seeing the dress uniform on her, he decided it didn't look half bad. It was far fancier than anything he'd ever worn, but if he looked anything like she did, the effect would be a positive one.

There were several ratings behind her, and he could see one of the differences in the dress uniforms was that the ratings didn't have raised collars. Their tunics had standard lapels, and the dress shirts underneath had small bow ties, and rather than having bands to represent rank, they had emblems on the upper parts of their sleeves. Their belts also lacked the gold band.

To his surprise, they also had swords, though the tassels were silver.

Following them were a pair of Marines. They wore enlisted-style dress uniforms, with the difference being a scarlet stripe down the outside of their pants legs. They had swords but also had sidearms.

"I'm going to want a sidearm as well," Jack said. "I believe the idea of having officers armed while on duty is a good one. It can go behind the dagger. Do we have enough time to make that happen?"

Hutton nodded. "I thought you might go there, so I have what's needed right here."

He produced a fancy holster that he attached to Jack's belt underneath his jacket. It only took a few moments, and Jack could transfer his pistol from his standard duty uniform to the dress uniform. He provided another one for India.

"You look good, Jack," India said once they had her fixed up. "Like something out of an entertainment video but good."

"I'm sure you look far better in this getup than I do," he grumbled. "Still, I suppose it's the least we can do."

"Do you have any idea what you're going to say?"

He nodded. "Not the usual kind of thing, but I think it'll set the right tone for us to grieve for those we've lost while putting some steel into our spines for the challenges yet to come. Let's get your pistol. I'll want you and the other senior officers with me while I give the eulogy."

She grimaced but nodded. "I'm ready."

"Then let's go."

Jack headed for the hatch, trying to get used to how the sword affected his gait. It was time.

24

TINA ARRIVED at the small craft bay were using for the memorial service dressed in her best clothes. As a former spy—and maybe current once again—she'd annoyed her husband by bringing along a wide variety of clothes to suit different needs. That meant he'd had to figure out where to store everything, but she was well prepared for virtually any circumstance.

Including, regrettably, a mass funeral.

Small craft bays were enormous to begin with, but someone had taken the time to clear the vessels from this one, placing them somewhere else for the duration. Probably out in space since it had infinite room. That had to have taken days they could've been spent on just about anything else, but this was important.

That left plenty of room for roughly a hundred and fifty caskets. They weren't made of wood but of synthetic material that must've been stored aboard the ship. It was similar to wood but different enough that she could tell it wasn't at a distance.

While the caskets weren't made of wood, that didn't mean they didn't gleam. The exterior of each softly reflected the illumination of the overhead lights. Each also bore the flag of the Confederation across its center.

Even with so many dead, the caskets only took up a small amount of the vast space. The rest was available for the crew and passengers, who were even now arriving in large numbers. Jack would be speaking from a platform set up to one side of the room. There was no lectern, so whatever he said and did would be plainly visible to all.

While she was looking around at the impressive dress uniforms, Tina spotted Christine Hooghuis. The woman was clad in the somber gray suit, though she still wore her belt of many pouches.

Tina walked over to stand beside the other woman and watched as the naval and Marine personnel filled the large compartment.

"I thought the regular Navy uniforms were a bit overdone," Christine said, "but I see I'm going to have to reassess what my definitions of the word actually mean. These dress uniforms are far gaudier than I'd have expected. It will make for quite the visual in the recordings I'm making."

Tina looked around but didn't see any of Christine's drones watching over the crowd. She knew they had to be up there somewhere because there was no way the other woman would miss documenting this.

"Jack said you wanted to be a war correspondent," she said. "I suspect this is going to be a common occurrence once the fighting heats up."

Christine nodded. "I'm afraid so."

Tina had expected the crowd to stay away from the caskets, but they didn't. Instead, they flowed through them, looking for friends. Each of the dead was identified by a plaque.

Everyone did something different when they found whoever they were looking for. Some cried. Others placed their hands on the caskets and grieved. A few raged, their faces grim, no doubt swearing vengeance.

Revenge was a powerful motivator and, if properly harnessed, would bind this crew together for the fight ahead. That was up to Jack to manage that—if he chose to—and it would be interesting to see how he went about doing it.

One thing she was sure of was that he wasn't going to miss the opportunity to bring his people together. The idea of simply having a mass funeral with as many people present as possible almost ensured that. Her husband certainly wouldn't have missed the chance to put a bug in his ear on the subject.

Within half an hour, the compartment was utterly packed. There had to be three or four thousand people jammed together, and she knew many others would be watching the ceremony remotely.

Finally, Jack and the other senior officers came in as a group with an honor guard of Marines resplendent in their dress uniforms surrounding them. She wasn't surprised to see the newly minted Lieutenant Calvo among them. She'd heard a bit about the fight after she'd gotten back aboard, and he'd impressed her. That young man would go far if he survived.

Jack made his way to the center of the platform, and his officers arrayed themselves beside him. The Marines accompanying them spread out in front of the platform and faced the caskets, drawing their swords and sharply whipping the blades in front of their faces in salute.

"Today, we gather to bid farewell to friends and comrades," Jack said loudly enough to be heard throughout the compartment. "We've lost far too many for me to say something about each, no matter how much they deserve it. I wish I'd gotten to know them all, but they were taken from us too soon. That was both a tragedy and a crime.

"Those who perpetrated this travesty will pay for their treachery, but we'll still have to heal from the wounds they've inflicted. Sadly, with more battles stretching out ahead of us, this is likely only the first time we say goodbye to those we care about. That will be hard, and I want you to remember you're not alone. You'll never be alone again."

He turned and gestured toward the caskets. "We need to remember those who gave their lives for us because one day it may be our turn to do the same for others. The Locusts have invaded the Confederation, and no one understands their endgame. There are uncountable people in the cluster depending on us, and we *will* free them. In doing so, we only have one another to depend on. We must all strive to be worthy of what destiny demands."

To Tina's surprise, Jack stepped off the platform and walked to a casket directly in front of him. He placed a hand on its surface and looked down at the plaque.

"Lieutenant Laura Dubsky of the Confederation Marines gave her life defending this ship and everyone aboard her. Of all the people we lost, I suspect I knew her the best, so it's only fitting that I make a pledge to her."

He reached under his jacket and pulled out a knife with a long blade and a very wicked point. He jabbed it lightly into his thumb and then held up his hand so that everyone near him could see the scarlet drop that welled out of his flesh. "No one who has bled for me, my people, or the Confederation will ever do so without knowing that I will do the same for them. This I swear on the blood that binds us together."

He pressed his thumb on top of the casket, undoubtedly leaving a bloody thumbprint. Then he stepped back, and Captain MacKinnon stepped forward, pulling out her own knife and stepping to a different casket.

"Lieutenant Larry Kroll of the Confederation Marines died defending the Confederation. I promise to do the same if needed. This I swear on the blood that binds us together."

In turn, each of the officers stepped forward and repeated the ceremony. Tina had never seen anything like it. This wasn't a rousing speech in the form that she'd anticipated. No. This was something *far* more powerful. They were dedicating their lives to this cause—and to one another—with a blood oath.

"Do you have a knife?" she asked Christine in a low tone.

Her friend turned and blinked at her in confusion. "As if I'd go anywhere without one."

Tina held out her hand, and Christine dug up a small folding blade. Timing her moment to when the last officer had finished making his oath, Tina stepped out of the crowd to the nearest casket and looked down at the name on the plaque.

"Spacer Jessica Bergstrom gave her life for me, and I in turn pledge mine to this ship and all of you," she said in a tone loud enough for all to hear. "This I swear on the blood that binds us together."

She jammed her thumb—perhaps a little too enthusiastically based on the amount of pain that shot through her hand—and showed her now bloody digit to the crowd before pressing it on top of the casket.

Christine stepped forward with a handkerchief, exchanged it for the knife, and repeated the pledge at a different casket.

The crowd seemed to take a deep breath, and they all began spreading throughout the caskets, seeking people they knew. They called out the names of the dead and swore their own oaths, binding themselves to those who had gone before and those who would come after.

Tina saw Jack had returned to the platform and someone— David most likely—had found a handkerchief for each of the officers to staunch their wounds. He watched the crowd with somber eyes until they'd finished.

"Each of us is bound to one another by blood, and I give you my solemn word that our enemies will pay dearly for each drop they spill. This I swear on the blood that binds us together."

That finally got a shout from the crowd as they raised their knives into the air.

When the roar had died down, Jack raised his own knife in salute before sheathing it. "Our dead will remain here with a Marine honor guard for the rest of the day so that anyone who couldn't be here can come to say their own goodbyes. Dismissed."

With that, he and his officers marched off the platform and out of the compartment.

The only one who stayed was Derek Calvo. He walked through the caskets until he found two specific people and swore his oath to them again. His expression was grim, and tears streamed down his face. Once he'd finished, he joined the streams of people leaving to return to their duty stations or their quarters.

"That was some powerful stuff," Christine said. "Do you think it's going to work?"

"Sometimes, all you have to do to accomplish great things is get a crowd moving in the same direction. Now, rather than thinking about everything that's happened to them, they're thinking about the people around them and how they can pay this forward.

"Many of these people never expected to serve with one another, and now they have to form a fighting crew to beat the Locusts. The blood spilled here today will bind them to that task and one another. Even the civilians are going to remember this day."

"*Everyone* will remember it if we make it back to the Confederation," Christine said. "My drones have it recorded for posterity. Now all we have to do is beat the Locusts."

"Words to live by, sister," Tina said with a lopsided smile. "Let's get out of here so other people have a chance to grieve.

Besides, I jabbed my thumb good, and I think I need to put something on it."

Christine chuckled and threw an arm around Tina's shoulder before leading her toward the hatch. "I happen to have some sealant and strips in my quarters. As someone who works with her hands, I'm cutting myself all the time. Let's go get you fixed up."

Tina cast her eyes back over the crowd one final time as they left and wondered if this would truly be enough to bind them all together. If so, this might very well be the turning point in the war.

She certainly hoped so. That was probably the only way they'd survive, much less triumph.

25

JACK HAD nightmares about the attack—and he suspected that he would for quite some time—but he suspected his paled to what so many of his crew were suffering through. He had his eye on Derek, but the boy was only one of so many that were hurting.

It would take time and therapy for them to get past that. They needed closure, which brought him to the distasteful yet inevitable duty he now had to carry out. He'd delayed justice long enough.

Jack sat in the command chair on the bridge with India beside him. Even though they weren't at combat stations, all consoles were occupied. It seemed no one wanted to miss this moment.

That was fair. They'd earned the right to see this finished.

"How distant is *Hawkwing?*" he asked.

"Three hundred thousand kilometers, sir," Calvo said from the helm console. The young man's voice was brisk and emotionless. If he felt any horror or satisfaction about what was to happen, it didn't show.

"Are all vessels clear of the detonation zone?"

"Yes, sir."

The Marines had carted the surviving pirates out to the disabled vessel and shoved them aboard once *Hunter* and the other ships were clear of the detonation zone.

One final pinnace had brought Magri to the place of his execution. He'd still been wearing his Navy uniform, stripped of all rank and insignia because those were the only clothes the Marine force recon personnel had allowed him.

They didn't care if he'd gotten dressed either. They'd have taken him naked if that's what had been required.

Once they'd shoved the screaming man through the airlock and disengaged to return to *Hunter*, that had placed everyone responsible for killing and wounding his people aboard a vessel with an armed self-destruct device.

He'd had India and the former chief engineer go over the vessel with a fine-toothed comb. Engineering was in vacuum, and there were no protective suits on the ship. The computers had been stripped out, along with anything else that might've been used to disarm the charges.

There would be no escaping justice today.

He stood and stepped over to the communications console. With no fanfare, he pressed the button they'd indicated would send the self-destruct signal. It was his responsibility, and he'd shoulder the burden of executing Magri and the surviving pirates.

The screen at the front of the compartment showed a brief spark of light as the explosives detonated. Then it vanished as the vacuum of space killed the flames. There was nothing left except for scattered debris flying off in every direction.

"Those who shed our blood have paid for their crimes," he intoned. "May God have mercy on their souls."

After a few moments, he made his way back to his chair. India put her hand on his arm as he sat but said nothing.

"Have we confirmed that everybody is aboard?" he asked.

"Yes, sir," she said. "I sent the Marines back through every ship to ensure we didn't leave anyone behind. They're all on a course to take them into the system's outer reaches, so the Locusts might miss them if they do come looking."

"Take us out to a good jump range, Lieutenant Calvo. I assume you've got a course already laid in?"

The young man turned and nodded. "Yes, sir. We'll be able to get most of the way to our destination without having to interface with any occupied systems. The trick will come at the end because we can't get to the depot system without going through one of the occupied systems—New Copenhagen— which also held the concealed gate that led to the depot system.

"We should be able to jump into it at a location that'll keep us from being observed unless we're damned unlucky. With a little bit of luck, we can travel to a jump-off point to the depot system before they can intercept us."

"We can certainly hope for luck, but we can't count on it. We'll just have to do the best we can."

He pressed the button on the arm of his chair that opened a channel to engineering.

"Engineering," Danek said.

The sour note in her voice made him smile just a little. She hadn't taken the surprise promotion very well. Apparently, she'd been serious when she'd indicated she thought the rank came with more problems than it solved. Nevertheless, he'd pointed the metaphorical finger at her and turned her into a commander.

Or maybe she was still annoyed because he'd decided not to indulge her experiment with expanding the quantum bubble. The scientists had said the theory sounded plausible, but it was a dangerous unknown he wasn't willing to risk for the sake of taking along a few civilian ships.

"Bridge here. Are we ready to jump?"

"We're ready, sir," she confirmed. "I still think we should try taking at least a couple of the civilian ships with us."

She was nothing if not determined.

"Your concerns are noted. If we decide that's what we have to do, we can come back for them. We've got a few months before the Locusts will likely get here. Let's go see what we can find before making that kind of decision."

"You're the boss, boss. Engineering stands ready to provide all the power needed for this jump. The new fusion plant is operating at full power."

"Then let's make the magic happen, Commander."

He could almost hear her eyes roll through the audio connection. "Engineering out."

"Is it just me, or did she sound a little testy," India asked with a bit of a smirk.

"One thing you'll learn about Commander Danek is that she *always* sounds testy. It's just one of those things you have to learn to love about her."

He turned his attention back to the helm officer. "Jump at your discretion, Mister Calvo."

"Aye, sir."

The young man was seated next to *Hawkwing*'s former helm officer. Jack had worked with Lieutenant Commander Alexey Golousenko for several years and had absolute trust in the man. It was interesting watching someone with that much experience pay absolute attention to every step the boy was taking him through.

Calvo wouldn't be initiating this jump. He was walking his new superior officer through the steps and explaining what they were doing and why. That would take a bit longer, but Jack was more than willing to wait the extra few minutes it would take.

When they were ready, it was Golousenko that turned toward him. "We're ready to jump, Commodore."

"Take us out of the system, Commander."

The man took one deep breath and pressed the button. There was a gratifyingly slight twitch, and the massive battleship instantly moved eight and a half light-years to a new system.

Jack slowly let out the breath he'd been holding. If they'd been unlucky, one of the power plants could've gone bad, but everything seemed to have gone smoothly.

Of course, they still had almost a dozen jumps ahead of them, and there was still plenty of time for something to go horribly wrong.

He stood. "Commander Golousenko, you have the conn. See us moved to the next jump location and notify me when you're ready to go."

"Yes, sir."

Jack noted the man didn't move from his current location. He was going to be maneuvering the ship and learning what the potential pitfalls of doing so would be as well.

Along with him on the bridge, Lieutenant Commander Ahmed Adel was seated over at the tactical console getting an education of his own, even as Lieutenant Commander Charlie Ferrero was shadowing Danek around engineering. They all had a lot to learn, as did he.

Leaving them to their work, Jack walked out of the bridge with India at his heels. They retreated to his office, where he poured them each a little bit of whiskey. That done, he sat in the comfortable seat across from her.

"I wish Lieutenant Kroll had made it," he said. "His loss was painful, but now that we've lost Lieutenant Dubsky as well, we'll have to rely on Mac Turner and his people to provide the backbone of leadership for the Marines. How do you think they're going to react to that?"

India snorted. "Is that a joke? Turner is a retired Marine force recon officer. He was a major, for God's sake. If anyone can handle the job, it's him.

"As for what our people think, they revere him. Force recon is the ultimate goal for a Marine, so he's been there and done that. There's no doubt in my mind that he's going to get one hundred and ten percent support."

She sipped a little of her whiskey and then set the glass down. "Things are just so unsettled, Jack. I understand that's why you feel nervous, but you're going to have to accept that our people will gel around the leaders we have. Under ideal circumstances, maybe we'd have more seasoned officers, but we don't. We'll make do.

"Do you think we're going to run into trouble when we get to New Copenhagen?"

"Based on our track record? Yes."

She chuckled. "I assume we're going to stop short of the system, make a bunch of contingency plans, and then jump in and see what we find on the other side. How ready are we for it if we get into a fight?"

It was his turn to take a sip of his whiskey and think. "We've got our people working on getting as many lasers into operation as possible. I think we'll probably be above ten percent of our available firepower at that point. While that sounds like a low percentage, it's a rather large number of laser batteries in absolute terms.

"If we can control where we emerge in New Copenhagen, we can minimize our travel time, even at the reduced speeds we'll need to use. Unless they've got ships scattered right out at the jump limit, odds are we'll be in and gone before they can reach us. Even if we can't, I doubt we'll have overwhelming force land on us all at once."

"Then it sounds like we're doing everything we can," she said after a moment. "That means it's time to stop worrying about what could happen and focus on what we need to do. It'll take us more than a week to get to New Copenhagen, so let's focus on making everything as good as it can be.

"We've got the civilians under watch, and Hutton has certainly got a lot of them busy sorting our cargo and spare parts. The time isn't going to go to waste."

"No, I suppose it's not. I'll order a stand down for a full forty-eight hours before we go in. There's no reason to rush, and I think having everybody rested and ready will pay dividends."

Of course, that would depend on what they found on the other end. Things could get ugly when they saw the reality of what the Locusts were doing in New Copenhagen.

Could he really just pass by if they were doing something horrific? He didn't know.

The smart thing would be to wait and see exactly what was happening, get *Hunter* refitted and rearmed, and then come back and kick their asses. Sadly, there was plenty of evidence that he didn't always do the smartest thing.

He hoped they didn't find an atrocity in progress when they got there, but deep inside, he doubted the alien machines were there to just secure the space around the occupied worlds. There'd be something else going on. Something terrible.

"Let's get something to eat and make a tour of the ship," he said after a few minutes of silence. "Everyone needs to see us."

They tossed their drinks back and stood. Morale demanded they make a pass through the ship. Their people needed to be at their best when it came time to fight again. And he had no doubt it would come far sooner than any of them would prefer.

26

THE NEXT WEEK and a half went by far faster than Derek had anticipated. He had a lot on his plate and not enough hours in each day to do what he needed to do. Not only did he have to train the helm personnel from *Hawkwing*, but he was also still responsible for learning what he needed to know to run watches more effectively himself.

That often meant that Commodore Romanoff and Captain MacKinnon technically led a watch while he sat in the command chair. Sometimes they'd be observing him directly, other times remotely from their offices. He knew they were paying attention because they'd deliver the occasional critique about something he'd done or failed to do.

He also was grappling with nightmares. He'd wake up in the middle of the night with his heart racing. He swore he could smell blood and burnt gunpowder as he sat there gasping for breath. The screams of the wounded and dying seemed to still be ringing in his ears, and all the while, the memory of ordering the ship to fire on the pirates dominated what he could recall of the dream.

When that happened, he knew better than trying to go back to sleep. Even with medication, it just wasn't happening. That quickly led to him becoming exhausted, and the commodore had finally shoved him into the medical center to speak with his mother.

Derek wasn't certain what he'd expected from her, but she was much like her son. She could be very direct, but she also listened carefully to everything he said and gave him what he was sure was excellent advice.

He just didn't know how talking about what had happened would change anything. It only seemed to dredge up the emotions he was trying to bury. It felt as if he was chasing his own tail, yet he had no choice but to endure.

That problem would eventually sort itself out. It had to because he couldn't focus on it with everything else demanding his attention.

The ship made it just short of the New Copenhagen without any issues. The commodore then parked the ship for a full forty-eight hours with minimal watches while everyone got as much rest as possible.

Everyone except for the maintenance personnel. They'd been working hard on restoring as many of the laser clusters as possible, and to his astonishment and the commodore's pleasure, they had about fifteen percent of the ship's defensive armament functional by the time the ship was ready to jump.

That was still only a drop in the bucket compared to the missile batteries they couldn't use, but one had to work with the tools they had. Maybe once they got to the depot, they could begin refurbishing some of the stockpiled missiles and gain some true offensive capability, but for the moment, they were limited to what they could make work.

When it came time to jump into the occupied system, he was at the helm with Lieutenant Commander Golousenko at his side. The man had been putting in a lot of time both on the bridge and in the simulators in the operations center.

Derek had to admit he was impressed. The older man had begun to grasp the basics of maneuvering the massive battleship and had even started to understand some of the limitations and capabilities of the independent quantum drive.

He wasn't nearly as proficient as he needed to be in manipulating the controls, but the man's experience was definitely showing. The commander would get there faster than he'd initially expected.

"Are we ready to jump, Derek?" the commodore asked.

"Yes, sir," he responded without taking his eyes off the controls. "We can go at any time."

"Take us in at your discretion."

Even though he'd be responsible for what they did once they got into New Copenhagen, Derek gestured for Commander Golousenko to set up the jump just as he had the last few times. The man managed it, though he was slow. To Derek's pleasure, the solution was within the appropriate tolerances for a successful jump this time.

"Good job, Commander. This would've gotten us there, though I'll optimize it somewhat. You'll need to keep working on your speed, but it looks like you have a decent understanding of the process at this point. Well done."

The man grinned but shook his head. "That's kind of you to say, but I've got a long way to go. I wasn't nearly as certain about some of the parameters as I should have been. I'll need to do this more effectively before I'm satisfied. You don't need to be worried about me taking over your spot for quite some time, I think."

"Believe me, I'll be happy when you don't need supervision, sir. Some extra off time would be nice. Why don't you hit the button and take us to the other side?"

The commander pressed the button, and the universe seemed to twitch. Derek scanned the console and saw they'd successfully made it to New Copenhagen.

"Successful jump," he told the commodore. "No ships in our vicinity. Beginning passive sensor scan of the system. It will take us a while to correlate the data, but I've got our specific targets dialed in, and I'm feeding the information to the operations center.

"Based on our exit point, velocity, and course, we should be able to reach the jump-off point in approximately eight hours."

"Excellent. Since there isn't anybody in our general vicinity, I'll leave the watch in your capable hands, Commander Golousenko. Stand the ship down to normal operations for the moment. If there's any change in status, wake me at once."

"Yes, sir," Golousenko said as he rose from the helm station. "Keep doing what you're doing, Mister Calvo."

"Yes, sir." Derek dedicated some passive sensors to pulling information from across the system because one never knew what one would find in the dark corners. Surprise attacks happened because you weren't seeing what was out there.

Everything they saw from near the habitable world was hours old, but that was good enough for him. It meant that the enemy wouldn't potentially notice *Hunter*'s arrival until they'd been there for a while.

They were going a bit farther than they needed to because the commodore had decided to make it seem like they were jumping for a different system, even though the Locusts wouldn't be able to tell their destination just from watching them.

No one wanted to highlight the depot system for the alien machines. Far better for them to go hunting in the wrong location and wonder if *Hunter* had simply continued on to some other system.

Even though he wasn't responsible for parsing the information from the human-populated world, he kept a close eye on it. This was the first opportunity he'd had to watch what the Locusts were up to without being in the middle of the battle.

They'd subdued this system weeks ago, so the fighting was long done. What were they doing now? It was far too distant to make out individual ships, but there was enough activity in orbit for him to see it.

Thankfully, the same wouldn't be true of *Hunter*. The nickel-iron asteroid it was constructed from was very effective at blocking signs of power generation. The only thing they had to worry about giving them away was their fusion drives.

They'd come into the system at a location that should allow them to move without directly exposing their fusion drives to ships around the planet. If the Locusts had other ships in the system, that wouldn't do them any good, but there was only so much they could do to mitigate that. Crossing enemy-held territory was dangerous.

He frowned as he took in all of the activity. He had no idea what would be normal under circumstances like this, but there was a lot going on in orbit around New Copenhagen.

Were they constructing something? Did they have ships going down to the surface? Something so alien that he couldn't imagine what it might be? Whatever it was, it was certainly a change from everything he'd learned about the first invasion.

Luckily, he didn't have to figure out what was happening. That was up to Tina Chen and her husband in the operations center. David Chen was a retired intelligence analyst, and she was a former operative, so if anyone could pull some useful explanations from the data, it would be them.

It was far better for him to focus his attention on the things in the system that were less obvious. He wasn't an intelligence analyst and didn't have much experience at finding hard-to-discover objects, but there were scenarios inside Locust War Online that revolved around doing those very things. He'd manage.

One of the things he was interested in were the quantum gates. Or where they'd been, at least. They didn't know their status at this point because they assumed the signal Vice Admiral LaChasse had sent had propagated throughout the entire cluster, destroying every gate. This was their opportunity to confirm or disprove that assumption.

According to the maps, this system had been a transit point between many different locations inside the cluster and had four quantum gates. By focusing some of the passive scanners on each of those locations, he should be able to determine if there had been any explosions in the recent past.

In short order, he'd determined there *had* been explosions at all four locations. While some of that might have been caused by ships lost in combat, he didn't believe so. The readings were too consistent.

If they'd had anything like probes to verify what was there, he'd have been happy to use them, but they didn't. That technology hadn't been used during the first invasion, and *Hawkwing* had lost her probes due to battle damage.

They could've launched a few small craft to scout the locations, but that was chancy at best. They'd been training people to fly the small craft, but they didn't have that many working. Also, it hadn't been something the commodore had been interested in risking, and Derek didn't blame him

Interestingly, the quantum gate that led to the depot system didn't have any explosive remnants that he could detect. That implied it might still be intact. That was interesting and troublesome.

He turned toward the command chair. "Commander, I've been going over the passive data, and while I can detect what looks like explosive remnants from the quantum gates, I'm not detecting anything like that from the concealed gate leading to the depot system. Sir, it might still be there."

The officer scowled at the smaller screens attached to the command chair. Then he stood, walked over to the helm console, and looked over Derek's shoulder. "I wish I could manipulate the controls on the command chair the way I want, but I'm not there yet. Show me."

Derek made the passive sensor scans larger and enhanced the explosive remnants he'd seen at the first four locations. He let the fifth zone stand on its own for comparison. Looking at them side-by-side, it was obvious there'd been no explosion at that location.

"Good eye. We'll leave the final confirmation of that to the Chens, but I agree with your initial assessment. Annotate the passive data stream with what you've discovered so it's brought to their attention."

"Yes, sir. Based on the direction of the hidden gate, we have the option to send a single active pulse from our sensors in that direction to verify whether there's anything there or not."

Golousenko shook his head. "No. The commodore would never authorize anything like that, and neither will I.

"Try to refine as much data as you can using just the passive sensors. I know we're too distant to see the gate itself, but you might find other signs of its destruction. If it's still there, that presents us with new opportunities and challenges."

"Yes, sir."

Derek spent the next hour refining as much data as he could.

In the end, he was certain there hadn't been an explosion at the gate location. It was still there.

The gate sat above the plane of the ecliptic and farther out than one would normally expect something like that to be. Based on its location, scanning it directly wasn't much of a risk, but Derek understood the concept of taking no chances at all.

Interestingly, while he didn't detect anything from the area near the gate, he did pick up something faint from an adjacent location. He'd have missed it if he hadn't been looking at the one area so intensely.

It was closer than the gate and came across as an active fusion plant. It wasn't operating at full power, but it was there. It was distant enough that the readings were almost too weak to pick up.

"I've got something else, sir," he said once he'd confirmed what he'd seen as well as he could. "I've discovered an active fusion plant. It's nowhere near the planet, and it's not operating at a very high level of output."

"Is it a Locust mothership or drone?"

"I don't think so. First of all, they'd be operating at a significantly higher power output, but they're also shielded. Not as well as we are, but more than what I'm detecting here. The fusion plant I'm looking at doesn't seem to be putting out that much power, but I'd be very surprised if it's shielded at all. The signals are weak but crystal clear."

The older man considered him for a moment and then gestured toward the main screen. "Show me exactly how it sits in the system relative to where we are, as well as the planet itself. In fact, populate the screen with all the data we've been able to gather at this point and our projected course. Let's see where everybody is."

It took a minute for Derek to get everything positioned the way he wanted, which was a little embarrassing. He should've been ready for that request.

He expected Golousenko to chide him about it, but the man didn't say anything. It was obvious to Derek he was making allowances and that he recognized Derek knew he'd made a mistake. Oh well, that was part and parcel of becoming an experienced officer and one more thing Derek needed to remember going forward.

Once he had everything up on the screen, the situation became even more curious. While there were undoubtedly patrols of drones out in the system, they were nowhere near the area where the fusion plant was located. They must have detected it, yet they didn't seem concerned.

Deciding he needed to make sure the watch officer recognized how unusual that was, he spoke up. "The Locusts should be able to detect the fusion plant, but they don't seem worried about it, sir. None of their ships are anywhere near it, and they don't seem to have any curiosity about it whatsoever. From what I remember about the first invasion, they didn't tolerate any human shipping or stations. Why is this different?"

The man pursed his lips. "If they don't tolerate human traffic in the systems they control, that implies what we're looking at isn't human. Could it be a damaged mothership?"

Derek shook his head. "Even at its lower output settings, this seems like too much energy for a mothership. The readings are all wrong. It's almost like we're detecting a large fusion plant with no shielding operating at minimal power."

Golousenko considered the screen for a moment and then looked down at the arm of his chair. "I think we need to wake the commodore. This is something he might be interested in. Send the location and your suspicions to operations so they can start going over the data and either confirm or eliminate the possibilities you've thrown on the table. Again, excellent work."

Derek nodded and got busy. He wondered how the discovery would change their plans. Well, he'd find out soon enough.

27

Jack frowned as he stared at the scant data on the main screen. "What could that thing be? It's obviously artificial, but the Locusts would've destroyed it already if it was a damaged ship. A human ship, anyway."

Alexey nodded his agreement from where he now stood beside the command chair Jack sat in. "That means it's not human. I suppose the only other option is that it's a Locust vessel, though not a mothership, according to Derek. It's not maneuvering at all, just sitting there. Why?"

They'd have to take a risk if they wanted to know what that thing was, but they could take steps to mitigate the risk. He made a rough guess at the distance to the wreck and then examined how close they'd come to it. Not close enough to make much of a difference unless they angled more in that direction.

Under ideal circumstances, he'd probably have dispatched

some of the small craft to take a better look, but in hostile space, that was too dangerous. No matter how they approached this problem, odds were the Locusts would see them and attack. He had to be ready for that outcome.

There were, however, ways they could make this a little bit safer. The downside would be that it added to their travel time and made them more vulnerable because of lost speed.

Unlike the Locust motherships and drones, one did not simply accelerate a kilometer-long asteroid quickly. At least they'd already achieved some of the acceleration they'd been hoping for, so perhaps it wouldn't be that bad.

"Cut our acceleration to one-third and change course to make a closer pass of the unknown ship," he ordered. "There's still a risk that ships near the planet will detect our fusion drives, but it should be more difficult for them to do so. If they spot us, we'll go to full acceleration and deal with any of the drones that catch us. Hopefully, it won't be too many.

"Derek, how long to get into the vicinity of that ship?"

The young man tapped at his console for a few seconds. "At the reduced speed, approximately eleven hours, sir. I have to warn you that even though we'll be going slower, the chances of attracting unwanted attention might be higher than you think.

"Since those ships are robotic, they're always looking for something that fits their attack parameters, even though they know this system is empty. Just the slightest hint that we're out here will draw them in, where it might be written off as a sensor ghost by a human."

"If you have any indication they've spotted us, go to

maximum acceleration immediately," Jack ordered. "Whatever that thing is, I'm sure it'll provide useful information, but our ultimate goal is to safely pass through this system. Is the new course going to bring us close enough to look at the hidden gate to the depot system?"

The young man nodded. "If we use active sensors, yes, sir. I recommend that if the Locusts come after us, we go to active sensors and sweep the entire system. That way, they don't see us looking at anything in particular, and they'll have no reason to search that specific area.

"If we have to go to maximum acceleration, we can get to the area near that ship in about three and a half hours. It's sitting just outside the jump limit, so we'll be able to get an excellent look at it right before we jump while still misleading the Locusts about our destination."

"What is the soonest they'd be able to spot us?"

"The ships around the planet would get the first indication of our course change in a little less than ninety minutes. They can catch us just short of the jump limit at maximum acceleration. If we can accelerate at the lower speed for an hour past that potential detection point, we'll likely get clear, even with that sprint capability they've already demonstrated. Anything in the middle is a crapshoot."

It would be a risk, but they desperately needed to get intelligence about what the enemy was up to. They weren't going to run and hide every time the enemy had the capability to strike at them.

"Do it," he ordered.

As the young helm officer began changing course, Jack leaned back in his command chair and considered what they were looking at. Information from the first invasion was extensive, and Derek had been correct. This didn't match anything he'd ever heard about. Neither did whatever the Locusts were doing in orbit around New Copenhagen.

David and Tina Chen were busy trying to decipher what they could about the activity near the planet, but he didn't hold out much hope they'd get a lot of hard details using the passive scanners.

If they'd genuinely wanted to gather intelligence here, they'd have to find a way to get a ship into the system and send it on a ballistic course without risking the enemy being able to detect fusion drives or an active fusion plant. Even some of the civilian ships could probably have completed the task successfully, though there'd have been more risk.

He supposed bringing some of the civilian ships for that purpose might have been worthwhile, and he'd been the one who'd made the call to leave the ships behind. Now that was biting him in the behind.

Once they finished working on the weapons in the depot system, they'd have to come back and settle the Locusts here. Maybe they'd be able to figure out what the damned things were up to at that point. Whatever it was, he was sure he wouldn't like it.

The other troubling issue was the quantum gate leading to the depot system. It didn't seem to have been destroyed along with the others. Odds were it had never had the self-destruct option installed.

He had no idea why the Navy would've singled it out, but it was possible the Locusts would discover it and come swarming through. He'd have to think hard about destroying the gate on the other side to keep them safe.

Time seemed to drag right up until the situation changed. He'd been rooting for Derek to get the full hour he wanted, but deep down, he hadn't expected it. Sadly, he was right.

They'd been accelerating for just more than two hours when Derek stiffened and began manipulating his controls.

"Activity around the planet indicates they've detected us," the young man said. "I've increased our speed to maximum. Going to active sensors."

"Time to intercept?" he asked. "How close will we get to the jump limit before they reach us?"

"It depends on if they have the sprint capability they demonstrated during the first fight. If only certain of their ships have it, we might be able to handle the wave that reaches us without too much difficulty. If they all do, things could get hairy.

"Based on the speed they're demonstrating right now, they're not using the sprint capability, but they didn't use it until they got close the last time."

"We'll go to battle stations half an hour before they reach us," he said with a grimace. "No need to get everybody up when they can't get to us yet. Are we detecting any other drones coming after us?"

"There's only one patrol closer to us than the planet at the moment. They should detect us in the next five minutes. Everyone else will be a little late to the party, but I expect them to come swarming in from every direction based on what we know about their behavior."

That didn't surprise Jack at all. In fact, it didn't even displease him. He wanted to give the weapon systems another test, and that smaller group of ships would be just what the doctor ordered.

"What about the activity around the planet? Now that our sensors have gone active, how long until we get more detailed information?"

Calvo turned in his seat to face him. "We're just as limited by the speed of light as they are, sir. I figure we'll start getting firm data maybe ten minutes before we're ready to jump. That will give operations a chance to record everything, but we'll need a lot of time to parse the data to understand what the Locusts are doing there."

"Since we're closer to the unknown ship, I assume we'll get data on it sooner. How long do you think before we know what it is?"

"We'll start getting active returns from it in less than an hour, sir. That'll be around the time the first patrol catches up with us."

Jack nodded and stood. "You have the conn, Commander Golousenko. I'm calling a staff meeting for the senior officers for right now, and I want you and Derek to participate remotely. Make certain everybody gets the word. I want to hear about it as soon as we have any information about that unknown vessel."

Alexey nodded and took the command chair. "Yes, sir."

Jack left the bridge, keeping his worries to himself. A combat commander couldn't let himself be paralyzed by the possibilities. They were fighting for humanity, which meant they'd have to take calculated risks.

Was the ship sitting out there worth the chances they were taking? He wouldn't know until they learned more about it. It might be some type of new Locust vessel, and if that was the case, they needed to find out everything they could about it.

Jack made his way to the briefing room adjacent to his office. It wasn't nearly the same scale as the dining room next to his quarters, but it was more than sufficient to hold his senior staff.

He didn't bother taking off his hat or greatcoat, simply sitting at the head of the table and waiting for everyone else to arrive. It only took a few moments for India to arrive. She must've been in her office even though she'd been off shift.

"I hear the fecal matter has hit the rotary impeller," she said as she took a seat to his right. "Are we going to be able to get out of here without engaging the Locusts?"

He shook his head. "It's an open question whether the larger force can get to us in time, but a smaller patrol will intercept us in about an hour. That'll give us a chance to test our weaponry and see if they display the same sprint mode that the other ships used during the fighting at the gateway system."

She grimaced. "My memory of that battle isn't a pleasant one. They were all over the sky, and no matter how many of them we shot down, there were always three to replace every one that was destroyed. Our sensors were mostly offline by the time you got into the fight, so I'm looking forward to seeing how well everything works."

"I'm not worried about the first group," he assured her. "We've got three times more lasers working than we had during the first fight, and we handled a group that was bigger than the patrol easily enough back then. It's the second group that's going to give us trouble. There'll be a lot of firepower coming our way from the planet."

Joby Hutton and Kelly Danek came in, with Charlie Ferrero right on their heels. Ahmed Adel and Amanda Harris followed them in. Harris was definitely the junior in this meeting, but she had far more experience with the tactical aspects of the upcoming fight than any of them, so she'd earned a seat at the table.

Jack opened a channel to the bridge so that Alexey and Derek could hear them and contribute when called upon while the newest arrivals took their seats. "Okay, everyone, let's bring you up to speed."

He filled them in on everything they'd discovered to this point and what their current plans were. That didn't mean much considering how sparse the data was, but he could sketch out the situation as it sat.

"Now," he said once he'd finished, "the question becomes what we do next. When we jump out of the system, we should still be able to make them think we're going somewhere else.

"They don't understand how our independent quantum drive works, or the fact that we don't have to be on a course toward the destination system or even be pointing toward it to make the jump. If there's a way of determining our destination, the

Confederation never figured out how to do it, so I don't think the Locusts will do any better.

"The real question is what we get intelligence-wise before we leave. And, of course, making sure we thrash any drones that catch up with us. The last thing we need is to take major damage here."

He looked over at Harris. "Why don't you run the numbers for us, Amanda. What are we looking for in this first fight?"

The young woman looked a little uncomfortable but launched right into her briefing. "Based on the numbers in the initial group of drones, we won't have any difficulty taking care of them, sir. We have three times the firepower we had the last time, and there are less than half the drones we faced at the battle then.

"The bigger question is how soon the larger force will catch up with us and what its composition is going to be. It has a swarm of motherships with it, and they are somewhat slower than the drones themselves."

"What kind of numbers are we talking about?" India asked. "How does it compare with what the rear guard was fighting back in the gateway system?"

"I don't have firm numbers for how many drones you fought before we got there, but the wave that overwhelmed the cruisers was probably about three times larger than what we've got behind us now. That's still a lot of drones."

"How can we minimize the damage we take while maximizing our offensive capability?" Jack asked. "If they have the sprint capability, they're going to catch us before we're ready to jump. If they don't, they may still be within laser range.

"Our laser range is greater than theirs, so we'll be able to hurt them before they close the distance, but it's all going to be a numbers game, isn't it?"

The young woman nodded. "Yes, sir. The new technology is the wildcard. If every single one of those drones is equipped with sprint capability, we're going to end up jumping out of the system under heavy fire. We just won't have enough lasers to defend ourselves against them all.

"That doesn't mean we don't have options, though. Depending on how we orient the ship and rotate our fire among the attackers, we should be able to deal them some heavy damage. They're not going to be able to come at us from every angle, so we'll be able to optimize our fire as they close the distance. Again, it's going to involve rotating the ship as we go, and that's going to be in Derek's wheelhouse."

"I've been running some simulations on that," the young man said over the communications unit built into the table. "There's going to be an element of luck involved, and I don't like that. We can test out some of the patterns on the patrol when they close with us, but it's going to reveal what we're doing before the enemy gets to us in large numbers. I'm not sure if that's what we want to do."

"Let's hear what you've got," he said. "We'll keep working on this right up until the enemy gets here."

And that's exactly what they did. Derek presented several options they could use in the upcoming fight, and they debated the pros and cons of each, then settled on what they hoped was the best options.

Jack was pleased to see no one seemed panicked, even the young Harris. Everybody was focused on what they needed to do and how they needed to do it.

"The drones in the first patrol are about five minutes away from our extreme laser range," Derek said when they'd finished going over the last option. "If you want to continue with the briefing, sir, the commander and I should be able to handle this fight. The number of enemy drones isn't going to threaten us, and I'll be able to tell him what the risks are as we proceed."

"And we can call if we need assistance since you're right down the corridor," Alexey said. "I concur with Lieutenant Calvo, sir. We can handle this."

Jack was very tempted to turn that offer down, but he needed to trust that his officers knew how to fight the ship if he wasn't there.

"We'll monitor the fight from here and then continue the briefing," he decided. "Have any of the drones used sprint mode?"

"Not yet, sir," Derek said. "There's still time, but I would've expected them to have already used it if they'd had it. That's good news."

"Carry on and let me know the moment it's done."

India reached over and clasped his hand once he'd muted the channel. "They're going to do fine, Jack. Alexey is an experienced officer, and Derek isn't going to steer him wrong. They've got a full crew up there and should be able to handle this.

"Think of it as a simulation. This is what they used to call a smoke test. You've got to turn it on and see what happens."

"That's not very reassuring," he said. "Still, you're right. The time may come that they have to fight without me. Hell, during the first fight, I might've been in the command chair, but it was Derek and his team doing the fighting."

He looked over at Amanda. "Head to the bridge and take over gunnery. We want our A-team on duty for this fight."

"Yes, sir," she said, then she rose to her feet and walked out of the briefing room with Ahmed at her heels.

"They say war is a young person's game, but I'm not sure this is what they meant," Jack said with a dark chuckle. "I still have trouble getting used to the fact that our youngest officers have the most experience fighting this ship. It's turning every aspect of what we thought we knew on its head."

Sitting there for the fight was just as hard as he'd expected it to be. He and the rest continued going over their plans until the bridge announced they were opening fire. He'd already brought the wall screen to life, and it showed a swarm of drones attacking them.

Derek had been right. There weren't nearly as many as the last time, and his ship was better armed than it had been, so the fight was short, one-sided, and brutal.

The incoming drones tried to come at them from two different directions, but Derek rotated the ship, and Amanda fired laser clusters at the incoming hostiles, decimating their ranks before they even reached range to fire back.

Jack noted with approval that the turn kept the enemy from threatening the fusion drives. They were protecting the most vulnerable section of the ship and doing it well.

They lost some laser clusters in the fight, but it didn't change the outcome. Every single drone was wiped out shortly after coming into *Hunter*'s primary laser range. The ship then turned back to its original course and continued accelerating as if nothing had happened.

"Amanda, how many lasers did we lose in the fight?" he asked over the communications channel once he'd unmuted it.

"We had more than fifteen percent of our total laser armament operational at the start of the fight, and we're down to about fourteen and a half percent now. Maybe a third of those are completely destroyed, but we should be able to get some of that firepower back online before the next wave of drones reaches us."

"Were there any hull breaches?"

"No, sir," Alexey said. "We didn't sustain any additional damage."

"Excellent work," Jack said. "Pass along my congratulations to everyone and stand down from battle stations until we're just short of being engaged again. Romanoff out."

He was about to dismiss everyone when his comm unit went off. It was Tina Chen.

"Romanoff," he said once he'd accepted the call.

"We need you in operations," she said. "We have the readings from the ship with the operational fusion plant, and you need to see what we're looking at."

"On my way."

He put his comm away and stood. "Back to your duty stations

or beds if you were off shift. I'll see that you get a summary of what we've found and what we're doing next."

And with that, he headed for operations. It was time to see if the anomaly had been worth the damage they were going to take to have a look at it.

28

Tina barely glanced up when Jack came into the operations center. She and her husband had taken over a pair of consoles that were larger than the ones she'd seen on the bridge because they'd have more space for them to work with. She had a lot of displays open so she could interpret everything the sensors were giving to her.

Frankly, she still wasn't sure what to make what they'd found.

"What have we got?" Jack asked as he stepped up beside her.

"It's definitely a ship," she said. "A big ship, about a third the size of *Hunter*."

Jack frowned and leaned over to look at the sensor data for himself. "That is a big ship. It could be a freighter, but it seems unlikely the Locusts would've allowed a human-built freighter to stay out here.

"That must mean the Navy damaged a new class of Locust

ship during the invasion. I don't understand why the Locusts left it sitting out here, though. Shouldn't they have dragged it into planetary orbit? Is it so badly damaged that it's worthless to them?"

"We're not going to be able to figure that out without getting closer," she said. "Assuming that is a Locust ship, what is its purpose? We've never seen anything larger than a mothership. What is it, and why is it here?"

David shrugged. "Based on the unshielded fusion plant, it doesn't seem like it served a military purpose. That's not how the motherships or drones are built, so if those are meant for fighting, perhaps this ship isn't."

"I want you to do your best to confirm that it is a Locust design," Jack said. "I realize that may be difficult, but we absolutely have to know."

"And if it is?" she asked. "How does that affect what we're doing?"

He grimaced. "If it is a new class of Locust ship, I'm going to have to do something I'd hoped to avoid. Danek told me she believes we can extend our quantum bubble behind the ship in roughly the same size as what we're looking at. That might blow another fusion plant, but at least we'd be in the depot system."

He headed for the hatch. "Draw in as many people as you need. You have carte blanche, so make the magic happen."

After Jack had left the operations center, Tina looked over at her husband and shrugged. "I think getting Kelly Danek to take a look would be useful. Second, the professor's insight would be worthwhile. And lastly, Doctor Wilson and her team."

She pulled out her comm unit and called the chief engineer. "Kelly, this is Tina. We need you in the operations center immediately."

"I'm a little busy," her friend said. "It's going to have to wait."

"It can't wait. The commodore has given me instructions to call in anyone that can tell us if a ship we're looking at is of Locust design. I'm also calling in the professor and the researchers, but you're the engineer, and I need you.

"And before you start arguing, Jack has already said if this is a Locust ship, he's going to use that little trick you thought up to snag it, so you've got some skin in the game."

"Why didn't you say that up front? I'm on my way."

She called the professor's com, and he picked up immediately. As soon as she'd explained what they were looking at, he said he was on his way and disconnected. The older man sounded excited.

Her last call was to Wilson. "I'd like you and your assistants to give me a hand looking at something that might be of Locust origin. If you could tag one of the Marines guarding your lab, they'll get you to operations. This is an all-hands-on-deck sort of thing, and I'd appreciate it if you could arrive with all dispatch."

"We'll be there as quickly as possible," the woman said. "Can you give me an idea of what we're talking about?"

"We think we might have found a new class of Locust ship, but we only have a short time to make an assessment of it. The sooner we do, the better the chances we'll be able to recover it."

"We're leaving now."

Her husband grinned at her. "You certainly have a way of

getting everyone all excited."

Danek arrived first, but the professor was right on her heels, hobbling along with the aid of a cane. The old man could move pretty fast, considering his injuries.

"Let me see the data on this new ship," he demanded.

Tina set up the console she'd been using to show what they were looking at. The professor and Danek took seats and began discussing what they saw among themselves. That left Tina free to handle Wilson and her research assistants when they arrived a minute later.

She set up another console with the exact same data and gestured for the newcomers to take a look. David was at her side because Danek and the professor didn't need their assistance working the equipment, whereas Wilson and her people did.

"This is definitely a Locust vessel," Danek said. "There's enough information coming in from the fusion plant to rule out human manufacture."

"And it's completely and utterly different from anything we've seen before," the professor said with a grin.

"It looks like a cargo carrier to me," Wilson said. "My people and I have traveled on a lot of freighters over the years, and the way the vessel is laid out implies it's meant to carry a lot of cargo.

"Whether that's its actual purpose, it's got a lot of space for equipment and items that would be of unimaginable value in understanding our enemies."

"It looks lopsided," Danek said. "I think we're looking at the stern of a much larger ship. The front end is cut off unevenly, so it's not the original prow."

Tina looked at the data. She could see how rough the front was, but that didn't mean anything to her. She'd have to accept the other woman's expertise.

"So, if this ship was once larger, how much so?" Prescott asked.

Danek shrugged. "Hard to say. Somebody could've just shot off the tip, or it could have been several times longer than it is now. It's definitely wide enough to support a long hull.

"In any case, this ship had to come from wherever the Locusts came from. That means it has got a hyperdrive big enough to move a ship this large, or potentially much larger."

"Leaving aside the technological aspects," Wilson said, "the fact we're looking at a ship that's radically different from the robotic probes implies the possibility that this ship was once manned by sentient beings. They might have left something aboard that ship. Hell, there might still *be* some aboard it."

"How would this method of moving it with us work?" Tina asked Danek. "We'll have drones all over us by the time we reach that wreck. How delicate and time-consuming is the process going to be?"

Danek grimaced. "It'll take a lot of skill to make something like that happen, but it's possible. It will entail greater risk than just picking up a similar amount of mass and taking it with us. If something goes wrong, we may blow another fusion plant.

"I've got to crunch some numbers and talk with Derek Calvo. The maneuver I'm thinking of will require some serious flying, and I need to know if it's even possible. Tag me if there's anything new I need to know about."

And with that, Danek headed for the exit.

Tina let the academics continue discussing what they were looking at and stepped over next to her husband. "It sounds like we're going to be trying something dangerous, dear. I thought you told me this would be a pleasure cruise."

He smiled wryly. "When have I *ever* taken you on something as boring as a pleasure cruise? You'd be tearing holes in the bulkheads."

She laughed. "I knew there was a reason I loved you. Now, let's see about getting something to eat. I'm starving, and none of us are going anywhere until this is done. We might as well pull as much data out of the system as we can while we have the opportunity. It might prove invaluable later."

Tina considered the other data while David headed out to get the food. The lack of radio signals in this system was worrying. That meant no one on the surface of New Copenhagen was transmitting anything powerful enough to reach them, and that was ominous.

Taking everything off the air likely meant the Locusts had attacked the transmitters, which hadn't happened during the first invasion. What were they up to?

And then there was the cloud of drones headed their way. That was a lot of firepower, and if Danek's maneuver was as dangerous as she'd implied, they might not successfully make the jump.

If they didn't, they were about to get their asses shot off.

Tina hoped her friends were as good as she thought they were, or this would be the shortest war ever.

29

"I'M STILL NOT a big fan of your plan," Jack told Danek with a grimace as they talked at his command chair on the bridge. "We blew out one of our fusion plants the last time and completely lost power when the rest went down in a cascade failure. What if that happens again, but we don't make the jump? Being trapped in this system would be a really bad thing if we had no power."

"Sir, that ship is probably a trove of intelligence about the Locusts," she argued. "If we don't take the opportunity to snag it while we can, we won't get another chance. And, honestly, the damned thing is just sitting there *begging* us to take it with us."

"I understand that, but I have to consider all the possibilities here. Give me the most conservative assessment possible. What are our chances of being trapped here if things go badly?"

It was her turn to grimace. "I honestly don't think it's even possible, but conservatively, maybe ten percent. We'll be pulling the energy we need for the jump and executing it in one go. The fusion plants—if they're going to have any trouble at all—will almost certainly have it on the other side.

"You're right in that this is going to be risky, but not for the reasons you're thinking. We've got to position that ship directly behind us to pick it up. We've only got a small area of space to play with, and that calls for a maneuver no one in their right minds would try."

She sighed and began pacing. "To make this work, Derek will need to cut our fusion drives at the critical moment as we swing past that ship and have it at our backside. I'm not even sure that's possible, so all of this might be for nothing."

Jack felt himself frowning as he tried to figure out exactly how something like that would work. He'd been a helm officer for most of his career, and if he'd tried to do that with a cruiser, it would've been difficult. With a kilometer-long nickel-iron aster-oid? It sounded impossible.

Time to ask the expert.

"Mister Calvo, if you could join us for a moment?"

He waited for the helm officer to rise and noted that Alexey Golousenko rose to come with him. This would be a very amusing conversation if he got the reaction he expected from his old helm officer.

Once they were at his command chair, Jack laid out exactly what they would have to do to retrieve the alien wreck. As expected, Alexey's eyes almost bugged out.

"Is this a joke, sir? That's not even possible."

"If it's not possible, we're obviously not doing it, but if it's merely difficult, we're going to have to try. Derek?"

The young man frowned in concentration. "It's not going to be easy, but if we can tweak our approach vector enough, I *might* be able to use the computers to assist me in timing everything just the way we need it. At the speeds we're talking about, we're only going to have seconds to execute everything perfectly."

Now it was Derek's turn to pace while thinking. He was silent for ten seconds before he started speaking again. "We'd need to kill the fusion drives just after I made a lateral thrust to swing our stern to line up with the wreck. I've seen ground vehicles do something like that when they drift into places they're not supposed to be.

"This will be something very similar, and I'd have to execute the jump as part of the maneuver, which adds another level of complexity to the process."

"But it's possible?" Jack stressed. "If not, I won't risk this ship."

The young man nodded. "Possible, yes. Easy, no. This will be the most difficult thing I've ever tried to do. I'll need every bit of time I can get to make this happen, and when we engage the drones, it's going to complicate matters significantly. Everything will happen on the fly, and I'll need to keep adjusting to the situation as it exists at that moment.

"It's going to be the hardest thing I've ever attempted. I have to be honest and say that I think I've got a better chance of blowing it than succeeding."

The young man looked like he was chewing on a lemon as he said that. He obviously didn't want to admit there was a significant chance he wouldn't be able to do what they needed him to do.

"Being honest about the possibilities is a strength," Jack said. "I realize we're asking you to do something miraculous, but it's far better to understand just how low the chances of success are rather than thinking we've got this in the bag."

Derek nodded. "I'll do my best."

The young man looked over at Alexey with a regretful expression. "I'm afraid this isn't something Commander Golousenko can help me with. In fact, I'm going to have to ask that he not be at the console so I can focus completely on what I'm doing. Sorry, Commander."

The older helm officer held up both hands in a gesture of surrender. "I wouldn't want to be a distraction."

Derek smiled and nodded to them before heading back to his console.

"Doesn't he know this is impossible?" Alexey asked Jack in a low tone.

"When I was a boy, my mother told me one of the great benefits of having new blood in any endeavor was that they didn't know their limits," Jack said with a smile. "Not knowing something was impossible, they'd do things us older folk never even considered.

"Do I think this is going to work? I certainly hope so, but if we're going to have any chance at success, it's going to be because of people like Derek doing something incredible."

Alexey considered the young man working at his console. "He's frighteningly young, but he's got great skill when it comes to flying this ship. He told me his team played at the highest level of competition in Locust War Online, and I believe it. If anyone can make this work, it's him."

"Let's hope so. Now all we have to do is deal with all the drones coming our way. That's going to be more serious than anything we've fought to this point. We've also got to shield the wreck from their fire as much as possible."

"Shouldn't we turn around and engage them away from the wreck if that's our goal?"

Jack shook his head. "It wouldn't take them any effort at all to divert a portion of their attacking force to take out the wreck. As things sit, we'll probably engage them around the same time we get there. That allows us to take the wreck with us, though it's not guaranteed.

"If some of these drones have that new sprint mode, it's going to make things significantly more challenging. It also depends on how single-minded the damned things are. Are they programmed simply to attack us? Will they ignore the wreck because it's a known quantity? We just don't know."

Alexey nodded. "If you don't mind, I'll head to auxiliary control to keep an eye on exactly what's going on and try to learn something from Derek without being underfoot."

Once the helm officer had departed, Jack brought up the small tactical display on his command chair. They were roughly an hour and a half away from the wreck at the speed Derek had settled on. The computers calculated the drones would likely catch up to them shortly after that, but if any of them had sprint mode, they'd beat those odds.

There was a cloud of motherships following the drones, but they wouldn't get there in time to add anything to the fight unless things went badly wrong. They just didn't have the speed of the smaller craft.

Amanda was busy working with her tactical team, and he knew she'd do everything possible to mitigate the damage the drones could cause. That didn't mean there wouldn't be any, and he'd have to accept that the valuable wreck would likely sustain even more combat damage than it already had.

He hoped it would survive the experience because having it blown out from under them right at the last moment would suck.

Jack excused himself to get something to eat and used the head. Then he ordered the bridge crew to cycle off shift to do the same. Everyone was going to be fueled and ready for this fight when the moment came.

Derek made a run to the head but declined food. The boy could eat a damned survival bar if need be, but one couldn't ignore a full bladder.

At about twenty minutes short of the wreck, Amanda spoke up. "Status change. About one-third of the drones pursuing us have entered sprint mode. I estimate they'll have us in range just before we reach the wreck.

"My team and I have been going over various scenarios and planned for something like this. If they focus their attention on us, we should be able to eliminate them before they cause serious damage to the target. The trade-off is that we're going to take damage in return."

"We're also going to have to maneuver, which will delay our

arrival at the wreck by a little," Derek said. "It could also complicate our approach vector depending on their attack pattern. Even so, I think we'll still be able to carry out the primary mission before we jump. It just may complicate the timing and execution."

"Understood," Jack said as he leaned forward a bit. "This is it, people. Focus on the task at hand and don't worry about the side issues. We'll adjust as needed to make this work. When will you get active sensor data back from planetary orbit?"

When Derek didn't answer, Amanda tapped her screen and seemed to do some mental calculation. "We should start getting returns in about five or six minutes, sir. Based on how I see this fight and the approach to the wreck playing out, we may get about ten minutes' worth of data before we jump. We're recording everything, so we can focus on it later."

"Does it look like the drones are interested in the wreck?" he asked.

"Not at this point, sir," she said. "That's pretty damned short-sighted of them, considering how important it probably is. I expect that behavior to change when we get closer to it.

"We might even trigger a defense initiative built into them that forces them to defend the wreck from us. I'm not certain exactly how much more aggressive they can get, but we have to keep in mind that we don't understand what makes them tick."

"Other than firing their lasers at us, what could they do? Ram us?" he asked.

Then he blinked. "Of course they could. Amanda, work that into your calculations. It's entirely possible they'll run kamikaze attacks on us. If they do, that will cause significantly different forms of damage, and we need to have everyone ready. Make sure damage control is informed, and we need to have vacuum protocols in full effect."

"On it, sir."

They wouldn't suit up on the bridge, though they had a suit locker if they needed it. If the drones breached the bridge, the entire ship was compromised.

He leaned back in the command chair and considered the prospect. If the drones began suicide runs, their impacts could cause significantly greater damage in limited zones. When their fusion plants failed, there would be explosions, and if they happened at a vulnerable location, the effects could be drastic.

"Derek, protecting our fusion drives just became a lot more important," he said. "Adjust your plans to take that into account. Amanda, I assume we've got a lot of lasers that would normally protect our stern. Have they been a priority in the repair regimen?"

She turned and nodded. "Yes, sir. Out of our fifteen percent operational laser batteries, five percent of them ring the stern. After the pirates, I figured we'd want to emphasize protecting our most vulnerable area and asked Commander Danek to focus on them."

"Excellent thinking. Marines, seal the bridge hatch and put us on our own life support."

He was grateful Danek, and her people had been able to repair the bridge hatch. Being without it would've left them a lot more vulnerable to decompression.

Jack pressed a button on his armrest, and an alarm began sounding throughout the ship even as the all-hands channel opened. "General quarters, general quarters. This is not a drill. All hands to battle stations."

Jack watched the tactical display as the sprinting drones closed on them. None of them split off to go after the wreck, but he knew the odds of some of them shifting their attack to it were high. Harris would have that in mind and target any of them that tried to bypass *Hunter*.

His ship was both a target and a defender at this point. It complicated what they needed to do, but it should still be possible to pull this off if they were lucky.

The first group of drones caught up with them when they were still short of the wreck. Now that they were close, Jack could see a lot more detail about the derelict ship, and it was definitely like nothing he'd ever seen before.

And since the damage was obviously laser hits, not plasma, it hadn't been the Confederation Navy that had disabled the ship. *Hunter* was the only ship in service that used lasers.

He had absolutely no idea why the Locusts would do that to one of their own ships, and he needed to know. The answers might be critical to winning the war.

When the drones entered *Hunter*'s extreme range, Amanda began picking them off. Jack noticed her accuracy had improved since the last fight, and she seemed a lot steadier. Having been in a real slugfest had calmed the woman down.

Hell, she was a veteran now. They all were.

As he'd feared, a number of the drones bulled their way

through the fire and came at them hard. They used their lasers to blast at *Hunter* and then charged in to ram.

It was a damned good thing he'd mentally prepared himself for something like this because the explosions as the drones impacted *Hunter*'s hull were powerful enough to send tremors through the ship.

The engineering officer on the bridge started calling out damage reports where some of the access corridors leading to the surface had lost pressure, and there was radiation damage inside, including casualties.

They'd lost some laser clusters, and Jack was sure they'd also lost some of their personnel. There would be time to mourn their deaths later, but this fight was shaping up to be rougher than anything they'd dealt with so far.

On the positive side, the increased number of laser clusters—particularly at the stern—kept the drones mostly at bay. The fusion drives probably took some laser hits, but they were built for that.

None of the drones attempting to ram the ship's stern made it through, though some of the close calls blasted the fusion drives with radiation. That was problematic, but their thrust seemed unaffected. He hoped that remained true.

About a quarter of the attacking drones attempted to bypass *Hunter* and go after the wreck. They did manage to get within their own extreme laser range of the derelict and pepper it with more shots, but it was a big vessel and withstood the damage.

Amanda and her people focused a good portion of their lasers on the drones attempting to take out the wreck and blew them to pieces. All that was left now was seeing if they could escape their pursuers before they caught up to them.

"ETA to jump?" he asked.

"Ninety seconds," Derek said in an almost mechanical voice, his attention totally focused on what he was doing. "I've adjusted course for the best final approach. If we've got more drones incoming, you're going to have to keep them off us without maneuvering the ship, or I'm going to miss the damned thing."

"Amanda?"

"We're going to have drones in range at that point. We won't have to deal with any trying to ram us during the maneuver, but we may take some hits from their lasers."

"Understood. Execute the plan, people."

At this point, there was nothing more he could do. Jack's people knew what had to be done, and they'd do it. The only question was whether they'd successfully snag the derelict in the process or take critical damage before they jumped.

Amanda and her people took advantage of the prepro-grammed maneuvers that Derek had put into spinning the ship and opened fire on the approaching drones at *Hunter*'s extreme range. The drones couldn't return fire at that point, and they began dying.

That didn't keep them from reaching extreme range of their own, and their return fire began notching more damage on the derelict and *Hunter* herself. Jack kept half an eye on the damage control board but was primarily focused on the timer. They were under thirty seconds from jump, and the wreck was growing huge in front of them at an almost terrifying speed.

At the ten-second mark, one of the drones got lucky and disabled one of *Hunter*'s fusion drives, making the massive ship lurch. Jack could see Derek feverishly working his console, and he hoped the young man could compensate.

"Here we go," Derek said. "Lateral thrust at full in three... Two... One... Zero... Killing the fusion drives in Three Two... One... Sliding into place and... Jumping."

To Jack's relief, the lighting didn't even fluctuate. He saw from the damage control panel that all the fusion plants were still up and running. Apparently, Danek had been right.

"Did we get the wreck?" he asked.

Derek tapped on his console and then turned to face Jack with a grin. "We got it!"

A cheer went up from everyone on the bridge, and Jack was half inclined to join them. He didn't because it would've been out of character for a commanding officer with the nerves of steel, but inside, he was cheering.

"What have we got around us?" he asked instead. "What can we see?"

"We didn't come out where I'd planned to because of the last-minute maneuvering, but it's definitely the depot system," Derek said.

Then he leaned forward and frowned at his console. "I'm picking up radio signals, sir. Lots of them. It looks like human traffic."

"Go dark," Jack snapped. "Were our active sensors on when we jumped?"

Amanda shook her head. "No, sir. Standard procedure is to

kill active scanners before we jump. We came in dark, though it's possible someone could pick us up because of our fusion drives or the radiation leaking off of the hull from where the drones rammed us.

"Still, we're pretty far from the radio sources, so the imprecise arrival works to our advantage. We're at least nine hours away from the depot at full acceleration."

Full acceleration that they might not have because they'd lost a fusion drive. One more thing to check on.

Jack considered the situation and took a deep breath. "It looks like someone beat us here, or perhaps a bunch of refugees went through the quantum gate. If those are human transmissions, at least we're not dealing with Locusts.

"With the gate being inactive, what are the chances of the drones in New Copenhagen discovering it?"

Amanda shrugged. "I can't say, sir. The odds are low because it's in an unusual location, but it's not an impossible scenario now that we've stirred them up and led them partly in that direction."

They'd need to figure out a way to deal with that worry by either destroying the gate or booby-trapping it in some fashion. That was something he'd have to think about. For now, he needed to know exactly who was in this system and what they were up to.

This was an unexpected complication, and based on their track record thus far, it wasn't going to be a pleasant surprise. The best they could hope for was that these were refugees, but since the system was also where a lot of the drone and mothership debris was stored, he wouldn't be surprised if criminal elements were present.

Well, there was only one way to find out. They had to get there, which meant they needed to get the wreck moving without destroying it. Time to make more magic happen.

Or he could order someone else to make the magic happen and give them some valuable experience.

"Derek, turn your console over to your backup and head to engineering. Get me a status on the damaged fusion drive, work up a plan with someone there to safely move the wreck, and get an exploration team together to start assessing it. We need to know what we're dealing with."

The young man stood. "Moving it might be premature, sir. Way out here, it's safe from discovery. The fusion plant isn't shielded, but at low output, we're too far from the depot for it to be detected without dedicated and very keen sensor operators looking at this specific section of space.

"Since there aren't any other gates here, the odds of that are pretty slim."

"Good point, but I want you to look at the situation more closely before recommending any course of action. Don't go into things with an outcome already decided."

The young man nodded and opened the hatch. "Yes, sir. I'm on it."

Jack let him go and brought the ship back down to a normal operational status. It was time to see how bad they'd gotten hurt for their prize.

30

DEREK ARRIVED in engineering to find a scene of controlled chaos as the engineers tore one of the fusion drives apart at the compartment's rear. That would be the one that had taken a hit on final approach to the wreck, almost throwing his exquisitely planned maneuver into the trash.

It was a bloody miracle he'd managed to pull it off after that.

He knew better than to distract the chief engineer at a moment like this. She had her attention focused where it needed to be. Instead, he found the new assistant chief engineer, Lieutenant Commander Charlie Ferrero. He was keeping an eye on things but wasn't buried neck-deep in the work like Danek was.

The man raised an eyebrow as Derek approached. "We're a little busy right now, Lieutenant. What can I do for you?"

"I'm sure this is a bad time, but the commodore wants a status on the fusion drive. I figure he wanted to make sure

Commander Danek wasn't disturbed, so he sent me to get the word. What can you tell me?"

The man grimaced and looked back toward the work party. "The fusion drive shorted out the way it was supposed to, which protected the unit from exploding, but something on the interior caught fire. That's supposed to be impossible, but these drives were built two centuries ago, so they might have used materials that wouldn't pass muster these days.

"Commander Danek will have to give the commodore the final word about the drive once she's had a chance to look at everything, but it's probably something we can fix. There's going to be some fried equipment and damaged parts, but we should be able to make it happen with time and effort. Until then, we're down about eight percent of our allotted acceleration.

"Did we make it to the depot system?"

"It was touch and go, but we made it," Derek said. "We even brought the derelict Locust ship with us. That's the next thing I need to look over.

"When you have time, please put a bug in Commander Danek's ear about possibly needing to move the wreck deeper into the system. It's almost a third of *Hunter*'s size, and we don't want to damage it, so I'm sure that's going to be a challenge if it's even possible."

The man nodded, his eyes going unfocused as he likely began considering possible solutions to the problem. "I'll pass that on, and we'll get the commodore an update as soon as possible. Thanks for giving me a heads up about the wreck. Do you want some of our people to go with you?"

"I'd appreciate it. I'm not sure what we'll find over there, but having a few engineers along would help since we know it has an operational fusion plant. Thanks."

"No problem."

Ferrero called out to two men and a woman working at the fusion drive. That earned him a glower from Danek, but nothing else. The officer quickly told the engineers what they were doing and sent them for equipment and vacuum suits.

"Where should I send them?" he asked Derek.

"Small craft bay four. The Locusts researchers probably know more about the technology, so we'll leave from there."

"Will do. Good luck and be careful."

"Careful is my middle name."

"I think you need something a bit more intimidating," the officer said with a laugh. "I'll start a pool and see what the crew comes up with for you." And with that, he headed for the damaged fusion drive.

Derek hoped that was a joke. He hated nicknames.

Task one done, he headed for the secret research lab. He called the bridge while he walked and gave the commodore all the information he had and updated him on his plans.

Once he arrived at the lab, he found Wilson and her team going over something at one of the tables. There were cups of coffee and a small platter of what looked like baked goods with icing. The sight made his stomach rumble. He'd skipped eating because he hadn't wanted to chance anything screwing up his maneuver to pick up the derelict.

"Can I have one of those?" he asked as he walked up to them.

"You're the man of the hour, so you even get coffee," Wilson said. "That was your flying, wasn't it? Good work."

"I had something to do with it," he said with a smile as he poured himself some coffee and grabbed a gooey dessert. "We made the jump, and now we're ready to send an exploratory party over to the wreck.

"You and your people are our resident experts since the professor is still healing, and I figure taking him on an excursion into vacuum isn't the best idea. He can yell at me later."

"And yell at you he will," Wilson said with a chuckle. "Still, I suspect you've got the right of it, though. Once you finish fueling up, we can get everybody outfitted and take our cutter over to see what we've found."

Derek took a big bite of the pastry and found it to be excellent. He washed it down with some passible coffee. For researchers, these people knew how to eat.

"Get your gear," he said once he'd wolfed the pastry down, "but we're taking a Marine pinnace. There's too much risk of something happening, so I'm bringing along a few Marines to make sure we're ready for any eventuality. We'll also have a few engineers."

The older woman stared at him, frowning. "Absolutely nothing we've found thus far indicates the Locusts ever put anything dangerous into their spacecraft, other than the self-destruct devices on the hyperdrives, and even those are only a risk to the drive itself. What makes you think this ship will be any different?"

"This is unlike any Locust ship we've ever seen. Those other ships were obviously robotic in nature, but this one might have had living beings on it. I'm not willing to assume anything at this point, and for your safety, you shouldn't either."

Wilson thought about that and nodded. "I suppose you're right. In any case, you're the boss. Everyone, into your vacuum gear and gather up every bit of recording and scanning gear we've got. It's time to go explore a spooky Locust derelict."

Derek stepped out of the repair bay and over to the Marines guarding it. He didn't know either of them, but they looked like recruits.

"We're heading to a wrecked Locust vessel of unknown design, and I need a pinnace with a group of Marines in armored vacuum suits just in case there's trouble."

The young woman nodded. "I'll call it in, Lieutenant."

"Thank you. We'll also have some engineers going with us, so keep an eye out for them."

That accomplished, he headed for the small craft bay they'd been using since the beginning of this adventure. The suits there had all been inspected and certified, so he'd rather use one of them than take a chance with any of the suits here.

Eventually, they'd get around to certifying them all, but it hadn't been a high priority. With all the combat they were getting into, it might be best to make that happen sooner rather than later. He made a mental note to bring that up with someone.

He made it back and got fully suited up just in time to see an old-style Marine pinnace with a faded image of *Hunter*'s emblem on the stabilizers come ghosting through the small craft bay hatch and settle to the deck nearby. Its hatch opened, and Major Mac Turner stepped out, suited in a modern armored vacuum suit with his helmet tucked into the crook of his arm.

He grinned at Derek. "How do you like my ride?"

"It's nice, but I thought we had a few new ones. Why go old school?"

"We've got a few new models from the academy, but this one works well enough. We'll save the few modern units for emergencies. What are we expecting to see over on the Locust ship?"

"I haven't got the slightest idea, and that's the problem. We don't know what it's carrying, what purpose it was intended to fill, or how dangerous it's going to be. We literally know nothing about it other than it has an operational fusion plant."

"Well, that's not exactly helpful, but we'll be ready."

Wilson and the research assistants came out in their civilian model vacuum suits, lugging a lot of equipment. Their timing was good as the engineers arrived, also in their suits and carrying their gear.

Derek spoke briefly with the new people and briefed them on what was happening. Then he made his way into the pinnace as he seated his helmet into place.

The seats were configured to carry people in armored vacuum suits, so there was plenty of room. It was also set up to carry cargo at the rear as well.

A pinnace was significantly faster than a regular cutter, heavily armored, and armed in case it needed to fight something in space. In all, Derek was relatively certain this was overkill, but once again, they wouldn't know until they took a look at exactly what they were dealing with.

Everyone strapped themselves in, but he headed for the control area. They had very few people certified to fly the old-style small craft, so he wasn't surprised to find Richard Klein in the pilot's seat.

The older man—who wasn't in a suit—turned and grinned at him, gesturing to the copilot's seat. "Park it, kid. That was some good flying you did today. You ever run one of these?"

"Only in Locust War Online," Derek said as he strapped himself in.

"That's better than most. Take us out, and I'll keep an eye on you."

Derek was familiar with the controls, but flying a real ship was different from playing a simulation, particularly for small craft. He didn't allow himself to hesitate or second guess himself. If he did something wrong, Klein would let him know.

At first, there was a bit of a bobble, but he smoothed out the lift and headed for the hatch, triggering it to open as he approached. There was a screen in place to keep the atmosphere in, but the pinnace slid through it cleanly and exited the ship through the other hatch at the end of a short tunnel.

Once in space, Derek quickly oriented himself and headed for the derelict. It looked bigger than he'd expected. *Hunter* was an asteroid that had been mined out to create a ship, and it looked mostly natural.

The wreck was a third of *Hunter*'s size and entirely artificial. It just felt bigger than its actual size because living beings had made it.

Turner came into the control area and looked out the front port. "That's big. Do you have any particular point you'd care to board?"

"Going in through engineering might be best," Derek said. "That means we'll start off in an area with power, so at least we'll have lights and potentially gravity."

Turner raised an eyebrow. "That might not be the best idea if they have anything to defend the area, such as an automated weapons system and such. Like you said, this is a different kind of ship, and we don't know what to expect.

"Still, I can't say you're wrong because any part of the ship could be set up as a trap. When we lock onto the hull, I'll send my people in first. We'll make sure everything is clear before we have you join us."

The Marine force recon officer returned to the personnel compartment.

Derek flew the pinnace around the wreck and whistled at the damage. The Locusts had shot it almost to pieces. There was no way they'd be able to move it without crushing it. The ship was toast.

Every section had been shot with lasers, and wide gashes in the hull were everywhere. At best, there wouldn't be anything more than a few scattered compartments with pressure. The odds of finding survivors were almost nil.

He eventually settled on a large cut across the engineering

section. It would provide access without forcing their way through an airlock.

The approach was ticklish only because he took things slow and steady. He wanted to latch on with the magnetic grapnels on the first try and not jar anyone in the back. Thankfully, many long hours of doing all things helm-related in Locust War Online gave him simulated experience, and he pulled it off.

Once they were down and locked into place, Klein punched him lightly on the shoulder. "Well done, kid! I'd say we have another pilot to call on in a pinch, though I know you're too busy for that. We don't have any kind of formal certification on this old gear, but consider yourself one of us."

"I'm happy to be of service," he said as he unstrapped himself. "This was fun. Now it's time to explore the spooky alien ship, so I'll let you keep an eye on the pinnace while we see what's over there. Thanks for letting me fly."

The Marines were gathered at the airlock when he stepped into the personnel compartment and sealed the hatch to the control area. They bled off the atmosphere, opened both airlock doors, and made their way onto the alien ship's hull.

The sharp, unblinking stars all around them made the scene even stranger than it might have otherwise been. He'd never been on a spacewalk before either.

Turner waved to get his attention and then flashed a series of numbers using his fingers. That would be the channel they'd be using.

He set his comm to the channel. "Comm check."

"Loud and clear," Turner said. "I'll leave some Marines with you while we go in and make sure the coast is clear."

And with that, the Marines examined the gash in the hull and made their way into the ship, careful not to risk their suits on the edges.

Derek expected it to take a while, but a Marine returned in less than ten minutes. It took a little bit of careful maneuvering, but he was able to make his way into an engineering space that was as large as the one aboard *Hunter*.

The overhead lights were dimmer and somewhat skewed more to the violet spectrum, but most everything was clean and tidy, except where the lasers had burned through and melted things.

The equipment around them was similar to what he'd seen in their own engineering compartment, but it was, of course, of alien design. This was definitely not a human ship.

Several of the Marines were off to one side of the massive compartment examining something, and Turner gestured for him to come over. Thankfully, the alien ship had artificial gravity similar to what was used aboard *Hunter*—though it felt somewhat lighter—so walking over was an easy task.

He looked between the Marines and saw a humanoid lying on the deck. *Definitely* not human. It was wearing what seemed to be utility coveralls and, by all the evidence, had died due to exposure to vacuum.

Derek had seen dead people—humans—before, but he still found the sight sickening. Even if this thing had been responsible for the invasion, he could regret the manner in which it had passed. The fact he'd been responsible for killing a lot of pirates in the same way still weighed on him.

"It looks like this guy—if it really is a male—died when the Locusts attacked the ship," Turner said. "Or, if these are the people that created the Locusts, maybe they're the Locusts. We're probably going to have to come up with some new terminology."

If the sight of the body disturbed the Marine force recon officer, it didn't show.

Wilson and her team arrived at that moment. "Is that one of them," she asked in a hushed tone. "I have to admit, I never expected to see any of the creators. It doesn't look like its death was pretty, but I suppose no death is."

"We'll need to take it back with us when we leave," Derek said, surprised at how even his voice sounded. "The medical people will have to do an autopsy if that's the right term. We need to know more about them."

"We'll get it bagged up," Turner said. "There are other bodies in here, so we'll take them all."

The engineers headed deeper into the compartment, with a handful of Marines watching over them. They'd focus on examining things they were familiar with—and take readings of the things they weren't—so he'd leave them to it.

Wilson turned toward a large hatch on the bulkhead. "We'll need to look into the rest of the ship and see what's there. This vessel was moving something, and if it had living beings aboard, there might be survivors.

"Just think of how valuable it would be to get our hands on living creators. There are so many things they could tell us."

"If they're willing to talk to us at all, and we could understand what they were saying," Derek agreed. "Major, do you have any emergency airlocks? If we're looking at possible survivors—however unlikely that seems—we don't want to inadvertently blow out the pressure on the other side and risk killing them."

The man nodded. "I've already got some of my people getting one right now. You're the officer in command of this mission, but I recommend we only take a quick look around, gather what intelligence we can, and then head back to *Hunter* to go over everything in detail. We'll have plenty of time to sort this out without rushing."

"So long as we can let the engineers and researchers scan as much as possible, I have no objection."

While he waited for the emergency airlock, Derek squatted beside the body and closely examined it. It had two arms and two legs, but the hands had thumb-like appendages on either side of the palm and three fingers between them. The digits also had an additional knuckle when compared to a human's and were longer.

Its head sat at the end of a long, slender neck, but it was radically different from a human's. The jaw at the bottom of the face opened vertically rather than horizontally, which was creepy looking, and there was a slit in the skin above the mouth that might have something to do with its breathing.

Higher up, two bulbous eyes had ruptured in the vacuum. Derek couldn't tell anything about them, other than they were significantly larger than a human's. The head was covered in what looked like a mixture of gray, brown, and white fur that was patterned almost like an animal pelt.

The being had a tool belt around its waist that held all kinds of interesting looking instruments and tools he suspected would be of use in an engineering setting. The professor would have a field day going over everything.

While he'd been examining the being, the Marines had returned and begun setting up the emergency airlock. The process went quickly, and once they were done, a pair of Marines entered the transparent bubble.

They examined the hatch and attempted to manipulate its controls. It took a couple of tries to figure out exactly how the mechanism worked, but the hatch eventually rolled aside.

It was thick and looked even more impenetrable than the one the pirates had blown apart on *Hunter*'s bridge. There was no gush of air, so the other side had already been in vacuum.

Derek opened the emergency airlock, stepped inside, and walked to the large hatch. To his surprise, there wasn't a corridor on the other side. Instead, it opened onto a spidery catwalk spanning a colossal chamber.

There were small open-sided elevators that went from one level to another, but everything inside the tremendous compartment was visible from where he stood. The vast area was filled with large pods stacked one upon another. Massive cables and conduits went from one to another, trailing across the open spaces like old-style powerlines.

This ship hadn't been prepared for a fight. This kind of

construction was the sort of thing that led to a disaster in combat, which had obviously happened here.

He turned toward Turner. "I want to take a closer look, so I'll need a tether in case I come off the walkway."

The Marine promptly produced a tether and found a spot to tie it to the bulkhead. The hole he'd found was too large for the clip, but the Marine was able to run the line through and manually tie it into a sturdy knot.

Once Derek had the line attached to his belt, he slowly walked out onto the catwalk. As flimsy as it looked, it supported his weight without any give. A little more confident, he made his way to the nearest pod and looked inside through a clear port.

A soft green glow came from inside the machine, and an alien much like the dead one lay unmoving on a red couch. Its eyes were closed, and Derek wagered it was in some kind of suspended animation. Unlike the dead one, this being seemed unclothed, though he could only see it from the chest up.

He turned and looked out over the large chamber and saw that the vast majority of the pods didn't have any interior illumination. Only a handful at the very back of the compartment seemed to still have power.

Or, he supposed, the rest could be empty. There was only one way to find out.

The nearest one without any illumination was a dozen meters away, so he walked to it and looked inside. The interior was exactly like the previous one, except there was no light, and the alien inside was obviously dead.

This one had what certainly looked like breasts, so it was

likely female, though he hesitated at assigning gender to an unknown alien species. That was for the doctors to determine.

Its eyes were wide open with what he'd have described as a look of terror. The being's limbs were contorted with what he imagined had been a final struggle to get out of the pod. Not that coming out into a vacuum would've saved its life.

Considering that these beings were likely responsible for creating the Locusts that had devastated the Confederation twice now, he found it difficult to feel bad for its end. Karma could be a stone-cold bitch.

Satisfied that he'd seen enough and ready to let the researchers do whatever they needed to do, he walked back to engineering.

Turner was waiting. "What did you see?"

"A lot of dead aliens, and a few living ones, though they seem to be in suspended animation. I suppose the rest of the pods could have some empties, but my guess is that this ship is a giant tomb.

"It looks like we might end up with some living Locusts to ask pointed questions to if we can figure out how to wake them, so that's going to fall to the researchers and the engineers."

He looked over at Wilson. "Get your people recording everything. We'll work for a few hours and then head back to *Hunter* and brief the commodore. Let's make the most of our time, shall we?"

31

JACK EXAMINED the image of the alien displayed on the wall monitor in his briefing room. Humanity had often wondered what the creators of the Locusts might look like, and now they had an answer. Still, he wasn't certain what that gained them.

He turned his attention to Professor Prescott, Doctor Wilson, India, Derek, Sara, and his mother. They were also expecting Kelly Danek, but she was running late.

He decided not to wait. They could talk about the biology of what they'd discovered first and come back around to the engineering aspects of the ship that we recovered.

"How many of these things are over there?" he asked Derek.

"Based on the one chamber we saw and the fact that there are six more just like it, I think the low hundreds of thousands," the young man said with a grimace. "We don't have to worry about the vast majority of them because other than just a few pods at the very back of the ship, all the rest lost power. Each of those pods seemed to have been occupied, and the beings inside them are now dead.

"All told, we've got a dozen functional pods with living beings still inside them. We've got three additional pods that seem to be functional, but they must've been punctured by debris because the occupant is dead."

"I have to note there are some differences in the pods we found at the rear of that last compartment," Wilson said. "They have a strip of green around the viewports whereas the vast majority have a strip of orange. There were only a few hundred with the green striping—including all the survivors—so the difference must mean something fairly important."

"I'd have been happy to look around to see if I could find anything unusual," Prescott said. "That was if *someone* had bothered to inform me you were going in the first place."

He shot a glare at Derek with the last sentence. The young officer flushed a little but didn't say anything.

"I happen to agree with Derek's judgment in this matter," Jack said. "You're still recovering, so it makes sense to be careful with you. Looking at the video they recorded, is there anything that stands out?"

"It's a colony ship," India said, sipping some of her coffee. "That much is obvious. Why did the Locusts feel it necessary to bring their civilization here to conquer us?

"They had to go past any number of systems before they got to us. Surely some of those worlds would've been suitable for their needs. Why come all the way to the Confederation to start a war? Hell, to start *two* wars."

"That's the question, isn't it?" Jack mused. "Mom, have you discovered anything about the alien since you started looking into its biology?"

"We've discovered a lot of things," she said with a smile. "Unfortunately, we're not sure what's important at this point, and we've only scratched the surface. This is an entirely new species, and we have to build a knowledge base from scratch. We know nothing about their dietary needs, atmospheric requirements, or literally anything else about them.

"One of the problems with doing that workup is that it's not going to happen quickly. We'll be able to determine some things about them, but I'm not sure how useful that will be in the short run. What are you hoping we can tell you? I'm certainly willing to focus on the things you think are critical."

Jack shrugged. "My concerns deal with fighting the war. I need to know why they chose to invade us. I'm not sure their biology is going to tell us anything, but if we're ever going to wake up the living ones for us to question, that's going to require understanding how to feed them and making sure their physical needs are met."

"I should be able to examine the equipment in the engineering space and determine what the atmospheric mixture was supposed to be," Prescott said. "The lighting is functional, so I should be able to recreate an environment that's at least moderately comfortable to them. Figuring out the appropriate temperature might be a little dicier, but we'll figure something out.

"That's not going to be a quick process either. First of all, the surviving pods are in vacuum. We have no idea if there is even a safe method to relocate them, much less the procedure to bring them out of suspended animation. Attempting to do so is going to be risky."

The hatch slid open, and Kelly Danek strode in. "Sorry I'm late. I was going over the information my team sent from the wreck. What did I miss?"

Jack gestured toward the carafe of coffee and launched into a brief summary of what they'd just been talking about while she poured herself a cup.

The engineer took an approving sip of her coffee and nodded as she sat. "Everything you've just said is correct, but I believe we can at least get around one of those problems. The pods have a battery backup built into them. To test whether or not it would last long enough to relocate the pod from the wreck to *Hunter*, I had them disconnect one of the damaged ones that still had power and move it over to our engineering department for study.

"Everything was decontaminated, so don't worry. It's still going, so I believe it's probably safe to relocate any of the functional pods once we get some power cables of our own rigged up to host them in an out-of-the-way compartment."

"There is a danger of contamination once we bring them out," his mother confirmed. "That said, it shouldn't be considered a high risk. Humanity has been to many worlds, and the ability for alien pathogens to infect us is extremely low. We're not the target audience, if you will.

"We'll still want to take all reasonable precautions, but let's not blow the risk out of proportion. The chances of a cross-species plague taking us down is infinitesimal."

"We're not going to rush this," Jack said. "We've only got a few opportunities to get this right, and any one of those individuals could be critical to winning this war. Since I doubt this was the only colony ship to arrive in the cluster, we need to know what they can tell us soon.

"I suppose one of the most important things we need to figure out is why their machines turned on them. Something obviously went very wrong, and while my sympathy for their plight is limited, I want to know why the homicidal machines are behaving in the manner they are."

"I can't tell you about their motivations, sir," Danek said, "but we found some interesting things in their engineering section. The first was a full-blown schematic of the original vessel.

"It looks like that ship was originally *Hunter*'s size. Which makes the second thing we discovered all the more intriguing. It has a *massive* hyperdrive. It doesn't look to be damaged or booby-trapped either. I guess they thought their machines would protect them. Oops."

That set the scientists to chattering amongst themselves. Jack wasn't so enthused.

"That's interesting but not relevant to us in more than an academic way," he finally said, interrupting their conversation. "The more pressing matter from an engineering standpoint is the status of our damaged fusion drive."

"Partially repaired," Danek said, her expression falling somewhat. "We'll be able to get it back up to a reliable eighty percent thrust, but I wouldn't want to push it beyond that. I'd like to replace some of the parts, but we don't have spares. We're going to have to get to the depot for that.

"On the positive side, it's only one out of twelve drives. It shouldn't negate more than a few percent of our speed, even with the imbalance. If I might ask, Commodore, what's our plan going forward? When will I have an opportunity to start rummaging around the depot looking for parts?"

"That depends on who's in this system and what they're doing," he said with a sigh. "We've detected significant radio traffic, and it's not just coming from the depot. These folks have been here for quite some time, and we have absolutely no idea who they are or what their endgame is. Until we know more, I'm going to be cautious."

He used his controller and took the image of the dead alien off the monitor. He put up a map of the system as they knew it in its place.

"The depot is about three and half hours away from the quantum gate leading to New Copenhagen. We're about nine hours away from the depot but only seven hours away from the gate.

"When we wrap up with our initial exploration of the derelict, we'll head for the gate. The last thing we can afford is to have the Locusts break into this system. It seems this particular pair of gates wasn't booby-trapped by the Confederation, so we're going to take care of it ourselves."

India frowned and leaned forward to examine the map. "How exactly are we going to do that? I wouldn't think this ship had a lot of explosives aboard. And, even if we did booby-trap the gate, it would have to be something automatic because we couldn't wait to detect them coming in from hours away. What do you have in mind, Jack?"

"Honestly? I think the best idea is simply to destroy it. We can't afford to take chances."

He checked his chronometer. "We need to wrap up the initial inspection of that ship and collect anything we want to take with us. My skin is crawling because we can't control access to this system."

"What do you consider critical for us to recover from the ship?" Danek asked. "All the functional pods? I can have an area set aside for them with appropriate power feeds—based on what the professor tells us we need—in about an hour. It might take a few hours to relocate them all, though.

"If we want to take the thing's hyperdrive, that'll take significantly longer to disconnect and disassemble because we don't know anything about it. We'll have to proceed slowly and take care not to break anything. It would be like an archaeological dig where we're disassembling something and noting where it came from so we can put it back together later."

Jack shrugged. "Then we'll leave it here. Once we have the pods relocated and collect any computers on board, we'll shut the fusion plant down and leave the wreck here. As long as no one knows it's here, it should be safe enough. We can come back at our leisure to finish taking everything apart."

Danek wasn't happy to hear that, but she obviously recognized what the priorities were.

Jack looked over at his mother. "We'll need to recover some bodies for you and your people to examine. I don't want us to get hung up on something that might be an individual variation among the dead, so I'll have people recover as many bodies as you think you'll need."

She grimaced. "Autopsies were never my favorite thing, but I suppose you're right. We'll need at least a few dozen specimens, preferably spread out among the genders. The one you brought over was male—at least that's the closest I can match it to one of our genders—so there must be a female of the species.

"There may be additional genders, but we're not going to find out unless we look at a wide selection. Better too many than too few."

He nodded. "Derek, see to it. Klein said you did a fine job flying the pinnace, so take a cargo shuttle out and have people trained in vacuum operations recover fifty bodies. Spread out the search to all of the compartments and find females and males in roughly equivalent numbers. If you spot something that looks like it might be a different gender, bring a similar number of them along."

It was a very distasteful task, but the young officer only nodded. "Like I told Mister Klein, I've done plenty of simulated flying, but I haven't actually taken one out in person before today. I'll be careful, but I wanted you to know."

"You're one of the very few helm officers I trust flying my battleship, and we have very few pilots skilled in the old equipment. I trust your judgment. If you feel like you don't know something, stop and call Klein. You need the experience of operating solo, and this seems like it should be safe enough."

Sara, who had been quiet until then, smiled a little. "As my people are underutilized right about now, we'll act as a clearinghouse for the information. You keep your eye on the ball, Jack. We'll make sure the rest goes smoothly."

"That'll help a lot. Thanks."

Jack stood. "Now, if you'll excuse me, I think I need to talk to the Chens and see what they've been able to determine about our new friends before we come calling."

32

TINA SAT at one of the consoles in the operations center and listened on the headset she'd had someone dig up for her. She was monitoring someone in the system giving an update on their course and speed. To whom, she had no idea. The woman sounded bored, and her word choice had a very casual air.

It definitely didn't sound like someone in the Navy. Based on where the transmission was coming from, this person's flight originated in the outermost of two asteroid belts, and they were headed toward the depot. Considering her origin point, odds were she was coming from a mining operation or refinery.

According to Jack's data, there were no habitable planets in the system. That was probably one of the reasons the Navy had chosen it. It didn't even have an official name, just a catalog number.

The depot orbited a relatively cold gas giant. She supposed

the other mothballed battleships would be in orbit around the gas giant as well. It was certainly large enough to have them strung out in a single orbital plane.

Tina switched to a different channel and listened to someone nearer to the depot. This time it was a man, and he seemed to be reading a grocery list. Or at least he was ordering foodstuffs from somewhere. Not like a personal order, but enough to supply a large group of people for quite a while.

She slowly created a map of the system on her console based on the origin points of the transmissions. It looked as if some of the battleships might have squatters.

That definitely wouldn't please Jack, but with as many people as she'd already heard moving around the system, this place hadn't been a secret for a while. At least not to the people occupying it.

She wondered why the Navy hadn't sent anyone to check on things. This was embarrassing. A secret naval facility taken over by squatters? Heads should roll. If they hadn't already.

"I think I've put together something based on the sensor data we got from New Copenhagen," her husband said. "Take a look at this."

She walked over to his console and looked down at what he'd put together. There were a lot of ships in orbit, but most of them were gathered at two locations and seemed to be constructing something.

"What are they building?" she asked as her brows furrowed. "Space stations?"

"Space elevators, I think."

She tilted her head to the side a little and stared at the images he'd put together. She didn't know much about space elevators since no one had ever built one because the materials needed were still out of reach.

Theoretically, there would be a line going down to the planet and a counterweight going beyond the station to balance everything out. Those would be large construction projects.

"Why build something like that?" she asked. "This is a spacefaring society, so they could just go down in small craft like we do."

"Just because we do it doesn't mean it's necessarily what an alien race defaults to," he countered. "And just because it's what we do doesn't mean it wouldn't be better to use space elevators if we could. Once one was constructed, the energy expenditures would be significantly lower, and one could move quite a bit more cargo.

"In the end, we have to remember these are aliens. They do what they do, and it may not make sense to us. We can guess why they do something, but we don't have enough information to be sure."

"Did you detect any other ships like the one we found?"

He shook his head. "I saw what looked like a few larger ships, but nothing in the same category as the wreck. Not even close.

"What about you? What's going on in this system?"

"A lot. I'm detecting transmission sources across the system, including the outer asteroid belt. I'm also picking enough transmissions around the gas giant that I suspect several of the battleships and the depot have been occupied. I even heard somebody ordering up a bunch of food, so the squatters are numerically significant."

David grunted. "That's going to make Jack happy."

"What's going to make me happy?" the man said as he walked into the compartment. "If you've got good news, I'd love to hear it."

Her husband turned in his seat to face Jack. "That was more the nature of sarcasm. I'll let my wife fill you in."

She gave Jack the rundown of what she'd discovered thus far and watched her friend's expression sour. By the time she'd finished, he was pacing.

"Well, that's an unwelcome complication," he grumbled. "How are we supposed to rearm this ship and get everything repaired when we're dealing with squatters? And you know these people are going to be pirates or smugglers. Probably both. Not the kind of people willing to work with us."

"You're going to have to improvise. Whoever these people are, you can't just wish them away. You've got to deal with them."

Jack threw his hands up. "I need facts to deal with them. How do we get them?"

She smiled. "You won't like my solution. We've got to send someone in for a closer look. Based on the number of small craft moving around out there, an extra cutter isn't going to make any difference. It's not like they're expecting someone to just sneak into a closed system."

"No," Jack said. "That's too dangerous."

"While there may be some danger involved, it's much more dangerous for you to take this ship in fat, dumb, and happy. They might have been here long enough to get some of the weapon systems operational. What if they have missiles and you don't? What if they have a lot more lasers than you do?

"No, it's far too dangerous to take the only functional warship we have into a situation where we have no data whatsoever. That's what scouts are for. And spies."

Jack looked as if he'd bitten into a lemon. "Out of all the complications I planned for, this wasn't on my sensors. It's a secret system. How did they even *find* it? Do you have any estimates on how long they've been here?"

"A significant amount of time," she said. "They've set up a mining or refining facility in the outer asteroid belt. That doesn't happen overnight. With as many people as were likely looking at and as casual as they're sounding, I'd wager they've been here for years.

"The one thing I will bet on is that they're not pirates. I've been listening to a lot of conversations—none of which were encrypted—and they just don't sound like pirates. These people are too relaxed. They've known safety and security for a long time, and with pirates, you're always waiting for someone to stick a knife in your back. This doesn't feel like that."

"I'm sorry to rain on your parade, dear, but that's an educated guess," David said. "You're reading what you want to hear into the situation. These *could* be pirates, and they've just worked together so long they've built this kind of rapport with one another.

"That orbit could be full of pirate vessels. The only way to be sure is to take a closer look, and that's going to be a risky proposition."

"What would you do instead?" she shot back.

"The same thing you're suggesting, only I wouldn't send my wife. If this is just an information-gathering expedition, there's no reason for you to be there. They can forward everything to us via tight beam.

"You want to go because you want to get involved. What's your plan? To slip into the stream of ships going from place to place and maybe even board the depot? That's it, isn't it?"

She smiled at him. "You know me so well. I'm relatively confident I can blend in and get the information we need.

"I know the two of you feel like this is utterly crazy, but it's what I'm trained to do. I'm a covert agent, and I have the knowledge and skills to slide into places I'm not supposed to be and act as if I belong there."

That set Jack to walking again. "I don't like it, but I can see the logic of what you're saying. Have you got any idea what kind of small craft they're running? Are they using scavenged small craft from the battleships, or are they modern? You're not going to be able to blend in if you don't know what to look for."

"I'm hoping we'll eventually pick up a video signal that will give us an idea. At worst, I'll take a modern cutter and an old one, and we'll go in slowly until we can determine which one is appropriate.

"These people aren't worried about the traffic that's already in the system, Jack. Their idea of traffic control is significantly more minimalist than most places. They're not going to notice me."

"You *assume* they're not going to notice you, but they might," Jack countered. "What will you do if they catch you?"

She smiled at the Navy officer. "Then I'll negotiate. I'm not their enemy. I'm just trying to find out who we're dealing with. If it turns out to be someone reasonable, I'll do what's needed to make introductions."

Jack sighed but eventually nodded. "I can't argue with your logic, but I want you to take some of Turner's people with you. They can use concealed weapons and provide some level of protection for you."

"That works if we're dealing with a society that respects that type of force projection. What if this is something more benign? I might need someone along that doesn't raise other people's suspicions. I'm not going to argue about taking Turner's people, but I think it might be prudent if I have someone that looks a bit more innocent.

"Why don't I have Derek fly the old-style cutter? Once we get close enough, we may have to leave it parked away from everyone else and go in with the modern one, but his young face will certainly lessen people's suspicions if this isn't a criminal organization."

"I've already got him doing something, but I suppose I can put Klein on the shuttle. I want you to wait at least an hour and see if you can narrow down what kind of small craft you'll need to take. If you can figure it out in advance, that reduces the potential complications."

She nodded and looked over at her husband. "Do you have any objections beyond the obvious ones?"

He shook his head. "How can I argue with the woman I love being who she is? This is what you do, and you're very good at it. Just be careful."

"Oh, I'm *always* careful."

Both men laughed a bit derisively as Jack headed for the hatch.

She harrumphed, but she also grinned. How well they knew her.

Well, this was going to be fun. She wondered who she'd find when she got to the depot. Pirates, smugglers, or something completely unexpected?

Whoever it was, she'd need to fit in and get the information they needed to survive. The Confederation—even humanity itself—was depending on them.

33

UNABLE TO RESIST TAKING a look for himself, Jack took a pinnace over to the alien wreck. Since he knew they'd also appreciate a look at what they were dealing with, he brought Sara and India along.

They weren't going alone, of course. There was no way Turner would countenance the senior officers being unescorted on an alien vessel. They had a squad of Marines in armored vacuum suits along to make sure they could be hustled out if there was any danger.

Based on everything he'd heard about the wreck and its condition, Jack didn't find that outcome likely, but professional paranoia had its time and place, and protecting one's bosses in a potential combat zone certainly qualified.

They landed on the hull near a massive gash at the ship's stern. Unless he was mistaken, that was where Derek and his people had made their entry into engineering. There were several small craft near it and people constantly going in and out.

Those going in were carrying tools and equipment, and those coming out brought alien gear for study. A cargo shuttle floated in the void nearby, and it was the recipient of all of the recovered Locust equipment and artifacts.

Everything would be taken back to *Hunter* for study. Wilson and her people were helping guide the engineering team to what might be useful, so it was possible he'd run into them during their tour.

Back aboard *Hunter*, the professor was expanding his laboratory while simultaneously giving directions about expanding the secret one down in small craft bay four. They'd have to set up Marines at all access points, and its existence would become common knowledge—if it wasn't already—that they were examining items recovered from the wreck.

If this system hadn't already been occupied, they'd have nudged the wreck closer to the depot and examined everything there. Since that wasn't an option, they'd just have to make do.

Tina Chen, Derek Calvo, and a pair of people from Turner's Marine force recon group had departed for the depot half an hour ago. He was worried about them but had to trust in the woman's skills. If anyone could sort out what was going on without getting caught, it was her.

She'd finally gotten confirmation—based on hearing someone complain about how their old-style cutter was constantly breaking down—that there were old-style small craft in use, so his people were in one of *Hunter*'s old cutters.

They'd picked one with extremely faded exterior paint, and the mechanics had done everything they could to make it fade even further without being obvious about it. Still, if someone looked, they'd see *Hunter's* emblem on the tail, so he hoped she was as good at slipping into places she wasn't supposed to be as she'd advertised.

In any case, he had to focus on his own tasks because he couldn't affect the outcome of her mission. She'd do what was needed, and so would he.

Once the pinnace had grappled to the hull, everyone verified their vacuum suits were good and they made their way into the alien ship. Someone had sprayed something along the edges of the hull breach to reduce the chances of anyone cutting their suits, but they were still careful.

As they'd seen in the images, the interior of engineering was spacious, though it was oddly lit in an almost violet shade. The chamber was in vacuum, so the shadows were razor-sharp and deep black.

The only thing missing were the bodies they'd found there. Those had been extracted and taken to *Hunter* for examination. They wouldn't be able to do anything with the rest of the dead aboard this ship, but the process of extracting the operational suspended animation pods was almost done.

On the whole, everything was going well, and he hoped that trend continued.

"It certainly looks odd," Sara said. "After hearing and seeing so much about the Locusts over the last month, it's difficult to imagine living beings associated with them. Do you think we're ever going to understand why they did what they did?"

India gestured toward the engineering team examining what looked like a computer. "Even if we can't wake the survivors, as soon as we shut down the fusion plant, we'll be able to pull that computer. I'd wager it's got some details that'll help us understand why all of this is going on.

"From what I understand, the professor cracked the method of accessing the data, even though we don't understand the formatting for a lot of it. With Wilson and her people's assistance, we might be able to make more progress. It would be nice to understand what the hell is going on."

Jack spotted Danek walking around the fusion plant in question with some of her people, so he changed course and headed toward them. She acknowledged his presence with a slight wave while talking to her people.

When she was done, she turned toward him. "You must be desperate for an update if you're tracking me down. Either that or you're bored."

"I'm definitely not bored," he said with a chuckle. "I want to get moving, and to do that, we've got to get the computer out of here. That means we've got to extract the last of the functional pods and shut this fusion plant down.

"We're taking a look around while this place still has lights and gravity, but we need to get this wrapped up ASAP."

"I hear you, sir," the woman said. "Everything is proceeding as smoothly as I could ask for. Word is they'll have the last pods extracted in the next thirty minutes. Once they're done, I believe I know enough to safely initiate a shutdown.

"I'll send most of my people back to *Hunter* when we do that, but I doubt anything I can do to this plant will cause it to blow up. It has to have safety systems of its own that will shut it down if I do something wrong, which will have roughly the same effect as what I was looking to accomplish."

"We could still do without any drama," Jack said. "Let's be as safe as we can. What about removing the computer?"

"We've located two primary computer nodes. The one back here almost certainly controls the hyperdrive and other systems in engineering. That's going to have a treasure trove of operational data if it's not encrypted.

"The second is almost at the front of the ship as it is now, which means it was more toward the back third of the original ship's length. There may have been other nodes when this vessel was whole, but it's the only one we could locate. It seems to be a major unit, so it may have been the primary computer system. In any case, both of them seem to be intact."

"Is extracting them going to be a problem?" India asked.

"No. The professor has done a lot of work with Locust computers. While these are somewhat different—and significantly larger—they share a lot of things with those found on the motherships, minus the equipment meant to lobotomize them.

"Once the power is down, disconnecting the equipment and getting it out of here will be a straightforward process. I estimate that's going to take a minimum of two hours.

"I understand you want to get out of here, but there are limits to how fast I can make things happen. I'm sorry if that's more of a delay than you're looking for, but if we cut corners, we're potentially damaging irreplaceable equipment."

That wasn't what Jack wanted to hear, but he couldn't argue with what she was saying. Everything about the ship was unique, and it might hold the clues they needed to fight the Locusts more effectively.

"Don't cut corners," Jack said with a sigh. "Once you've extracted the last of the operational pods, I'll start *Hunter* toward the gate. You'll have plenty of small craft here to catch up with us once you've extracted the computers, but I'm not comfortable leaving the gate outside our control any longer than we have to.

"I'm sorry if that feels like we're abandoning you."

"I can work with that, sir. Now, if you'll excuse me, I'll get back to figuring out what I need to do with this fusion plant, and you can take a look around. You might be able to see them extracting the remaining pods if you hurry."

Jack let Danek get back to what she was doing and led India and Sara toward the large hatch to the bay forward of engineering. He stepped out onto the narrow catwalk and was amazed at how solid it felt. These people knew how to build things.

There was a gap in the pods directly around them where some had already been removed. People were working on disconnecting the last of the functional ones and moving them using straps and antigravity lifters.

Even as they watched, another pod began the trek out of the ship through a massive cut at the forward end of the compartment. Based on what he could see, there were only four left to move, and they were being worked on.

It looked as if the work crew might beat Danek's estimate. That meant he should get back to *Hunter*, but he still stood watching them while he thought.

Why had these people come all this way to attack the Confederation? Were they fleeing a natural disaster? Were they simply the kind of people that had to invade others and take what didn't belong to them? Something else that was so incomprehensible he'd think them insane?

He was looking forward to waking one of these beings so he could ask a few pointed questions.

"If you two have seen enough, I think we'd best head back to *Hunter*," he finally said. "If removing the remaining pods goes smoothly, we might be on our way within the half hour."

The two women nodded, and they headed for the hatch. He spared the dead arrayed throughout the ship one final glance.

He hoped the living aliens could help him find a way through this war to eventual peace. If not, he and his people might end up just as dead as these poor bastards before much longer.

34

Derek consulted the map Tina Chen had provided for the traffic in the system. There were several places small craft seemed to be traveling between, so he selected a location that would allow him the best chance to slip into traffic unnoticed.

Since these people thought they were alone, that turned out to be somewhat easier than he'd expected. If anyone was monitoring the sensors running on the depot, they didn't see him.

Tina sat in the copilot's seat, working on a tablet he'd connected to the cutter's network. He was willing to lay odds she was monitoring communications through her headset. The more information she could pull in to build her cover, the better the chance of going unnoticed.

He breathed a sigh of relief when he'd nudged the cutter onto the course he'd chosen between the asteroid belt and the depot. The rest of the small craft were running active sensors, so he needed to do something similar, or he was going to call attention to himself.

The trick would be doing so in such a manner that he didn't suddenly pop up on someone's screen and make them wonder where he'd come from. To do that, he decided to bring the sensors online at a low level and gradually increase the signal strength until it was at full power.

He went through the process methodically, nudging the power of the sensors up slowly but surely over about half an hour. He still didn't breathe easy until an hour had passed, and no one had attempted to contact him or changed their behavior. At that point, he was happy to assume he'd escaped their notice.

With active sensors running, he was getting a lot more data about the system layout and the small craft ahead of him in the queue. They were definitely old-style Navy cutters and cargo shuttles. Their signatures were unmistakable. That meant he and his cutter were going to blend right in.

It took another two hours for him to get close enough to the gas giant to get an idea of what was there. They'd hypothesized that the depot and battleships were in orbit, one proceeding another as they circled the planet, and the data confirmed that.

He stared in awe as he saw battleship after battleship slowly pass in front of the gas giant. This fleet had crushed the Locust invasion two hundred years ago, and it was waiting for them to bring it back online to once more sally forth and engage the enemy.

If, of course, they could figure a way of doing so without rousing the anger of whoever was in control of the depot.

He almost laughed at his earlier thought about bringing all those ships online. They barely had enough people trained to get *their* ship operable for combat. Even if they split their crew multiple times and trained the civilians, it would be impossible to get more than a couple into operation with minimum crews.

Also, none of those ships had been maintained over the last two hundred years. They'd been left here to rot. Hell, with all the unknown people, someone might've been salvaging things from them.

That would suck, but he couldn't rule it out without a lot more data. Data he doubted they'd be getting any time soon.

"That sure looks like a lot of firepower," Tina said. "Do you think anyone stripped them of weapons to plant around the gas giant? Wouldn't that make sense?"

"It would be easier just to get the weapons systems operational on the ships themselves," he said. "If they get even a single fusion plant operational, they've got more than enough power to use the lasers, and we've already seen that a single battleship can deal out damage at short range with enough lasers.

"If they've got the missile launchers working—and refurbished some of the missiles—that gives them a significantly larger offensive envelope. Even one ship having a small segment of her weapons working would be more than capable of protecting this entire fleet. They could gut *Hunter* before she even got into range to fire."

Tina pursed her lips. "Not good. When we get there, pay close attention to what I'm doing and follow my lead. We don't know who these people are, and while I think I've got enough information to blend in, we've got to be cautious.

"My advice is to keep your mouth shut unless you absolutely have to say something. If you do need to speak, keep it innocuous."

"What about our Marine friends? They don't look very innocuous."

She laughed. "No, they don't. Once we've brought the cutter into the small craft bay on the depot—if we can get aboard—we can assess what kind of people are walking around and see if bringing them with us will stand out. If so, we'll leave them on the cutter.

"Again, we're not there to cause trouble. The best possible outcome is if the folks on the depot never know we're there at all."

He nodded and automatically tweaked his course to follow the cargo shuttle in front of him a bit more closely. "Let's say that works. This seems like it's going to be a bit more involved than a quick pass through asking questions. What's your long-term plan?"

"You're smart to recognize that I need one. If possible, I'll set myself up on the station doing something. Maybe I'll keep one of Turner's people with me, but the ultimate goal is to establish myself as an intelligence asset in their midst.

"As you'd guessed, that's not something that'll happen quickly. It takes time and care to develop contacts, and the only way I'm going to find out the true story here is to become one of them.

That might take a couple of days. Maybe a week. Hell, maybe a month. I'm not going to guess."

"And me? Do you need me to stay here and provide a quick escape if needed?"

"If they discover I'm an outsider and capture me, you need to get out of here as quickly as possible and get back to *Hunter*. Under no circumstances are you to stage any kind of rescue effort. All that's going to do is get you captured or killed. Understood?"

Derek pursed his lips and considered her for a moment. She wasn't in his chain of command, so none of the orders she gave technically carried the force of law, but she had the commodore's confidence.

"You're the boss," he conceded. "We'll be coming into the area around the gas giant in another hour. Before we get there, I'm good to set up a directed transmission toward where *Hunter* is now. We can give them information about the situation until it's not safe to do so anymore."

"Shouldn't they have moved by now?"

"They are moving. They're far enough out that there's almost nothing to see, but I know what to look for. Because of the light-speed delay, they're running ahead of the location I have them at, but I can plot their correct location. Piece of cake."

She smiled more widely. "Aren't you the smart one? Okay then. Let's focus on slipping into the area around the depot without drawing any undue attention. Are you picking up any communications from traffic control yet?"

He nodded. "They're not exactly trying to hide their presence. I think you've already listened in on it because it was one of those you had listed. I'm paying close attention to how they're talking to one another, and it's a very casual affair. These are obviously not trained traffic control personnel or pilots. Not in the normal way that we'd mean the term anyway."

"I'll leave that to you while I gather more data, and I'll attach it to the transmissions you're sending to *Hunter*. Let me know a few minutes before you cut off the transmissions entirely. I want to send a final update with everything I've been able to put together."

"You've got it."

Derek kept a close eye on the traffic around the depot and decided it was getting too dangerous after about forty-five minutes. He let Tina know, and she sent everything she had, after which he gave his own final report and killed the transmission.

He then wiped it from the logs so no one could tell they'd been spying after the fact. She hadn't told him to, but it sounded like something a spy would do.

By then, they were close to the gas giant, and he started paying more attention to the traffic around the depot. First of all, the word depot didn't do the space station justice. It was *significantly* larger than Navy headquarters at Faust. If it had been fully manned, it was supposed to hold full crews for a dozen battleships. That was a lot of people at five thousand a pop.

And that didn't even count all the support personnel that were supposed to be present during a heightened state of alert. The station was large enough to hold three hundred thousand people in comfort—at least as the Navy saw it—as well as all the repair parts and reloads required for the logistics of the battleship division during a full-scale invasion of the Confederation.

It was monstrous, dwarfing the battleships in the same orbit. It was lit and its sensors were running. Hell, it was probably armed too. There was no reason for a military station to be unarmed, so it would have lasers and missile batteries.

It was an open question whether the squatters had the technical know-how to get those systems online, but it wasn't entirely out of the question.

Now that he was close enough to get a good look, there were dozens of small craft flitting between various battleships and the depot. That meant whoever was living here was either doing work aboard the battleships or living there themselves. It would fall to Tina to figure out what they were doing.

"It's about time to announce ourselves," he said. "Let's hope they don't find our arrival unusual or unexpected."

"Are they asking anybody else where they came from? It doesn't look as if they're organized at all."

"They're not, really, but I'm not willing to count on good luck favoring us. Here we go."

He activated his transmitter on the traffic control channel. "Station, this is a belter cutter inbound," he said, his tone laconic. "I need a slot in the small craft bay."

There were a few seconds of silence, and then someone responded. "Flash your locator beacon, belter cutter."

Derek flipped his locator beacon on and off several times.

"We've got you. Maintain course for now. You are seventh in line to come in, so just follow the rest and no hot-dogging."

"Spoilsport. Thanks."

He was relieved they hadn't sounded the least bit suspicious. Now he and Tina just had to get aboard the depot without tripping over any unexpected social niceties.

Time seemed to drag as they made their way to the depot, and he eventually brought the cutter through one of the enormous hatches. There were undoubtedly more small craft bays on that station than *Hunter*, but they only seemed to be using one.

That probably meant they didn't have the traffic to need a second one running, so that put a cap on their maximum population. He mentioned it to Tina and got a nod in return.

Up close, the enormous space station dwarfed anything he'd ever seen. Derek took sensor readings until he had to shut off the sensors because they were going in. That data might be useful at some point.

Once through the hatch, he spotted someone manually directing traffic. They sent him to a parking slot.

This was the most ticklish part of the operation because he couldn't afford to look like he didn't know how to fly. Derek hovered the cutter into the designated parking space and set it down on its landing gear more smoothly than he'd expected.

He breathed a sigh of relief once it was down and started shutting down. As he did so, he examined the people he could see walking around the bay. They didn't look all that unusual.

Nobody was in uniform, and they looked like any other group of civilians he'd seen. There were men, women, and children, as well.

The fact there were young ones implied this wasn't a pirate stronghold because he couldn't see them being family types.

He unstrapped himself and followed Tina back to the hatch. He was dressed in civilian clothes borrowed from some of the merchants they'd rescued. If they had an opportunity to pick up clothing here, he might see about getting something that would blend in even better.

Tina triggered the hatch and went down the steps to the deck. He followed close behind her and felt the Marine force recon people trailing him.

A woman walked over from what looked like a kiosk set up in the middle of the deck. She looked bored and held out a hand. "Landing fee."

"Remind me again how much that is," Tina said as she began pulling out a small clip with Confederation dollars.

The woman snorted as she stared at the money. "As if that's any good now. You know the drill. All fees are to be paid in coin."

Derek had no idea how the covert agent would talk herself out of this because it certainly seemed like their cover was about to be blown. He forced himself not to tense up, but he did step a little to the side so that the armed men behind him could act if needed.

The next few seconds were going to shape how this entire mission played out, and he was suddenly afraid everything was going pear-shaped.

35

WHILE JACK COULD HAVE GOTTEN to the quantum gate more quickly, he decided not being detected on their approach—either by the depot or ships potentially guarding the gate—would be better. They still had no idea who these people were, and an uncontrolled confrontation with them might make things impossibly difficult for him and his people.

Yes, there was a chance the Locusts would find the quantum gate and use it before he arrived, and that would be a disaster. They hadn't located it in the last several weeks, though, so he thought the odds of that happening to be reasonably low.

At least he hoped so. Their fight might have stirred the Locusts up enough to locate it, which would definitely be the worst-case outcome.

Even though the gate had been about seven hours away from their arrival point, it took *Hunter* almost ten hours to arrive in its vicinity at the slower speed he'd ordered. That gave Danek and her people plenty of time to catch up without drawing attention to themselves.

At that point, he had the helm officers—Alexey Golousenko and a young minder working as a pair—cut their speed even further. If there were ships out there watching the gate, he didn't want to appear out of nowhere and start a firefight.

"Ahmad, using passive sensors only, can you tell me if there's anyone out there?" he asked the tactical officer. Ahmad Adel had Amanda supervising his work in case things dropped into the crapper, too.

"I'm seeing evidence of shielded fusion plants," the man reported, turning in his seat. "Someone is keeping an eye on the gate."

"Can you narrow down their locations with more observation time?"

"Roughly speaking, I believe so, sir. As we get closer, the picture will get clearer. The risk is that someone's going to notice a big honking asteroid maneuvering near the gate. That's *probably* going to cause some consternation."

Jack chuckled at his friend's humor. "I'm sure it will, but we'll deal with it when it happens. Right now, I need to know if there is a single ship or a dozen."

"Probably not a dozen, but more than one. All I can say for certain is that someone went to the effort to shield their fusion plants from casual observation. That says either military or pirate to me."

"That's a complication I'd hoped we wouldn't have to deal

with, but I'm betting on pirates," Jack said with a sigh. "Alexey, bump our speed up some. Be ready for any hostile responses, Ahmad."

The two tactical officers stiffened less than five seconds after Jack had finished speaking. Amanda cut her superior officer off moments before he could say anything. "Hostile incursion at the gate! Locust motherships detected emerging and deploying drones!"

So much for doing this the easy way.

"General quarters," Jack snapped. "Helm, take us to flank speed. Tactical, how long until extreme laser range?"

"We're at least ten minutes from being able to engage the gate itself, sir," Amanda said as the alarm began sounding. "There'll be a lot of enemy vessels in our space by then. I hope our unknown friends had the gate rigged to blow."

"Go to active sensors," he ordered. "Let's turn *Hunter* into a beacon. I want them coming after us and not the depot."

Even as his crew scrambled to bring the ship up to readiness for battle, Jack watched the tactical display and saw that it didn't matter how many ships their unknown squatters had parked around that gate. They hadn't destroyed it, and there was now a fight between what looked to be six vessels and far more drones and motherships than Jack would ever want to face in their shoes.

The battle around the gate lasted less than thirty seconds before all the defenders were gone. They must not have had the gate rigged to blow because it was still there. Either that or whatever they'd used had failed to detonate.

All that mattered was that motherships continued to pour into the system, building a cloud of drones that would be anyone's nightmare.

Thankfully, the gate was a bottleneck, and if they could get there soon, they'd be able to destroy access to this system. Drones couldn't use the quantum gates without a mothership to carry them, so there were now far more motherships in the system than he liked.

Even if they destroyed the gate, those motherships could still use their hyperdrive to get the word out. They had to be the priority.

"It looks like the Locusts have picked us as the next target, sir," Alexey said.

"What kind of numbers are we looking at?" Jack asked as he eyed the swarm on the tactical plot.

"A lot, sir. We're talking thousands of drones and hundreds of motherships at the rate they're pouring through. That's a far bigger force than we've engaged to this point."

Jack wished they had missile capability because that would've made this fight a lot easier, but they didn't. They'd have to do this the hard way. He was grateful his ship was tough because she was about to get the crap kicked out of her.

"Begin firing at them as soon as we get into extreme range," he ordered. "I don't want you to look like you're doing it, but make sure every single mothership that comes into range gets enough love to vaporize it. We can't allow any of them to escape back through the gate or into hyperspace, or we're toast."

He hadn't considered it before, but one of the benefits of charging directly into an enemy formation was that your fusion drives were as hard to hit as possible. If they could destroy the Locusts before they got past them, their vulnerable engines wouldn't be at risk.

If they couldn't stop them all, they might lose some of their ability to maneuver, leaving them at a serious disadvantage with the people in this system. It was a trade-off that he hoped he didn't have to make.

"Entering extreme laser range," Amanda said, taking over the tactical console. "Firing."

The tactical display lit up with markers for drones and motherships as they were destroyed in the initial round of fighting. The drones and motherships had less powerful lasers than *Hunter*, so they couldn't fire yet. He'd enjoy that advantage while he could because it wouldn't last.

These had to be the drones that had faced his ship before because they went right for the kamikaze maneuver. *Hunter*'s lasers took down a large percentage of them, but even more continued to pour in as the first wave slammed into his ship with explosions of plasma from failed fusion plants.

"Status?" he asked.

"We've taken out every mothership that's come into range," Amanda said. "They're coming at us with the drones, so we'll have a chance of a clean sweep if they don't twig to our plan. The gate will be in range in about two minutes."

That left an awful lot of time for even more Locust drones and motherships to get in this system. Sooner or later, one of them would pick up some signal from the gas giant and break off to chase it down.

If and when that happened, he'd have to send a message warning the squatters what was coming and hope they had enough defenses to stop them.

And, true to form, thinking about something bad made it happen.

"Some of the drones must've detected the activity around the gas giant because they're breaking off and heading that direction," Alexey said. "They're outside of our range, and we're not going to be able to engage them. I estimate their arrival at the gas giant in about three and a half hours."

"ETA to the gate?"

"One minute and five seconds."

"How many motherships are going with the breakaway force?"

"None at this time," Amanda said. "It looks like we're still the most popular dance partner. Fifty seconds until gate engagement."

The cloud of drones peppering them now was so large that they couldn't shoot them all, and some of them flew past. They tried to engage his engines, coming under fire from the lasers at the ship's stern.

Those were unbloodied and better able to deal with the drones, but that didn't mean they were invulnerable. The ship's acceleration stuttered.

"One of the drones took out a fusion drive," the engineering officer said. "Thrust down roughly eight percent."

"Helm, do what you can to keep them off our ass," he ordered. "Tell me we're about ready to engage the gate."

"Less than thirty seconds away, sir, but our forward batteries have taken a pounding," Amanda said. "We've lost two-thirds of our forward-facing lasers, and that number is dropping every time they ram us. We're not going to have much left by the time we get there."

"Hull breach!" the environmental officer said. "Hull breach in the forward quarter. Emergency hatches have slammed shut, but we're going to have casualties."

"Fifteen seconds to extreme laser range on the gate," Amanda said. "Locust mothership count is now at ten. Scratch that. Eight."

Jack held his breath as they bulled into firing range on the gate. He watched the marker on the tactical plot and saw it vanish about twenty seconds after she'd spoken.

"Quantum gate destroyed," Amanda said. "Mothership count now three. It looks like they're trying to disengage and go to hyper. Took one out."

"Slewing us around to bring stern lasers into play," Alexey said.

"Got another one," Amanda continued. "The last one is about to go into hyper… Got you, you son of a bitch! Who's your Momma?"

Amanda punctuated her shout by pumping her fist in the air.

"Let's keep the celebratory fist bumps to a minimum until we get the last of these damned drones off of us," Jack said in a repressive tone he didn't feel. Her success thrilled him. They'd kept word of where the gate led from the Locusts and prevented any leakers from getting out of the system. That was an unvarnished win.

Hunter jerked again.

"We just lost another fusion drive," the engineering officer said, sounding a little sick. "A drone rammed us, so there may be other damage back there. Thrust down thirty percent."

Their power hadn't flickered, so engineering was still mostly intact. That didn't mean there wasn't serious damage, though.

Jack watched the tactical plot as the drones around them broke off and tried to join their fellows headed toward the depot. His ship was able to pick off ninety percent of them, but some escaped to join the others.

"What's the final count on the number of drones headed toward the depot?" he asked, his stomach clenched tight.

"One hundred and six, sir," Ahmed said. "That's a lot of firepower, and we're not going to be able to catch up with them. I hope whoever is squatting there managed to get some of the weapons online.

"Me, too. Open an audio channel to the depot, communications. Cue me."

The communications officer held up a finger. "You're live in three... Two... One..." He pointed at him.

"Attention in the system," Jack said. "This is the Confederation battleship *Delta Orionis*. The quantum gate has been breached by Locust forces, and one hundred and six drones are on their way to your location. Your protective force has fallen, and you need to prepare a defense immediately.

"We're following as quickly as we can, but we're not going to be able to help you. Whoever you are, Godspeed."

He gestured for the communications officer to kill the channel. This had gone far worse than he'd hoped. He'd have been better off charging to the gate at full speed. Now others were going to die because he'd underestimated the enemy.

"I want a full damage report," he said. "Get everybody helping damage control rescue anybody trapped in the decompressed area. Communications, send an encrypted signal to our cutter. Maybe that will give Derek, Tina, and the rest time to escape."

If they didn't get the message, he hoped they were still alive when *Hunter* got there.

36

Tina smiled at the woman. "You know how it goes. I forgot to bring the coin. What can I do to make this right until next time?"

"You can head back to wherever you came from," the woman said without the slightest bit of sympathy. "It's been weeks since they made the change, and you've got no excuse for trying to pass off that trash as money now. Either pay up or get out before I impound your cutter."

This was going to make things more challenging.

"Here now, Lydia," a man drawled from behind Tina. "There's no cause to be such a hardass. People are just trying to get by, love."

Tina turned and found an enigma. A man a little older than Jack stood behind her and the men accompanying her. He was of average height with dark red hair that flowed down to his shoulders, framing a pale face with a splash of freckles and green eyes.

He was a handsome man, she had to admit, but it was the way he dressed that made him stand out. If she'd thought the crew aboard *Hunter* dressed archaically, then this man took it to an entirely new level.

Whereas Jack and his people looked like old time sailors from some entertainment video, this man was dressed like a pirate from all the way back to the age of sail. From his boots with many buckles, dark trousers, white shirt with lace at the cuffs and neckline, and the dark blue greatcoat he wore, and ending with the black tri-cornered hat on his head, he was a walking anachronism. All he needed to complete the picture was an eye patch, a cutlass, and a flintlock pistol.

And maybe a parrot.

If the man's appearance seemed odd to the woman trying to throw Tina out, it didn't show. She didn't even blink. It was as if she saw people dressed even stranger than this all the time. Or, perhaps she was just intimately familiar with the man.

"I don't think we've met," Tina said with a smile as she extended her hand. "Tina Chen."

"Mark Connor, and I'd certainly remember if we'd met before. I'll tell you what, Miss Tina. I'll pay your landing fee, but you'll have to make it up to me. You see, I've developed a powerful thirst. Join me for a drink right now, and we'll call our scales settled. What say you?"

She allowed her grin to widen. "You've got a deal."

The man reached into one of the inner pockets of his greatcoat and produced two gold coins. Actual gold coins. Tina had never seen anything so archaic in her entire life.

He handed them over to the woman, who rolled her eyes and walked back over to the table, scanning the coins underneath some device before giving him a thumbs-up.

Gold was useful for certain industrial purposes, but it was far too plentiful in the Confederation to be valued as money. With the ability to mine ores in space, one could find a *lot* of gold.

She didn't understand what was happening, which was part of the problem. She was walking into a strange situation without any information at all. The chances of screwing something up through ignorance were a lot higher than she'd anticipated. Connor's arrival could be both a blessing and a curse, so she'd best be careful.

The flamboyantly dressed man gestured for her and her companions to accompany him through the small craft bay's primary exit. She took a look around and verified nobody else was playing dress-up. That meant that this guy was the exception rather than the rule.

"So, Connor, I don't get out very often, and I don't think I've seen anyone dressed the way you are," she said as they walked. "What's with the getup?"

He grinned back at her. "You like it? It took me quite a while to settle on a look I cared for. Here's a piece of advice for you, young lady. If you look like everyone else, you become everyone else. If you've got a desire to forge your own path, you should do whatever it takes to present the world with the face you want them to see."

"And you want to present yourself as an old-time pirate?"

"That's what it might look like to the uninitiated, but I'm no pirate. As you no doubt know, pirates aren't welcome here. Still, none of those scalawags would dress in something so grand as this, so there's little risk of me being taken for one.

"No, I much prefer moving hard-to-find cargoes that the authorities frown upon without ruffling their feathers. And what about yourself? What do you do, and what brings you to Port Royale?"

The name sounded vaguely familiar to her, so she'd probably be able to look it up when she had an opportunity. For now, she'd just have to pretend she'd known that all along.

"We just came in from the belt. You know how lonely it can get out there, and we don't get to Port Royale all that often."

He nodded. "Indeed I do. Each of us has a part to play in ensuring our little society has everything it needs. Though, I do have to say that it surprises me that you came from the belt and didn't have any doubloons. That's where the damned things are made, after all. They're pretty much your stock in trade, aren't they?"

"I thought Derek had what we needed, and he assumed I did. It was just an oversight."

"Not that she'll ever let me forget it," Derek said with an eye roll. "Make one mistake, and a woman will never let you live it down."

Connor laughed before clapping Derek on the shoulder. "There's the truth of it, lad! Learn that lesson early, and your life will be a lot simpler. If there's a mistake made, it's the man that made it."

Tina expected Connor to take them to a dive, but the place

he went to was just outside the small craft bay and looked completely and utterly normal. It wasn't a bar so much as a restaurant that served alcohol. She'd seen any number of places like it scattered throughout the Confederation.

The young woman manning the entryway nodded to Connor and the party as they came in. "Welcome back to Handor's, Captain Connor. I'm afraid someone's already at your usual table. Would you like to wait, or can I seat you somewhere else?"

"Someplace with a view would be perfect, Adele. Thank you so much."

He slipped the young woman a doubloon with a wink and followed her into the restaurant.

The young woman, for her part, acted as if this happened every day. She didn't even blink at the way Connor dressed or spoke. Looking around, the man got his share of attention from the other patrons, but the level of gawking was low.

It seemed Mark Connor was a known element, and his eccentricities didn't stand out enough to cause a scene. That didn't stop people from occasionally pointing and talking about him, so he wasn't an everyday experience.

They ended up at a table with a view of the concourse. It was filled with people going about their day-to-day lives.

These weren't squatters. They'd been here for some time, and there were a lot of them. It was as if they were valid residents of this system. At least they certainly acted as if they were.

As soon as they were seated, a young man wearing a white apron came up. "Welcome to Handor's, Captain. What can I get you and your guests?"

"I think I'll start off with a beer, Jason," Connor said, spreading his arms expansively. "Then some chips and salsa. I feel like something spicy, so bring enough for everybody."

Tina followed his lead and ordered a beer. The quality of one's alcohol said a lot about their society. The Marine force recon guys and Derek followed suit.

In less than a minute, the beer and chips had arrived. Connor took a drink, then selected a chip to heap salsa upon and stuffed it into his mouth. He closed his eyes in pleasure as he chewed.

"I tell you, there's nothing like a good salsa to set you up for the rest of the day," he said as he washed it down with a sip of his beer.

Tina followed suit and had to admit that salsa was good. The beer was also decent. She grabbed another chip and scooped salsa while thinking about how she wanted to proceed.

Connor, though, spoke before she could. "You said earlier that you don't get to Port Royale all that often, and I'd say that must be true. Honestly, I think this is probably your first visit here. Am I right?"

She wasn't sure admitting that would be appropriate, but it would certainly explain why she had no idea what was going on. She took a chance and nodded.

"Thought so," he said. "Society here on Port Royale can be a bit odd to the uninitiated. There are little pitfalls here and there that someone who doesn't know any better would wander right into. Almost as soon as I laid eyes on you, I knew for a fact that you were new."

He grinned a little bit wider. "In fact, you're not from the belt either. Why don't you do an old smuggler a favor and tell me who you *really* are?"

It wasn't unusual for a covert operative to have her cover story challenged, so she didn't crumble. Instead, she smiled back. "Just because I haven't seen everything doesn't mean I don't belong. Nobody can know everything."

He nodded. "True enough. Let's start with something easy then, shall we? Port Royale doesn't have what anyone would call a standard leadership structure, and it's one most people wouldn't understand if they just rolled in.

"You, being a resident here, of course know everything. Why don't you just tell me who runs Port Royale? A simple question that everyone knows the answer to but an outsider wouldn't have a clue to."

Put on the spot, Tina knew her goose was cooked. She hadn't had an opportunity to get *any* information, and now Connor had her pinned down hard. No matter what she guessed, it wouldn't match the facts.

So, she decided to go big.

"You've caught me," she admitted after taking a drink of her beer and digging out some more salsa. "I slipped into the system when no one was looking. My friends and I were fleeing what was happening in the cluster.

"We're not looking for trouble, and we want to do our part, but with the Locusts out there, we were lucky to find this place."

He considered her for a long moment, pursed his lips, and nodded. "You know, I think you might just be telling me the truth, if not the whole truth. You see, I've got an eye for when people are trying to hoodwink me. It's part of being a smuggler, you understand. You get a feel for when people are playing you.

"And while you're certainly playing me, I can hear at least a hint of the truth coming through. There's nothing to be ashamed of in running from the Locusts. Still, the leadership here has the hidden gate plugged pretty thoroughly, so I'm not sure how you could've slipped through. Perhaps you'd care to satisfy my curiosity."

Before she could answer, the man's communicator went off, and he held up a finger while he plucked it out from underneath his coat and answered it. "Connor."

Tina couldn't hear what the person on the other end was saying, but it made the redheaded man frown.

The call only lasted fifteen seconds before he signed off, put it away, and stared at her with hard eyes, his easy-going expression gone. "Personally, I'd have rather kept playing this game a bit longer, but I'm afraid I'll have to insist on a straight answer from you, lass.

"It seems the Locusts have penetrated the hidden gate and destroyed our guard force. While we can't see precisely what's going on, it's obvious there's still a fight in progress, and it's none of our people doing the fighting. That leads me to believe it may be the mysterious ship that brought you here."

He smiled without a hint of humor. "Time is short, and I need you to tell me who you are and what you're doing here because we're going to be in a fight for our lives in a bit more than three hours.

"The time for word games has passed, and your answers will

decide if you walk out of here free and clear or if my friends take you somewhere to ask again less politely."

With that declaration, the dozen people eating and chatting at the tables around them stopped whatever they were doing and focused their full attention on Tina and her friends. They didn't reach for weapons, but she had no doubt they had them.

Tina was impressed. She hadn't sensed even a single hint they were paying attention to her table at all. They were good, and the game was truly up.

The Marine force recon people tensed, so she spoke to them before they did anything hasty. "It's okay. Sometimes the truth is better than a good story. Hell, sometimes the truth is a great story, too."

"Well, I do like a good story, but I'll need the abbreviated version. Does it at least have a swashbuckling hero?"

"It does. His name is Romanoff and—"

Connor held up a hand abruptly, cutting her off. "Romanoff, you say? That wouldn't be Jack Romanoff of the Confederation Navy, would it?"

Tina blinked in utter surprise. "You know Jack?"

The man grinned even more widely. "Oh, Jack and I go way back. It's been years, but I'm sure he remembers me. That happens when people pull guns on one another."

Well, that sounded ominous. She'd have to find out what that meant once the Locusts were dealt with though. As concisely as she could, she started telling their story.

37

JACK SPENT the next few hours watching the drones race toward the depot with a growing sense of dread. The entire situation had come down to a roll of the dice. No matter how things turned out now, it would mean trouble down the road.

First, it was possible the Locusts would utterly destroy the depot and rob him of all the weapons and parts he needed to fight this war. He didn't know how they'd turn this whole thing around if that happened.

The other option was that the squatters had gotten some of the weapons online and would be able to defend themselves. That introduced a whole different set of complications.

Hunter was in pretty bad shape after the fight, and whoever these people were, they might outgun him now. If that happened, he might not be able to get the resources he so desperately needed.

"The Locusts are about to enter the depot's extreme missile range," Amanda said. "If they have their missile launchers operational, they could open fire now."

"But they'd be smarter to hold fire until the Locusts get closer, right?"

"Yes, sir. I'm just saying they *could* fire, not that it's the best idea. They're about ten minutes from the outer edge of their primary missile envelope. At that point, they'd start getting much better results."

Over the next ten minutes, it became apparent that either the squatters had no missiles at all, or they had someone with an idea of what to do with them. He wouldn't know which until they used them or the Locusts got into laser range.

It was a good five minutes past the edge of the primary missile envelope before Amanda said anything. "Multiple missile launches detected. The depot has fired on the drones."

Jack watched as the depot launched three salvos of thirty missiles. It was a small number, but they'd be able to reach the drones much farther away than the drones could return fire. Maybe they had a chance after all.

The drones tried to take out the missiles as they approached, but the Navy designers had built in some decent electronic countermeasures and defenses—even considering the age of the weapons—to dodge that sort of thing.

The first salvo took out twenty drones, the second took out twenty-three, and the third took out twenty-five. He expected more salvos to eliminate the rest, but there were no more missiles.

He wasn't sure if that was because they had a limited supply or they had enough lasers to deal with the leakers.

When the remaining thirty-eight drones reached laser range, the depot proved it had the same exact lasers *Hunter* had. That meant they got off several rounds of fire before the drones got into their own range.

Their accuracy was crap, but each salvo took down a couple of drones. By the time the drones were in range to return fire, their numbers had been reduced to less than a dozen. The drones opened fire on the depot and scored some hits, but the defenders quickly eliminated them.

And that concluded the fight with the drones but led to the next stage of this operation. It was time to talk with the people in the system and figure out exactly what kind of accommodation could be made.

He was surprised they hadn't sent any kind of message after he'd warned them the attack was inbound, but they'd sent no messages to him. It was time to end the silence and see what they had to say.

He opened his mouth to tell the communications officer to hail the depot, but the officer turned around and spoke before he could do so. "We have an incoming communication from the depot, sir. Audio and video. Be advised there is a five-second lightspeed transmission lag."

"Put it on the screen. Helm, stop us here."

The main screen changed from showing a tactical view of the general area to a close-in view of a seated man. Oddly, he was dressed just like a pirate from an old entertainment video and looked even sillier than Jack did in the old-style navy uniforms.

"Welcome to Port Royale, *Delta Orionis*. It's neighborly of you to drop in, but I wish you'd have closed the door behind you. We don't like bugs here. Now, I'll pause until I get a signal from you."

"I regret we caused you problems, but I'm glad you managed to handle the issues. I'm sorry you lost ships and people at the gate. I'm Commodore Jack Romanoff. Who might I be speaking with?"

Rather than directly answer the question, the man grinned even before Jack's opening could have finished getting to him, though he had the courtesy to wait for him to finish before replying.

"I never thought I'd see the day. Here I thought I was the most fabulously dressed man in the system, and you've come to try and prove me wrong. That's not very neighborly, Navy."

"I assure you that that wasn't my…"

Jack's voice dragged to a halt. Stripped of the ridiculous costume, Jack realized that he *knew* the man.

"Connor?" he asked.

The man's grin widened after the ten second round trip. "Jack! It's been fifteen years, if it's been a day. When we last parted, you'd pulled a gun to arrest me. I wonder if that's how today is going to play out.

"And before you get all excited, it would probably turn out just as poorly for you this time too."

The last time Jack had seen the man had been when he'd been a lieutenant trying to save a freighter from pirates. It turned out that Connor—the freighter's captain—had turned out to be a smuggler. A smuggler who'd managed to get away with most of the valuables aboard his ship and leave Jack the unenviable task of explaining to his superiors how he'd let the man and his crew escape.

The only thing that had saved Jack from serious repercussions was that Connor had turned on the pirates because they'd been trying to take receipt of Locust drone lasers. The man apparently had issues with that kind of thing.

They'd been allies of convenience, though it hadn't ended up being all that convenient for him.

Jack's eyes narrowed when he'd finally processed the man's reaction. "You don't seem very surprised to see me."

"It would be a poor host that didn't know his guests. Now, before you get all worried, I ran into a friend of yours, and we had a long chat over lunch. She told me this incredible story about a man who turned a museum into the last functioning warship in the Confederation that could fight the Locusts.

"I have to tell you, Jack, that kind of derring-do brings a tear to my eye, but the premise might not be entirely accurate. Remember when I told you I'd track down where those weapons had come from and deal with the pirates trying to deal in them. I found them here."

Jack blinked. "Here? In this system?"

"The very same. It seems the pirates had chanced upon the hidden quantum gate and moved in. When I found out what they had at their disposal, and what they intended to do with it since it didn't seem as if the Confederation even remembered this place existed, I undertook a little quest of my own to make sure not a single one of them made it out alive.

"Once I'd accomplished that, somebody had to make sure the pirates never came back, so I moved in. I have to tell you, this place certainly makes a great haven for smugglers. Over the last ten years, we've brought in others that didn't quite fit under the Confederation's thumb, and now we've got a thriving civilization of our own."

The man leaned forward, and his genial expression vanished. "And we're not going to be letting it go just because an old friend has shown up at the door unexpected like.

"As I see it, we've got a few options, Navy. We can fight and see who comes out on top, which wouldn't be my preferred choice. Or, we could once again become allies of convenience and deal with our common foe before we settle our differences."

Connor grinned. "What's it going to be, Navy? Shall old comrades take up arms again and fight off the things threatening our way of life? I'll remind you that the last time we did so, I kept my word to the letter, and I'll do so again.

"And as proof of that, I think it's an appropriate time to bring in your friends."

The view from the camera pulled back and showed that Tina, Derek, and the two Marine force recon troops were standing off to Connor's side. None of them looked injured, and they weren't even bound.

"I'm sorry, Jack," Tina said. "They caught us when we tried to sneak in. Apparently, smugglers keep a much better eye on the ships around them than one would expect.

"Your old friend intercepted us right as we came aboard, so we sat down and had a nice long talk about current events and how the two of you met. You never told me you had such a dashing encounter in your past. I'm jealous."

To say that Jack was off-balance was an understatement. He couldn't have possibly planned for this situation and wasn't sure how to approach it.

After the incident with Connor, he'd kept an eye out to see if anyone ever captured the smuggler, but there'd been nothing, and he'd forgotten about the man. Now it looked like he'd have to figure out how to deal with him all over again.

"It's going to take me a little time to adjust to this," Jack finally said. "I'll tell you right now that I'm not here to shoot up innocent people. That's not who I am."

"Never thought you were, Navy. You're a good man at heart, which makes working a deal possible. You were responsible for luring the Locusts here, but you also stopped them, which counts in your favor.

"The two of us need to have a nice long chat about our mutual goals and how we can achieve them. As I said, we can come to an arrangement if we're willing to compromise on a few things."

Once again, the man leaned forward and grinned. "What do you say, Navy? One more fight for old times' sake?"

Jack sighed. This was *exactly* the kind of complication he'd been hoping to avoid. Now that that wasn't possible, he'd have to figure out some sort of path forward that let him fight the Locusts.

"I'm willing to talk, Connor, but I'll need some assurances. Safe passage in and out when we decide it's time to go."

"You have my word. As your friend can vouch, I know a place with excellent beer to go with their chips and salsa. And if you're in the mood for a meal, their enchiladas are amazing. Come on over, and we'll chat."

"Tina, send Derek to pick me up. I'll only bring a handful of people with me. Trust has to start somewhere, I suppose, and I want to sit down with you and my senior officers so we can assess what's going to happen next. Don't make me regret this."

"We're old friends, Navy," he said, his tone expansive. "You've got nothing to fear from me. See you shortly."

The transmission ended, and Jack pinched the bridge of his nose, trying to hold back a sudden headache. Just when he'd thought the situation would start getting simpler, it took a hard left turn. Everything they were trying to achieve was now at risk, and he'd have to negotiate a deal with a criminal.

This was just perfect. Absolutely perfect.

He stood and looked at India, who was staring at him with wide eyes.

She smiled a bit wickedly. "You make the most interesting friends, Jack. I want to hear how you met. Tell me *everything*."

"Let's get Sara, and I'll tell you on the cutter," he said with a sigh. "I hope you like enchiladas."

"Don't forget Christine. She'd kill you if she wasn't there to record this."

They headed out for a meeting with the criminal that controlled everything they needed to fight the war. A negotiation that he couldn't afford to screw up. It was shaping up to be a perfect day that wasn't going to end anytime soon. They'd won this battle, but another was looming fast on the horizon.

Well, he'd figure it out. Humanity was counting on him.

Amazon won't always tell you about the next release. To stay updated on this series, be sure to sign up for our spam-free email list at jnchaney.com.

Jack and the crew will return in ALPHA STRIKE. Available to preorder on Amazon.

CONNECT WITH J.N. CHANEY

Don't miss out on these exclusive perks:

- Instant access to free short stories from series like *Backyard Starship*, *Sentenced to War*, and more.
- Receive email updates for new releases and other news.
- Get notified when we run special deals on books and audiobooks.

So, what are you waiting for? Enter your email address at the link below to stay in the loop.

https://www.jnchaney.com/last-hunter-subscribe

CONNECT WITH TERRY MIXON

Check out his website
https://terrymixon.com

Connect on Facebook
https://www.facebook.com/TerryLMixon

Follow him on Amazon
https://www.amazon.com/Terry-Mixon/e/B00J15TJFM/

ABOUT THE AUTHORS

J. N. Chaney is a USA Today Bestselling author and has a Master's of Fine Arts in Creative Writing. He fancies himself quite the Super Mario Bros. fan. When he isn't writing or gaming, you can find him online at **jnchaney.com**.

He migrates often, but was last seen in Las Vegas, NV. Any sightings should be reported, as they are rare.

Terry Mixon is a #1 Bestselling Military Science Fiction author who served as a non-commissioned officer in the United States Army 101st Airborne Division. He later worked alongside the flight controllers in the Mission Control Center at the NASA Johnson Space Center supporting the Space Shuttle, the International Space Station, and other human spaceflight projects.

He now writes full time while living in Texas with his lovely wife and a pounce of cats. Visit **terrymixon.com** to learn more.

Made in the USA
Middletown, DE
14 April 2024

53018160R00235